PRAISE FOR THE CALLIOPE REAPER-JONES NOVELS

the golden age of death

"I could not have been more delighted with where this series has gone. Benson knows how to tell a good story, and she ratchets up the tension with every page."
—Seanan McGuire, *New York Times* bestselling author

how to be death

"You may know Amber Benson from her stint on *Buffy* as Tara, but her talents are multifaceted, making this series a favorite."
—*RT Book Reviews*

"*How to Be Death* will make you an instant fan of Amber Benson . . . Not only will this novel amuse you, but Benson has crafted a well-written page-turner mystery. Full of colorful characters and hilarious dialogue, this is a series supernatural fans will devour."
—*Fresh Fiction*

"Reads like a clever and complex whodunit . . . U̲ asy fans should not miss this lighthearted. ev m

"A true suspenseful m̲
with some seriously co
book and a wonderful a̲ ̲ ̲es
series. 5 stars!" ̲ *Textuality*

serpent's storm

"Calliope Reaper-Jones is hysterical. One can't help but root for her to get the man, save the world, and get her heart's desire in the process. This character-driven addition to the Reaper-Jones series is truly fantastic." —*RT Book Reviews*

"Amber Benson shines through her novel and entices readers. Calliope's personality is genuine, and readers will definitely love her." —*Nocturne Romance Reads*

continued . . .

"Fast-paced but filled with humor and pathos. A powerful, action-packed thriller." —*Genre Go Round Reviews*

"Benson has brought the series to a new, impressive height—dark, startling, and [with] plenty of shocking surprises. Urban fantasy fans should not miss this fantastic series."

—*SciFiChick.com*

cat's claw

"Callie bounces from twist to twist as she explores Benson's richly imagined world, where multiple mythologies blend and the Afterlife is run as a corporation." —*Publishers Weekly*

"An entertaining, frenzied fantasy frolic that will have the audience laughing at the chick-lit voice of the heroine, who is willing to go to Heaven on a hellish cause."

—*Genre Go Round Reviews*

"Benson is back with a second helping of her refreshing take on death and Purgatory . . . Callie's offbeat humor and viewpoint guarantee a madcap romp." —*RT Book Reviews*

death's daughter

"Amber Benson does an excellent job of creating strong characters, as well as educating the reader on some great mythology history . . . A fast-paced and very entertaining story."

—*Sacramento Book Review*

"An urban fantasy series featuring a heroine whose macabre humor fits perfectly with her circumstances. Sure to appeal to fans of Tanya Huff's Vicki Nelson series and Charles de Lint's urban fantasies." —*Library Journal*

"A beguiling blend of fantasy and horror . . . Calliope emerges as an authentically original creation . . . The humorous tone never gets in the way of the imaginative weirdness of the supernatural events." —*Locus*

the golden age of death

AMBER BENSON

ACE BOOKS, NEW YORK

THE BERKLEY PUBLISHING GROUP
Published by the Penguin Group
Penguin Group (USA) Inc.
375 Hudson Street, New York, New York 10014, USA

Penguin Group (Canada), 90 Eglinton Avenue East, Suite 700, Toronto, Ontario M4P 2Y3, Canada
(a division of Pearson Penguin Canada Inc.) • Penguin Books Ltd., 80 Strand, London WC2R 0RL,
England • Penguin Ireland, 25 St. Stephen's Green, Dublin 2, Ireland (a division of Penguin
Books Ltd.) • Penguin Group (Australia), 707 Collins Street, Melbourne, Victoria 3008, Australia
(a division of Pearson Australia Group Pty. Ltd.) • Penguin Books India Pvt. Ltd., 11 Community
Centre, Panchsheel Park, New Delhi—110 017, India • Penguin Group (NZ), 67 Apollo Drive,
Rosedale, Auckland 0632, New Zealand (a division of Pearson New Zealand Ltd.) •
Penguin Books (South Africa), Rosebank Office Park, 181 Jan Smuts Avenue,
Parktown North 2193, South Africa • Penguin China, B7 Jiaming Center, 27 East Third
Ring Road North, Chaoyang District, Beijing 100020, China

Penguin Books Ltd., Registered Offices: 80 Strand, London WC2R 0RL, England

This is a work of fiction. Names, characters, places, and incidents either are the product of the author's
imagination or are used fictitiously, and any resemblance to actual persons, living or dead, business
establishments, events, or locales is entirely coincidental. The publisher does not have any control over
and does not assume any responsibility for author or third-party websites or their content.

THE GOLDEN AGE OF DEATH

An Ace Book / published by arrangement with Benson Entertainment, Inc.

PUBLISHING HISTORY
Ace mass-market edition / March 2013

Copyright © 2013 by Benson Entertainment, Inc.
Cover art by Spiral Studio.
Cover design by Judith Lagerman.
Interior text design by Tiffany Estreicher.

ISBN: 978-0-425-25615-2

ACE
Ace Books are published by The Berkley Publishing Group,
a division of Penguin Group (USA) Inc.,
375 Hudson Street, New York, New York 10014.
ACE and the "A" design are trademarks of Penguin Group (USA) Inc.

PRINTED IN THE UNITED STATES OF AMERICA

10 9 8 7 6 5 4 3 2 1

ALWAYS LEARNING   **PEARSON**

For "The Shamers"—
I would never have finished without you

acknowledgments

I want to thank a bunch of people, not just those who helped push along Book #5, but people who have been integral to the creation and longevity of Calliope Reaper-Jones. To Christopher Golden, who encouraged me to write books, period. He makes being a novelist look easy—even though it's anything but. To Ginjer Buchanan, my tireless editor, who not only gave Callie and me a home but also listens graciously to drunken, brokenhearted authors and always offers the best advice. To my agent, Howard Morhaim, the word "debonair" was created for you—thank you for fixing past mistakes and treating me like a real writer. To the ladies of Ace/Roc: Rosanne Romanello, Erica Martirano, Jodi Rosoff, and Katherine Sherbo—you gals give "classy" a run for its money. To Anton Strout, my brother-in-arms—Callie and I thank you for sharing signing space with us and only laughing at us occasionally. To Robert Busch, the best proof-pages reader around. Every typo I miss, he sees. To Jennifer Vineyard, Jordan Katz, Kate Rorick, and Sarah Kuhn—you guys read the books before the world gets ahold of them. Your love and advice is invaluable. And, finally, I want to thank my Aunt Beverly, my sister, and my mom and dad for putting up with my preoccupied and bizarre mind. I love you guys.

There are so many people out there who helped shepherd Callie along on her journey. Way too many to name in these pages—but you know who you are, and you know you have my eternal thanks.

And most important of all: Thank you to the readers. You guys are the real rock 'n' rollers.

Nevertheless they perished, and became as though they had not been, and their souls descended into She'ol in Tribulation.

—THE BOOK OF ENOCH

prologue

Gerald had many duties at the dispensary, but the one he liked best was making "deliveries." He would come into the shop and work the register when they needed him to—that was a given—but when they asked him to go out in the field, well, that was even better. He looked forward to those days like a little kid gearing up for Christmas morning.

Luckily, he had no competition in the deliveries department because he was the only one with his own transportation: Molly, a bright red Vespa he'd bought with his own money. Money he'd earned from three years as a paperboy, doing a hideously early paper route that meant getting up at the butt crack of dawn and bicycling all over his neighborhood until every last paper had been delivered. He liked the biking part and the throwing-the-newspaper part, but he hated the early-morning part.

That sucked.

It was the reason he'd applied for the job at the dispensary: The place didn't open until eleven in the morning.

And sleep was something Gerald prized very highly. Especially after being deprived of it for the last three years. Not that he was out all night partying or anything—he just liked to stay up and watch movies. And getting up early conflicted with this.

The paper route had conflicted with it, too, but he guessed he'd just wanted to buy a Vespa more than he wanted to get sleep.

Oh, Molly, Queen of the Vespas.

She was the apple of his eye: cherry red with black trim and shiny chrome details. She purred like a little baby kitten and rode like a dream. He loved that machine more than anything else in the world.

Riding her around town, doing the deliveries for the store . . . he was The Man. He got to look cool and wave at the old ladies who congregated outside Mable's Beauty Parlor and gun the engine when he passed the kids playing outside the elementary school.

Damn, he loved his job.

But today there was no time to tool around town and make the rounds. Today, he was traveling outside of his normal area, over to the Pacific Coast Highway to make a delivery to one of those fancy beach houses wealthy people lived in, but only on the weekends.

It took him twenty minutes to reach his destination, a small bungalow—smaller than he'd imagined a rich person would own—between a stand of other mini bungalows, their identical beige stucco jobs a bland attempt at the trendy adobe style that was all the rage in town. He pulled Molly off the highway, wheeling her into a protected spot over by a row of tall hedges, then headed up the private road leading to the bungalow's tiny carport.

Of course it was only *after* he'd already rung the bell he realized he'd gotten the bungalow number wrong. He waited, hoping no one was home so he could just jog over to the right bungalow and make his delivery without some irate rich lady yelling at him for disturbing her.

He counted to sixty, and when no one came to the door, he decided he was home free. He was just about to turn around and go when he felt a pinch in his lower back. This quickly turned into a burning sensation that spread across his torso and down his legs. He tried to scream, to call out for help, but a gloved hand appeared in front of his face, covering his mouth and muffling his cries.

He made one last attempt to escape, thrashing against his attacker like a fish on a line, but he was hooked fast.

After that, he didn't remember anything.

one

CALLIOPE

My name is Calliope Reaper-Jones and if I were a dessert, I like to think I'd be "Death by Chocolate." Not that I'm looking to turn myself into a chewy, gooey, sugary mess anytime in the near future, but if you know me, then you also know my choice of "dessert self" is not only literal, but kind of meta, too. Because even though I'm still an ocean away from my late twenties, I am the sole proprietor of a *bizarre* business. One I can honestly say keeps me on my toes twenty-four/seven/three hundred and sixty-five days a year:

I am the twenty-first century Grim Reaper.

Death *Not* by Chocolate.

Seems like a joke, right? I assure you it's not.

I am the president and CEO of Death, Inc., a multinational conglomerate specializing in the collection and transportation of the recently deceased from Earth to the Afterlife. Once there, the souls are released into their own cultural and/or religious sections of Heaven and Hell, where they are rewarded or punished for their Earthly deeds before being recycled back into the soul pool for reassignment.

My dad was Death before me—I inherited-slash-won the job after he was kidnapped and then murdered by the Devil and my older sister, Thalia. And though it wasn't a career path I would've previously seen myself pursuing, I've actually discovered I'm not too terrible at the gig.

Don't get me wrong, I'm still learning—but, luckily, I have peeps in my corner who keep me from embarrassing myself on a daily basis: my brilliant, techno geek, younger sister, Clio; my Executive Assistant, Jarvis, who has an encyclopedic knowledge of the Afterlife; and my talking hellhound pup, Runt, who makes life better just by existing—though she hasn't been around nearly as much as I'd like because she's been helping her dad, Cerberus, and my boyfriend, Daniel, clean up Hell.

After the Devil was deposed from office for trying to take over Heaven, God installed Daniel as the acting "Steward" of Hell, with Cerberus, the former Guardian of the North Gate of Hell, as Daniel's second-in-command. Together, they were dismantling the old bureaucracy and setting up a new business model based on the platform my dad used to revamp Death, Inc. Their plan included a complete overhaul of Hell—which required doing a lot of community outreach to get the populace involved.

I hadn't had a chance to go to Hell to see what they'd accomplished because I'd been so busy running Death, but my Executive Assistant, Jarvis, said they were making slow progress.

The kind of reformation Daniel had planned for Hell had occurred in Purgatory decades earlier when my dad had taken over Death. Back then, the Afterlife had been a much more archaic place, and Purgatory, in particular, was a cesspool. Instead of being a way station for the recently deceased, it'd been used as a penal colony of sorts, where the dead were locked away in antiquated prison cells on an indefinite basis, with absolutely no recourse to get themselves released back into the soul pool for recycling.

My dad had changed everything, forcing the old guard out so he could then bring Death into the modern era, creating a whole new Purgatory modeled after a corporate business structure.

Thus Death, Inc., was born.

Those who chose to continue their gainful employment with Death had to change their way of thinking—because the new

Death, Inc., had more in common with Wall Street than Riker's Island.

The last holdouts were the Harvesters and Transporters—they're the guys who do the actual collecting and shepherding of souls into the Afterlife—and they liked things the way they were. They had zero interest in changing their mindset, preferring the old, heavy-handed techniques to my dad's new logic-based, corporate way of doing business.

When they got wind of what my dad was proposing, they did the only corporate thing they would ever do: They unionized.

They thought this would give them some control over my dad's "invasive" changes. And though it gave them more leverage than they would've otherwise had, it never brought them the ultimate power they were seeking.

The union *did* fight and win the right for the Harvesters and Transporters to continue to wear their Victorian "ghoul garb"—as my dad called it—on the job. My dad thought their over-the-top Victorian costumes and props made the wrong impression on the newly deceased, but he'd had to cave to their demands when the union had promised to defend their rights to "free dress" by going on strike. Once they discovered this technique worked, the union used it to strong-arm my dad into doing what they wanted on a regular basis.

In the little time since I'd been appointed president and CEO of Death, Inc., Uriah Drood, the all-powerful head of the Harvester and Transporter's Union, had twice pulled the strike card out and waved it in my face. We'd been at loggerheads from the moment we'd met, and he was just looking for an excuse to make my life miserable. Well, at least ours was a mutual "unappreciation" society: I didn't like his sneaky, underhanded way of doing business, and he just didn't like me, period.

It made me proud to think someone as abhorrent as Uriah Drood found me so nauseating—though perhaps it wasn't the wisest choice to add him to my roster of enemies. He was the vindictive sort, and I knew our strained relations were going to come back and bite me on the ass some day.

But I kinda felt that way about a lot of the enemies I'd made, including my arch-nemesis, the Ender of Death.

The Ender of Death was the only one of my enemies I hadn't personally cultivated. He wanted me dead purely because it was in his job description. To this end, he'd officially challenged me to a single-combat throw down where only one of us could come out alive. I'd hedged, putting the challenge off for as long as I could, but the day of reckoning was fast approaching—and I was pretty sure the outcome was not going to be in my favor. I was a lover of fashion and food, not a fighter of supernatural bad guys. A fact that Marcel—Marcel was the human name the Ender of Death went by in this incarnation—was well aware of.

I didn't want to die, but I'd made a bargain with Marcel and now it was time to pay up.

You see, my older sister and the Devil had staged a coup on Death, Inc., and Heaven, and I'd asked Marcel to back off the "kill death business" until I could stop them. To my surprise, he'd agreed to my request, so long as I promised to duke it out with him once I'd set Death, Inc., back to rights.

He'd been true to his word, staying out of my business while I did what I needed to do. But now that everything had (mostly) returned to normal, my verbal promissory note had finally come due.

I didn't like it—I mean, who liked getting killed?—but this fight to the death was going to happen and there was nothing I could do to stop it.

Jarvis told me I was being a fatalist, but I was pretty sure this was what one would call "pragmatic" thinking. I knew my chances for coming out of the duel with my life intact were pretty slim and I just wanted to get it over with. I'd done some checking with my friend, Kali, who was a member of the Board of Death, and she'd reassured me that upon my untimely end, at least two (or three) "possible" Deaths would be called up to vie for my job.

I'd worried my boyfriend, Daniel, would be up for the job again—he'd been a challenger my first time at bat—but since I'd drunk from the Cup of Jamshid and been a sitting Grim Reaper through one annual Death Dinner, Daniel was safe. After being the Devil's (now former) protégé for so many years, Daniel was too involved with the politics of Hell to want to take over the reins of Death, Inc. At least he didn't have to worry about that now.

To reassure me even further, Kali had done something

highly illegal. Something that could've gotten her kicked off the Board of Death if anyone had discovered her transgression: She'd dipped into the Death Records and retrieved the names of two "possible" Deaths. Thankfully, one of them allayed my fears and gave me the faith to finally accept my fate.

If I died during my battle with the Ender of Death, I would leave this Earth knowing that at least one of the next "possible" Deaths was more than fit for the job.

And how did I know so much about a random name Kali pulled from the Death Records, one might ask?

Well, because this "possible" Death was anything but random.

She was my baby sister.

Clio.

Though it was almost unheard of for two siblings to be "possible" Deaths within successive generations, Kali said it *had* happened once before. As a member of the Board of Death, privy to certain secret information, she'd had her suspicions Clio was a "possible" Death. But she hadn't known for sure until she'd pulled Clio's Death Record and read what was written inside. She'd wormholed to Sea Verge—my familial home in Newport, Rhode Island—immediately after reading it, so she could let me know what she'd discovered.

I don't know why, but after she left, I decided not to tell anyone what I'd learned. Not even my most trusted friend and Executive Assistant, Jarvis.

No one really believed I'd be out of the job so quickly that the next generation of "possible" Deaths would need to be called up—and maybe the need *wouldn't* arise. Maybe the impossible would happen and I'd kill Marcel instead of him killing me. Stranger things had happened . . . but I wasn't betting on it. I was prepared to meet my end—and knowing Clio would have the opportunity to battle for my job made me feel kind of okay about my (possible) impending demise.

I'd never really wanted to be immortal, to live forever while my human friends slowly withered and died. Though I knew firsthand Death wasn't the be-all and end-all—heck, I was the gal in charge of making sure human souls got to their preordained Afterlife destinations—it still didn't stop me from disliking the process.

On more than one occasion, I'd asked Jarvis why the Afterlife worked this way. Why humans needed to die and be reborn, why each body a soul is housed in gets its own personality, and when that body dies and the soul is recycled, that personality is destroyed, never to be used again? But all he had to say on the subject was this: That's the way things are and we shouldn't question it.

Well, screw that. I *lived* for questioning things. So I'd done a lot of thinking about God's system and I'd come up with a few hypotheticals that might give an answer to my unanswered question.

The one I liked best went something like this: God just wanted to experience everything. Through us, his/her creations, he/she gets to do every job, be every kind of personality, try every kind of sex, be in and out of every kind of love, feel every emotion, enjoy every kind of pain or bliss.

I've decided that maybe God is just the biggest voyeur in the history of History—and instead of chasing down meaning, we should just enjoy our lives as best we can, so that God can then enjoy them through us.

Radical, I know, and probably not right, but it was my hypothesis and I was sticking to it. There was an order to the world. One I couldn't see, but at least, as Death, I was privy to the Afterlife, so that, though I still missed the people I loved who'd died, I knew their energy lived on.

That somewhere my dad, and even my older sister, would be born into other human bodies and get to restart the game of life.

And who knew, maybe I'd accidentally run into them again—or if I was feeling sly, I could cheat and access my dad's Death Record to find his next incarnation. (I was still angry with my sister for almost murdering me, so I would not be seeking out her Death Record.)

But I kept these thoughts to myself because no matter how much I wanted closure with my dad, if I found him again, well, it wouldn't be him anymore. Whatever magic it was that made him "him" would be gone, and, in the end, it would just be me being selfish, wanting to hold on to something that didn't exist anymore.

And if I'd learned anything from my time as Death, it was this: Being selfish sucked.

two

Jennice McMartin stood at her desk, umbrella in hand, marveling at her good luck. It was after regular business hours, and she'd only been in the office by chance, but when the call had come in she'd somehow had the foresight not to let it go to the message machine—or maybe she should just chalk it up to her inability to let a ringing phone go unanswered. Either way, her actions had worked in her favor and the windfall had landed right in her lap.

"Easterly Realty, *we* sell the home you don't want to. This is Jennice speaking, how may I help you?"

Jennice thought the Easterly Realty tagline Brett had come up with did more to hurt their business than help, but since she was only a junior real estate agent, no one listened to her opinion. Forced to say something she thought was stupid, she did her best to put a cheery face on it, trying very hard to keep her voice light whenever she answered the phone—especially when Brett or Calista were in the office. They liked her to sound chipper and "can do" whenever she talked to a prospective client.

"Is this Jennice McMartin?" the voice—rather snooty with a slight British accent via Brooklyn—inquired.

This was already shaping up to be an odd call because no one ever asked for Jennice by name.

"Yes, this is Jennice. How may I help you?"

"The family I work for would like to commission you to sell their home."

Jennice frowned, imagining the only property—a trailer out at the Shangri-La Mobile Home Park—that Brett and Calista had let her sell by herself.

The owner was a crotchety old man who'd been very vocal about how much he hadn't liked the color of Jennice's skin (mocha-caramel). She'd ignored his bad attitude and gotten him a reasonable offer on his property, which he'd taken without once telling her "thank you" for all her hard work. At first Jennice was hurt by the old man's snide remarks and ill temper, but after she'd gotten her commission check and seen the number on the dollar-amount line, she'd felt a lot better. Still, the Shangri-La experience had made her leery of potential clients.

"Are you a referral from Shangri-La?" she asked, keeping her tone bright.

"Shangri-La?" the voice on the other end of the line asked, sounding confused.

"The mobile home park," Jennice added. "Are you calling about listing a trailer?"

There was a derisive snort—maybe this wasn't a Shangri-La referral after all—and then the voice said:

"If you are referring to Sea Verge as a trailer, then I—"

"Sea Verge?" Jennice squeaked into the phone, cutting the speaker off midsentence.

This had to be a joke. Sea Verge was one of the old stately mansions on Bellevue Avenue—and it was worth millions and millions of dollars.

"Yes, I represent Calliope Reaper-Jones, the heiress of the Reaper-Jones fortune," the voice continued, as if Jennice hadn't squeaked at all. "And she would like for you, personally, to sell her family abode. Does that sound like a task you might be up to?"

Jennice nodded before realizing the man couldn't see her nod over the phone.

"Uhm, yes, I could . . . do . . . that. But," she said, her good sense taking over, "I'd need to see the property, meet with Ms. Reaper-Jones."

There, she'd covered her butt. If this was a hoax, then the man would hang up. Or make up some elaborate excuse about how Ms. Reaper-Jones was away on business. *Or something.*

"Can you be at Sea Verge in twenty minutes?" the man on the phone said, a pleased note to his voice.

Jennice almost nodded again.

"Yes, I'll get in my car right now."

"My name is Jarvis. I'll meet you at the front door."

There was a *click* as the line went dead, but Jennice continued to stand at her small, untidy desk for a few seconds longer, clutching the sweaty phone in her hand.

Her mind couldn't help but tabulate the commission on a home like Sea Verge. The number was so large she could hardly fathom it. Unshed tears collected in the corners of her olive green eyes as she realized her prayers had been answered, that a miracle had occurred—and she'd only stopped by the office, a shabby little rattrap in the not-so-nice neighborhood of Newport Heights, by sheer chance.

On her way to the hospital to see her mother for evening visiting hours, she'd realized she'd forgotten her umbrella at work. Normally she would've just left it there under her office chair, but the weather report on the radio had called for heavy rains later in the night and she'd decided, on a whim, to stop by and pick it up.

I can pay for momma's care now, she thought, the tears running down her apple-round cheeks.

Her mother had the beginning stages of Alzheimer's and two nights earlier she'd fallen in the shower, breaking her hip—and nothing Jennice tried could fix it. This was something that'd never happened before and part of her wondered if it was her mother's way of letting her know she was tired of life, that Jennice should just let her go. The thought made her shudder. She couldn't imagine a world without her mother in it.

Unhappily, Jennice had gone with the ambulance to the hospital, all the time worrying about how exactly she was going to pay the bill. Medicare only paid for so much and the kind of care her mother was getting was going to add up *very* quickly.

She'd spent the past two nights sitting vigil at her mother's bed, wondering if it might be better to pray for the end, rather than the speedy recovery that would just extend her mother's pain. But she couldn't do it.

Instead, she'd prayed to God for something to happen, that someone would find it in their heart to help her. What she was really asking for, though she hated to admit it to herself, was for a miracle—and now it'd happened. She knew she shouldn't count her chickens before they hatched, but in her heart she was certain this wasn't a false hope. This Calliope Reaper-Jones had been sent by God specifically to help *her*, Jennice McMartin.

Praise the Lord, she thought as she finally set the phone receiver back in its cradle.

Holding the umbrella tightly to her chest, she walked toward the exit, her whole body shaking with relief as the heavy weight of desperation fell away from her shoulders for the first time in almost forty-eight hours.

As she stood by the door, Jennice gave the cluttered office one final look before flipping off the overhead light switch.

She had a funny feeling she'd seen the last of Easterly Realty.

there was someone in the house.

Not that anyone else would have known it, but Edgar Freezay had a sixth sense about these things. With the sensitivity of a seismograph, he could feel the hum of another entity, low and regular, coming from somewhere inside the bungalow. There weren't many rooms in the place—a bedroom, a miniature kitchen, a bathroom and a living room looking out over the ocean—so it wouldn't be too hard to flush the uninvited guest from their hiding place.

"I know you're in here and, frankly, my dear, I don't give a damn," he said, the sound of his voice echoing in the emptiness.

He'd always had a strange fondness for Clark Gable—and for *Gone with the Wind*, actually—so he liked to trot out the quote whenever possible. Besides, it was the truth. He really didn't give a damn who was in his house.

Setting his keys down on the white-tiled, eat-in bar linking the kitchen to the living room, he went about his business—his business being fixing himself a drink. He picked up a heavy-bottomed highball glass from the drying rack next to the kitchen sink, then extracted a bottle of scotch from the nest of (mostly empty) liquor bottles on the mini wet bar in the living room, pouring himself three fingers of the golden liquid and gulping it down in one swallow. He poured himself two more fingers and, thusly fortified, he went to sit on the gray twill couch, his eyes locked on the swell of the ocean below his window.

Freezay sipped from the highball glass, eyes forward, but his other senses were on alert, waiting for the telltale signs his mysterious guest was about to show himself. He knew it was a man and not a woman because of the smell, the slight hint of musky English Leather aftershave (his *own* aftershave, probably stolen from his *own* bathroom) that lingered in the air. It was stronger by the couch than it'd been in the kitchen, probably because his visitor had sat here, looking out at the ocean in much the same way Freezay was doing now.

It made Freezay wonder how long his guest had been in residence. Surely the man hadn't slept here the night before, taking Freezay's absence as an invitation to use his bed. (God Freezay hoped not.) Still, it wasn't outside the realm of possibility. It was his fault anyway. He wasn't supposed to have spent the night in Los Angeles, ensconced in all the luxuries the Sunset Downtowner motel had to offer (that number was zero), but he'd been too tired after a day of pounding the sun-baked sidewalks of Hollywood Boulevard to drive the three and a half hours back to the Central Coast.

He'd opted for the motel because, at the time, it'd seemed the lesser of two evils. Maybe it hadn't been the wisest of decisions. A man had to sleep, though, and it beat having your car shoot over a cliff because you fell asleep at the wheel—now that was just a stupid way to get yourself and your car mangled up for nothing.

"I don't know who you are, but why don't you have a seat," Freezay said, not turning his head as he gestured with the highball glass for his guest to take the brown leather armchair kitty-corner to the couch.

He felt his mysterious guest leave the safety of the hall, the man's sock-footed tread making no whisper as he stepped into the sunken living room and took the seat Freezay had pointed out.

Finally, Freezay turned his head—and if he recognized his guest, he gave no indication.

"So you slept in my bed last night, didn't you," Freezay began. It wasn't a question.

The kid—Freezay amended his description because he could hardly call the thick-necked teenager a man—nodded, deciding to play the honesty card.

"Why?"

The teenager shrugged, the stink of English Leather pervasive. Freezay realized someone had used the English Leather to hide the rancid stink of dead body lying just below the musky tones of the aftershave. Probably not the kid. Probably someone who'd left the kid here for Freezay to find.

"Do you know what you're doing here?" Freezay asked, careful to keep his voice casual. He didn't want to freak the kid out.

The kid looked down at his hands. They rested in his lap like two limp, flesh-colored fish. Freezay sighed and sat back against the couch cushion, rubbing his left temple with his free hand. The other hand just held the nearly empty highball glass more firmly.

"I can't help you if you don't talk."

"Who says I need your help—" the kid spat back, his voice raw.

Freezay shrugged, getting up to refill his glass.

"Then no help it is."

The kid's brow furrowed, and Freezay could see the kid hadn't meant to get so testy. He was probably freaked-out and that was fueling the bad attitude. Freezay could empathize. His stomach growled angrily in his gut, reminding him he hadn't eaten since the plate of greasy ham and eggs he'd shoveled down back at the Downtowner's grimy café. Barring the bags of peanuts and pretzels he liked to munch while he drank, Freezay never kept any food in his place, enjoying all of his meals out—and since he didn't own a television it was the only entertainment he got.

"Well, I'm hungry," Freezay said, leaning against the mini wet bar and sipping his drink.

The kid rubbed his belly.

"Me, too."

Freezay knew this was just a residual feeling. The kid was never going to be eating anything again.

"We should maybe do something about it, then," Freezay said, scratching the bristly goatee covering his chin. It matched the white-blond hair on his head perfectly.

"I'm a vegetarian," the kid added. "Nothing with a face."

"Well, I'm partial to a wet meal, so there's that."

"Like cat food?" the kid asked, confused.

Freezay supposed what he said could be misconstrued, if taken literally.

"Like alcohol."

"Oh," the kid said, nodding. "That's not like cat food at all."

Freezay took the half-finished drink to the kitchen and deposited it in the otherwise empty sink. He picked up his keys and gestured for the kid to get up.

"Let's get out of here. Get ourselves something to eat."

The kid got up, a look of mild excitement on his face. Though he knew better, Freezay decided not to shatter the kid's illusions of hunger.

The dead don't eat. It was a fact—and Freezay reckoned (correctly) the kid's body was back in the bedroom, silently decomposing, so food was the least of their worries. But the idea of food seemed to calm the kid so he humored him, thinking it would keep his charge occupied until someone came to collect him.

And Freezay could get something to eat for himself, too.

"Hey, I never got your name?" Freezay said, not that it really mattered, but it was a good way to establish a rapport with the kid.

"Gerald," the kid said.

"Freezay."

"That's a weird name."

"No weirder than Gerald," Freezay replied.

They left through the front door, Freezay locking it securely behind him—but he seriously doubted this would keep out the

Harvesters and Transporters who, by now, had to be on their way to pick up the dead kid's soul.

while freezay dealt with the dead, Clio Reaper-Jones was up to her neck in the living.

"Can you hand me the panko?"

Why she'd agreed to host Indra's dinner party was beyond her. If she thought back to the moment she'd said yes—no, she'd been so busy the past few days she didn't even *remember* saying yes to him, but apparently she had.

Twenty people. She was cooking for twenty people! This was insanity.

"Which cabinet is it in?" Noh asked, pushing her long brown hair out of her face, her nose twitching.

"Behind you, two cabinets over," Clio said absently as she measured five cups of flour into a red ceramic bowl and began to look around for the eggs.

She was glad to have an extra set of hands tonight, but she felt bad about dragging her sister's best friend into her dinner party preparations—especially since Noh had barely stepped off a transatlantic flight two hours earlier. But she was desperate and if Noh was going to be taking up space in the kitchen anyway . . . ?

Over by the sink she found the eggs she and Noh had purchased at the grocery store on the way back from the airport, still in their gray crate. She moved the carton to the island and lifted the lid, studying the rounded, brown bodies before selecting ten of the dozen to crack into another, smaller, red ceramic bowl.

"Here ya go."

Noh set the box of panko on the butcher-block island, pushing it forward with her fingers so Clio could reach it. Dripping egg goo everywhere, Clio grabbed the box and dumped its contents into another bowl along with two cups of crushed pistachios she'd ground to a pulp earlier in the afternoon.

"Thanks."

"Any word from Callie?" Noh asked. "She knows I'm here, right?"

"I would assume so," Clio said, reaching toward what appeared to be a mountain, but what was really a pile of boneless, skinless chicken breasts resting on a piece of parchment paper in front of her. "Jarvis called me this morning and specifically asked me to pick you up at the airport then bring you to Sea Verge. I didn't tell him we were going to stop by Indra's place first, though, so I'm surprised no one's calling to bug me about where we are."

"That's odd."

Clio had always thought Noh was a bit odd, if they were going to talk about levels of oddness. The girl was bone thin and paler than any living person had a right to be. With her long brown hair, pixie face, and the odd moon-shaped scar that ran from the right corner of her mouth to just below her chin, she looked like a broken porcelain doll someone had tried to put back together with super glue—but there was nothing in the least bit delicate about the girl. She was as strong as an ox and whip smart, the best friend Callie had made while she was away at boarding school.

"Well, there was the Death Dinner and then she had this, uh, *thing* with Marcel, the Ender of Death, so, you know, she's been busy . . ." Clio trailed off as she dipped a raw chicken breast into each of the bowls—egg, flour, then the breadcrumb and pistachio mixture—before placing it on one of the two aluminum-foil-lined baking sheets that sat, empty, on the counter next to the stove.

"The last time we talked," Noh said, her eyebrows scrunched up in concern, "she seemed really distracted. Like she was only half listening to what I was saying."

That sounds exactly like Cal, Clio thought, amused. She loved her older sister dearly, but Callie was not known for her ability to focus—something Noh knew well from experience.

As if she'd read Clio's mind, Noh added:

"I know she can be a flake-in-the-butt sometimes, but Callie's way more attentive on the phone than she is in person. The fact she was so distracted was odd."

A flake-in-the-butt? Clio thought as she picked up another chicken breast, the raw meat almost slimy in her hand. There was a reason Noh and Callie were best friends: They both liked to make up weird combinations of words and then pretend like their made-up phrases were part of the everyday vernacular.

"Sure . . ." Clio replied, letting the word hang between them.

Noh continued to look at her expectantly, waiting for Clio to elaborate. She sighed, realizing her silence came from the fact she didn't have an answer for her sister's friend. Callie *had* been acting strangely and Clio was just so busy she'd ignored her sister's flakey behavior.

"I think she's overwhelmed," Clio said after a protracted pause in the conversation, where the only sound was the slap of raw meat on wood. "She's got her hands full running Death and doing all of Dad's Grim Reaper duties . . ."

She paused again, the grief she felt at her father's loss still so raw it made her catch her breath.

"I hear that," Noh agreed. "She's in intense-land, but still . . ."

Noh was right. Clio hadn't actually seen her older sister in the flesh, or even talked to her on the phone except once or twice. Everything had been via e-mail or text. The most impersonal way of communicating that existed.

"You know," Clio began, resting her elbows on the butcher-block island, her gaze thoughtful. "I feel like I haven't talked to Cal in ages. When did you talk to her last?"

Noh's lips thinned as she scrolled through the past few weeks, trying to remember when she'd last spoken to her best friend.

"Was that the last time?" she murmured under her breath, shaking her head as if to jog some memory loose. "Nope, that's not it either . . . we spoke right before the Death Dinner and she was trying to decide if she should take this swimsuit—a bikini, actually—or if it was too slutty to wear to an official Death thingamabob—"

"And that's the last time you talked to her?" Clio interrupted, unconsciously smearing a streak of flour across her cheek as she reached up to scratch the tip of her nose with a magenta fingernail.

"Yes . . . no! No, it was after that. I called to tell her I was coming to town to visit, gave her the flight info and that was that. She seemed happy I was coming."

"That must've been before Marcel," Clio murmured, her brain spinning.

"Oh," Noh said thoughtfully, then added, in what was a total non sequitur: "I told her to take the bikini. That slutty wasn't necessarily a bad thing for a business trip."

And I wonder if she took your advice, Clio mused, but instead of exploring this sidebar, she returned to the matter at hand.

"I think we should go over there now. Check in."

Noh nodded, thoughtfully.

"I'm game. I don't think it's a bad idea. It's almost like we're supposed to, actually."

Clio couldn't have agreed more.

"Then let's go," she said, plunking the last of the chicken breasts on the aluminum-covered baking sheet before shoving it into the refrigerator.

Wiping the excess flour and egg on her apron, Clio ran the tap and washed her hands, the last vestiges of the raw chicken circling down the drain.

It was time to pay Sea Verge a visit—dinner party be damned.

three

Bernadette hated roller coasters.

Hated them with a passion. In the entirety of her life she'd only ever ridden on one of the horrid things and the experience had been painful enough to make her swear off the hulking machines for the rest of her days. But now the promise she'd made to herself never to climb aboard another rickety, wooden roller coaster had been rescinded, all self-imposed restrictions lifted because the person she loved more than anyone else in the world had asked the impossible of her.

Bart, her nine-year-old grandson, wanted his maw-maw to ride on the Big Bellower with him.

Bernadette knew *impossible* was a big word, probably best not used by a doting grandmother from Ohio who was no more than a malleable hunk of clay where her grandson was concerned, but if anyone other than her grandson had asked her to ride on a roller coaster, "impossible" would've been the answer she'd have given.

Anyone else would've known better than to ask her.

But Bart was all wide-eyed wonder and excitement, his childish curiosity so catching, Bernadette could only grin like an idiot whenever she was in his company—and because of this she'd found herself agreeing to the impossible. Against her better judgment.

She wasn't a small woman. Getting on the darned ride had not been easy. Thank God Bart was no bigger than a cattail, so they'd been able to squeeze in together, her much larger bulk taking up the vast majority of the cold fiberglass seat. She knew she was in trouble when she heard the quiet *swoosh* of the protective bar sliding over their heads, and she felt her whole body begin to sweat.

Bart was immune to her fear. His light mocha face was full of excitement, the black of his pupils so wide they overtook the brown irises. He was giddy, his tiny body shivering with anticipation.

"Maw-Maw, Maw-Maw, look!"

Bernadette's gaze followed the crook of Bart's finger. He was pointing upward, toward the cloud-filled sky where a murder of crows, like a synchronized swim team, flew above them, their black bodies in silhouette against the blinding light of the sun. Bernadette welcomed the distraction, perfectly timed to match the lurch of their roller-coaster car as it shot forward.

Bart let out an excited squeak as the Big Bellower creaked underneath the weight of the cars and the ride began. It was all Bernadette could do not to shriek as fear lanced through her soft, pink body and her face broke out in foul smelling perspiration. She felt very much like a pig headed to slaughter.

As the car began its long, slow climb up the first steep hill, Bernadette let her eyes return to the crows, hoping their perfectly synchronized flight would help calm her. She was surprised to see two of the crows break away from formation, dropping down and away from their brothers as she watched them.

"Maw-Maw, this is fun!" Bart screamed in her ear over the *clickity-clack* of the roller coaster's hydraulics. But Bernadette wasn't paying attention to him. She was too transfixed by the sight of the crows falling steadily earthward—their bodies like large black stones—to process what he was saying.

She opened her mouth to say something to Bart about the crows just as they sailed over the crest of the first hill and her words melted into a hysterical scream, gravity sending her stomach flying into her esophagus, choking her. Beside her, Bart shrieked with delight, a thrill junkie in the making.

The car began to build up speed again as it soared toward the next obstacle: a giant, round loop that would turn them upside down in their seats. Bernadette saw the loop looming ahead of them and terror tore at her heart. She looked around wildly, trying to find an escape, but there was no exit—she was trapped.

Her bowels turned to jelly as their car sailed onward, hurtling them inextricably toward the loop. Whistling currents slammed against her upper body as she flew through empty air, eyes stinging in the wind. She let her gaze rise, her thin gray hair plastered against her cheeks and mouth, and then she gasped.

The two crows were flying straight toward them.

Ice-water shock filled her veins as she realized what was about to happen. With a silent prayer to God, she threw her arms around Bart, covering the tiny boy with her considerable girth just as the missile-like crows dove into them, the impact taking her head clean off her shoulders.

Later, one of the detectives at the scene of the accident would marvel out loud at the old woman's quick thinking. She was a real hero, saving her grandson's life like that.

Sitting on a nearby bench, Bernadette's ghost shook her head. She wasn't a hero. She'd just done what she'd needed to do to protect Bart—and she'd have done it all over again without batting an eyelash.

She continued to watch the police and emergency crews swarm along the base of the now silent Big Bellower like busy worker ants, but they didn't notice her.

Stupid roller coaster, she thought, shaking her head again. *Stupid, stupid roller coaster.*

sea verge was empty.

Well, not *exactly* empty, Jarvis corrected himself.

There was still some furniture, but what was left of the beautiful, old pieces—antiques lovingly accumulated over decades of habitation by the Reaper-Jones family—were now draped like ghosts in protective swathes of white sheeting, left to molder in abandonment. As things had progressed, he'd been forced to watch the pieces begin to disappear around him. This wasn't shocking. He'd expected as much, in point of fact.

But what *had* surprised him were the left behinds. How they were suddenly covered in those god-awful white sheets, as if by magic. Well, it was a magic of sorts, actually, but that was neither here nor there. What bothered Jarvis enormously was that there was nothing he could do about it. The place was becoming a veritable ghost town and he was helpless to stop it.

It also meant *things* were still up in the air, and Calliope might not be able to stop them as they'd hoped—but he banished the thought immediately from his mind.

He focused on Sea Verge instead. On the young woman Realtor Calliope had forced him to invite over to see the house, and, ostensibly put it on the market. But that wasn't the real reason Calliope had wanted Jennice McMartin to come to Sea Verge. Not by a long shot—

He was interrupted midthought by a sneeze, his entire body rattled by the size and sweep of the thing. He knew the dust that'd settled over the rooms since Calliope had decamped from Sea Verge the previous night only exacerbated his allergies, but the knowledge didn't make the sneezing any more manageable.

He was well into sneeze number two when the doorbell rang.

"Oh, blast," Jarvis sighed unhappily as he pulled a monogrammed handkerchief from his breast coat pocket and blew his hawkish nose. "One moment!"

He knew whoever had rung the bell couldn't possibly hear him—the study where he'd been working was far removed from the front entrance—but he still felt compelled to offer up the placating words. He tucked the used handkerchief into his coat pocket and set the petite book he'd been dusting back on its shelf, sliding it in with the other tomes, where it sat, looking innocuous—though it was anything but.

This was the original copy of *How to Be Death: A Fully Annotated Guide*, written in the tongue of the Angels. It was a death sentence to any mortal who dared touch it, and it'd almost fallen into the wrong hands five times over when Jarvis had attended the annual Death Dinner at the Haunted Hearts Castle with his boss, Calliope Reaper-Jones.

It gave him the willies to think of anyone other than the rightful Death (that being his boss) having the book in their possession. But if Edgar Freezay, the ex-detective for the Psychical Bureau of Investigations, hadn't stepped in and helped Calliope solve the mystery of the book's disappearance, well, that would've most likely been the outcome.

A book that could jump-start the End of Days lost to the hands of someone who would use it for their own gain. Jarvis shuddered at the thought.

Though it'd only been hours, it felt like forever since Calliope had gone, leaving the tiny book in his possession. He didn't like being the keeper of the book, but he would do it until Calliope came back to collect it, or—

The doorbell rang for a second time, interrupting his thoughts.

Jarvis made sure to drape the white sheet back over the bookcase that held the original *How to Be Death* before leaving the confines of the study behind him.

"That should do it," he said as he studied his handiwork, satisfied no one would realize the book was hidden in plain sight.

He wiped his hands on his pants then turned and left the room, the doorbell ringing again, more insistently now, as he traversed the empty hallway, the loud chimes cutting through the hollow echo his wingtips made on the polished surface of the floor.

"I'm moving as fast as I can," Jarvis murmured under his breath, though he did pick up his pace a little.

He was sure the Realtor was the culprit. All the obsessive bell ringing stunk of over-excitement. He looked down at his watch—yes, just as he'd expected, the woman was fifteen minutes early. She must've already tallied the commission check she would receive if she successfully sold Sea Verge, and the ridiculously large number had her chomping at the bit to get the show on the road.

The woman had no idea she was never going to get to sell anything.

"Coming!" Jarvis called, as he neared the front entrance to the house. He couldn't ever remember feeling this unsettled when he'd been in the service of Calliope's father, the previous Death. True, her father's Reign was nowhere near as fraught as the one Calliope had inherited, but still, it'd had its rough patches, too.

But Calliope? Calliope was another story altogether. Jarvis was certain she'd been created just to thrust his well-structured existence into utter turmoil.

Not that he didn't love the girl like a daughter—which was an odd statement given the body he now possessed was that of a twentysomething hipster, clearly closer to Calliope's age than to her father's. He'd been born a faun, the progeny of an anonymous coupling at a Bacchanal, but during his time as Calliope's Executive Assistant, he'd been killed and brought back to life, losing his older body and acquiring this newer, younger model in its place.

It was an "almost" adequate exchange—the large, emaciated hipster frame for the tiny faun haunches and humanoid upper body—though he did miss his Tom Selleck–inspired mustache. To his extreme consternation, the body he now inhabited did not seem capable of growing anything but scruff.

The doorbell chimed again and again, insisting that someone, somewhere acknowledge its existence.

Jarvis turned the doorknob just as the last chime died away, throwing the wooden door wide open. To his surprise, the visitor on the other side was not the one he'd been expecting.

Well, he'd anticipated this guest's appearance, but he'd just assumed he would be the last to arrive because he was traveling the farthest.

"Jarvis, where in God's name is my girlfriend?" Daniel, the former Devil's protégé and newly minted acting Steward of Hell, said as he stood on the front doorstep, looking anything but happy.

He didn't wait for an answer, just pushed past Jarvis and strode into the foyer.

"She's not here and I have no idea where she went," Jarvis said, jogging behind Daniel, as the Steward of Hell made for the stairs, taking them two at a time in his haste to reach the second floor.

"I don't believe you. I think she told you to say that."

Jarvis shrugged, not that Daniel was paying any attention to him.

"But I'm going to check her room just to make sure—"

Daniel didn't bother knocking, just pushed the door open and stepped inside.

Then he got quiet.

The room had been cleared out. No sheet-covered furniture like the rest of the house. Absolutely nothing had been left inside.

Daniel turned around slowly, his brow furrowed, eyes demanding an answer to his unspoken question: *What the Hell?*

Jarvis sighed, leaning his bony shoulder against the wooden doorframe.

"She's gone—"

"I see she's gone," Daniel interrupted, his ice blue eyes chilling. "Where?"

Jarvis was prepared for this eventuality. He and Calliope had spoken about what he would say when Daniel and Clio and Noh arrived—and they would all be here soon enough.

"Calliope has departed"—Daniel started to protest, but Jarvis held up his hand for silence, so he could finish. "And I don't know where she intended to go, so it's no good interrogating me. But she's asked that you remain here until she returns."

Jarvis could almost hear Daniel grinding his teeth in frustration and he empathized with the other man's situation—not knowing where someone you loved had gone could be frightening.

"You don't know where she is or you won't tell me where she is?" Daniel pressed.

Jarvis shook his head, his caterpillar eyebrows bunching together as Daniel paced back and forth in front of the bedroom door like a caged tiger.

"I don't know. Honestly, I don't."

Jarvis felt sorry for Daniel and he felt sorry for himself, too. He hated being the gatekeeper when he didn't agree with what Calliope was doing—but he was still her Executive Assistant and that meant he had to do her bidding, regardless of how he personally felt about her orders.

"This morning I opened my mail to see that Callie had iTunes gifted me this very, I assume, *prescient* Dolly Parton song called, 'I Will Always Love You,'" Daniel said, roughly dragging his hands through his dark hair so that a few pieces stood up like a cockscomb. "Now I show up here—knowing something's wrong if she's sending me that song—only to find the place empty. It's extremely confusing."

Jarvis wished Daniel would stop expressing his anger and take a moment to calm down. The right question asked, would set all explanations into motion. Though Jarvis had been truthful when he'd said he didn't know where Calliope had gone, he was chock-full of lots of other extraneous information . . . including why Calliope had seen fit to go in the first place. And many, *many* important things could be gleaned from understanding Calliope's reasons for leaving. But until Daniel was ready to listen to him, there was nothing Jarvis could do to ameliorate the other man's worry.

Daniel strode past Jarvis and sped down the hallway. Jarvis knew there was nothing for Daniel to find at Sea Verge, so he kept his pace to a trot, already feeling exhausted by what was ahead of him.

"I'm checking the study—" Daniel called back to Jarvis as the two men hit the circular stairway.

"Be my guest," Jarvis replied, shaking his head. There was nothing in the study, but the last of the sheet-covered furniture. *And the book.*

He decided there was no need to chase after Daniel, so he slowed his pace, letting the other man get ahead of him. He took the stairs one at a time and kept a leisurely pace as he moved down the hallway, so that when he finally arrived at the study, Daniel was already there, leaning against the massive sheet-covered desk Calliope had inherited from her father.

"I don't understand," Daniel said, his voice strained. "Where's Callie?"

"As I said before, Calliope is gone and I have no idea where she is—"

Jarvis saw Daniel's mouth open, as if he were going to argue, but then he closed it, starting to pace in front of the desk, instead. Finally, he stopped and turned to face Jarvis.

"Okay, you don't know where she is. Got it," Daniel began. "But if you don't know *where* she is, then do you maybe know *why* she left?"

"That was the very question I'd hoped you would calm down enough to ask—"

Jarvis was interrupted by the peal of the doorbell. He knew who would be at the door this time.

The damned Realtor.

He took a deep breath and gave Daniel an encouraging smile.

"I need to answer the door, but you can come with me," Jarvis said.

Daniel didn't need to be asked twice.

jennice kicked the wheel of her tiny Ford Aspire and cursed the day she'd bought it. A friend said it "aspired to be a car" and she'd laughed, but it wasn't far from the truth.

She'd bought it used. It'd looked good in its pictures on craigslist, but the reality wasn't nearly as pretty. It'd driven fine the first two months and then it'd just begun to sputter and shudder its way into falling apart. She took it to a mechanic who'd openly laughed at her, pointed to the odometer, and told her someone had reset it. Which meant the car had seen way more than the thirty thousand miles the seller had claimed.

Then the mechanic had given her the estimate for fixing everything on the clunker, and the figure on the piece of paper was so exorbitant all she could do was try not to cry. It far exceeded the amount of money she had in her bank account.

Head swimming, she'd asked him how much to get it running, no bells and whistles. He'd quoted her another number— still high, but a little more manageable—and she'd pulled out her checkbook.

Six months later and here she stood, on the side of the road, the Aspire's prospects looking very uncertain.

Jennice pulled out her cell phone, remembered she'd let her AAA membership lapse and that there was no one to call, then dropped the phone back into her bag. She was just gonna have to hoof it the rest of the way to Sea Verge and hope the police didn't impound the Aspire. That would cost her even more money she didn't have in her bank account.

Maybe after she'd sold Sea Verge she could buy herself a new car. Nothing expensive, just something that ran well and didn't break down every time she drove it. That thought gave her something positive to hold on to and she used it to begin the long slog to Bellevue Avenue.

She hadn't gotten ten steps when a little green Honda Element swooped past then slowed down and pulled onto the shoulder in front of her. A woman with long, dark hair and the palest buttercream skin Jennice had ever seen jumped out of the passenger seat and jogged toward her, the woman's brown boots making crunching noises as they churned up the dirt.

"Your car break down?" the woman asked—and as she got closer, Jennice realized she wasn't much older than she was. Twenty-five, at the oldest.

"Yeah, it's been on borrowed time for a while now," Jennice said, hands on hips. "I guess it was finally time to pay the piper."

The woman laughed and extended her hand.

"I'm Noh. My friend, Clio, and I can drop you off somewhere if you need us to."

Jennice took Noh's proffered hand, it was cold as ice and there were hard calluses on the ridge of the palm.

"Actually, I'm just going to Bellevue Avenue," Jennice replied. "If you guys wouldn't mind dropping me there, it would be much appreciated."

Noh wrinkled her brow.

"That's odd. We're going to Bellevue Avenue ourselves."

Jennice smiled. It must be her lucky day after all.

"Well, that works out, then," Jennice said, pleased not to put Noh and her friend too much out of their way.

"Come on," Noh said. "I'll let you have shotgun."

As she followed the strange young woman back to the Element, she couldn't help wondering what Noh's story was. Jennice loved to make up imaginary lives for the people she met. She didn't really have any friends, mostly because she'd spent her teenage years looking after her mom, but she liked to pretend the people she made up stories about—who they really were and the fascinating secret lives they led—were actually characters in a giant tapestry she was weaving . . . and there was something about Noh that inspired a fairytale-sized addition to her project.

"By the way," Noh asked as she climbed into the backseat of the car, her face turned away so Jennice couldn't read her expression. "You don't happen to be going to Sea Verge, do you?"

All Jennice could do was nod, strangely frightened by Noh's question.

Maybe this wasn't her lucky day, after all.

four

The name? What was the name of the card game they were playing?

The old man had a terrible memory, but that hadn't always been the case. When he was young and spry, he could recite whole passages from the King James Bible like he was reading out a grocery list. But these days he was lucky if he could remember to put his own pants on.

The thought made him look down at his legs just to make sure he'd *actually* put his pants on. Yep, they were on. At least, he'd remembered to do that this morning.

Ever since his wife, Flora, had died six months ago, he'd been getting steadily worse. He had moments of lucidity—like right now—but those didn't last and they were always followed by long stretches of lost time.

Lost time. He wondered where it went? He knew it had to go somewhere . . . he just couldn't put his finger on where that might be.

He looked around the room, his brain trying to remember how he'd gotten to the recess room, but for the life of him he couldn't fathom how. He knew he was safe, that the other denizens of the Shady Glen Row Home For The Aged were all around him, enjoying the extracurricular activities and supplies that abounded in the recess room: cards, board games, books, painting supplies, clay to mold . . . even a television set for the lazy ones. There was a wealth of things to do if you wanted to participate—and he wanted to participate.

He looked down at his gnarled old hands, the skin coated with liver spots the size of silver dollars, and was disgusted. When had he gotten so old?

It was a question he asked himself on a daily basis.

He sighed, wishing he were anywhere but in the old, worn down body he was in—and that's when he noticed the lightness. It was in his fingers and toes, inching its way up his arms and legs toward his core. He'd never experienced anything like it before. He tried to speak, to let the woman sitting beside him (he had no idea what her name was) know there was something wrong with him, but words just wouldn't come.

A stroke? Was he having a stroke?

Not long before Flora died, they'd watched an old woman having a stroke at lunch. It'd been awful, the woman's face going slack as her body shook, then she was pitching forward into her plate of oatmeal. The aides had run over as quickly as their crepe-soled shoes could carry them, but the woman was already dead. He'd known it, Flora had known it, all the other old people around them had known it . . . because being so elderly themselves, when Death came to cull one of the herd, it tipped its hat to all of them.

He tried to get a word out, any word, but his vocal chords weren't working. He looked around, eyes fluttering in their sockets, trying to catch someone's gaze, let them know he was in trouble, but no one seemed to be paying him any attention.

The lightness quickly overtook his body and he knew there was no coming back from it. Whatever had ahold of him wasn't going to let him go.

Liddy had noticed Howard nod off, but she hadn't thought much of it. He usually fell asleep halfway through gin rummy, leaving the others to finish the hand without him. But the game had ended now and Howard was still asleep, his chin resting against his concave chest.

"Howard . . . ?" Liddy said, reaching out a stick-thin arm, the skin hanging off the bone like a flesh drape.

She poked Howard in the fatty part of his upper arm, but

instead of a startled, sleepy response, Howard remained inert, his chin continuing to rest against his chest. Liddy didn't need to poke him again. She had a pretty good idea Howard wasn't going to be playing gin rummy with them anymore.

"It's all right, Liddy," Howard said as he stood above her, the sight of his own, lifeless body a bit hard to take.

He reached out a hand and placed it on Liddy's shoulder, but it just went right through her like a shadow. He lifted up his hand, surprised to see that the skin was still old and liver spotted. He'd hoped his ghost would be in the image of his younger self.

"Oh, well," he murmured, just glad the pain from the rheumatoid arthritis he'd been battling these past five years was finally gone.

He waited patiently for Liddy to collect herself. It took her a few moments of deep breathing before she was calm enough to sound the alarm. Her voice came out in a tight, nervous curl, but the two on-duty orderlies heard her and ran toward the table, their dark eyes sad with the foreknowledge that their efforts would be futile—and then, as the two men in their crisp white orderly uniforms began to probe his dead body, looking for his nonexistent heartbeat, Howard slowly backed out of the room.

freezay and his charge didn't make it to the car. They were attacked the moment they set foot outside—well, the moment *Freezay* set foot outside; the kid was a ghost, whether he knew it or not, and didn't have a corporeal form.

The assailants moved so quickly Freezay didn't have time to prepare for the onslaught, instead, all the years he'd spent as a human policeman, and then as a detective for the Psychical Bureau of Investigations, kicked in. Slamming his fist into the face of the first man who'd dared to step into his personal space, he watched the man's nose explode into a Rorschach of blood. The man dropped to his knees, cupping his ruined nose in his hands as if this would stop the blood from flowing out.

Freezay didn't have time to feel bad about ruining the man's face. Someone else was already grasping his shoulders and trying to knock him off his feet. Keeping his weight on the balls of his toes, he sent a back kick into the guts of the new attacker, his heel connecting solidly with the man's solar plexus. Instantly the pressure on his shoulders slackened and he turned around to catch the shocked look on the other man's face as he tried to draw breath, his eyeballs nearly popping out of his eye sockets.

To his consternation, a third attacker descended on him now—this one bigger and more lethal looking than the first two combined. Freezay tried to fend the larger man off, but his blows only seemed to antagonize the giant. The fight—if you could call the undefended pummeling Freezay gave the giant's chest—only lasted a moment or two and then Freezay was airborne, the man's meaty hands gripping him around the middle and hoisting him heavenward.

The giant began to spin in circles, his feet as nimble as a dancer's, the forward motion making Freezay's stomach lurch—and then the giant sent him flying. Unprepared for the abrupt dismount, Freezay's back and head slammed into the brick wall separating his property from his neighbor's and he saw black. But his vision cleared pretty quickly when he realized the giant was on the move again. Ignoring the throbbing in his head, he used the wall to drag himself back onto his feet.

His front doorway was obscured from the road—and his nearest neighbors—so there was no chance someone would see the fight and call the police. Besides, the fog had already begun to roll in, coating the world in a thin film of cloudy gray. Even if the attack had happened farther out on the driveway, the likelihood of anyone noticing them would still be slim.

Freezay couldn't count on the kid to help him, either. The boy was merely a ghost without any ability to affect human reality. Which meant Freezay was entirely on his own. With that realization, he quickly decided that, yes, the best defense was really going to have to be a good offense. Rather than waiting for the giant to make his next move, he would have to get the jump on the big man first. And that meant he was going to have to make a full-frontal assault on the giant if he was going to have any chance of taking him down.

He steeled himself for the pain he knew was about to come, and, head bowed, burst off the wall like a swimmer, crashing into the big man with enough force to knock them both off their feet. The giant didn't know what hit him. He landed hard on his back, cracking the brick on the paved walkway. His body was so overgrown with steroid-created muscle he flailed like an upside-down turtle as he tried to right himself.

Freezay used the pause in action to reassess the situation. Out of the corner of his eye, he saw the ghost boy taking off down the driveway.

Good luck with that, kid, he thought, then turned his attention back to the fight already in progress.

The giant was out of commission and the goon with the ruined face had beat a hasty retreat, but Solar Plexus was still lying on the ground trying to catch his breath. Freezay walked over to him and placed his large black boot on the man's chest. He pressed down, lightly at first, and then with more pressure. The man started wheezing, eyes wide with fear. He had red hair and a weasely face boasting two protruding front teeth that made him *seem* dopey—though Freezay knew looks could be deceiving.

"Who sent you and what do they want?" Freezay demanded.

His head was pounding and he'd somehow managed to knock a front tooth loose, so it wiggled helplessly in his gum as he spoke.

Weasely Face shook his head.

"Get . . . off . . . me."

Freezay increased the pressure and the man cried out as one of his ribs cracked.

"I don't want to dispatch you, but you're pushing it, buddy," Freezay said, shaking his head.

Out of his peripheral vision, he saw the giant struggling to get up.

"Don't even think about it or I'll come over there and put you permanently out of commission," Freezay shouted and the giant ceased his struggles, a hangdog expression on his face.

"Now, you," he continued, grinding the heel of his boot into Weasely Face's chest. "Tell me what I want to know before I crack another rib."

Weasely Face raised his arms in supplication and Freezay eased up with his boot. A shudder ran through the prone man's body.

"Supposed to take you . . ." he wheezed, "back to Death, Inc. Someone there wants to talk to you about something."

Freezay slid his boot off the man's chest.

"Why didn't you just say that?"

Weasely Face coughed and sat up, cradling his side. It was apparent it hurt him to even draw a breath.

"The President and CEO of Death, Inc., requested your presence personally."

Freezay nodded. He'd expected Calliope to come harass him about the job offer she'd made him up at the Haunted Hearts Castle—Head of Death Security or something equally as nebulous—though he wouldn't have pegged her as the kind of gal to send out the Goon Squad to pick him up.

"If Calliope wants to talk to me, she can just wormhole herself over here and say hi," Freezay replied, offering Weasely Face a hand up, which the other man took hesitantly.

Behind them, the giant had begun to struggle again like a bug on a pin.

"Calliope?" Weasely Face said, his grip tightening on Freezay's hand. "You must be mistaken, brother, there's no Calliope . . ."

"No Calliope?" Freezay echoed, confused.

"There's only Death and his name is Frank."

With that, Weasely Face grinned, revealing those dopey-looking buckteeth of his again. Then all pretense of submission dropped from his face as he reached out and slammed his fist into Freezay's gut, penetrating the flesh and sliding into warm, gooey innards. Freezay blanched, the pain unbearable as he felt the goon's fingers maneuvering inside his guts.

"Fuck . . . off," he wheezed.

Which only made Weasely Face laugh.

"Not so much fun when the shoe's on the other foot, is it?"

He began to tug on Freezay's small intestines as if he could extract them in one long, sausage-y string.

"You like the gift we left you?"

"What . . . gift?" Freezay grunted, his body in agony.

"The body in the bedroom." Weasely Face giggled. "Poor kid didn't know what hit him."

"Bastard," Freezay growled—and then he spat at Weasely Face.

The gob of saliva and mucus hit the goon square on the cheek, soft as a kiss. Weasely Face started, but the surprise didn't last long and was quickly replaced by raw anger. Freezay watched the rage build inside of the other man, hatred boiling over as he reached up with his free hand and wiped the spittle away, smearing it against his jeans.

"You shouldn't have done that," Weasely Face said—and now he was grinning, but there was no mirth in his cold, dark eyes.

"Why not?" Freezay said, arranging his face into the smuggest expression he could muster.

Trying to beat the smirk off of Freezay, Weasely Face backhanded him; the blow was hard enough to make Freezay's head snap to the left with a sickening *crunch*—and then he saw stars as Weasely Face yanked at his guts with the hand that was entrenched in Freezay's innards.

"Too bad you didn't know it was a 'dead or alive' kind of invitation," Weasely Face said, his jack-o'-lantern grin splitting his face in two.

The last thing Freezay saw before he blacked out was Weasely Face leaning in toward him, his hot breath sweet and sour as he spoke:

"Sayonara, buddy. Long live the rightful Reign of Death!"

jarvis opened the door, once again expecting only the Realtor, but instead, found himself staring at a trio of very powerful-looking women. Obviously, he knew Clio because he'd been her father's Executive Assistant (as he was her sister's now) and had known her all her life, but the other two women were strangers to him. Though, there was something strangely familiar about the girl with the long, dark hair and the livid scar running across her face.

"Where are your manners, Jarvis?" Clio said. "Are we supposed to stand on the doorstep all day?"

"Yes, of course, come in," Jarvis said, flustered as he opened the door wider so the women could step inside.

"I think you've meet Callie's best friend, Noh, before"—that was why the girl looked so familiar; she'd just grown up since the last time he'd seen her—"and this is Jennice . . . the *Realtor* you called to sell Sea Verge?"

The annoyed question mark at the end of her sentence was a not-so-subtle demand for answers.

"Hi," Jennice said, sticking out her hand for Jarvis to take.

As her warm fingers slipped in between his own, he decided Jennice wasn't at all what he'd expected from a Newport real estate agent. She was young for one thing—in her early twenties, if that—and she had a round, pleasant face. Her dark eyes were fringed with thick black lashes and her mouth was pleasingly full and bow shaped. She was wearing a long, cotton dress in a rich mulberry color that did nothing to accentuate her curves, but, instead, hung like a potato sack on her Rubenesque frame.

What a shame to hide all that beauty under a bushel, Jarvis thought, his appreciation for the larger-bodied woman no secret to anyone who knew him. If his heart hadn't already been attached to another, he would've most definitely given Jennice the masculine attention she richly deserved. As it was, he was taken, so all he could do was give her a warm smile and tell her it was lovely to meet her.

"Thank you," she said, eyes downcast with embarrassment.

Luckily, Clio cut the awkward moment short when she noticed Daniel lurking in the hallway behind Jarvis.

"What are you doing here?" she asked, confusion ripe on her face.

"Your crazy sister sent me something weird this morning, so I hightailed it up here to see what was going on."

"Where is she?" Clio asked Daniel, as she stepped into the foyer.

Daniel shook his head.

"She's MIA, and Jarvis is keeping his lips locked."

Clio turned on Jarvis, raising an eyebrow in consternation. Jarvis knew he was in for the third degree because once Clio had her mind set on something she was like a pit bull, holding on until she got what she wanted.

"Why doesn't everyone go into the kitchen," Jarvis said, gesturing toward the back of the house where the state-of-the-art kitchen was located, "and I'll get Jennice started. She's going to want to look over the house immediately, I'm sure."

Clio scowled at him, sensing some kind of subterfuge, but Jarvis only shook his head and looked over at Jennice, trying to telegraph to Clio his intention of removing Jennice from the others, so they could talk openly and not frighten the uninitiated Realtor.

"I would love to take a look around the space," Jennice said, pulling a tiny notebook from her pocket as she followed Jarvis over to the staircase that led to the second floor.

"Off you go," Jarvis said, shooing Clio and the others away. "Clio, why don't you set the kettle to boil and we can have some tea?"

Clio gave him an odd look, but finally nodded.

"Sure thing, *Jarvi*."

She stressed the nickname he hated, and that she and Callie loved to use behind his back, knowing he would get the message: *Let's hurry this thing up.*

"I'll be there in one moment!" he called after them, as they left him alone in the foyer with Jennice.

"You'd better be!" Clio yelled back, before disappearing down the hallway.

"I'm sure you don't need my help," Jarvis said, turning his attention back to Jennice. "It's rather self-explanatory, I hope."

Jennice smiled at him.

"I think so. I'll do the upstairs first and then move to the lower floor."

"Excellent!" Jarvis said, as he watched her begin to climb the stairs, excitedly making notes in the notebook she'd brought along with her.

He turned to go, but Jennice caught him before he could get too far away.

"The crown molding is just gorgeous," she breathed, pointing to the ceiling as she turned to smile down at Jarvis. "Do you know anything about it?"

Jarvis returned the smile and nodded. He was an encyclopedia when it came to Sea Verge.

"All the molding in the house was hand carved especially for Sea Verge in Brienz, Switzerland."

Jennice made a notation in her notebook.

"Thank you," she said, turning back to admire the crown molding again. "You know, it's all the little details that are so important in making a good listing."

No one can be that excited about crown molding, Jarvis thought, but apparently Jennice was the rare exception.

"Have fun," Jarvis said, but Jennice was already moving up the stairs, lost in the grandiosity that was Sea Verge.

Satisfied that Jennice would be out of their hair for the duration, Jarvis turned and followed the sound of raised voices back toward the kitchen.

"Well, neither Noh nor I have spoken to her," Clio was saying as Jarvis entered the room, catching her in the middle of filling a silver teakettle she'd pulled down from one of the cabinets.

"Yeah, she's been incommunicado for a while now," Noh agreed, as she watched Clio set the kettle on the stove to boil.

Even though it was the most modern room in the mansion, Jarvis still loved the huge, open-plan kitchen at Sea Verge best of all. There was just something about the space that caused him to relax as soon as he'd crossed over its threshold, stepping into the dewy, yellow warmth from the overhead lighting fixtures.

Maybe it was the large center island encircled by a quartet of comfortable wooden stools, or its pristine white-tiled walls, or the gleaming appliances soaking in the sunlight that streamed in through the large bay window overlooking the backyard, but whatever it was, it inspired instant familiarity and a feeling of togetherness.

"We've just both been so busy," Daniel was saying—rather lamely, Jarvis thought—from his perch on one of the barstools.

The sound of five teacups being set down on the counter drew Jarvis's attention away from Daniel and back to Clio, who was now pulling a bag of English Breakfast tea from the cabinet and setting it beside a pretty white and pink-flowered enamel tea pot.

Not for the first time, Jarvis noticed how much she'd begun to look less like a punk rocker and more like a normal teenage girl. The change had occurred in tandem with her starting to date the Hindu God, Indra, but Jarvis believed it wasn't just love that made Clio change her style. She was growing up, maturing into a young woman, and the shaved head and ripped clothing just didn't jibe with her more adult self—although she was still holding on to her chunky, black-framed Buddy Holly glasses for dear life, so she hadn't completely changed her fashion sensibility.

Still, Jarvis thought she looked rather lovely in the pale blue kimono dress and black skinny jeans she was wearing, Buddy Holly glasses only complementing the ensemble.

"What's going on, Jarvis?" Clio said, turning to look at Jarvis as she accepted the teapot from Noh and filled the strainer with the loose leaf tea.

Jarvis opened his mouth to reply, but Daniel beat him to it.

"Wrong question, Clio," he said. "We already played this game and the right question to ask is: Why?"

"Why what?" Noh said, brushing away bits of loose-leaf tea that hadn't made it into the tea strainer.

"Why did Calliope leave Sea Verge," Jarvis said, all eyes now trained on him. "That is the correct question."

"Something's going on here and you better start spilling it," Clio said, as the kettle whistled and she removed it from the stove top, pouring its contents into the teapot before setting it back on the eye.

Jarvis was prepared to be as frank as possible. Now that they were all assembled at Sea Verge, he knew he had to keep them here for the next twenty-four hours—something that would not be an easy task once they'd heard what he had to say.

"The 'difficulty' came to Calliope's attention the day she met the Ender of Death for their duel," Jarvis said. "Though the thing seems to have started long before that."

"Okay, can you be more ominous?" Clio asked.

"I am not being dramatic," Jarvis replied. "I am trying to be as accurate as I possibly can."

"Just go on," Daniel said, shooting Clio a "cease and desist" look. "No one is going to interrupt you again until you're finished."

Jarvis seriously doubted Daniel's ability to control Clio when she was upset, but he decided to keep that thought to himself.

"Wait," Noh said, suddenly. "Before you start talking, tell me one thing."

Jarvis hesitated, not sure what the girl was going to ask of him.

"Yes?" he asked, waiting for her to continue.

She looked him dead in the eye, her gaze probing and intense, then she spoke:

"Why are you in the wrong body?"

This was the last thing he'd expected her to say.

"I, well, I—" he spluttered, but Clio swooped in to save him.

"How do you know he's in the wrong body?" she asked Noh.

Noh shrugged.

"I can just tell."

She left her spot at the island, walking over to Jarvis and taking both of his hands in hers—and Jarvis shivered because her fingers were so cold.

"What are you doing?" he asked when she suddenly lifted both of his arms up into the air.

"Callie never told any of you what I do, did she," Noh said matter-of-factly.

When no one answered, she smiled.

"I'm a clairvoyant . . . or, if I'm feeling more whimsical, I just say that I see dead people."

"I didn't know that," Clio said, picking up the teapot and pouring out tea into each of the mugs as though it were an everyday occurrence for human beings to see dead people.

Jarvis had known Clio her entire life—and he didn't think anything ever fazed her.

"It's how Callie and I met. We were part of the Strange Brigade at the New Newbridge Academy. There were a bunch of us odd kids, kids who didn't quite fit in with the rest of the student body, and we just sort of found each other and became friends. Actually, less like friends and more like family, really."

She returned her gaze to Jarvis, giving his hands a quick squeeze before letting them go.

"So because of my abilities, I can see that your soul doesn't fit in this body. It pops out in all kinds of weird spots," Noh added, poking at his side. "Like here."

"That tickles," Jarvis said, backing away.

"And here and here," she continued, ignoring Jarvis's skittishness as she pointed to his neck and head.

"Is that a bad thing?" Clio asked.

Noh shook her head.

"There's absolutely nothing to worry about, but it's just a

very, very curious phenomenon, something I haven't really seen before."

"Thank God," Jarvis said, sighing with relief. He didn't need any strange body issues cropping up in what was already proving to be an untenable situation.

"You can go on with your story now," Noh said, her whole face lighting up as she gave him a shy smile—and Jarvis thought she was truly beautiful in that moment.

"Thank you," he said, returning her smile. "As I was saying, it started with the duel. We all know Calliope had promised Marcel, the Ender of Death, she would meet him in one-on-one combat. The promise was given so he would back off and give her the space she needed in order to stop the Devil and Thalia from staging their coup on Death, Inc., and Heaven—"

Jarvis suddenly found his mouth was dry as a bone, and he paused here to take a mug of tea from Clio.

"And then, later, at the annual Death Dinner and Masquerade Ball, Marcel called her out on her promise. Obviously, she was scared of meeting him in battle—we all know she's an incompetent fighter—but she knew she had to keep her promise," Jarvis said, sipping on his tea as his mind wandered back to that fateful day. "But it was the only way to keep Marcel in his place . . ."

five

CALLIOPE

"But it's the only way to keep Marcel in his place," I said as I slid the body armor Jarvis had given me around my midsection and fastened it in place. "At least for a little while."

Jarvis nodded, his gangling frame wrapped in a heavy fur parka so thick I had a hard time seeing his face because of all the fluff. I shivered in my own lightweight wool-lined Zero-Loft jumpsuit, wishing I were wearing a similar ginormous parka. But since I needed to be free to fight, a parka of any kind was not in my future. Jarvis had kindly created a special warming spell for both of us so we wouldn't freeze—add to that the molded titanium body armor I was now fastening myself into—and I was as warm as I was gonna be, given the situation.

The situation being a battle to the death with Marcel, the Ender of Death.

Lovely.

We were meeting in a location of his choosing, but only because he'd been "kind" enough to let me push the date a little. Originally, we were supposed to do our "battle to the death" the day after the annual Death Dinner and Masquerade Ball, but Jarvis had felt this was a tad hasty and wanted me to postpone. The only way Marcel would agree to the postponement was for him to get to choose the duel's location. Neither Jarvis, nor I was pleased about this, but what could we do? I'd been impulsive and now I was going to pay for it.

In Antarctica.

Why the wily Frenchman had chosen this desolate spot—Ridge A, it was officially called—I had no idea, but it would definitely not have been my duel spot of choice. If I'd had *my* druthers, I'd have staged the thing at Barney's, so at least I could die amongst the designer clothes I loved. But, alas, the choice of venue was not mine and I'd ended up in "cold town" instead of "clothes town."

Jarvis, ever the fastidious Executive Assistant, had done his research on Ridge A and had gleefully told me the average temperature hovered around negative ninety-four degrees Fahrenheit—well below the point a normal human body could withstand without some supernatural help.

That was how I'd ended up in the crazy-ass jumpsuit, really wishing I'd peed before we'd wormholed it out of Sea Verge. Of course I would never give Jarvis the satisfaction of letting him know he'd been right (as usual) and, yes, I should've hit the head before we trekked out to the middle of nowhere. So, I was just going to have to be a good girl and hold it.

"Well, I believe you are as ready as you ever will be," Jarvis said, handing me a titanium scythe that bore a razor-sharp diamond blade.

"Do I really have to use this?" I said, taking the scythe and feeling its heft. "I think this choice of weaponry is a little too on the nose, even for my taste."

"It was Marcel's choice," Jarvis sighed—and I knew what he was thinking: Once again Calliope's impetuousness had backed her into a corner.

Of course Jarvis was right. If I hadn't let Marcel rush me into setting a date for the duel, then I'd have had a lot more leverage.

Instead, I was forced to cater to Marcel's weird flights of fancy . . . like this stupid scythe. A scythe being the predominate weapon of choice in pretty much every artist's rendering of Death.

"I know. It's all my fault," I said. "One more Calliope Reaper-Jones cock-up."

Jarvis snorted, eyes bright within the fur of the parka's hood.

"You were well-intentioned," Jarvis conceded, trying to make me feel better.

"That I was," I concurred, stepping away from Jarvis and giving the scythe a few practice swings. "Shall we do this thing?"

Jarvis nodded.

"Yes, I believe we shall."

I took a deep breath—wishing I was anywhere else—then I began to march toward what was a more than probable death, Jarvis trailing behind me, acting the part of my very reluctant "second."

Wanna talk about freezing your balls off? Well, this was a place where that phrase actually carried a little weight. The air was calm, but so cold I could totally feel the snot crystallizing on my upper lip. The visibility was amazing; clear enough to see the powdery blanket of white coating every spare inch of the place.

I noticed the ice and snow wasn't as slick as I'd expected. Of course, the special boots I was wearing added to my stability, but the ice pack would've been firm and maybe not too terribly hard to walk on even if I weren't wearing them.

"I see him," I said suddenly, pointing ahead of us to where Marcel and his second were standing out in the center of the ice, waiting for us.

Marcel's second was wearing a parka similar to Jarvis's so I couldn't see who or what it was, but Marcel looked chipper, shifting his scythe back and forth between his hands. To my surprise, he was wearing only a leather singlet, which left his arms and legs totally exposed to the elements. I knew he was probably all spelled up to keep himself warm, but still, his lack of clothing was kind of intimidating . . . and distracting.

If I hadn't known Marcel, hadn't experienced his bad behavior personally, hadn't seen him do terrible things—like behead my father in cold blood—then I might've found his slim body *very* attractive. To the uninitiated, he was heartbreakingly beautiful, with blond curly hair and a cherubic face, all angelic and pure looking—but to me he was a lowlife, the skankiest of skanks, and the less I had to interact with him, the better.

It made me ill just to look at his smarmy face.

"You made it," Marcel purred when we reached the appointed spot and stopped.

"What were you expecting?" I asked. "A no-show?"

Marcel laughed, spinning the handle of his scythe between his fingers.

"Your predecessors have always been so humorless. You, at least are never at a loss for words."

I decided to take that as a compliment.

"Thank you," I said, giving a condescending little bow, which only made him laugh again.

"I must say you truly have proven to be more than a worthy opponent. When I first met you all those years ago, I would never have believed it."

I'd met Marcel—he was calling himself "Monsieur D" back then—when, as a kid playing hide-and-seek at Sea Verge, I'd unwittingly stumbled across a doorway leading into the deserts of Hell. Unbeknownst to me, my father had trapped Marcel there in order to keep me safe—and little did he or I know that my childhood visit would have such serious repercussions, proving to be the catalyst that eventually destroyed my father and sealed my destiny forever.

Very heavy stuff, indeed.

"You were selfish, shallow, self-involved, vain—" Marcel continued. "Yet, you have survived and flourished as the new Death. Even now it amazes me."

"Oh, shut up and let's just do this thing," I snarled, annoyed by Marcel and his condescending, backhanded compliments. "If I'm going to die, then I want to get it over with, okay?"

Marcel grinned, shifting his scythe into his right hand and giving it a playful swing.

"If you insist."

"I insist."

Marcel waved his hand at his second and the parka-covered thing backed away. As much as I wanted Jarvis close by in case things got really bad, I knew I had to follow the rules of the duel.

I gave Jarvis a nod and, bowing his head, he did as I asked, falling back just as Marcel's second had done.

When the two seconds had reached a safe distance, Marcel offered me his bare hand. I took off my right glove and met his bare skin with my own.

"May the best man win," he purred.

"May the best *person* win," I corrected.

Marcel released my hand, so I could slide my glove back on.

"Ready?" he asked.

I swallowed hard.

"Ready."

Marcel was quick as a flash, bringing his scythe down on me like a sword. Instinct took over and I jumped out of the blade's way.

"Don't you think using scythes is a little on the nose?" I called out as I sliced at him with my "on the nose" weapon.

Marcel shrugged, easily parrying my attack.

"I thought it was fitting. Death coming to death by his own blade."

"*Her* own blade," I corrected again.

I was Death and I was a woman. Marcel needed to get that through his thick head.

"*Excusez-moi,*" he shot back at me. "Touchy, touchy, Miss Death."

Distracted by my anger, I almost opened myself up to a killing blow, but luckily I was able to dodge Marcel's scythe as it whistled by my head. Still, it was a close call.

Too close.

Wheeling around, I gathered all my anger and used it to launch a frontal assault. Raising my scythe behind me like a hockey stick, I ran at Marcel, catching him off guard. I had just enough of an offensive surprise to be able to shove the butt end of my scythe handle into his stomach, the blow sending him sprawling. He hit the ice hard, but rolled just out of my reach as I struck at him with the pointy end of the blade.

I hit ice instead of the soft flesh I'd expected, and it jarred me, sending a shockwave of pain up my forearms.

"Damn it! Stop being so wily," I yelled, frustrated by my inability to get him.

"Never!" he shouted, climbing to his feet and charging at me, a bull in a spectatorless arena made of ice and snow.

I wasn't prepared for his full body blow and I went flying, but was still able to twist in the air so I hit the ice with my side and not my back. I felt more than saw Marcel's scythe as it plunged toward my head, the cold spray of ice letting me know I'd managed to jerk my face out of the line of fire just in time.

Marcel swung his blade at me again and I borrowed his

trick, rolling away so he couldn't get at me. I quickly climbed to my feet, using the scythe pole to balance myself, but Marcel kicked it away, sending the weapon flying out of my hands. I didn't give him time to pounce, but dove for my lost weapon, sliding across the ice on my hands and knees, grasping like a blind man until I felt the scythe's handle, and yanked it back into my possession.

"You have a terrible job," I said, as I backed away from Marcel and his advancing blade.

"Why ever do you say that?" he asked, his cheeks red from exertion. It made me happy to think I wasn't making this easy for him.

"Because you spend your whole existence chasing Death, trying to put a stop to the natural order of things," I said, jumping back to evade the sweep of his blade.

"It's not so bad," he said, swinging at me with the handle of the scythe. "True, it did suck to be trapped in Hell, tied to a fucking palm tree, but who doesn't have a few shitty decades in their immortal existence?"

Marcel's immortality was very different from mine. His physical bodies came and went, but his soul, or ego, was always the same. *I* was tied to my corporeal form. When someone used my immortal weakness against me and I died, that was it. No more Calliope Reaper-Jones.

If my arch-nemesis killed me today—aside from my one immortal weakness, the Ender of Death was the only other thing that could destroy me—then all the near-death experiences I'd managed to scrape my way out of these past few months would be for naught.

It was kind of a bummer.

"Whatever you say, Marcel. I've never been tied to a palm tree, so I'm just gonna have to believe you on that one."

I blocked his next attack with my scythe handle, his diamond blade skittering off it—and that's when I saw my opening: Marcel's forward momentum had left his lower extremities totally vulnerable. I didn't hesitate to take my shot. I struck out at him with my left knee, catching him right in the balls. I heard a guttural *croak* come from deep inside of him, and then he dropped to the ground, a look of unimaginable pain washing across his face. I slid the edge of my scythe under his chin, pressing the sharp part of the diamond blade into his throat, drawing a necklet of blood just above his Adam's apple.

He stared up at me, eyes bloodshot—and I thought I saw a spark of amusement in his gaze.

"Stop!" I heard someone shout behind me.

I turned in the direction the voice had come from, still careful to keep my blade firmly pressed against Marcel's throat.

"Do not kill him, Mistress Death!"

It was Marcel's second, running across the ice toward us. Not one to be left out of the action, Jarvis was jogging back to us from the opposite direction. I couldn't see his face, but I knew he must be worried this was some kind of ploy to distract me and give Marcel the upper hand.

"Tell me why I shouldn't kill him," I yelled back at Marcel's second, whose identity was still obscured by the parka. "Give me one good reason!"

"Because your very existence might ride on this man's life," the second said as she threw back the hood of her parka.

I gasped, shock filling my gut as I realized Marcel's second was none other than Anjea, the Vice-President in Charge of Death for the Australian Continent—and an employee of Death, Inc.

My employee.

"Anjea? What is the meaning of this?" Jarvis cried as he reached us, his own shock as palpable as mine. He put a protective hand on my shoulder, but did nothing to encourage me to release Marcel.

"Jarvis De Poupsey," Anjea said, nodding her head at Jarvis, her long, unkempt hair bouncing in approval. "You have the voice of reason within you. You will understand."

She was a commanding presence, though her papery mocha complexion and thick Aboriginal features looked bizarre set against the icy backdrop of the Antarctic tundra. The tiny brown owlet on her shoulder, her familiar, I supposed you called it, nuzzled against her neck.

"I shall try to understand," Jarvis said, but he looked uncertain, confused by this surreal turn of events.

Anjea bowed her head, the soft folds of skin below her eyes and at her neck the only indication of her true age.

"You may release him now," she said, gesturing I should let Marcel go.

"Why should I do that?" I asked, knowing Marcel wouldn't have hesitated to take my head off my shoulders, were the situation reversed.

"What does your heart tell you to do?" she asked, looking deep into my eyes, almost as if she were trying to read my mind.

I'd only had limited dealings with the Goddess, but even in the little time I'd spent with her, she'd proved herself to be wise and selfless. I tried to do as she asked, tried to listen to what my heart was telling me, but it was so hard to hear its voice when my brain was screaming at me that this was the man who'd murdered my father.

I drew a shaky breath.

What *did* my heart say?

My heart said I just wanted to be left alone to do my job in peace.

I hesitated a moment longer, feeling the power of the blade as it sang to me, begging me to take Marcel's lifeblood, but then I did as Anjea asked, lifting the blade from Marcel's throat.

He scuttled away from me on all fours like a retreating crab. When he was clear of my reach, he lifted his hand to probe his wounded neck, his fingers coming away bloodied. I expected him to shoot me a nasty, hate-filled look, but, instead, I was surprised to find him appraising me, a newfound respect in his eyes.

"You were right, after all," he said to Anjea, his voice full of wonder. "She is the *balance*."

"The *balance*?" Jarvis and I both said at the same time.

"It was divined at your birth that your existence would herald the beginning of the next Golden Age," Anjea said. "This was why your mother was convinced to give you up, though she was despondent over it. It was for your own protection."

I'd only recently learned the woman who'd raised me wasn't my real mother. It'd explained a lot about my personality, why I didn't quite fit in with my family, and why my sisters and I were so different. It was kind of a relief to know I wasn't the black sheep of the family, that there was someone more like me out there. Still, it'd been tough to reconcile all the years I'd spent without my real mother in my life.

"She really wanted me?" I asked Anjea, unable to help myself.

Even though Caoimhe, my birth mother, was back in my life now, I still carried some doubts about her feelings for me. I knew I was being childish and insecure, but I found myself needing as much reassurance as I could get that she'd actually wanted me, that giving me up had not been her choice.

"Of course she wanted you," Anjea said sharply. "You were, and are, a very loved child."

I hadn't intended to cry, but Anjea's words cut me to the quick. To have her confirm I was wanted—by both of my parents—felt like washing away the pus from a festering wound. I guess I hadn't really understood how disconnected I'd felt from the woman who'd *actually* raised me. I knew she cared for me, but she'd always been so much closer to Thalia and Clio—her daughters by blood. I'd spent my life trying to please her, to make her love me as much as she seemed to love them. I didn't know this was an impossible task. That I was a constant, living reminder of something terrible from her past: her beloved husband's infidelity.

"But that is neither here nor there," Anjea said, yanking me out of my thoughts. "Those who seek to keep the world in decline and humanity trapped in its darkest phase, they want to destroy you, Mistress Death. Because with your destruction comes the blackest time of all."

This was a lot to take in.

I turned to Jarvis, expecting him to know what Anjea was talking about, but from the look on his face I realized this was news to him, too.

"Did Calliope's father know about this?" Jarvis asked.

Anjea nodded.

"It was why he fought so fiercely to keep Calliope free of her fate for as long as possible."

Jarvis nodded, digesting her words.

"And how does Marcel fit into all of this?" I asked, curious as to what her answer would be.

"He is the Ender of Death, true," she said. "But we have made a bargain, one you have just sealed for us."

I raised an eyebrow. I didn't like bargains that concerned me but I had no voice in.

"If you chose not to spare the creature that murdered the person you loved most in the world—your father—then you would blacken your soul with revenge. The balance would be destroyed and those who sought to keep humanity in the dark would have no further beef with you. Though they would still seek to unseat you as Death, but for personal reasons only."

"That doesn't sound very good," I said, kind of glad now Anjea had stepped in when she had.

"It would be a catastrophe, Mistress Death, for us all," Anjea agreed.

"But I did spare him, so what does that mean?" I asked.

"It was why we came here, to this desolate spot, so we would not be observed, or interrupted if we reached this summit. Now we must decide if the deal is to be finalized, or not."

I shifted my gaze from Anjea to Jarvis, trying to gauge what he was thinking, but he looked as confused as I felt.

"And what is this deal you would like struck?" Jarvis asked on my behalf.

"The Ender of Death will put away his directive for the next thousand years. He will become the Champion of Death, and he will fight on your behalf," Anjea said. "And believe me— when you leave this place, you will have much need of a champion. Someone is seeking to merge our universe with another, one where your old nemesis, Frank, is Death. You don't exist in that universe, so you will be destroyed utterly if the two are allowed to come together as one. You must stop this."

"That makes no sense," I said, shaking my head as I tried to comprehend what Anjea was saying. Instead, I focused back on the Ender of Death. "The whole point of the Ender of Death is to kill Death. Why would he agree to something like this?"

"It was a trick," Marcel said, wading into the conversation for the first time. "I didn't think you would last two seconds in battle and Anjea believed otherwise. We made a wager and I lost. Now I am bound by my word."

"There has to be a catch," I said, finally, because I'd been hanging around the Afterlife long enough to know you never got anything free. There were always strings attached.

Anjea looked down at Marcel, who nodded—and I knew

she was about to tell us all about the dreaded "strings" that came with this pretty little deal.

"There is always a catch, Mistress Death," Anjea agreed. "When the Golden Age is over, if you are still the reigning Death after those thousand years, you will bend your neck to Marcel and he will have the satisfaction of chopping your head off, rescinding your immortality."

I just stood there, trying to take in what Anjea had said, but I was dumbfounded. What she was implying sounded more like handcuffs than strings. Jarvis saw my distress and squeezed my shoulder, letting me know he wanted to speak to me, alone.

"Let me discuss this for a moment with my Executive Assistant," I said, holding up my hand.

"Hurry, Mistress Death," Anjea said, "even now those who seek your demise are on their way."

I grabbed Jarvis by the parka collar and dragged him a few feet away from where Anjea and Marcel were standing, waiting for my answer.

"What do you think?" I whispered.

"I don't know what *to* think," Jarvis said, his voice low and uncertain.

"I mean, it's definitely stamping an expiration date on my ass," I continued, "but if it'll bring about this Golden Age, then maybe it's what's supposed to happen."

Jarvis nodded then immediately shook his head.

"No, I think we should ask for more time to think it over. We have no idea if this is just a ruse to keep Marcel's head in place, or if there is truth to what Anjea is saying."

I trusted Jarvis implicitly—if he said to ask for more time then we'd just go ask for more time.

"You're right," I agreed. "We'll ask for more time then we'll go home and get the crew together, see what they think."

And by crew, I meant Clio, Daniel, my friend, Kali, and my talking hellhound pup, Runt.

"Agreed," Jarvis said.

Satisfied with our decision, we broke our huddle, and turned around to let Anjea know what we'd decided—but my words froze in my throat. The ice behind us was covered in arterial blood . . . Anjea's arterial blood.

Her body lay on its side, blood gushing from the gaping hole where her head should've been. I spotted the head—eyes wide, mouth in a terrible rictus of pain—resting a few feet away, where it had landed after it'd been forcibly removed from her shoulders. A flash of brown wings crossed my field of vision and I stepped back as Anjea's owlet flew past my face then zoomed upward, disappearing into the frozen white sky.

I shifted my gaze away from the owlet and found Marcel, scythe flashing, as he battled a man wielding a golden ax. I knew the man hadn't been there when Jarvis and I had gone into our huddle, so I surmised he'd just wormholed in for a surprise attack.

"Gold must have been Anjea's weakness," Jarvis whispered in my ear, as he pointed to the golden ax the stranger was using like a meat cleaver.

I nodded, my eyes riveted on Marcel. He cut a graceful figure as he used his diamond-bladed scythe to slice away at the man who'd murdered Anjea, beating him farther and farther away from where Jarvis and I were standing.

"Get out of here!" Marcel yelled back at us, startling me out of my state of inaction. "I'll find you—I always make good on my word!"

Jarvis yanked my arm, pulling me behind him as he tried to distance us from the carnage.

"I guess that means we're accepting the deal," I said weakly.

Jarvis ignored me, focusing on the spell he was using to call up a wormhole and get us the hell out of Ridge A.

"Jarvis, are you listening to me?" I said, having a hard time focusing on what was happening.

"Of course I'm listening to you," Jarvis said, as the air around us began to shimmer and quake. "It means, Mistress Calliope, someone is out to get you. Someone very, *very* bad."

I watched as the wormhole finally coalesced into being in front of us, the beginnings of hysteria gnawing at my insides. Suddenly, I felt something wet on my cheeks and I reached up with tentative fingers, terrified I'd find blood on my face.

But when I looked down at my hand, there was no blood.

Only tears.

six

"And so we returned to Sea Verge," Jarvis concluded. "And everything had changed."

The tea in his hands was cold and he had barely tasted it. He set his mug back on the kitchen island and waited for the unhappy response he knew was coming.

"Calliope would never do that," Clio said.

Behind her, Daniel had begun to pace again, the echo of his heavy tread filling the otherwise silent room.

"This is bullshit. Cal would never get involved with the Ender of Death. He murdered our dad," Clio continued.

"Be that as it may," Jarvis said. "It is what happened. And as much as I detest it, it cannot be changed—"

"How is it possible for someone like Anjea to be killed and, yet, no one in Hell heard a word about it," Daniel said. "She's the Vice-President in Charge of Death for the Australian Continent—"

After they'd returned from Ridge A, Jarvis had had the exact same thought, so he'd done some checking, making an incognito trip to the Hall of Death on Calliope's behalf.

But there'd been no mention of the Vice-President's demise in her Death Record, and this had given Jarvis pause.

He knew what he'd seen with his own eyes, and that included the beheaded corpse of the Vice-President in Charge of the Australian Continent. He'd been present as Marcel battled her murderer, giving Jarvis and Calliope a chance to escape, unscathed.

None of it made any sense. Death Records didn't lie and their magic was intractable, making it impossible for anyone to tamper with them.

In the end, he hadn't been able to come up with a plausible answer as to why Anjea was still listed among the living—but somehow she'd managed to cling to some semblance of life up on Ridge A.

"That was my first thought, as well: How could there be no uproar over Anjea's murder? So I went to the Hall of Death and checked her Death Record myself," Jarvis said.

"And there was nothing?" Clio asked, concern growing steadily in her eyes. "No mention of her death in her record. That's impossible. I interned at the Hall last summer and I got to know their system pretty well. It automatically records all births and deaths, including the ones for immortals. No one— not even Death, herself—can mess with those things."

"I know," Jarvis said. He was as confused by the situation as Clio and Daniel were.

Only Noh remained silent, observing the others through half-lidded eyes.

"The records are indestructible," Clio said, setting her mug down hard on the counter, the sound jarring to everyone. "They can steal them. They can salivate over them. They can molest them. They can try to destroy them, but they can't change them. It's impossible."

"I know."

This was all Jarvis had to say in reply to Clio's angry tirade—because she was right. The Death Records only recorded the truth.

"Does that mean Anjea's alive somewhere, then?" Daniel asked as he leaned against the kitchen island. "That she engineered this whole fake death thing in order to trick Callie into making this deal with the Ender of Death?"

"I need to get to Purgatory and look at the records—" Clio said, starting to get up from her stool, but Jarvis laid a hand on her shoulder, staying her.

"You can't wormhole from Sea Verge," Jarvis said as Clio stared at the restraining hand on her shoulder. "It will destroy the protective spell Calliope asked me to create around the mansion before she left . . ."

Clio narrowed her eyes.

"And you won't be received warmly when you get to Death, Inc.," Jarvis continued. "I almost didn't make it out myself. Except for Kali, the Board of Death has been co-opted by Uriah Drood and his minions. The Harvesters and Transporters are doing his bidding, too. All in direct opposition to Death, Inc., protocol. All because they've presented the Afterlife with another version of the truth: a new Death."

Clio stared at him as though he were speaking in tongues. She didn't want to believe what he was saying—and he couldn't blame her. The whole thing sounded entirely implausible, even to his own ears.

"That's impossible," she said, finally, stepping away from him.

"The balance of power has shifted," Jarvis said. "And Calliope Reaper-Jones is being written out of the annals, her deeds eradicated as if she never existed. Uriah Drood is even now in the process of installing his new Death in her place."

Three pairs of disbelieving eyes were locked on him now, waiting for him to continue. It wasn't that he hadn't expected their disbelief—he'd been mentally preparing himself for it, in fact. But the reality of having people he cared about look at him as though he were a liar, was much easier imagined than experienced.

"Drood has tapped into something great and terrible. He's using the knowledge inside of the original copy of *How to Be Death* in order to create a giant collision between our universe and another. And in this other universe, Calliope Reaper-Jones does not exist. There, Purgatory is under the control of a different Death. One who exists in our universe, as well, but in a different capacity."

"You're not talking about me, are you?" Daniel asked, a worried expression on his face.

Daniel and Calliope had both been in the running to become Death after Calliope's father was kidnapped, but Daniel had forgone the opportunity, deciding to help Calliope win the job, instead.

"No, you're not Death in this other universe," Jarvis said reassuringly.

"How do you know what you're saying is even scientifically possible?" Clio asked, eyes narrowed as she tried to logic out the problem. He'd known that she, alone, would want hard, scientific proof—this was the way her mind worked—but it wasn't something Jarvis could give her.

"I have nothing but my word to give you, Clio," Jarvis said. "Kali came here, she spoke to me and your sister. Everything I've said came directly from her mouth. Drood has done what your sister and the Devil, as outsiders, could not do. He's taken over Death, Inc., from the inside out."

"It's Frank, isn't it?" Daniel said, suddenly, nostrils flaring with anger as he looked around the room, begging someone to contradict him.

Jarvis felt bad for him. He knew Frank was the man Calliope had almost ruined her relationship with Daniel over, and it would be like someone sprinkling salt on an open wound, having Frank reintroduced into his life like this—but, sadly, the acting Steward of Hell was correct.

"Kali said that in the other universe, Frank is a despotic Death—one who abolished Death, Inc., and returned Purgatory to the Dark Ages, destroying all the improvements your father, Clio, instated when he took over the job in our universe."

"If this is true. If what you and Kali say is really happening is *really* happening," Clio said. "Then we have to do something about it. We can't just sit here talking and not acting—"

Clio had never lived in a world where Death, Inc., didn't exist, where the management of Purgatory was overseen by dictatorial, power-hungry madmen who did as they liked without any thought to how their craziness might affect the rest of the Afterlife. But Jarvis had been around long enough to remember the darker days, before Clio's father had taken over Death, and he knew he would do anything not to have Purgatory plunged back into the Dark Ages.

"—so let's go to Death, Inc., and do something. It's very

simple. We've fought these assholes before and we can do it again."

Jarvis appreciated Clio's enthusiasm, but there was nothing "simple" about this situation.

"So this is why Callie's room is empty," Daniel said. "Because her life is being erased?"

Jarvis nodded.

"She won't exist here much longer unless something drastic is done to stop the two universes from joining. And as they get closer to becoming one, the more things will change."

Noh had remained mostly silent during the course of the conversation, but now she spoke:

"It's the truth. It seems illogical, but I feel in my bones that it's right."

"Then let's go," Clio said, striding toward the door.

"Wait," Jarvis said before Clio could reach the threshold.

"What?" she said, turning back around to shoot him a look of annoyance.

"Calliope. Your sister," Jarvis said, trying to find the right words. "She has empowered me to keep you here at Sea Verge."

Clio rolled her eyes at him.

"That's ridiculous. You can't dictate what I do or don't do—" she began, but Jarvis cut her off.

"You and Jennice, the Realtor upstairs, are two of the next 'possible' Deaths."

Clio froze, her body rigid as she tried to take in what Jarvis was telling her.

"Calliope wants the two of you protected, here at Sea Verge," Jarvis said, the words difficult for him to get out. "If she is killed before the universes merge, then the game is changed completely—"

Clio stared at him, uncomprehending. Only Daniel seemed to understand what Jarvis was getting at.

"She'll ask the Ender of Death to kill her before the universes merge, Clio," he said. "That way you, the possible 'Deaths,' will rise up in this universe in the wake of her death. The two of you must exist in both realities, so you'll be able to continue the fight against Frank for her."

He fixed his gaze on Jarvis—and it was all Jarvis could do to nod.

"She'll sacrifice herself for our world," Daniel finished. "And she needs you, and that girl upstairs, alive and well, so if that happens, you can save the rest of us."

Clio shrank visibly as Daniel's words sank in.

"No . . ." she said, her voice strangled by emotion.

Then she turned tail and fled the room.

Noh started to go after her, but Jarvis held her back.

"Give her some space. It would be a difficult thing for anyone to digest. Let alone when the person sacrificing themselves for you is someone you love."

Jarvis knew this from experience—because he did not want to imagine their world without Calliope in it, either.

freezay opened his eyes and saw only a black void. Then he realized there were little twinkling things in the darkness and he felt slightly better.

Stars meant he was still alive.

As his eyes adjusted, he became aware he was lying outside, not too far from his front door. Not too far from—

He reached down and felt around for the gaping hole in his gut, the one Weasely Face had made when he'd stuck his hand into Freezay's very vulnerable intestinal cavity. But to his surprise, he found nothing but unblemished skin and tattered fabric. Fabric, he decided, that had once constituted the bottom of his shirt.

"I made them go away."

Freezay watched as a woman's head came into view above him. He squinted, trying to place her, but then he realized he didn't know the face. Because he would've remembered a face like this one: high cheekbones, pale ivory skin, light eyes whose color he couldn't discern in the dark. Her hair was damp, framing the beautiful features of her face like a moonlit halo. She smiled down at him then reached out with a tentative hand to stroke his hair. That was when he noticed she wasn't wearing any clothing, just a small, red-jeweled pendant hanging from her neck like a scarlet teardrop.

"Who are you?" Freezay asked, struggling to sit up.

Her fingers fell away from the white-blond strands of his hair as she stood up from where she'd been kneeling beside him, and he realized, suddenly, he didn't want her to stop touching him; that he liked it.

She seemed to sense his interest in her and giggled, scooting a few feet away from him so he was treated to a limited view of her naked body, her breasts and hips covered only by the long tendrils of her pale hair.

He couldn't lie. It was a glorious sight, her curving silhouette outlined in moonlight. He found himself full of longing; the ache to be inside of another human being so strong he was frightened by the pull. He wasn't one to give in to carnal temptation so easily, but her nearness was severely testing his willpower.

"I'm Starr. And I made a promise to a friend I'd get you to Sea Verge," she said, drawing her pink lips into a perfect bow. "I hope you won't make a liar out of me."

Sea Verge? That was where Death, or in this case, Calliope, lived. He'd been there before when her father was in charge, but only on official business—never as an invited guest.

"What friend?" he asked.

Starr made a pouty face.

"Who do you think?" she asked, stepping back in his direction and offering him her hand so she could help him to stand. "Use your brain."

Once she got him standing, he realized that his head felt funny, all light and fuzzy, and he had to lean on her to keep himself upright. Something about the girl made the blood sing in his ears, only adding to his disorientation. It was lucky he was so physically incapacitated, or he'd have had a hard time not ravishing her right there on the carport.

"You still haven't explained who you are or why you're helping me—other than someone asked you to get me to Sea Verge," he said, as she led him over to the steps so he could sit down properly.

"I'm a Siren—and I'm Calliope's aunt. Is that helpful?" she purred as she sat down beside him, rubbing the back of his neck with her long fingers.

Of course! No wonder he was having all these misplaced sexual urges. Siren's were sexually intoxicating by definition. Whether they were sunbathing on rocks, luring sailors to their doom, or making an ex-detective from the Psychical Bureau of Investigations feel like a horny teenager, they were bad news.

Notoriously fickle, they were sly and only lifted a finger to help if it was in their own self-interest to do so, which made them excellent mercenaries. They loved shiny objects, so it was easy to buy their allegiance: Just hold some gold coins or sparkly jewels under their noses and they'd do anyone's bidding.

He knew the woman who'd raised Calliope was part Siren, as were Callie's half sisters, Thalia and Clio—so maybe the familial connection would negate some of Starr's more Siren-ish qualities. But until he'd spent more time with her, he would proceed with caution. Even if Calliope *had* sent her, it didn't mean she could be entirely trusted.

"Yes, very helpful," he said, better able to control his impulses now he knew his libido was being manipulated by the Siren's nearness.

Starr stared at him for a moment, then her pretty face became hard as stone.

"You think I like dirty old men getting all hot and bothered over me, don't you?" she said, standing up then glaring at him as he grasped her wrist to keep her from leaving. "Well, I don't. It's disgusting and I hate it. I mean, you would never blame a shark for being a predator. That's just how they were created— and I wish you humans would afford me the same respect."

Freezay found he couldn't argue with her logic.

"But every now and then," she continued, switching moods so easily Freezay got emotional whiplash, "you cross paths with someone you don't mind turning on."

She eased herself back down on the step beside him then leaned forward seductively so her wet, pink lips were inches from his own.

"And then it's kind of nice to know how easily you can wrap them around your little finger."

She kissed him then, before he could turn away—not that he *really* wanted to turn away—and the kiss was electric. It sent frissons of heat coursing through his body. He reached out, his fingers entwining in her long, sea-drenched hair, the taste and smell of the ocean filling his senses. He couldn't help himself and pulled her closer. Her naked skin, so soft and silky, made him want to weep.

"That's enough," she said, pushing him away as he hungrily clambered for more.

"What? Why?" he said, his voice thick with lust.

She gave her knuckles a very manlike *crack*, then grinned at him.

"I just wanted to show you what I could do to you . . . if you were nice to me."

He'd laughed as he realized he'd been molested on the whim of an egoist. Well, he'd had worse done to him.

Much worse.

He knew she was playing with him, trying to incite him into a frenzied state of sexual aggression. But instead of falling into the machismo stereotype she expected, he calmly changed the subject.

"So if that guy put his hand through my intestinal wall, why isn't there any damage?" he asked Starr.

If the Siren was thrown off her game, she didn't show it.

"I didn't make you an immortal or anything, if that's what you're getting at," she said. "I can't do that."

"But for all intents and purposes, I should be dead right now—" he said, pressing the point.

Her laugh was like the trill of a dozen tiny bells, all vibrato and treble.

"You should be dead. That's true. But I used my little jewel on you."

She grasped the tiny red stone at her throat, lifting it in the air for him to see.

"A wish-fulfillment jewel," Freezay said, reaching out to touch the dark red stone.

Starr nodded, pleased he knew what it was—but then her eyes went dark with suspicion.

"It's mine and you can't have it," she said, petulant as a child, snatching the jewel out of his line of view.

He wasn't about to take her pendant away from her. It was just a very rare artifact, and he was interested in getting a closer look at it.

"I've never seen one before," Freezay said softly, trying to seem as obsequious as possible in order to allay her fears.

He really had no intention of stealing the charm out from under her nose, but he did want to get another look at the jewel.

"That's because they're very rare," she said, relaxing her

hold on the pendant and letting it drop, so it fell into the hollow of flesh between her collarbones.

"Where did you get it?" Freezay asked, his curiosity aroused by the jewel.

"From a friend."

But that was all he could get out of her. She was on guard now, hyperaware of his interest in her charm.

"What about the kid?" he asked, changing the subject again.

"What kid?"

She didn't seem to have a clue what he was talking about, and this made him feel as though a weight had been lifted from his shoulders.

It's good she didn't see the ghost, he thought. *It means the Harvesters and Transporters finally came to collect the kid's soul.*

"Nothing," he said, pleased to be unburdened from looking after the ghost kid.

She narrowed her eyes, not buying his nonchalance.

"Maybe I should've just left you for dead," she muttered under her breath, obviously annoyed with him.

He decided it was a rhetorical question and didn't deserve an answer.

"Should we go to Sea Verge now?" he asked, instead, standing up. He was still unsteady on his feet, but he was actually starting to feel better.

"I thought you'd never ask," she purred.

jennice had never seen a more beautiful home in her life. It was like a museum or a castle . . . or something out of a *Masterpiece Theatre* miniseries.

There were views of the water from almost every window on the backside of the house, making Jennice wonder what it would be like to wake up in the mornings to such a beautiful vista. Probably made the start of your day more pleasant than waking up to a brick wall, which was what she saw every morning when she opened her eyes, because her bedroom window looked out onto the brick enclosure separating her building from the next building's Dumpsters—not a very inspiring sight.

She couldn't imagine why anyone would want to sell a place like Sea Verge. If it'd been her home, she'd have done everything in her power to keep it. Then she realized that if she'd grown up in a home like this one, her life would've been very different. Money would not be an issue, and she might not be so attached to one house, in particular, because she'd probably own like fifty more of them.

This was a sobering thought.

Well, if the house was going to be sold, then she was glad to be the one to do it. She would take good care of Sea Verge and make sure the people who bought her were worthy of her beauty.

"Oh, I'm sorry. I didn't know you were in here."

Jennice turned away from the view of the sea to find Clio standing in the doorway, her cheeks red and tearstained. Jennice, her big heart always getting her in trouble, couldn't help but reach out to the other girl.

"Are you all right?" she heard herself asking—which was a silly question because anyone with a brain could see she wasn't.

"I'm okay," Clio said, trying to smile, but the quiver of her lower lip undermined her words.

Jennice could feel the other girl's anguish radiating like heat, and before she knew what she was doing, she'd crossed the space between them and laid her hands on Clio's arm. She could feel the intense whirlpool of emotion percolating inside of the other girl, and where she touched bare skin, sorrow shocked Jennice's fingers like static electricity. It hurt, the pain making Jennice's eyes water, but it wasn't nearly as bad as when she worked on her mother, so she ignored the prickling sensation under her fingers and steadied her breathing. She gripped Clio's arm, squeezing the soft flesh as she corralled the anguish, forcing it to flow out of Clio and into her own body. She let it find purchase inside of her—and then it was over, Jennice dropping her hands and falling back against the wall, her breath coming in ragged bursts.

She had a terrible headache, but even distracted by the painful throbbing of her pulse in her temples, she was pleased to note Clio looked much better.

"What did you just do?" Clio demanded, her eyes brimming with uncertainty.

Jennice didn't know what to say. She'd never let a stranger see her power before. Had never had to explain herself to anyone.

Even as a baby, Jennice's mother had known there was something special about her child, and she'd been very protective of her. But then when Jennice was fourteen, her mother, already old at fifty-seven, had gotten sick—so sick the pain made it impossible for her to look after Jennice properly. Jennice had learned to take care of herself, to make sure her mother's disability checks got cashed and that there was always food on the table. Besides these chores, Jennice had become her mother's caretaker and nursemaid, using her powers to keep her mother alive—though even they could not dull the exquisite pain her mother experienced on a daily basis.

And then this last time . . . her mother had been so bad even Jennice couldn't fix it. They'd taken her away to the hospital, where Jennice prayed the doctors could make her mother feel better.

"I don't know what came over me," Jennice said, stepping away from Clio. "I'm so sorry."

Clio stood in the doorway, not making a move to leave. But at least the tears were gone, and she seemed like she was more in control of her emotions again.

"I feel better," Clio said, dropping her shoulders and rolling her head from side to side. "I can hardly even remember why I was so upset. I mean, I do remember, but it's like an old memory. So weird."

She trailed off, her brow scrunched in concentration.

"I was just worried about my sister," she said after a long pause. "I came up to her room to see if it was really empty."

Jennice had never had a sister. It'd just been her and her mom for as long as she could remember.

"It's pretty empty," she agreed, lamely.

"She just . . . disappeared, you know, without telling me what was going on," Clio said, a tear trickling down her cheek. "I don't know where she is, or what I can do to get her back."

Jennice realized emotions were not as easy to cure as, say, a bad ankle sprain.

"Sorry," she added, as she wiped the tear away and gave Jennice a weary smile.

"Maybe she had her reasons."

It was just something to say. Jennice had no clue about the inner workings of Clio and her sister's relationship, or of sisters' relationships, in general.

"I'm sure she did," Clio said.

As they stood together by the door, surveying the empty room, they would've been surprised to learn they were each thinking a variation on the same theme:

It was nice just to stand with someone in companionable silence, without having to explain yourself to them.

They stood there, watching as the late-afternoon light faded away, the sun melting into the horizon just beyond the bedroom windows.

Finally, Clio broke the silence:

"Tell me about what you do with your hands."

Jennice scanned the empty room, looking for something, *anything*, to take the attention away from herself, but there was nothing.

"Stop looking all around like a cornered animal," Clio said, seeming to sense Jennice's discomfort. "I'm not going to bite your head off. Just tell me about what you do."

Jennice did not talk about her gift. Mostly because there was no one for her to talk to about it, but also a little because she was scared if she blabbed about it, it might desert her. She didn't know where this idea had come from, or how she'd become so superstitious, but she had. She tried hard not to even really acknowledge she was doing anything "special"—even when she was in the middle of a healing.

"It's nothing," she said, feeling hesitant about talking to Clio about something so intimate.

"It's not nothing," Clio disagreed. "You're a healer, aren't you?"

She didn't wait for Jennice to answer.

"Wow, there aren't very many of you guys out there. I mean, a few, but most of them go crazy pretty early on and kill themselves—"

Clio realized what she'd just said and stopped herself.

"Oh," Jennice murmured, trying not to let what she'd heard scare her.

"Damn, I'm sorry," Clio said. "I should watch my mouth."

"I've never wanted to kill myself. I don't think so, at least," Jennice replied, softly.

Her mind was spinning, Clio's words ricocheting inside of her. She'd never wanted to kill herself. Had never even imagined doing something so heinous, but now the thought wouldn't leave her brain.

"Maybe they were just unhappy people," she added, not believing her own words.

Clio shook her head. She obviously didn't believe in not being blunt in order to spare someone else's feelings.

"No, it has nothing to do with their personality. It's the pain and suffering they get exposed to, it becomes overwhelming after a while."

Jennice understood what Clio was driving at—and she figured if she were healing a lot of different people all the time, then maybe things would be different. But she was only helping her mother, and as tiring as that could be, the love she bore for the woman who'd raised her lifted away any of the bad thoughts, probably protecting her from the burnout Clio had mentioned.

"I don't do it very often," she said, finally.

"That's probably why you're as well-adjusted as you are," Clio agreed. "For someone in the supernatural world, that is."

Jennice was very curious about the "supernatural" world Clio was referring to, but she didn't want to reveal too much about herself. And asking questions meant she'd have to give answers in return, something she didn't know if she was ready to do. So she decided to keep her mouth shut and not broach the one subject she was dying to know more about:

Where were the other people like her? And why had she never met any of them?

If she'd grown up with even *one* other kid who understood what it was like to be different, she knew her life would've been easier. Except for her mother, there'd never been anyone else to confide in, or share her secrets with, and it'd made for a very lonely childhood.

And this was when Jennice realized, to her own dismay, that she was tired of being alone. She wanted to reveal her secrets to someone else, someone who would understand—and she thought maybe, just maybe, Clio might be that person.

Filled for the first time with the desire to know who and what

she was—a yearning she hadn't even known she'd possessed—
she opened her mouth and asked what she'd never been able to
give voice to before:

"Tell me about the 'supernatural' world. I want to know
what I've been missing."

seven

Howard was not prepared for the next phase of his death. The first part, the leaving the body and becoming a ghost part had been easy enough. It was the "what happens next" that stumped him.

He'd stuck around the retirement home for a while, watching as the aides cleared out the other residents from the area. They'd mostly ignored his body while they tried to calm everyone down and get them back to their rooms. He supposed he wasn't really a priority since Medicare and Social Security wouldn't be sending the home a monthly check on his behalf anymore, but still he felt sorry for his former physical self. In his mind, his body resembled a limp marionette puppet waiting for its master to pick up the strings and make it dance—though no one would ever pick up Howard's strings again. They'd been severed and now he was free floating, a ghostly presence in the midst of the living.

He hadn't tried to get anyone's attention, figuring if they couldn't see him standing there, then he was long gone from the realm of human senses. It wasn't like he particularly wanted any of them to know he was still lingering around. None of them cared if he was dead or not. He hadn't felt close to another human being since his wife's death—

His thoughts ground to a halt as he found himself excited by something for the first time since he'd ceased existing among the living.

If he was a ghost, then maybe his wife was one, too.

He couldn't shake the idea, once he'd come up with it. It was like a record player stuck on repeat.

How did one go about finding other dead people?

He couldn't just get out the Yellow Pages and look her up, and there weren't any other ghosts to ask. He didn't know what to do. He sat down on one of the now-empty card tables, a half-finished game of UNO spread before him. He reached out, intending to flip one of the un-played cards over, but his fingers went right through it.

But I'm sitting on the card table, he thought, curious about the rules of being dead—could you sit on something, but not touch it? Then he looked down and saw he wasn't *actually* sitting on the card table. It was more like he was hovering over it, his butt and hips a few millimeters off the tabletop.

There was a flurry of activity at the back door and Howard turned to see what was happening. It was the two men from the funeral home. He'd seen them before when they'd come to collect the first and only roommate he'd had after his wife died. When she'd been alive, they'd shared a private room. But after she'd passed, the home had quickly shuffled him out of there and into a space that wasn't half as nice. Plus it already contained an occupant, a man called Benji, who was even older and more out of it than Howard.

They'd been roommates for two weeks. Two *long* weeks of watching Benji's family (three sons and their families) battle with the fact their dad was in the advanced stages of Alzheimer's and had no clue who he was anymore—let alone who *they* were or why they kept bothering him. It was very sad and Howard, as terrible as he felt thinking it even now, was glad when Benji had died one night, peacefully in his sleep.

Howard had woken up at four in the morning to pee, and he'd noticed Benji wasn't snoring like he usually did. Curious, he'd crossed the room and bent down near the other man's face. There was a funny smell, like rotten cheese, and he realized Benji wasn't breathing.

He knew he should've called for an aide and reported the

death, but he felt sorry for the guy, thought he deserved a little peace and quiet. So he went to the bathroom and did his business then climbed back into bed and fell asleep. Needless to say, the morning aide discovered the body promptly at seven when she came in to get Benji ready for the day.

These same two men had come from the funeral home to collect Benji's body. Howard was supposed to be out of the room, at breakfast, but he'd forgotten his hat and had gone back to get it. He'd walked in on them bagging the body—an oddly pathetic sight—and he'd quickly grabbed his straw hat, escaping the room as fast as he could.

But the image of Benji's bloodless face being zipped up inside the black body bag had stayed with him for a long time.

Now he was next in line for the same treatment.

Fascinated, he couldn't stop watching as the two men from the funeral home began their work. He wanted to swoop over and yell at them, tell them to leave him alone, but he knew it was pointless—and he should be focusing on how to find his wife, not watching a heavy black body bag envelop his body. He was so distracted by what the funeral home men were doing to his old body, he didn't notice the Harvesters as they appeared behind him. Only the doleful ringing of a tiny bell, an artifact one of the Harvesters was carrying in his hand, made Howard turn around.

He goggled at them, the two strange men dressed in Victorian clothing, their watered silk top hats resembling stovepipes. The fabric of their suits—one in puce, the other midnight smoke, both colors usually seen only with Halloween costumes—was elegantly stitched together, tailored to their bodies like a second skin. One of the men was very tall with an Adam's apple protruding from his throat like an obstruction. He was wearing the puce-colored suit, his long torso halved where the top of the pants met the bottom edging of the suit coat, making it appear as though he could split himself in two. Howard imagined himself shoving the man, pushing against his chest with both hands just to see if the top half would slide off at the waist—but he restrained himself.

"Are you Howard Fielding?"

The other man, the one in the midnight-smoke-colored suit, spoke first. He was average height, a shock of pale apricot hair sticking out from underneath his top hat, the tiny silver bell in his right hand. The vest he wore, the only normal color on either of the men, was apricot and Howard found himself wondering what kind of person color coordinated their clothing with their hair.

"I am," Howard said, standing up from the card table, but still keeping his distance from the Victorians. "And who wants to know?"

The taller one motioned for Howard to come closer and, almost against his will, he found his feet answering the call. He could see his reflection in the mirrored lenses of their tiny, round sunglasses, could see the uncertainty in his face as he moved unwittingly toward them.

"Who are you?" he asked again, his vocal chords tight with fear as, against his will, his feet moved him closer and closer to the tall man's beckoning finger.

"Why, we've come to take you to your wife," Midnight Smoke said, dropping his hand.

Instantly, Howard's forward locomotion stopped, but he was already so close to the two men he could smell the faint scent of lilies emanating from their persons.

"You can take me to her?" he found himself saying through his fear.

Both men nodded in unison.

"What's the trick?"

Midnight Smoke turned to his tall companion and smiled.

"There's no trick," he replied, his voice smooth as creamed butter. "You just have to come with us willingly and of your own accord. That's the only stipulation."

Howard watched, mesmerized by the sleight of hand, as a misshapen iron jar the size of a coffee mug replaced the tiny silver bell in Midnight Smoke's hand. The Victorian raised the jar toward Howard's face, letting him see there was nothing inside.

Howard nodded. *Yes,* he thought, *the jar's empty, but I still don't trust you.*

"All you have to do is jump into the jar and we'll take you to your wife," Puce said.

"You promise me she's there? Wherever you're taking me?"

The two men looked at each other again, but they didn't smile.

"We are taking you where all souls go," Midnight Smoke said, not really answering Howard's question, or making him any kind of promise.

Howard didn't want to be a ghost stuck wandering the Earth for eternity. He wanted to be with his wife, wherever she was, and these two men seemed to represent the only means of moving forward.

"Okay," he said finally, making his decision—for better, or for worse.

"Just close your eyes and will yourself inside," Midnight Smoke said, pleased by Howard's answer. "It's the simplest task in all of the world."

Howard did as Midnight Smoke instructed, closing his eyes and willing his spirit into the jar. It only took a second, and then Howard was gone—a wash of gray vapor sliding into an iron jar.

Once Howard was inside, Midnight Smoke set a piece of metallic fabric over the top, securing it in place with a silver ribbon.

"That was the easiest one yet," Puce said, his voice a low growl.

The Harvesters watched as the funeral home men slipped Howard's corpse into the body bag already laid out on the gurney to receive him. The cold hiss of the zipper knitting itself together over Howard's face bore the hallmark of finality.

"Yes, it was," Midnight Smoke agreed gamely, looking down at the iron jar.

"Easy as pie."

as soon as the fighting started, Gerald was out of there, braving the fog to find his Vespa.

His brain had been kind of fuzzy ever since he'd woken up in the bungalow. He'd felt strange, lighter on his feet somehow, but now he did what he could to shake off the lethargy. He had to find Molly and get out of there before anything worse (than getting hit over the head and being left for dead on a bed) happened.

He took off down the drive, running in the direction of the highway, his sights set on the hedges where he'd left Molly. He'd often been told he sounded like a herd of stampeding elephants whenever he ran, but to his surprise, he practically flew down the drive on silent feet. His body was as buoyant as a helium balloon, ready to sail up into the sky the moment someone let go of its string.

He wasn't even winded when he got to the hedges, but his heart froze as soon as he realized Molly wasn't there. Like a dog chasing its tail, he spun in a circle, eyes searching for the missing Vespa. A sense of panic overwhelmed him, but then he had a calming thought, one that kicked the panic's butt and gave him hope.

Maybe he was confused! Hadn't he gotten the wrong bungalow to begin with? Maybe he'd just gotten the wrong side of the hedges, too!

Feeling a lot better, he jogged around to the other side of the greenery, but his hope was immediately extinguished when he found no trace of Molly there, either.

He felt like he'd been punched in the gut . . . someone had stolen his Vespa!

"Damn it," he said. "God damn it!"

A lone car flew past him on the highway and he glared at it, wishing it was him and Molly speeding down the highway instead—and the thought made him want to cry.

Forgetting about the fight happening behind him, or his need to escape it, he ran down to the highway's shoulder, eyes scanning the carports of the other bungalows. But he saw nothing out of the ordinary. There was no trace of Molly. The panic he'd fought off earlier began to claw at his throat again, making it hard for him to breathe. He didn't know what he was going to do. He couldn't lose Molly. He just couldn't.

He started bargaining with God. If he found Molly, he would quit his job at the dispensary and never, ever deliver weed ever again. He would be a better son and take out the garbage without having to be asked. He would never run a red light or sleep past nine in the morning. But even as he made these promises in his head, he knew they weren't going to help.

He was being punished.

His mom had known something like this would happen.

She'd been against him taking the job at the dispensary from the beginning, warning him bad things would happen if he did. She said marijuana was the Devil's drug and his soul would be forever tainted by his proximity to it.

But he hadn't listened. He'd laughed at her, told her she was being silly. He wasn't going to smoke the stuff, just give it to the sick people who needed it.

Now he knew his mom had been right. If he hadn't been working there, none of this would've happened. He'd run on the wrong side of God and he was gonna pay for it.

With his Vespa.

The realization he'd probably never see Molly again hit him like a ton of bricks and he began to cry for real, hot tears blinding his vision as he stumbled down the road. He didn't see the red Fiat Panda as it rounded the bend in the highway and shot forward, speeding toward him at an aggressive clip, its daytime running lights like two evil eyes emerging from the fog. His own eyes red from crying, he looked up just in time to see the car barreling toward him. Unable to get out of its way, he just prayed the pain wouldn't be too terrible.

The driver of the Fiat didn't even touch the brakes as the car slammed into him.

And then that was it. The whole thing was over so fast Gerald didn't even feel it.

He looked up, astonished to see empty road in front of him. He spun around and his eye caught the Fiat's red taillights as the car rounded another bend and disappeared into the fog.

The car must've swerved, he thought to himself, his body numb with shock. But he knew that wasn't what had happened. There were no skid marks on the asphalt, and he'd heard nothing to indicate the car had even *seen* him, forget swerving to get out of his way.

His anguish at losing Molly was replaced by another emotion. The fear that maybe he, Gerald McKelvie, wasn't with the living anymore. Terror tunneled through his brain, and he began to shake uncontrollably. It was as though his body was made out of Jell-O instead of muscle and bone.

Then the day began to melt away and he blinked, rubbing his eyes to make sure he was really seeing what he thought he was seeing.

All around him sunlight was disappearing, the foggy ocean haze somehow consuming the light and excreting darkness in its place. He scanned the horizon, looking for the storm clouds he knew had to be gathering, but there were none. The darkness was being manufactured by something other than the weather.

There was a sonorous *crack* as a bolt of blue lightning shot across the sky, its electric light illuminating the empty highway, making everything look ghostly in the haze.

There was another *crack* and the air around him sizzled and shimmered. He jumped back, thinking he was about to be electrocuted, but instead, two women in slate blue ruffle-necked dresses manifested in front of him, their eyes obscured by round glasses with smoky gray lenses. They were both holding parasols above their heads as if they were expecting rain.

One of the women was shorter than the other, her long black hair pinned up at the back of her neck. She carried a long-handled butterfly net in her free hand, the exposed skin at her wrist, milky and white. Her neck was sapling thin behind the thick blue ruffles that sat up stiffly at her throat.

"Gerald McKelvie?" she said, a sultry smoothness to her voice.

He was so overwhelmed all he could do was nod.

The other woman smiled at him and lifted her left hand, revealing a tiny silver bell hidden within her palm. She was a little taller than her partner, but even thinner. Pale blonde ringlets as thick as sausages fell to her shoulders, the buttery yellow skeins glistening in the darkness.

"We can help you," the blonde said, her voice even more melodic than her partner's.

"You can?" Gerald asked, still bearing the irrational hope that if he could only find Molly, then everything else would be okay.

Both women nodded, but neither expanded on how they could help him. Instead, the blonde lowered her parasol, its shiny black material folding in on itself as she set it at her feet. She stood back up and smiled at Gerald before slipping a skeletal hand inside the blue ruffles at her throat, retrieving a small iron cylinder from the folds of the fabric. She uncorked the cylinder and let the top, which was strung onto a silver chain that hung from her neck, fall back against her concave chest.

"All you have to do is jump in," she said, holding up the cylinder as though it were a talisman. "It's the simplest thing in the world."

"And Molly will be there?"

The blonde's smile only lengthened, exposing shadowy dimples.

Gerald wasn't really expecting her to answer him. Besides, he'd already made his decision.

the man in Gray stood by the edge of the cliff, looking down at the valley below him. He'd had a human name at some point in his existence, but he'd expunged it long ago. Not that it really mattered. After a time, all names became obsolete. Besides why should a name remain eternal when the physical entity had been so transformed that it would be almost unrecognizable as its former self?

So now he was the Man in Gray.

It was really more the *absence* of color than the actual gray itself, that appealed to him. He appreciated how gray brought no unnecessary attention to its wearer, was utterly forgettable.

From birth he'd been an inconspicuous man. Not because he chose this, but because his features dictated it. Eyes slid over his countenance without registering what they'd seen: the light gray eyes, pale lashes and brows, the long nose, and thin lips. It was a gift from God, or an anomaly of human genetics—he didn't know which and didn't care. His innocuous features had served him well over the many years of his existence.

Below him, the swarm was growing. Like ants to an anthill they flocked and it was all because of him. He'd overseen the creation of *The Pit*, had chosen its design and its placement over his own, former, jail. Now he stood above it all, watching as the Harvesters and Transporters came in larger and larger groups to watch the cloud of power amassing above *The Pit*, the souls they'd collected pinned and wriggling in the holding corrals the Man in Gray had built just out of sight. He knew it wouldn't do for the prisoners to see their final destination; to know they were bound for utter annihilation.

When Uriah Drood had come to him with his plans, the Man in Gray had gotten excited.

Very, *very* excited.

He knew he was the only man in all of creation who possessed the knowledge necessary to do what Drood asked, so he'd bowed and nodded, obsequious as could be, listening as the rotund man had laid out his plans—but inside the Man in Gray was laughing. He'd spent countless lifetimes calculating his revenge, and now, without even begging, his dark prayers were being answered. Through the machinations of the weak, who could not see through their own greed, he would have this ultimate triumph.

Upon his agreement to do as Drood bid him, he'd been freed from his hidden prison, and then, unwitting fool that Drood was, he'd been given all the tools he needed to bring about the destruction of mankind.

For it was mankind's destruction he sought. Not the pathetic restructuring of reality his latest master had decreed. But soon the denizens of the Afterlife and all of humankind would know the Man in Gray's might—and they would rue the day Uriah Drood had set him free.

The thought made him laugh, the sound brittle even to his own ears. The laughter hurt his chest, bringing on the hacking cough he'd acquired after living in such a dank, underground prison for so many centuries.

Time is but an illusion, he thought.

An illusion that is about to end.

eight

CALLIOPE

An illusion.

That's what Jarvis had said after he'd gone to the Hall of Death to look at the Death Records and found no notation of an untimely death in Anjea's file.

"No one is allowed to tamper with the Death Records," he'd said, the muscle of his right cheek jumping against the bone. "It's not possible."

We were in my father's study, Jarvis sitting on one of the brown wingback chairs, hands clasped in his lap, looking pensive. He'd spent the day wormholing from Sea Verge to Death, Inc., and back. Now he just looked exhausted.

"You think Marcel and Anjea are in cahoots?" I asked, as I sat across from him in the other wingback chair, thumbing through an English copy of the original *How to Be Death: A Fully Annotated Guide.*

I'd spent the whole day reading the damn thing cover to cover and now when I looked at it, my eyes automatically started to blur. I thought (hoped) I'd retained most of the information I'd read, but I wasn't placing any bets on myself to do well if Jarvis sprung a pop quiz on me.

"I just don't know," Jarvis said, yawning.

Neither one of us had gotten any sleep since we'd been back. The whole experience in Antarctica had been too traumatizing.

"What do they gain by me accepting Marcel as my champion?" I asked, closing my eyes so I could rub my aching eyeballs with the heels of my hands. "I can't logic it out."

I opened my eyes to find Jarvis giving me a withering glance—I got the impression he didn't believe me capable of "logic-ing out" anything—then he stood up, his long body unfolding from the chair. As he stretched, the cords of his impossibly long neck stood out like guitar strings. He took a long breath, held the air in, then slowly let it run out through his nose.

"There has to be more to this than we're grasping," he said, shaking off his exhaustion as he walked over to my father's desk—my desk now—and picked up the tiny, brown book lying on the blotter.

"I wish I knew how to read Angel," I said, looking at the original copy of *How to Be Death* Jarvis was holding in his hands.

The English translation of the book in my own lap was safe for casual reading because it was missing the most important section: instructions from the Archangel Metatron on how to start the End of Days and destroy God's last creation (humanity) forever.

Death—or rather *me*, since the job was now mine—was responsible for the safekeeping of the original book, tasked with making sure no one or no thing with evil intentions could get ahold of it and start something that, once set in motion, could not be stopped.

"It would take you years of study, and even then it might not be possible," Jarvis said, but he was distracted as he spoke, the little book taking up all his attention.

"It would enable me to know exactly how to trigger the end of humanity. That might scare the shit out of anyone who wants to kick my ass."

Jarvis looked up from the book, eyeing me.

"That's a ridiculous statement," he said, not amused.

I sighed and sat back in my chair.

"I know."

Jarvis, seemingly satisfied I wasn't a complete idiot, went back to studying the tiny book.

"I would never trigger any kind of end of humanity situation," I added, just to clarify. "I hope you know that."

Jarvis didn't like it when I made light of important Death subjects. But what he didn't understand was if I could joke about the things that scared me, then maybe, eventually, I wouldn't be afraid of them anymore. It was Psychology 101, a class I'd snored my way through at Sarah Lawrence, but I *had* learned that humor was a defense mechanism.

I looked outside and was gratified to see the day had finally been replaced by a chilly, moonless night. Even though Jarvis had already turned on the overhead lights, I reached over and switched on the table lamp beside me, happy to have even more light to blot out the weird, disconnected feeling that was slowly stealing over my thoughts.

I was also exhausted, and I knew this had something to do with my morose mood. I really wouldn't have argued if Jarvis had suggested we table the conversation for tomorrow and go to bed. At seven thirty. Way too early to crawl under the covers and disappear for the night.

"That's nice to hear," he said.

"You're giving in way too easily," I said, suspiciously.

When I looked over, I saw Jarvis had put on his "serious" face—and I knew this meant I was about to get a lecture.

"Go ahead," I sighed. "Blow my mind with whatever you're going to say."

Jarvis ignored my snarky comment, settling on the edge of the desk and staring intently into my eyes. It was unnerving when Jarvis got all professorial and intense on me—but I held his gaze, determined not to make any stupid comments or harass him in any way until he was done.

"There are two possibilities, as far as I can see."

He paused, waiting for me to interrupt like I usually did, but I remained silent. He gave me a pleased nod and continued:

"So Anjea spoke of another, alternate universe where Frank is Death and you don't exist, probably because you were never born there. If our world and this other world were to merge, then there is a distinct possibility—and Clio would know the exact probability—"

"Let's leave Clio out of this for now," I said.

I hadn't told Jarvis what I'd learned from Kali, that Clio was one of the next round of "possible" Deaths. But now seemed as good a time as any to unburden myself.

Jarvis waited for me to go on and I sighed, accepting that he was going to be mad at me for asking Kali to dig into the Death Records.

"Because she has a more important role," I continued. "One that will become *very* important if, or really when, something happens to me."

Jarvis narrowed his eyes.

"Go on."

I looked down at the book in my hands, wishing I could spirit myself away and never have to deal with the responsibility of being Death ever again. But I knew that wasn't going to happen, so I took a deep breath and plunged into my explanation.

"Kali and I went through the Death Records"—Jarvis started to protest, but I held up my hand for him to listen—"I know it was wrong, but I wanted to make sure if Marcel killed me during the duel, there'd be someone who could take my place. Someone who was better equipped to run Death, Inc., than I was when I was tapped for the job."

Jarvis didn't jump all over me like I'd expected him to. Instead, he nodded his head, processing what I'd told him.

"There's more," I said. "I know about the other 'possible' Deaths, too. The ones Clio would be competing against—and I want to bring them here to Sea Verge. To give them the opportunity to work under me at Death, Inc., learn the ropes, get some experience under their belts."

Jarvis stood up, thought about what he was going to say, then sat back down again.

"Are you okay?" I asked.

"I'm fine," he said. "But what you're talking about. It's never been attempted before. Informing the other 'possible' Deaths before they're called up . . . it's just not done."

I knew he'd feel this way—anything that went against tradition was anathema to Jarvis.

"Still," he added, looking thoughtful. "There is some merit to what you're proposing."

"There is?" I asked, surprised.

"What you went through was very traumatic," Jarvis said.

"Bringing the 'possible' Deaths into the fold before they're called up—if they're ever called up—would alleviate this trauma."

This was exactly what I'd been thinking.

"So you think it's a good idea?" I asked.

"Good or bad, I don't know," he said, setting the tiny *How to Be Death* book down on the desk blotter. "Worth a try? Why not?"

Relief flooded through me. If I could convince Jarvis to give my idea a try, then I was pretty sure I could convince anyone.

"One of the other 'possible' Deaths lives here in Newport," I said.

If this surprised Jarvis, he didn't show it.

"I want you to invite her here tomorrow under the pretense I'm looking to sell Sea Verge."

"You can't really be—" he began, but I shook my head.

"I don't want to sell Sea Verge. The girl's a Realtor and it's a good way to get her here without raising any suspicions."

Jarvis saw the wisdom of my words and calmed down.

"Yes, that's a good plan," he agreed.

"Then you'll do it?" I asked.

Jarvis nodded.

"If it's what you wish."

"It is," I said.

We sat in silence after that, both lost in our own thoughts. Finally, Jarvis broke the silence:

"What about Marcel?"

His gaze was fixed on the window behind my head, eyes focused on anything that wasn't me.

"If he shows up here, then we listen to what he has to say," I said.

Jarvis nodded—then he looked at me. *Really* looked at me.

"What?" I said, starting to feel uncomfortable.

"It's just . . . I couldn't be prouder of you if you were my own daughter," he said.

"Why?" I asked, not understanding.

"You're all grown-up," he said, shaking his head. "It's very impressive."

I felt stupid. I didn't deserve the kind things he was saying about me.

"I'm just being pragmatic," I said. "It's important to me Clio comes out of this okay."

Jarvis nodded in understanding.

"I don't like what any of this means and I hope it's only a contingency, but I'll do as you ask," he said—and I could tell he still wasn't 100 percent happy about what I was asking of him.

"Thank you, Jarvis," I said, smiling at him before putting on my own "serious" face and changing the subject. "So, explain this probability thing to me again?"

I didn't think I'd ever willingly encouraged Jarvis to lecture me before, but there was a first time for everything.

"Oh, yes," Jarvis said, nodding happily. "As I was saying before . . . if these two, disparate worlds merge, then there is a strong probability that because you don't exist in the other world, you will cease to exist in the new merged world."

"Okay," I said. "I'll just *poof* and that's the end of me."

"In that world, after your father's demise, Frank must have become Death because you did not exist in that world to fight him or Daniel for it."

"Frank must be a piss-poor Death," I mumbled under my breath.

"Agreed."

"So how do they do this? This merging of two worlds?" I asked.

"The book," Jarvis said. "It explains how to harness the power of the dead, use their energy like a giant particle accelerator—"

"And you fuse two worlds together," I said, getting what Jarvis was driving at. "I cease to exist, the Golden Age doesn't happen, and humanity lives in the dark for a long, long time . . . but we have the book, so, right now, no one can use it to start any bad stuff, right?"

But this idea did start me wondering about the near loss of the book that had occurred at the annual Death Dinner and Masquerade Ball. Had someone been trying to steal the book for this very reason?

"There's another possibility."

"The second one you alluded to?"

Jarvis nodded, walking over to the darkened window so he could look out at the endless sea.

"Someone releases Enoch from She'ol."

I sat back in my chair, Jarvis's words meaning nothing to me.

"Well, that's not where I thought you were going with that," I said, pulling my feet up under me in the chair.

"Enoch translated the book you're holding there," Jarvis said, pointing to the copy of *How to Be Death* I still held in my hands. "And he put a lot of it into The Book of Enoch so the rest of humanity could be prepared for what might come."

"He could read Angel?" I said, surprised a human had mastered this most difficult of languages.

Jarvis shook his head.

"Only because Metatron willed it so. Supposedly, he took pity on humanity and gave the story to Enoch to impart to his brethren as a warning—or maybe a reminder of what could be. Sadly, no one, not even Enoch, knew what Metatron's true intent was."

"But there's none of the bad stuff in this book," I said, lifting it up in the air for emphasis.

"No, there's not," Jarvis agreed. "But Metatron gave Enoch special dispensation so he, as a human who normally wouldn't be able to touch the book, could read and translate it, minus the 'bad stuff,' as you call it."

"So why's he in this 'Shiz'ol' place?" I asked.

"She'ol," Jarvis corrected. "It's Hebrew for 'grave'—a place to stow away the living dead."

"He's a zombie?" I asked, surprised. I hadn't known zombies really existed.

"I wouldn't call him that, exactly," Jarvis hedged. "She'ol is one of the many prisons where they incarcerate those who have angered the Angels. Each religion, or philosophy of being, has a few specifically created for their believers."

"And just how many of these places are we talking about?" I asked.

"Too many to count," Jarvis said in a low voice.

"So you really don't want to piss off an Angel," I said.

Jarvis didn't answer. He seemed to be mulling over his words, trying to decide how best to respond.

"Enoch made a terrible error in judgment. Instead of forgetting the book's contents as he was asked to do by Metatron, he secretly memorized everything he read."

"And they put him in this She'ol/grave place for that?" I asked.

"Worse things have been done for much less."

Jarvis was right. I'd seen this firsthand with my own father, who'd abused his powers in order to protect me—but that didn't make what he'd done right. Imprisoning the Ender of Death down in Hell, violating the balance between Life and Death, Good and Evil, etc., etc.—these acts, done out of love for me, had destroyed him.

Life and Death weren't fair, but God had set up the world this way and we had to accept it.

"You really think, after centuries of imprisonment, Enoch would be able to remember all that stuff?" I said.

I remembered how delirious the Ender of Death had been after a few decades of imprisonment down in Hell. If Enoch had been in this She'ol for as long as Jarvis had implied, then surely he'd be a basket case by now.

"I'd stake my life on it," Jarvis said, the tic starting up in his right cheek again. "He'd been a favorite of the Angels, allowed to wander freely through their plane—"

"They just let him run around Heaven?" I interrupted.

I had a hard time believing this. The Angels had felt pushed aside when God had created human beings—and, to this very day, it was still something they hadn't forgiven God for. Allowing a human being unrestricted access to their world seemed out of character.

"You obviously haven't read The Book of Enoch," Jarvis said, walking over to one of the study's many thick, oak bookcases and retrieving a heavy, goatskin-bound tome from one of the shelves.

"A little light reading," he continued, dropping the heavy book in my lap.

Now I had two old books moldering in my lap instead of one.

"Holy my God," I said as I opened the cover only to have a cloud of dust float up into my face, filling my nostrils. Sneezing twice, I held the book away from me.

"How many decades since someone opened this thing?" I wheezed.

"Many."

"If I promise to read it," I said, crossing my fingers behind my back to negate the promise, "will you just give me a quick play-by-play?"

Jarvis raised an eyebrow, his gaze lingering on the hand I held behind my back.

"Crossed fingers don't make a promise null and void, Calliope," Jarvis said, as he sat back on the edge of the desk and surveyed me.

I removed my right hand from behind my back and held out a flat palm. No crossed fingers this time. It was a show of good faith—although, I believed once the crossed fingers had been invoked, they were good for at least a half hour, but I didn't tell Jarvis this.

"I promise," I said, trying to look chaste.

Jarvis sighed, resigned to my ways, but not *so* resigned he wasn't going to make me work for the information.

"In the end, I suppose it doesn't really matter if you read it, or not," Jarvis sniffed.

With those words, I knew I'd won. I could talk Jarvis into giving me the full Enoch story if I was willing to do a little cajoling in return.

"He was friendly with the Angels . . . ?" I asked, letting my words trail off.

"Mmh," he replied.

"Mmh," I thought, *is not an answer.*

"And he was friends with the Angels because . . . ?" I tried again.

"I don't know the how and the why of Enoch's relationship with the Angels," Jarvis said. "I just know he had one and was allowed into their world when no other human was."

It drove me crazy when Jarvis got purposely vague.

"You're mad at me for not wanting to read the book," I said, leaning back in my chair.

"No, I'm annoyed with you for being so childish," Jarvis shot back. "The crossed-fingers thing."

He added this as if he thought I'd have no idea what he was talking about.

"I'm sorry about the fingers thing," I said—and I meant it. "I just didn't want to read the book."

I batted my eyelashes at my Executive Assistant and caught the merest hint of a smile at the corner of his lips.

"I see that baby smile," I said, leaning forward in my chair and crooning at him in a high-pitched, singsongy voice. *"Yes, I do. I see that little baby smile."*

Jarvis looked at me like I was nutso—and he was probably right.

"Oh, stop it," he said finally with a shake of his head, but I think there was a part of Jarvis that actually liked how silly I could be at times. "Apology accepted if you stop goo-goo-gah-gahing at me."

"Done," I said, sitting back and smiling at him.

"Where, oh, where is the mature woman I was speaking to no less than five minutes ago," Jarvis sighed to himself.

"I'm mercurial."

That was all I could offer him.

"That you are," he agreed, nodding his head. "That you are."

The ring of the doorbell, its chime loud and sonorous, surprised both of us.

"Who in the world?" Jarvis asked, standing up.

He looked anything but excited that an unannounced visitor was putting in an appearance at Sea Verge.

"I'll come with you," I said, setting the copies of *How to Be Death* and The Book of Enoch down on the side table next to my chair and hopping up to follow Jarvis.

But when I got to the door, he shooed me away with his hand.

"Go sit back down. You aren't a parlor maid."

I glared at him, but then shrugged my acquiescence, allowing Jarvis to close the door before I turned around and flopped back into my chair.

But when the door to the study finally opened again, it wasn't Jarvis standing in the doorway as I'd expected. Instead, I found myself staring into the haunted eyes of Marcel, the Ender of Death. He looked haggard, his lean face pinched, the ends of his hair sticking up from the crown of his head at odd angles. He was wearing a pale baby blue T-shirt with the slogan "Revenge Is A Dish Best Re-Heated" emblazoned across the front and a pair of light gray linen slacks bunching at his ankles. The flesh-toned huaraches he had on were at least two sizes too big for him, showing off unkempt toenails and lightly down-covered feet.

But the shocker, the thing that totally blew me away, was the long black nylon leash he held in his right hand . . . and the creature at the end of it.

My hellhound puppy, Runt.

She looked as bad as Marcel, her black coat covered in dirt, the tip of her heart-shaped pink nose abraded and bleeding.

"Oh my God," I said, racing to the hellhound pup and wrapping my arms around her neck.

Jarvis came into the room hot on Marcel's heels, his face white as a sheet.

"Calliope—" he began, but I was intent on Runt and ignored him.

I let her nuzzle my face, her warm breath coming out in short bursts that tickled my cheek. I could feel her heart thudding against my arm and her usually warm body was chilly underneath her matted coat.

And that's when I felt the warm wetness soaking into my shoulder—it was the only thing besides her breath that wasn't cold as death. I sat back, confusion rippling through me.

"Your shirt," Jarvis whispered, pointing at my chest.

I looked down at myself and gasped. The front of my white T-shirt was soaked in bright, red blood.

"They went for her voice," Marcel said, eyes downcast. "There was nothing I could do."

I looked up at Jarvis and saw tears dripping down his cheeks onto the starched collar of his dress shirt.

This was bad. This was really fucking bad.

"Runt?" I said, my voice cracking.

But she couldn't answer me.

nine

There were things in his life that confounded Daniel. He didn't know why the automatic faucets in public bathrooms refused to work for him without a fight, or why he could never seem to hail a taxicab whenever he was in Manhattan. He could live with these minor complications. They were annoying, but survivable.

There was only one thing—it was a person, actually—that had the power to overwhelm and confuse him like nothing else in the world. One minute his mind was flooded with images of her: the way she laughed (cackled was a better word, really), the way her body looked when she was half-naked in front of him, dressing for the day, the smoothness of her skin and its warm vanilla musk arousing him even in memory.

The next minute he wanted to kill her.

She drove him that crazy.

She was chaotic and reckless. "Headstrong" and "stubborn" were just words—and they didn't even begin to describe her, or how tough it was to get her to do anything she didn't want to do. Sometimes when he thought of her, a picture of a mule would pop into his mind. He knew it was terrible, no one should ever imagine their girlfriend as an ass, but there were days— too many to count—when she deserved it. Because she was, without a doubt, the most exhausting and erratic creature he'd ever encountered.

But, God help him, he loved her anyway. There was just something about her that made him feel like he was home whenever he was with her. It'd been such a long, long time since he'd felt this way he was loath to let it go. Even when she'd fucked around on him, it'd almost killed him to distance himself from her. He'd been devastated, totally sideswiped by her selfishness and lack of respect for their relationship and he knew if he'd been his old self, he would've wrung her neck.

Literally.

Not that it would do any good. She was an immortal like him, though she'd been given her immortality at birth while he'd had to sell his soul for his.

Still, he'd suffered something fierce when he'd been forced to do without her. He'd tried to interest himself in other women, but he couldn't even manage a smile for any of them, let alone an erection. Instead, he'd thrown himself into his work, spending every waking second trying to restructure Hell. The Devil had been an awful manager, much more interested in his own pleasure than the day-to-day running of his dominion. Daniel and his friend, Cerberus, the former Guardian of the North Gate of Hell, had their work cut out for them as they'd begun to unravel all the twisted skeins of corruption the Devil had left behind when he'd been dethroned.

Even though they were making headway dismantling the old system, Hell was still not a place for the faint of heart. It had always been a bit of a dump, and even when they were through with the restructuring, it would still be a pretty miserable place, but it wouldn't be nearly as scummy as it'd been when he'd accepted the Devil's bargain all those years ago and become the de facto "Devil's protégé"—a title he'd loathed.

But back then his ambition had been great and he hadn't cared what he'd had to do to secure his immortality. He'd done truly terrible things at the Devil's behest, some of which would be burned into his soul forever. Others were just fleeting memories, like old newsreels flickering behind his eyelids whenever he was feeling weak, full of self-loathing and hatred.

He'd never shared any of this with Calliope. He knew, as flighty and kooky as she was, she'd cut him out of her life forever if she even guessed at the horror his former self had wrought. Sure, he was reformed now. No, *better* than reformed.

He was a zealot in the quest for good. But no matter how much good he did to make up for his past behavior, the taint of evil would never leave him.

His biggest worry was Callie would discover who he'd been and how black his soul was—and it would end their relationship forever. If her thinking he was some kind of Goody Two-shoes was the price he had to pay for her to remain unaware of his past, then so be it. He'd rather she find him milquetoast than *know* what a bastard he'd been.

But then she'd sent him that song, thinking he'd let her go willingly—and unaided—to her own death. What she didn't understand was Daniel had no intention of letting her go. He'd put too much time and effort into making their relationship work for her to go and just get herself killed.

Yes, he'd said "killed"—because even immortals had weaknesses that could be exploited in order to destroy them. And everyone knew Callie's was the rare earth element, promethium.

This was not a hypothesis he'd come to on his own. That's not to say he wouldn't have gotten there eventually, but he'd been encouraged down the path by someone who was in the perfect position to know what they were talking about: Watatsumi, the man who'd first clued the Afterlife in to Callie's immortal weakness.

He'd gotten the Dolly Parton song she'd e-mailed him, and, in his gut, he'd known something was wrong. But then the Japanese Water God, Watatsumi, had shown up, unannounced, at his office door and he'd understood the magnitude of what was happening to his girlfriend.

"What are you doing here?" he'd said standing up and looking to see who'd let the small Japanese man into his office.

Though they were still very understaffed, Daniel had been almost certain his secretary, Hans, had come in early, too—but when he'd looked past Watatsumi, he'd seen that his secretary's bland beige office was empty.

When the Devil was running the show, he'd spent most of his time at the Pleasure Castle he'd built for himself in the southern jungles of Hell. Daniel had never liked the Devil's

Pleasure Castle—it reminded him of an S&M version of the Winchester Mystery House—so when he'd been granted the Stewardship of Hell, he'd moved the whole operation to a compound of old ramshackle warehouse buildings just within the shadow of the Eastern Gates of Hell.

He didn't love the setting, how dilapidated the buildings were, or how hot it got inside them without air conditioning, but they were a much more appropriate environment for doing business than a sex castle had ever been.

"Nice building," Watatsumi had said, stepping into the small office and setting his palms down flat on the edge of Daniel's cluttered desk.

The smaller man's monotone cadence had always set his teeth on edge, and this time it was no different.

"What do you want?"

He was two seconds away from calling Cerberus and having Watatsumi shunted into one of the myriad of prisons dotting Hell's landscape, but the Water God sensed Daniel's intention and cut straight to the chase.

"Uriah Drood has brokered a deal with a creature called 'the Man in Gray.' This Man in Gray seeks to merge our world and another. It will mean the end of your Little Death"—Daniel realized he was talking about Callie—"and it will seriously uproot my own plans."

Daniel opened his mouth to interrupt, but Watatsumi wouldn't let him speak.

"I don't like you. You don't like me. But we share a common enemy. If we work together, we can stop the porcine Drood before he takes over our world."

Daniel knew Watatsumi was notorious for manipulating and double-crossing those he'd made "arrangements" with. There was no way he was getting involved with the Water God.

"I don't think so."

Watatsumi stood back up and shrugged his sagging shoulders. The black kimono he wore made him look smaller and older than the last time Daniel had seen him.

"I need your help," the Water God said, finally, looking beaten.

It wasn't a plea, exactly, but it made Daniel pay closer attention to what the Water God was saying.

"Why would I help you?" Daniel asked. "You nearly killed my girlfriend."

Under the guise of helping her, Watatsumi had slipped Callie a wish-fulfillment jewel full of promethium, and if fate—and her friends—hadn't intervened, she'd have died.

"I make no bones about that," Watatsumi agreed. "It is true. And I would do it all again. But now we need to help one another—"

He pulled a small orange jewel from his kimono pocket and held it up to the bright, yellow light coming in through Daniel's office windows.

"A wish-fulfillment jewel. I will give it to you if you will help me. Proof of my goodwill."

He set the small piece of orange beryl on Daniel's desk—and both of them stared at it.

"Help me? Help you? It's all the same," Watatsumi continued, shrugging again.

"How do I even know you're telling the truth?" Daniel asked, his eye glued to the jewel on his desk. "Maybe you're just trying to get to Callie through me."

Watatsumi nodded, as if this were a good question.

"Go to her and see. Then you will know."

This answer unsettled Daniel.

"But take the jewel," Watatsumi added. "If you decide to help, use it to call me. We will strike a bargain then—and I will tell you how we will stop the Man in Gray."

With his peace said, the small man turned and shuffled back out the way he'd come. Daniel got up and ran for the doorway, but Watatsumi was gone. The hallway as empty as it had been before the Water God's arrival.

Daniel went back to his desk and sat down, his mind racing, then he opened his laptop—yes, even in Hell, computers were a necessary evil—and put on the Dolly Parton song Callie had sent him, really listening to the lyrics and its "I will always love you" refrain.

That had been the decider.

After that, he hadn't stopped to think, he'd just acted, leaving Hell posthaste, not even stopping to let Cerberus, his second-in-command, know where he was going. If there was any validity to what Watatsumi had told him, he didn't want anyone to know where he was going. Also, he didn't dare go directly to Sea Verge in case someone was monitoring the wormhole channels. Instead, he chose to take a wormhole to the John F. Kennedy airport in Queens, New York, where he purchased a very expensive round-trip ticket to Boston that left him with three hours to sit at the airport and twiddle his thumbs.

Of course, there had been no thumb twiddling. He'd put his downtime to good use, finding a payphone—one that took all the change in his wallet—and soon he was speaking to an old and very well placed friend who owed him a favor.

In his previous "Devil's protégé" existence, he'd associated primarily with the high rollers and movers and shakers of the criminal underworld. Everyone knew where there was greed and ambition, there was usually someone willing to sell their soul to the Devil. These were the people Daniel preyed on, and these were the people he still had some pull with, though his influence was slowly waning as the men and women he'd partied and played with died off, their positions now filled by others.

As the Devil's protégé, soul collecting had been his purveyance. He'd targeted the underbelly of the human race, tricking his victims into selling their souls for Earthly riches, never realizing when they died, they'd become the Devil's property: shades without bodies, forced for eternity to do the Devil's bidding.

Daniel had been a master at the art of trickery, using human vanity and avarice to entrap his unsuspecting victims. In his heyday, he'd collected so many souls he'd eventually lost count. He'd had no conscience, luxuriating in the hunt and the kill, giddy with power.

And then one day it had changed.

It was a long story, but suffice it to say, he'd grown a conscience. It'd been a rude awakening, but he'd never looked back.

Until now.

Now he was forced to delve into his former life to save the woman he loved.

The flight to Boston hadn't taken long. When he'd arrived at Logan International Airport, a black sedan was waiting for him in one of the short-term parking lots, the key in the ignition, as promised. Marty, his old contact with the Patriarca Crime Family, was always as good as his word: If he said a car would be there waiting for him, it would be there. He hadn't wasted any time, just hopped in the driver's seat and headed for Newport.

But when he'd arrived, he'd found that Watatsumi was right. Calliope was gone and Jarvis seemed like he was on the verge of a nervous breakdown. Daniel worked very hard not to let anyone, especially Jarvis or Clio, see how unsettled he was. If they'd even guessed at his intentions, they'd have tried to talk him out of it.

So he'd put on his concerned face, acting as though he was as in the dark as the others were. It was a lie, of course, but thanks to Watatsumi, he had a pretty good idea about what was going on.

And then when Clio had taken off, leaving them all standing in the kitchen, Daniel had sensed now was the time to contact Watatsumi and set things into motion. He'd excused himself and gone to the bathroom, the orange wish-fulfillment jewel burning a hole in his pocket.

clio followed jennice back downstairs. She felt as though a great and terrible weight had been lifted from her shoulders. When she was stressed out—and she was in stress city with Cal being gone—all her tension went right into her left shoulder. It was a minor annoyance she'd learned to live with, functioning as though everything was normal even when all she wanted to do was put her life on pause and go get a massage. But after Jennice had touched her, the pain had vanished, gone almost as if it'd never existed in the first place.

This was miraculous in itself then add the emotional relief that came with her touch, and the effect was even greater—or maybe it was all tied together, psychological pain manifesting as physical pain and vice versa.

She'd reached the last stair, and was about to step onto the foyer floor when she felt a tap on her shoulder. She stopped where she was and turned back around to face Jennice.

"Please don't tell anyone. About . . . you know."

"I promise I won't say a word to anyone," Clio replied. "Not unless you want me to."

Jennice nodded, but she still seemed uncertain.

"I know we don't really know each other," Clio continued. "I don't expect you to trust me. Just try to believe me when I say your powers are your own business."

"I appreciate that," Jennice said, nodding. "I just don't want anyone to think I'm crazy."

Clio wished Jennice understood just what kind of odd company she was keeping here at Sea Verge.

"What exactly is it that your sister does?" Jennice asked, changing the subject.

"Nothing as bad as whatever you're thinking," Clio laughed. "Here, it's easier to show you than to tell you."

She gestured for Jennice to follow her as she hopped off the last step and headed down the hallway toward her father's—make that her sister's—study. As they passed room after empty room, Clio felt her heart ache for the old life she'd shared with her parents and sisters. It didn't seem like that long ago she was ensconced upstairs in her room, playing around on her computer, doing her homework, and generally driving her mom and dad crazy.

Just normal teenage girl stuff.

She'd always been aware she was the youngest daughter of Death, there was no way to escape all the weirdness that passed in and out of their house (unless you cast a Forgetting Charm on yourself like Callie had), but in her mind she'd also been just a typical angst ridden high school senior with no duties other than passing her AP English and History exams. Math and science had always come easily to her, and even when she was in Advanced Calculus and Theoretical Physics, she'd never had a need to study for them.

"This way," she said, leading Jennice down the long hallway as the shadowy claws of darkness from the outside windows chased them.

When they reached the study, Clio stopped, resting her right hand on the doorframe. Jennice stood beside her, both of them marveling at the emptiness of the room and the somber white sheeting covering what little furniture was left.

"It looks so . . . empty," Clio said as she rested her head against the doorjamb.

"Is this what you wanted to show me?" Jennice asked, her eyes on Clio instead of the room.

Clio stood up straight, flashing Jennice a sad smile.

"No, not the room. I just hope what I wanted is still here."

She stepped tentatively into the room, eyes roving the sheet-covered bookcases.

"Hmm," she said, lifting one of the sheets so she could peer underneath it.

She moved to the next one and repeated the process. It was only on the third try she found what she wanted, pulling a thick tome from one of the shelves and handing it to Jennice.

"Here," she said. "This should explain things more succinctly than I can."

She waited for Jennice to open the book, but the girl stared at Clio uncertainly.

"I don't know," she said, her voice hesitant.

"Just look at the title," Clio said.

Jennice looked down at the front cover, her lips silently forming the words as she read.

"A handbook for Death?" she said, as she raised her eyes to meet Clio's, a perplexed expression on her face.

Clio didn't know why she was showing Jennice the book. Not really. It'd been instinctual, something she thought Callie would want her to do.

"It belongs to my sister."

Jennice flipped through the book, her eyes skimming the pages so fast Clio doubted she was taking in any of what she was reading.

"Why?" Jennice asked, as she shut the cover of the book with a soft *thud* and looked back up at Clio.

Clio shrugged. There was only one answer—and either Jennice would believe her, or she wouldn't.

"Because she's Death."

watatsumi had known Daniel would call him. Once he realized the magnitude of the situation, he would have no other option—he just hadn't expected Daniel to call him to a bathroom.

"What do you want me to do?" Daniel asked, looking into the mirror above the sink where Watatsumi's image stared back at him.

Watatsumi hated dealing with earnest people, people who tried their best to not affect others with their needs and wants. These souls were so boring they made Watatsumi wish he could crawl inside his underwater grotto and seal himself off from the world.

He had always believed there were not enough bad people. Bad people were interesting and made Watatsumi's job enjoyable. He wished Daniel were bad instead of earnest. He knew that inside, in his true core, Daniel was black, but instead of embracing his true nature, he fought it. Painted over it with goodness.

It made Watatsumi sick to his stomach.

But at least he could force Daniel to do some bad things in, what he thought, was the name of good. This made Watatsumi not hate his existence so much.

"You will bring me the next three people who appear at Sea Verge. They will arrive soon. One of them has always annoyed me. I will punish him. The others, well, we shall see. But you will do as I ask and use the jewel to bring them all to me."

Daniel shook his head.

"I don't understand. What does this have to do with stopping Drood from merging the two worlds?"

Watatsumi didn't think it had anything to do with it, but instead he said:

"Just bring them to me. Use the jewel and it will guide you."

Daniel looked down at the orange jewel clutched in his hand.

"Do it," Watatsumi said, "and together we will stop this. I possess Pandora's Box, the only thing which can contain the creature who is trying to bring about the merging of these two disparate universes."

Daniel swallowed hard then nodded. If Watatsumi had Pandora's Box, then maybe they really could stop this whole thing from happening, saving Callie in the process.

"I'll do it."

Watatsumi was pleased with how easy it was to make good people be bad.

Now he was glad he wasn't walled off in his underwater grotto. For the first time in many weeks, he was excited. He would make Daniel do many more terrible things before it was all over.

And he would enjoy every minute of it.

ten

It was getting dark outside, the air shot through with a bone-numbing chill as the lights came on, illuminating the last few stragglers as they snaked their way toward the exits at the front of the park. Bernadette knew she should've been cold, that her body should've been shivering, but she felt nothing. She watched as the wind picked up, the amusement park pennants high above her head flapping like sails from their thick steel poles.

She'd been sitting on the same bench since the police had first dispersed the crowd, then later gone themselves, taking their equipment, but leaving behind a wide swath of crime scene tape and an order to keep the Big Bellower shut down indefinitely. She'd watched them all go—even her distraught daughter and grandson, who'd been escorted from the scene by a policewoman and two paramedics—and now she was left alone, wondering what was supposed to happen next.

She'd always believed in Heaven and in Jesus Christ's love for mankind. If anyone had talked to her before she'd died, she'd have told them she fully expected to go to the pearly gates, have a sweet little back-and-forth with St. Peter, and then join her heavenly father and all her dead friends and family as they frolicked through paradise. Sitting on a park bench—a ghost no one could see or interact with—was not anywhere in her plans.

Where was St. Peter? The Heavenly Host? The pearly gates?

She was mystified. Her rigid religious upbringing unwilling to let her accept the Afterlife might be very different from what her minister had preached, and what she'd imagined for herself.

The boom of thunder shook her from her thoughts, and she looked up to witness a slash of lightning, like a putrefying scar, split open the sky. The rain followed, the heavens opening up to unleash a flash flood of water that blanketed every inch of the amusement park, but left Bernadette dry as a bone.

She was so busy marveling at the water's inability to soak her that she didn't notice the black-clad women, one carrying a long-handled butterfly net in her hands, as they shuffled toward her. They stopped just behind the bench, close enough to touch the nape of Bernadette's exposed neck, but it still took Bernadette more than a few seconds to become aware of their presence.

Sensing something or someone was watching her, she turned around in her seat, her heart hammering in her chest. But she relaxed as soon as she saw the two women—girls really—in their high-necked Victorian dresses, their pale white skin luminescent in the moonlight. Identical twins, they both had long raven hair, button noses, and tiny round sunglasses with mirrored lenses making it impossible to look into their eyes.

"Are you Bernadette?" the one with the butterfly net asked. Despite the fierce wind and rain, not one hair on her or her sister's head was out of place.

Bernadette stood up, taking a few steps away from them. Something about these two, odd-looking girls bothered her. Her gut told her not to trust them.

"I'm not Bernadette," she heard herself say—her curiosity was piqued by this new ability of hers to lie without conscience. This was something she'd never been able to do when she was alive.

The twins looked at each other, their faces unreadable. They reminded Bernadette of two cats, sleek and sly and in possession of a secret they'd never share with you.

"You're lying," the butterfly net girl said, obviously speaking for both of them.

"I don't care what you think," Bernadette said, anger bubbling up inside of her. She didn't like being called a liar even if she was one.

She took a few more tentative steps away from the girls, and she realized her body felt funny. So light and effervescent, almost like she would float away if she stopped concentrating on remaining Earthbound.

"Don't run away," the silent (up until now) twin said, her voice kinder than her sister's.

She stepped forward, leaving her sister behind her then held out her hands, palms up in supplication.

"Let us help you," she entreated, moving a step closer to Bernadette. "We know you're scared. Death can be a frightening state of being."

Bernadette felt the tension loosening in her shoulders. Something about this gentle twin's voice was lulling. It made Bernadette feel like she should just give over to the girls, do whatever they asked of her.

"Who are you?" Bernadette asked.

She didn't really want to know who the girls were, or what they wanted from her, but remaining ignorant to the situation wasn't going to help anyone.

The gentle twin glanced back at her sister, and after a moment, her sibling nodded. The gentle twin returned her gaze to Bernadette. She smiled and lifted an empty hand to her sunglasses, hooking her fingers around the right temple and sliding the glasses down her nose, letting them rest there so Bernadette could see her eyes.

They were cornflower blue, the irises large and oval, framed by a sheaf of thick black lashes the same color as her hair. The girl blinked twice then replaced the sunglasses.

With the revelation of the girl's eyes, something inside of Bernadette seemed to relax.

"Come with us," the gentle twin said.

It wasn't a question now.

She reached out her hand and Bernadette took it without thinking. It was the first solid thing Bernadette had touched since she'd died—and the intimacy of the gesture made her shudder.

"Who are you?" Bernadette asked again.

The girl smiled.

"We work for Death. We're called Harvesters and we've come to take you away from here."

Bernadette nodded. It did seem like a logical explanation for what was happening.

"Will I see my parents again?"

The gentle twin squeezed her hand, but didn't answer, a strange smile twisting her face.

Something about the smile chilled Bernadette to the core. She dropped the girl's hand and backed away.

"Where are you going?" the girl asked.

But Bernadette didn't answer her—she just turned and ran. She didn't stop until she was at the other end of the amusement park, the neon green exit signs illuminating her way out of the park.

She hit the gates, racing through them before any of the attendants could offer her a reentry hand stamp. Not that they would have. She was invisible to them. Still moving swiftly, she happened upon a tram heading to the parking lot and climbed aboard just as it took off.

As the tram rambled up and down the empty rows of parking spaces, Bernadette started to relax, her pulse slowing and her breathing returning to normal. But she still refused to look back to see if the twins had followed her.

She was too scared.

clio had not taken things well.

As soon as he'd finished his explanation, she'd left the room without a word.

He'd turned to Daniel, but the former Devil's protégé was already heading to the other end of the kitchen.

"I'll be right back," he said, flustered, as he opened the side door and stepped through into the back hallway. "Just gonna use the restroom."

Jarvis didn't think now was the most appropriate time to run off to the restroom, but who was he to dictate what Daniel did or didn't do.

He turned back to Noh, expecting her to try and escape his

presence, too, but instead, she was looking up at him intently, her dark eyes large and curious.

"What can we do to help Callie?"

She leaned back against the kitchen counter, balancing her elbows on its edge, waiting for Jarvis to answer her question. When she realized no answer was forthcoming, she sighed and said:

"She needs our help. And I'm down to do anything but sit here and wait it out."

Jarvis sighed, too, pulling out one of the stools and sitting down. He was exhausted already and there was still so much left for him to do.

"I promised her I would look after Clio and this Realtor girl. If we leave Sea Verge, I can't enforce that promise."

Noh nodded, still leaning back on the counter.

"Okay, I hear you. Your hands are tied."

She didn't say it condescendingly, or as if she thought he was being silly. There was no judgment in her tone—and for this, Jarvis was grateful.

"Thank you," he said, resting his chin in his hands and sighing deeply.

Suddenly, from somewhere at the back of the house there issued a loud *crash* followed by a piercing female scream. Jarvis was immediately on his feet, heading for the kitchen door, Noh hot on his heels.

As he entered the foyer, he could hear raised voices coming from down the hall. Using the voices as his guide, he jogged until he found Jennice blocking the doorway to the study. She looked bewildered, and didn't move out of the way as he pushed past her and entered the room. Inside, he found one of the bookcases on its side, Clio crouched over it, her hand extended toward a large bear of a man who was sitting on the floor, a dazed expression on his face. A completely nude, blonde woman was sprawled on the floor beside him, a bloody gash etched into the flesh of her right cheekbone.

"Freezay?!" Jarvis cried, shocked to find the ex-detective here at Sea Verge.

"Good to see you, too, Jarvis," he said, letting Clio help him to his feet. "But I'm afraid we might be bringing a shit storm with us. I was attacked back at my place by a bunch of thugs and they seemed to think someone other than Calliope was in charge of Death, Inc."

Jarvis was not surprised by the news. It was only the beginning of the end, as far as he was concerned. Still, he was rather relieved to be able to finally share his predicament with someone he trusted—and out of everyone here at Sea Verge, Freezay was the only one he trusted implicitly.

They'd been close friends for many years, but after Freezay had helped Calliope root out the murderers who'd tried to steal the original copy of *How to Be Death* at the annual Death Dinner, Jarvis had held out hope they would become colleagues, too. In fact, he'd been rather aggressively pushing Calliope to hire Freezay as Chief of Security for Death, Inc.

He knew she'd offered Freezay the job—and that he'd asked for some time to think it over—but now it looked as though he was going to be dragged into their world, whether he liked it or not.

"Sorry about the mess," Freezay added, running his hands through his blond mop of hair.

"Don't worry," Jarvis said, shaking his head. "You're joining a mess already in progress. The 'shit storm,' as they say, has achieved full residence here, my friend."

Freezay nodded his understanding then turned his attention to the blonde woman at his feet.

"Are you all right?" he asked.

"Hit my cheek on the bookcase when we wormholed in," she trilled, her voice light and feminine.

"Sorry about that," Freezay said, looking contrite.

She waved away his apology as she accepted an egg-yolk-colored handkerchief from Noh. She placed the handkerchief against her cheek, and the yellow cotton fabric slowly turned brown as it soaked up the blood.

"Where's Callie?" Freezay asked, turning back to Jarvis.

"She's not here," he said. "She and the Ender of Death have gone to try and head this thing off."

"The Ender of Death?" Freezay asked, surprised.

"Uriah Drood has gotten ahold of a way to merge our universe with one in which Calliope doesn't exist," Jarvis said. "The Ender of Death has become Death's champion until we can stop this thing—"

"He's on our side for *now*," Daniel said, pushing past Jennice so he could step into the room.

From the look on his face, Jarvis could tell Daniel wasn't happy about finding Freezay and the strange, naked woman sitting on the floor.

"That does appear to be the case—" Jarvis tried to add, but Daniel ignored him, stepping over his words.

"—but when this purported 'Golden Age of Death' Callie's supposed to usher in is finally over then he gets to murder her without contest. Just a little bargain she, Jarvis, and that crazy old bat, Anjea, made," Daniel finished, scowling at Jarvis.

Jarvis found himself becoming rather annoyed with Daniel. He hadn't had *anything* to do with Calliope's ultimate decision to indebt herself to the Ender of Death.

"We have to get out of here. Something's coming."

The voice belonged to the blonde woman on the floor. She was sitting up now, her long legs folded underneath her, hair draped around her shoulders like a cape.

Jarvis found the woman's words oddly chilling as they echoed through the nearly empty room—but only Freezay seemed to be the one to glean their importance. He tried to usher everyone out of the room, but it was too late. A loud explosion tore through the room, followed by a flash of blinding white light that was eyeball-searing.

Throwing his hands up to cover his eyes, Jarvis took an involuntary step backward, slamming into another solid body and losing his footing. He went down hard, his right elbow caroming off the floor. Waves of pain shot up his forearm and into his wrist. He cried out, reaching for his wounded appendage, but something leapt on top of him, driving him back down to the floor.

"Remove yourself!" he cried, using his good hand to push his assailant away.

Still blinded from the explosion, Jarvis could only make out his attacker's silhouette, a large shadowy outline looming above him. He heard a low, guttural *snarl*, one that chilled the marrow in his bones, and felt his attacker's full weight descend on his chest, his senses enveloped by the stench of rank, hot animal breath. It was a meaty and decaying bouquet, and his nostrils fought to keep the smell out of his sinuses, but it was impossible.

Ignoring the pain in his right arm, Jarvis tried to shake off the creature, but it was a losing battle. Whatever had ahold of him was much stronger and more vicious than he was.

As his vision cleared, he was finally able to see his attacker—and he wasn't surprised to find a male Vargr (a hybrid human/wolf creature) sitting astride him, its long, snapping jaws dripping saliva onto the front of his freshly starched dress shirt. Without missing a beat, Jarvis pulled back his left fist and punched the Vargr in the snout, making the creature shriek in pain.

But he didn't stop there.

He drew his knees in toward his chest and kicked out, the bottom of his shoes connecting with the beast's unprotected belly. He felt the soft flesh give way and the creature shrieked again before rolling off of him.

He climbed to his feet and kicked the creature in the head, twice, sending geysers of blood shooting across the floor—then he looked up to find the room in total chaos.

The explosion had heralded the arrival of a massive wormhole, one large enough to transport a whole pack of Vargr into the study. He looked to his right and found Clio and Noh back-to-back, battling three female Vargr. Clio was using a spell to repel two of them, while Noh was using her bare knuckles to punch the third Vargr in the eye.

"Are you all right?"

Jarvis turned around to find Daniel standing behind him, holding a bloodied Vargr head by the snout.

Before Jarvis could answer, Daniel had cocked his arm and thrown the head like a fastball pitch at the back of the skull of one of the Vargr Clio was spelling. The creature fell forward, whimpering as it crumpled to the ground.

"I'm fine," Jarvis said, instantly forgiving Daniel for being such a prick a few minutes earlier. "And that was a lovely shot."

"We need to get the hell out of here," Daniel said, his eyes scanning the room.

Jarvis knew exactly what Daniel was seeing: They were massively outnumbered by the Vargr.

A scream ripped through the chaos, catching their attention, and Jarvis turned to find Jennice standing in the doorway, hands out in front of her like she was pushing something away—only there was nothing to fend off, just a large, male Vargr lying inert at her feet.

She looked up at the two men, her eyes glistening with tears.

"I killed it," she moaned, her whole body shaking as she leaned against the doorjamb.

Jarvis nodded at Daniel, letting him know he'd handle it. Daniel took off and Jarvis made a move toward Jennice, stopping along the way to pull the original, Angelic copy of *How to Be Death* from one of the overturned bookcases. He slid the book into his suit coat pocket, then ran across the room, barely evading the clutches of another, smaller male Vargr, as it headed toward Jennice.

But luck was with him.

Freezay was suddenly at his side, grabbing the creature by its hair and swinging it in the air until its neck snapped. As soon as the Vargr went limp, Freezay dropped it on the ground then ripped its head from its shoulders.

Jarvis didn't stick around to admire the carnage. He took off, reaching Jennice just as she began to lean sideways against the doorframe, eyes rolling up into her head.

"It's okay," Jarvis said, pulling the young woman into his arms, as her heart fluttered against his chest like a wounded bird.

"I killed it," she whispered. "I didn't mean to. It just happened."

Jarvis stroked her hair.

"Shh, you did the right thing."

She didn't seem to hear him.

"I didn't mean to do it," she moaned. "It was an accident."

Jarvis knew nothing he said would reach her right now, so he decided the best thing he could do was just get her out of there. He tried to pull her from the room, but she seemed rooted in place, her body rigid.

"We have to go," Jarvis said calmly, his lips close to her ear.

"Let us help you," a voice said—and he looked up to find Clio and Noh standing beside him.

He nodded, letting the girls each take an arm while he

pushed from behind. Together, the three of them were able to drag Jennice out of the room, but not before some of the Vargr had noticed their attempt to escape.

"Stay back!" Clio screamed, raising her arms in the air as a spiral of electricity shot out from her hands, engulfing the Vargr that'd moved toward them.

The creatures writhed in the electrical storm, their muscular bodies shuddering as they were whipped into the air and then blasted backward. There was a *crack* as the creatures hit the ceiling, their blood arcing out in waves from the impact point.

Jarvis was impressed by the level of power Clio seemed capable of wielding. But then she'd caught his eye and shaken her head, letting him know she, too, was shocked by the extent of what she'd just done.

"We'll talk later," Jarvis said, ushering the three women farther down the hallway.

"Where are we going?" Noh asked—she and Clio each holding on to one of Jennice's arms.

Jarvis opened his mouth to say, "I don't know where to go," but he didn't get the chance to speak because suddenly Kali, the Hindu Goddess of Death and Destruction, was blocking their path.

"Dipwad told me you wouldn't need my help," she said, cocking an eyebrow at them. "That you could 'handle' things. All I have to say is: *ha!*"

Then Kali bared her pearly white teeth—in what Jarvis could only term a "horrific grimace"—and raced past them. Her eyes were glued on the husky, male Vargr that'd been slowly sneaking up behind them, its jaws open wide for the kill.

"Die, Vargr, die!" she screamed as she bit into its throat, tearing out its esophagus with her bare teeth.

Jarvis turned away, the sight of so much blood and viscera enough to turn even the strongest of stomachs, then he gave a silent prayer of thanks to whatever turn of fate had brought Kali into their midst.

starr did not feel any guilt about what she'd done. After all, she wasn't responsible for the Vargr attack. That was someone else's work. She'd just gotten Edgar Freezay to Sea Verge. That was it—and it was only because Frank had promised to fork over many special things in return for her help. Otherwise she would've just as happily said, "no."

Not that she really cared whose side she was on. It was more about what benefited her needs best. That was the Sirens' creed: Only do the things that benefit you directly. She knew it sounded harsh, but this golden rule had been working to the Sirens' benefit for as long as they'd ruled the sea.

Speaking of the sea . . . *thank God* Sea Verge was right on the water. She wondered if her half sister had made use of the proximity—she doubted it; the woman had always been so touchy about her half-Siren heritage—but Starr would have to ask her about it the next time she saw her. Not that she'd seen much of her half sister since the woman had returned to the sea. Death's widow had become a real hermit these days, hiding out in some godforsaken cave over by the Mariana Trench, isolating herself from her Siren family, and not even *once* inviting Starr over for a visit.

Well, her half sister could just have her hermit-y little cave. It wasn't like she'd been in Starr's life much before she'd come back to the sea anyway. No, she'd chosen to live on land with the humans, to marry Death, and ignore everything *Siren* about herself.

Pushing away thoughts of her ungrateful half sister, Starr decided now was as good a time as any to make her exit. She had zero interest in becoming entangled in the violent free-for-all happening around her. She would be sorry to leave the detective behind because she loved a sexy man-challenge—and Edgar Freezay, that strapping specimen of human manhood, would definitely be a tough nut to crack. Especially now he knew she'd lied to him and had ulterior motives for bringing him to Sea Verge. It made her feel powerful that she'd been able to beguile him, but now she was sad she wasn't going to get to do naughty things to his muscular body.

As the fighting heated up, Starr took a moment to scan the room, looking for the most direct escape route. If she wanted to avoid the craziness, the best way would be to smash open one of the windows and jump. It was probably a little extreme, but she thought escaping a full-on Vargr-pack attack called for extreme measures. She looked around for something to smash the window with, but there were only a few large pieces of furniture, nothing she could pick up without a lot of effort.

She decided there was nothing to do, but use her own body as a battering ram.

Clearing her mind, she took a running start and threw herself at the window, the glass shattering on impact. Shards of translucent glass rained down on top of her as she landed in one of the shrubs encircling the side of the house, its branches cushioning her fall. As she tried to extract herself from the shrub, waxy emerald leaves edged in prickles tore at her skin and hair, one of them even stabbing itself into the wound on her cheek, sending a shock of raw pain through her jaw.

She bit her lip to keep from crying out, then began to drag herself from the plant's grasping branches. It was a fight, the shrub seeming to like the taste of her skin and blood, but she was finally able to free herself, landing in the grass and skinning her bare knee. A trail of blood ran down the front of her calf, but she didn't dare waste any time inspecting her wounds, just climbed to her feet and, ignoring the pain in her cheek and knee, began the short jog across the lawn toward the water.

She could hear the sound of the surf crashing against the rocky shoals—and the knowledge the sea was so close drove her forward. The glamour she'd used to create human legs began to fade as she neared the water, and she had to push herself to reach the cliff's edge before she lost control of the spell and transformed back into a mermaid.

She ran faster, the edge of the cliff now only a few feet away. Closing her eyes as she stepped off the edge, she felt the land drop away underneath her feet. Savoring her triumphant return to the water, she squealed with joy as her body began the long drop down to the sea.

eleven

CALLIOPE

He spoke slowly and without emotion, almost as if he were giving a deposition and wanted every last detail nailed down so he wouldn't be accused of perjury. And, somehow, this emotionless retelling made the story even more horrific:

"It was Anjea who made the 'Golden Age of Death' prediction upon the news of your mother's pregnancy," Marcel said. "So she knew she would be a target. But there was no reason to suspect we'd been followed."

"Everyone's always shooting the messenger," I said, my thoughts bleak.

We were all in the kitchen: Marcel on a barstool next to the kitchen island, Jarvis futzing by the stove top. Runt and I were splayed out on the floor below the sink, my back pressed up against the kitchen cabinets.

"I've made it my business to keep tabs on Anjea, to always know what she was thinking," he said. "But I didn't know she was aware of how closely I watched her."

"She knew," Jarvis said.

"Yes," Marcel agreed. "I realized this when she came to me and proposed I make an alliance with you—she was many steps ahead of all of us."

"She was a seer," Jarvis said to me, as he began the preparations for a magical poultice he thought might draw out Runt's voice. "Your father consulted her on many occasions."

"Then why didn't she know they were coming for her?" I asked.

No one seemed to have an answer for this.

"Who's to say *what* Anjea's intentions were," Marcel said. "She's gone now and that's all the outcome we need to know."

"So you followed the man who beheaded her?" Jarvis asked. "That's how you came upon Runt?"

Marcel nodded.

"I believe someone is trying to systematically take out anyone who might be of help to you. I'm surprised your assistant is still living. He'd be the first creature I'd dispatch if I was going to cut your legs out from under you."

"Great," I said to Marcel then I turned to Jarvis: "I think he's trying to say you're a pretty special dude, Jarvis."

Jarvis rolled his eyes.

"I was able to piggyback on the killer's wormhole," Marcel said, his eyes on the microwave above my head as the timer slowly counted down to zero.

The Ender of Death had expressed his hunger to Jarvis, and Jarvis had obliged him by putting together a plate of leftovers from the refrigerator that he'd then shoved into the microwave, setting the timer for five minutes.

"I had no idea he was going after your hellhound," Marcel added, one eye still locked on the revolving plate inside the microwave.

I let Marcel's words wash over me. What kind of bastard went after a defenseless puppy?

Hard at work at the stove preparing the poultice, Jarvis shook his head, and I knew he was thinking the same thing.

The microwave chose that moment to finish its cooking cycle and Marcel leapt to his feet, extracting the plate of steaming food and sitting back down in two seconds flat. He didn't seem at all bothered by the sizzling sound the food was making, just picked up his cutlery and dug in.

"She was alone, guarding the entrance to the South Gate of Hell, which made the attack easy," Marcel said, in between bites of food. "There were already two men there when we arrived. One of them, the one I assumed was the leader because he never got his hands dirty, looked like a weasel. The other was just the muscle. A big mountain of a man."

"What about the man you were following?" I asked.

"I had the element of surprise," Marcel said, grinning wickedly. "He didn't expect me to follow him. He probably thought I'd wormhole after you. Since no one knows of our alliance, they'll continue to assume that it's you I'm after."

"You killed him?" I asked

"I wrung his neck. And then I wrung the neck of the Mountain who slid his knife into your hellhound's throat."

His words were grotesque. Made more so by the lack of emotion he showed when talking about the men he'd murdered. I wanted to close my ears, but being oblivious to the harsh realities of the world I inhabited wasn't possible anymore.

"It's ready," Jarvis said, removing a thick cotton dish towel from a kitchen hook and dropping it into the bubbling pot.

It appeared as though the painstaking process of combining herbal elements over a super-heated flame (and intoning words only Jarvis knew the meaning of) had worked. The poultice was ready.

Runt struggled to her feet, thumping her tail against the cabinet as she watched Jarvis draw the dish towel from the pot. Carrying the steaming towel in his bare hands, he brought it over to Runt and laid it over the wound in her neck. The smell coming off the dish towel was intense, and something, one of the herbs probably, made Runt sneeze.

"Bless you," I said, and it felt odd to have my polite puppy—who always said "thank you" after a sneeze—remain silent.

"I'm so sorry, little one," I said, petting her side as she looked up at me sadly.

She leaned against me, her body pinning me to the cabinet door I was leaning against—and I was unprepared for how much growing she'd done since the last time I saw her. She was practically dog sized now.

"Do you think it will work?" I asked Jarvis, who was now busying himself over the sink, cleaning up the mess he'd made in order to craft the poultice. Behind him, Marcel ate the last bite of leftover turkey and mashed potatoes Jarvis and I'd had for dinner the night before.

"The poultice *may* work," Jarvis said.

"May?" I asked, as I watched him rinse out the aluminum pot before sliding it into the dishwasher.

This was a habit I'd never understood. It was called a "dishwasher" for a reason. Why clean the dish beforehand?

"I hope it will work. It's strong magic and it should be able to reverse the damage, but . . ." He trailed off, not meeting my gaze as he picked up another dish towel from the counter and dried his hands with it.

"So, why the *but* at the end of that sentence?" I asked.

"If everything Marcel told us is true, then the poultice will work," he said, deflecting my question on to Marcel.

The Ender of Death didn't seem fazed to have his story called into question.

"I have no reason to lie," he offered, wiping a dab of mashed potato from his chin. "It was exactly as I said."

I caught Jarvis's eye. Neither of us trusted the Ender of Death, but the fact he'd saved Runt's life made it harder to outright despise him—and he *had* saved her life.

There was no doubt about it.

If he'd been lying, she'd have done something to let us know. Instead, she'd lain on the floor beside me, panting slightly, but never once stirring as he'd relayed the story.

"How long do we have to wait before we know?" I asked.

Jarvis checked his watch, lips pursed.

"Five minutes, more or less."

Runt thumped her tail.

"It'll work," I said, giving her a squeeze. "I have faith in anything Jarvis does."

I meant what I said. I really did think Jarvis could fix anything. And if he couldn't help Runt, well . . . then I didn't want to think about it.

As if she'd read my mind and was telling me everything would be all right regardless of the outcome, she rested her chin on my shoulder and nuzzled my neck. I reached up and patted her head.

Blissed out, she closed her eyes and snuffled happily into my shoulder, letting me know I should continue the petting, which, of course, I did.

The poultice was closer to me now, though, and my nose

wrinkled at the smell. Runt didn't seem put off by the stink, but that wasn't saying much. She liked all kinds of weird, pungent scents I found disgusting.

"How much longer?" I asked, looking over at Jarvis.

"Three minutes."

It was a very long three minutes.

Inside, I was bargaining with myself: If Runt got her voice back, I'd quit buying sunglasses . . . I'd never act like a bitch ever again . . . I'd be a better Death.

Frankly, I would've done anything to guarantee Runt came out of everything okay. But God wasn't into bargains—and it didn't matter what I promised to do, Runt was either going to be healed, or she wasn't.

"One minute," Jarvis said.

"Once this has been decided, Death, we need to go," Marcel said, picking up his dish and taking it to the sink. "It's not safe here anymore."

"No, we'll go when I say we go," I said, not liking the idea of Marcel thinking he could just tell me what to do.

"I only say it because it's true," Marcel said, pulling "a Jarvis" and washing his dish before placing it in the dishwasher. "They will hunt you down if you stay here. Already they may be on their way."

"I just need you to back off for a minute," I said.

Right then, all I cared about was whether Runt was going to be okay or not. I didn't need Marcel's matter-of-fact voice hammering in my ear.

"I'm just saying—"

"It's time," Jarvis said.

He squatted down next to Runt.

"Let's see now," he said, removing the dish towel from Runt's neck.

I was hoping for a miracle, but when she tried to speak, nothing came out. Not even a sigh. She hung her head before I could see the resignation in her eyes—and I had to admit to myself the magical poultice hadn't worked.

I started to cry. I couldn't help myself. The tears just came of their own accord and I was unable to stop them.

"It's okay, baby," I said, brushing the tears away with the back of my hands. "It's gonna be okay."

Runt continued to look at the ground, mute. I reached out and pulled her to me, hugging her tightly to my chest.

At least she's alive, I thought. *You should be grateful for that.*

Alive for now, another voice whispered, ripping the last shred of my self-control away from me.

"They're going to come after every one of them, aren't they?" I cried, addressing my question to Marcel. "All the people I love. They'll kill every one of them, won't they?"

These weren't questions, more like the hysterical ramblings of someone who's scared and guilt stricken; someone who knows they're incapable of fixing the things that are happening to the people they love, and feels responsible for the fallout anyway.

"They will destroy all that you hold dear, Death," Marcel agreed. He was back at his spot by the kitchen island, his chin in his hands, watching me.

"No one you love is safe. Every person or creature close to you will be ferreted out and killed, unless you stop this."

He was right. Runt would've been dead, if he hadn't been there to help her.

"How do I keep them safe?" I asked, the hysteria having abated somewhat, so I could think more clearly.

"You can't," Marcel said, shaking his head. "You can only stop the two universes from merging. That's it."

"It's ridiculous," I said, his words rekindling my anger. "I can let them know what's happening, tell them—"

"They can't help you," Marcel said, interrupting me. "They can only get in your way."

"I don't want them to get hurt," I said, turning to Jarvis and hoping a calmer head would prevail. "Can't we bring them to Sea Verge and keep them safe here?"

Jarvis took my question into consideration.

"There is one possibility . . ."

I was ready to hear anything.

"We could call them and I could use a spell, a very old and powerful one."

Marcel snorted as he climbed off his chair. He knelt down beside me, running his hand over Runt's head and then scratching the spot she liked behind her ears.

"Then they will all die here together, Death," he said, leaning forward so that his lips were almost touching my cheek.

"No!" I said, shoving him away.

I found myself really wanting to punch Marcel, but I restrained myself.

"They won't die here. I can give you twenty-four hours in which Sea Verge will be off the grid," Jarvis said. "So long as no one wormholes here, the mansion will be impossible to pinpoint on any map or GPS unit—and it will only be visible to those who you've invited."

"You can do this?" I asked Jarvis.

He nodded.

"I can do it—but you have to leave first, so you won't be bound in the spell."

That meant I would be saving the people I loved, but I wouldn't get to tell them good-bye. I might never again touch Daniel's face or kiss his sweet lips; I might never hear Clio's voice, or spend time with my birth mother. I felt nauseous— and then I realized it was just my body reacting to the fact I might die without letting my loved ones know how much I loved them.

"So be it," I said, speaking with a strength I didn't really possess.

As soon as the words were out of my mouth, Runt began to whine. Hope against hope, I prayed the spell had somehow worked, after all, and that Runt had gotten her voice back. But as her whines subsided (without any words emerging from her mouth), I had to accept the spell had been a dud.

"Oh, Runt," I said, nuzzling her head.

"I'm sorry, Death," Marcel said, sensing my utter disappointment as he offered me his hand. "Now let your assistant do his work while we do ours."

I wanted to say something snarky in return, but I just didn't have the energy. Instead, I took his hand and let him lift me to my feet. Immediately, Runt stood up, too, but I shook my head.

"You're hurt. You have to stay here with Jarvis."

She stared at me.

"This is no fight for a dog—"

"She's a hellhound," Jarvis said, interrupting.

"This is no fight for a *dog* or a *hellhound*," Marcel replied. "This is between Death and me."

"And those ingrates who want to destroy Death," Jarvis mumbled. "Let's not forget that."

"Of course," Marcel said, nodding. "And as Death's new champion, I'll protect her from her enemies—"

"But we don't even know your true motives," Jarvis said.

"The need to know my motives is unnecessary—"

"Unnecessary?!" Jarvis said, looking put out by Marcel's answer.

"I am here to help and that's all you need to know," Marcel shot back, his voice even.

"Well, I think we deserve to know more than—"

"Stop it!" I yelled, surprising both men. "I mean it. Stop talking."

Jarvis kept his mouth shut, but Marcel didn't seem to understand I meant business.

"Nope, mouth shut, thoughts to yourself!" I said, heading him off before he could speak again. "I'm the one in charge here and you better listen to me if you want to be my new champion."

"Champion, nappy-in," Jarvis said, under his breath.

"Jarvis," I growled, warning him to keep his juvenile thoughts to himself—and he raised his hands in supplication.

Marcel glanced over at Jarvis and Jarvis shrugged in return.

"Stop looking at each other like that," I said. "I know what that look means and I don't appreciate it."

"Sorry—" Marcel said.

"Excuse me—" Jarvis mumbled.

I waved their apologies away.

"I don't care about that. Just . . . listen up. I'm gonna tell you what you're gonna do and then you're just gonna do it, okay?"

They nodded, two marionette puppets being worked by the same puppeteer.

Me.

They had no idea how similar they really were. They both liked to boss me around. They both loved to hear the sound of their own voices because neither of them knew when to shut up. Of course, I loved Jarvis, and considered him to be part of my family, while Marcel was on my permanent shit list, no matter how many of my friends he saved. The man had taken too much joy in killing my dad and I would never be able to forgive him for that, or for the murderous act, itself.

"Marcel, Runt, and I are going to get out of here and let you cast that spell," I said to Jarvis, pleased to see I was holding everyone's attention with the power of my words. "Your job is to keep everyone here for the next twenty-four hours. Marcel and I are going to find Uriah Drood and stop him."

At the mention of her name, Runt got up and padded over to me, nuzzling my hand with her snout. I knew this meant she was throwing in her lot with me, and I was grateful for it.

Jarvis nodded, but Marcel still didn't look convinced.

"But the hellhound's injured," he said. "She'll be in the way."

I shook my head to let the Ender of Death know this wasn't open for negotiation.

"I trust her," I said, patting Runt on the head. "I don't trust you. End of story."

He took this better than I would have, had the roles been reversed.

"Are you certain Runt is up for this?" Jarvis asked.

"If she wants to come, then I want her with me," I said, by way of an answer.

"All right, then," Jarvis said, letting me make the call—something I very much appreciated.

"I promise I'll keep her safe, Jarvis."

"I know you'll try your best," he said—and I could see he wanted to believe I could protect Runt and, by extension, myself, but I also knew he was worried. To my surprise, Marcel was the one who stepped in to reassure him.

"I won't let anything happen to either of them," he said with conviction. "We'll find the ones behind this and stop it. I want to kill Death fair and square—and I don't want anyone else beating me to it."

Jarvis looked ill.

"It's the closest thing to a promise he's gonna give you, Jarvis," I said, catching my Executive Assistant's eye. "I say you take it."

Jarvis and I've never really connected over humor—and this was just another example of him not "getting it" when I was trying to lighten the mood.

"Sorry," I said.

Jarvis scowled at me, but let it pass.

"So," I continued, giving Marcel my attention now. "Where to first?"

"We go right to the top," he said, looking thoughtful. "Uriah Drood, the head of the Harvesters and Transporters Union."

I'd already been thinking along those same lines, so I nodded, pleased with his choice.

"You know he hates me," I said. "That's why he's doing this."

"He more than hates you, Calliope," Jarvis said, somberly. "You and Freezay humiliated him in front of everyone at the Death Dinner."

"No, this didn't happen overnight," Marcel said. "He's been planning this for much longer."

"He despised your father," Jarvis said, nodding his agreement. "And he does seem the kind of man who would transfer those negative feelings for your father onto you—and you didn't help by tearing him apart at the dinner."

"Negative feelings?" I said, with a snort. "I wish that were the case. The guy wants to eradicate my very existence. I think his feelings run a little more deeply than just 'negative.'"

"I would love to stand around and debate how much Uriah Drood loves to hate you, Death, but I think we should take our leave now," Marcel said, heading toward the door.

But I didn't move from my spot. There was one thing I wanted to do before I left, and it was important and private. Well, just personal more than anything.

"I need to go upstairs," I said, not waiting for an answer as I took off for the foyer. "It'll only take me a minute."

I took the stairs two at a time, hit the landing and then sped down the hallway. When I got to my bedroom, I threw open the door, but stopped before clearing the threshold, my eyes not believing what they were seeing.

My room was empty.

twelve

Hearing about something and seeing it in the flesh were two very different things.

The creature was crouched in front of Jennice, snarling, its long, mottled gray snout dripping saliva onto the floor. It bared its teeth as it growled at her, and she discovered, to her horror, there were just too many teeth for her to count. She took an involuntary step backward, throwing her hands out in front of her as if this would somehow protect her from the werewolf-thing deciding to tear her throat out.

"Stay back," Jennice said, her mouth so dry the words came out in a whisper.

The creature took a step closer, muscles rippling in its shoulders as it inched forward. Jennice could see large teats hanging from its belly and she realized it was a female—though there was nothing maternal about the bloodthirstiness of the thing crouched in front of her.

"Please stay back," Jennice moaned, cringing as the beast growled at her again then sat back on its hind legs.

Before she even understood what was happening, the beast had leapt forward, its jaws snapping as they made a beeline for her throat.

Heart stop! Jennice's mind screamed, the thought coming unbidden from some unconscious part of her brain.

Immediately, the beast made a strangled cry and lost all its velocity, falling at her feet like a limp rag. She waited for the creature to roll over, or make some kind of move to let her know it was just taking a breather in between attacks, but not one muscle twitched as it lay there on the floor.

The creature was not moving and it would not be moving ever again. The thought triggered an outbreak of sweating all across her body, her fingers and toes going numb as, for a moment, time froze. It was all she could do to remain on her feet.

Don't be dead. Please, dear Lord, don't let it be dead, she prayed, though she knew it was hopeless when she looked at the creature and found two swollen, glassy eyes in its head.

The world around her blurred and her brain felt like it was running the three-minute mile with a body covered in molasses. She couldn't stop thinking about what she'd just done, about what she'd become.

A murderer.

She'd always been different, but then Clio had told her she wasn't alone, that everyone at Sea Verge was different, somehow, too. She'd been filled with excitement because she wanted friends, people with weird powers like hers, who understood what it was like to be disconnected from the rest of the normal world. But then she'd seen what those powers could do . . . and she was terrified.

She knew there were monsters in this new world that would eat you alive if you let them—she might as well have been one of them herself, now—and this knowledge made her want *out*.

But you couldn't just close the door on something once you knew it existed. You could live in denial and pretend it wasn't real (and this would mean denying her own powers, too), but eventually you'd have to face reality—and she wasn't ready for that just yet.

So Jennice's mind did the only rational thing it could do given the situation: It shut down.

She felt it happening and was incapable of stopping it. It was an odd sensation, like leaving your body and floating up above yourself. She could still see all the action—the blond bear of a man fighting one of the monsters, Daniel slamming his fist into the spine of another, Clio and Noh fighting together, back-to-back—but she couldn't hear any of the battle. There was just a steady rushing in her ears, one that reminded her of the ocean trapped inside the inner swirl of a conch shell.

Her own immobile body was below her and when she looked down at it, she wondered how her soul fit so comfortably inside something so large and unwieldy. Bodies, she decided, looked very weird when you weren't inside of them.

She watched as Jarvis made his way toward her, his marionette body moving with a fluid grace someone so awkward should not possess. His eyes were wide with worry as he barreled across the floor.

She felt a strong pinch in the spot where her forehead would be if she'd still been in her body, and, like a raindrop hitting hot asphalt, sound exploded in her head. Whatever made the sound return, it wasn't finished with Jennice—it began to pour warmth all over her, weighing her down with heaviness until, with a sharp yank, she found herself back in her body.

She blinked twice then looked at Jarvis as he pressed her against him.

"I killed it," she whispered into his chest. "I didn't mean to. It just happened."

"Shh, you did the right thing," he said.

She hadn't done the right thing. She'd murdered and that was not something she could ever take back.

"I didn't mean to do it, I didn't."

The words came out in a rush, but Jarvis only shook his head, trying to let her know it was okay. At this point, with her peace said, she stopped paying attention to what was happening around her. She just clung to Jarvis as if he were a human life preserver.

The guilt of what she'd done was so overwhelming she wished she'd never returned to her body. She realized she must be in shock. She felt like she wanted to cry, but there was nothing to draw from, no tears, no well of emotion to tap into.

She sensed other bodies surrounding her and she looked up to find that Clio and Noh had joined them. She blinked and the three of them were guiding her out of the room, taking her down the hall. She wanted to help them, but it was all she could do to keep her body upright.

She saw the Indian woman before the others did, but they all stopped short once they realized she was there. There was something frightening about the regal way she held herself—the lion's mane of curly black hair, the fierce stare, and the shiny silver sari only adding to her mystique.

Jennice wanted to ask Clio who the woman was, but then everyone was talking and the fierce lady was gone.

"We have to leave Sea Verge," she heard Jarvis say.

Jennice tried to focus on the conversation, but her eyes kept straying over Jarvis's shoulder to where the dark-haired woman in the silver sari was now ripping the heads off the werewolves as they came through the door, their muscular bodies hell-bent on destruction.

She's amazing, Jennice thought, watching the woman as she laid waste to the beasts, dispatching them one by one with her bare hands. Then suddenly Jennice was being dragged down the hall again, away from the fascinating woman.

She didn't want to go. She wanted to stay there, watching the Indian lady work. She'd never in her life seen a woman do the kind of things this one was doing. It was like getting ringside seats to a bout of Wonder Woman vs. The Beasts.

"We have to keep moving," Clio hissed in her ear, the intensity of her words jump-starting Jennice's feet.

She liked Clio and didn't want to upset her, so she let the two girls lead her down the hallway.

"Outside," she heard Clio say to Noh as they pushed her through the foyer and toward the door.

She started to float again, the world blurring as Noh grabbed the doorknob and turned it, slowly easing the front door open—but something outside the door caught Jennice's attention, forcing her back into reality.

And that's when she screamed.

the little turncoat was getting away. He could see her through the busted window, running across the back lawn toward the edge of the property and the cliff overlooking the sea. From there, all she needed to do was jump and then she'd be in the water, totally untouchable. He didn't want to leave Daniel and Jarvis in charge of the Vargr while he took off after the Siren, but if he didn't catch her, he might well be squandering a very important lead.

He'd seen the girls hustling a shell-shocked Jennice out of the room, so at least they weren't in the thick of it anymore, but still he had a hard time making the decision—and with every second he delayed, Starr was getting farther out of his reach.

"Are you gonna stand there all day, Copper, or are you gonna go kick that bitch's ass?"

He released the limp body of the Vargr he'd just strangled to death, letting it fall to the floor before turning to find Kali, dark hair slick with blood, standing behind him, holding two Vargr by the scruffs of their neck. As he watched, she slammed their heads together, both skulls imploding with the force of the blow.

"I got this," she added, winking at him with a gleeful face, her once-silver sari drenched in dead Vargr's blood.

He took her arrival as a sign to get his ass in gear. Stepping over a headless Vargr body and avoiding the shards of glass still stuck in the frame, he vaulted himself through the window and out into the yard. He landed in a large shrub, its prickly branches cushioning his fall, but he was out of its embrace in two seconds, his feet plowing through the grass. He could see Starr ahead of him, her long hair flapping behind her as she limped toward the cliff's edge.

He willed his body to move faster. If she got to the water before he got to her, he'd lose his chance. Because there was no way he could catch her once she'd morphed back into her Siren form, which included a very powerful fish tail and the ability to breathe underwater. In no time flat, she'd easily outpace his puny landlubbing body and leave him drowning in her wake.

He wasn't going to make it. He pushed himself even harder, but it just wasn't going to be enough. She was inches from the edge and he was still fifteen feet away; his hesitation had cost him.

The Siren took one step off the cliff—

Freezay was going so fast he had to swerve to the left in order to avoid the wormhole as it disgorged a frantic woman from its belly, one whose arms were stretched out like pincers. The wormhole had ejected the woman far enough ahead of him she actually had a chance at catching the Siren. She hit the ground running and didn't stop, reaching the cliff just as Starr began her swan dive into the sea. The woman grasped at the tiny, naked body, her hands encircling the Siren's slim waist. With all her strength, she yanked Starr away from the abyss, putting an end to the chase mere seconds before the Siren would've escaped forever.

Freezay caught up with them to find the woman holding on to the squirming Siren as though Starr were a flailing fish.

"Get off me!" Starr wailed.

The other woman ignored the Siren's pleas, throwing Starr to the ground then setting upon her with her fists. She was able to get in a few good punches, mostly to Starr's exposed belly, before Freezay lifted her off the sobbing Siren.

"Freezay, help me!" Starr cried, reaching her arms up toward him for help.

"Stop it," the woman hissed, jabbing the business end of her elbow into Freezay's ribs, and forcing him to let her go.

She was back on Starr in an instant, pummeling the Siren's face with her balled fists. Gasping at the pain in his ribs from the elbow jab, Freezay took a step forward, insinuating himself in between the two women.

"Enough!" he yelled, separating them with his body.

The mystery woman still wanted a piece of the Siren and Freezay had to shove her away to keep her from finishing what she'd started. She stumbled, falling backward onto the grass— and it was only then he recognized her, his heart giving a slight stutter.

"Caoimhe . . . ?" he said.

Her name felt slippery in his mouth.

She glared up at him, her dark eyes flashing—and Freezay thought she'd never looked more beautiful. Just like his brain always did whenever he saw Caoimhe, it flashed back to the first time he'd met her:

The memory was as vivid in his mind's eye as if it'd happened yesterday. But this might've been because Freezay revisited this slice of his past more often than he did any of the other memories he possessed. He would never have told anyone this because they'd have thought he was obsessed with something that could never be—and they were right. It was his most beloved remembrance, though it had happened at the beginning of the time in his life he regretted most.

Since he was a small child, Edgar Freezay had known he was different. He'd learned to keep these differences hidden, but they'd still been there, always on the periphery of his life, haunting him. At twenty-two, he'd been a cocky little shit newly appointed to the Homicide division, working cases with a partner double his age who treated Freezay with a snotty disdain that made the younger man wish he'd been assigned to the drug detail instead.

Not that he didn't enjoy the work.

The work was the thing that made life worth living—and, thank God, he was good at it, too. From what he could see, his future was set. He'd spend the next thirty, thirty-five years working murder cases in Detroit, then maybe accept early retirement, move to California where the weather was nice, and take up fishing. It sounded like both an uneventful and uniquely satisfying life, and he was looking forward to enjoying every minute of it.

Then one afternoon his world changed, his future becoming anything but certain.

He was sitting at his desk waiting for Farley, his overweight and self-satisfied partner, to come back from a doctor's appointment. They were slated to do a follow-up interview with a witness and, though he'd have liked to do the interview without Farley, he didn't want to incur his partner's wrath.

"There's someone here to see you."

He looked up to find an attractive female officer he'd never noticed before leaning against the front of his desk. Her long brown hair was twisted up in a chignon at the back of her neck and she was wearing a white button-down shirt and khaki pants seemingly better suited for a safari than a day at the police station.

She gave him a sly wink, as if she knew what he'd been thinking, then beckoned for him to get up and follow her.

He should've asked her for the visitor's name, or *her* name, or why she wanted him to follow her, but, instead, he'd stood up and tucked his chair behind his desk, letting her lead him down the hall. Neither of them spoke as they walked through the station. He was just happy to be in the strange woman's company. They left the bull pen, Freezay eager as a puppy to follow her as she made a right, taking them down a long hallway he'd never seen before. Still, he didn't ask her where they were going, just followed her gently swaying hips.

There was something magical about her, about the way she moved and smelled. Her perfume, a seductive mix of cinnamon and vanilla, enveloped him as they walked, bewitching all five of his senses.

"He's waiting for you in the interrogation cell," she said as she stopped in the middle of the hall, indicating the open doorway in front of them, letting Freezay know he should enter.

"What's your name?" Freezay asked, overwhelmed by the urge to find out more about the mysterious young woman standing before him.

She grinned up at him, her dark eyes fringed with thick black lashes. There was something mischievous about her gaze, about the way she was sizing him up. He wondered if she found him wanting, or if he was as attractive to her as she was to him.

"I'm just Caoimhe."

"Just Caoimhe," he repeated, liking the feel of her name on his tongue, though he wanted to feel more of her than that.

He reached out and took her hand, kissing the delicate skin of her wrist. Her smell was so enticing he was having a hard time thinking straight. Looking back, he knew he should've just ravished her right then and there, but he hesitated, letting the moment slip away.

"I think you should go in now," she said, leaning toward him, her voice a low purr.

He was mesmerized by her nearness, by her scent, by the glint of amusement in her eyes—but he didn't tell her any of this, just let her go, as if he had all the time in the world to see her again. It would take years of hindsight for him to finally realize he'd dropped the ball, his chance to possess her gone with his reluctance to speak. He had no way of knowing she would soon be pregnant by another man and all hope of making her his own would be gone forever.

That one meeting's hesitation would cost him so dearly.

Though he wasn't quite ready to leave her company, Freezay

did as she asked, passing through the doorway (so close to Caoimhe he could almost taste her) and into the cold, gray room. The room's sole occupant was a compact man with a silver buzz cut and a set of piercing green eyes, wearing a tailored black suit that fit him like a glove. He stood up as Freezay entered, extending his hand.

"So good of you to meet me."

Freezay nodded, not sure who the man was, or why he'd chosen to have their meeting in an interrogation cell.

"I'm Manfredo Orwell," the man said, giving Freezay's hand a firm shake.

The man exuded an air of importance and it permeated the air like scent. He smiled at Freezay and indicated he should take a seat. Freezay pulled out the cold metal chair and sat down across the interrogation table from Orwell. He heard the door shut behind him and his heart clenched when he realized he might never see Caoimhe again.

"I'm sure you're wondering why I'm here, why I wanted to speak to you?" Orwell said.

He was watching Freezay with a quiet intensity that did nothing to hide the curiosity in his eyes. It was a look Freezay knew well. It lived on the faces of the men and women he worked with: hyperfocus coupled with an instinctual inquisitiveness about the world. This was the quality which drew Freezay to police work; it was the defining characteristic of who he was.

"I can't even imagine what you want with me," Freezay heard himself saying.

Orwell nodded, as if in Freezay's position, he would've said the same thing.

"I run an agency very similar to your Central Intelligence Agency or your Federal Bureau of Investigation"—Freezay could detect a slight, lisping accent as Orwell spoke—"and we would like to offer you a position."

"And what's the name of this agency?" Freezay asked.

But he didn't get the answer he was expecting; namely, the kind of faceless governmental entity or cold war double agent, spy-busting operation that filled the pages of paperback pulp thrillers the world over.

"It's called the Psychical Bureau of Investigations. I doubt you've ever heard of us," Orwell said, his smile revealing a row of blocky white teeth. "You might say we work for a higher power then your United States Government. We police the Afterlife."

Somewhere in the back of his mind Freezay heard the proverbial "other shoe" drop—and he realized he'd been waiting for a meeting like this his entire life.

"Before you go any further, I want to ask you something," Freezay said, leaning forward in his chair so his elbows rested on the interrogation table.

"Of course," Orwell said, leaning back and crossing his arms over his chest—and Freezay couldn't tell if the move was a power play or not.

"This isn't a joke, or someone trying to screw with my head, is it?"

Orwell laughed, his eyes crinkling at the corners.

"It does seem as if that would be the logical answer, doesn't it?" he grinned, amusement dancing in his eyes. "But no, this is not a joke, I promise you that."

"I've spent my life hiding from something like this," Freezay said. "When I was a kid they sent me to a psychiatrist because my mother and my teachers thought I was crazy. So I learned to stop talking about the odd things I saw, and it kept the doctors away—and now here you are, finally, after all these years. Telling me what I've always known: I'm not nuts."

Orwell nodded.

"Indeed, you are entirely sane."

"So this Psychical Bureau of Investigations, what kind of work would I be doing there for you?"

Orwell gave him a slow nod.

"No other questions, then? Nothing about the nature of the business or of the supernatural world, in general?"

Freezay shook his head. He'd always known this day would come, when he'd find out the truth about himself and about the strange things he knew existed outside the realm of normal human perception.

"It's just nice to know all those years of psychotherapy were utterly useless."

Orwell laughed.

"You'll find the world is much larger than the human mind can grasp."

"But I'm not really human, am I?" Freezay asked, his body tensing as he waited for the answer.

"No, you're not," Orwell acknowledged. "Your parentage makes you a far more valuable specimen."

Freezay's mother was a normal human—it was why she'd been so quick to throw him into therapy when he'd begun talking about the monsters he saw walking down the streets of their suburban neighborhood. He was four years old, he just assumed what he saw was what everyone else saw. He didn't know it was an overlay, one superimposed over what normal human beings could perceive.

Of his father, he knew next to nothing. Only that his mother had met him in a bar one lonely night and nine months later, Freezay had been born. So when Orwell referred to his parentage, Freezay knew he was speaking of his unknown father.

"What was my father?" Freezay asked.

"He was and still is the Norse God, Wodin."

Freezay thought he was prepared to believe anything, but the idea his father was some kind of Norse God just seemed ridiculous.

"It seems improbable, but believe me when I tell you it's the truth," Orwell went on. "Your father is well-known for his predilection for mortal women. He has half-human bastards strewn around the world."

It was only later, during his time with the PBI, that he was able to confirm this fact for himself. His father was, indeed, Wodin, and Freezay truly did have half siblings scattered across the globe.

"But this is neither here nor there," Orwell amended, returning to the matter at hand. "You've lived in the human world, your knowledge and skill, coupled with the fact you are derived partly from immortal stock, make you an invaluable asset—so much so, we would like you to head up our new division. We're calling it: Crimes Against Humanity."

"I'm in."

He hadn't needed to hear more. He was willing to chuck his human future without further thought, this new fate impossible to ignore, now he knew it existed.

"I had a feeling you'd see things our way," Orwell said, looking pleased. "Welcome aboard."

They'd shaken on it—and this had marked the beginning of a long and enduring friendship.

As the years had worn on, the Crimes Against Humanity division had become legendary. They were brought in whenever there was an unusual crime, one that stumped the other departments—and their solve rate was through the roof; something attributed almost singly to Edgar Freezay and his uncanny knack for discovering the truth, no matter where it lay hidden.

And so the years had melted away almost without notice . . . but his feelings for the mysterious woman he'd met that day had never gone away.

Even now as she climbed to her feet later, her features distorted in anger, he couldn't stop staring at her, she was so breathtaking.

"Well, don't just stand there staring at me, Freezay," she chided him. "Let's rip this Siren's heart out."

It took everything inside of him not to oblige her.

even though this was the first time Noh had seen a Vargr, she wasn't in the least bit afraid of them. The rational part of her brain knew she should be terrified of the slavering beasts that could destroy her with one chomp of their jaws. They weren't just plain old bad guys, but competent killing machines taking infinite pleasure in the violence they wreaked.

But her animal side, the one that'd taken control of her body now, wasn't at all scared. It was fearless. It wanted to wipe the floor with the Vargr's brains, then eat their guts on toast points for breakfast. She wasn't usually so gory in her revenge plots, but she was worried about Callie, about what the shitheads were trying to do to her friend, and anger brought out the nasty in Noh.

As they reached the front door, she heard Clio say:

"We have to keep moving."

Noh looked over at Jennice, not sure the other girl was going to be doing much "moving" once they got outside. From her glassy-eyed stare and inability to connect to what was happening around her, it seemed like she'd gotten more information than she could handle and had blown a brain fuse trying to process it all. From the car ride up to Sea Verge, Noh had gathered Jennice possessed no knowledge of the Afterlife—which meant she must've been hella surprised when creatures like the Vargr showed up and started trying to eat her.

"Outside," Clio said, pointing to the front door.

Noh wrapped her fingers around the doorknob and felt a strange prickling sensation flow up her arm. She shivered and almost didn't open the door, but then Clio was shoving Jennice into her back and it was impossible for her not to open it.

Jennice screamed, and Noh saw what had caught the girl's attention: A pack of Vargr were waiting for them on the front stoop. Noh's survival instincts prevailed and she quickly slammed the door shut in the Vargr's faces. Then she turned back to Clio, waiting for her to issue another set of instructions, but the girl looked stumped.

"What should we do now?" Noh asked encouragingly.

Obviously they couldn't go back the way they'd come, and the front was just as dangerous. Her question went unanswered as a Vargr claw slammed into the front door, cracking the heavy wood separating them from the monsters outside.

Jennice screamed and cowered against Noh as another concussive *crack* splintered the wooden door even more.

"I guess there's no time like the present to open that door and beat the shit out of those disgusting mongrels," Clio said, swallowing hard.

Noh liked Clio's plan very much. If she had to choose between fight or flight, she'd go with fight every time.

"Aye, aye, Captain," she said, grasping the doorknob.

Then she let the front door fly.

thirteen

Daniel watched Kali make short work of the remaining Vargr. He and Jarvis had tried to help, but she'd yelled at them to back off. Apparently, she enjoyed a bloody fight way too much to share it. He didn't know if Freezay had caught up with Starr, but God he hoped so. He was pretty damn sure she was the reason the Vargr had shown up at Sea Verge. It was why he'd stayed away from the wormhole system to begin with. It was just another way to track someone or *be* tracked by someone else—and it was something he'd wanted to avoid until he'd found Callie and was assured of her safety.

The minute he'd set foot in Sea Verge, he'd sensed there was magic at work. At first, he'd hoped this meant Jarvis was cloaking Sea Verge to protect Callie's location, but when he realized she was gone, he knew the magic was being used for other purposes. Put two and two together—and it meant Jarvis had placed a spell on Sea Verge to keep unwanted guests from finding and accessing the mansion.

So, why had it been so easy for him and the girls to breach the spell?

The only answer he could come up with was they'd been wanted; left exempt from the spell so they'd be able to find the house without any trouble. Freezay must've been on the exemption list, too, but wormholing in with Starr (who wasn't) had probably been what destroyed the spell.

He was going to have to quiz Jarvis about this if they ever got out of Sea Verge alive. Not that he was worried about himself, or Clio and Jarvis. They were immortal and could withstand a vicious Vargr attack—but he seriously doubted Jennice and Noh (who were mortal) could. As for Freezay, he figured the man had to have some supernatural blood in his veins or else he wouldn't have worked at the PBI, but this was just an educated guess.

He felt a light touch on his shoulder and turned to find Jarvis standing beside him.

"I think Kali has this well in hand," Jarvis said, eyeing the Hindu Goddess of Death and Destruction as she plucked one of the dead Vargr's eyeballs from its head and popped it into her mouth.

While the two men watched, she chewed and then swallowed the gelatinous mass. Jarvis seemed amused by the strangely sensual act, and Daniel had to agree there was something compelling about what they'd just witnessed.

Though he'd never personally been attracted to the woman, when he was working as the Devil's protégé the Devil had liked to take on Daniel's appearance in order to seduce and torment women—especially the Goddesses he deemed to be "goody-two-shoes." Kali had been on the Devil's hit list, and now it made interacting with the high-strung, and rather violent, Goddess kind of awkward.

Kali, and the many other victims of the Devil's seductions, had been made aware of the truth, that Daniel wasn't the one to pin their anger on. And though they intellectually knew he wasn't the responsible party, he still couldn't help but feel weird whenever he walked into a room and they looked at him sideways.

The Devil had not made Daniel's post-protégé life very easy.

"Yeah, I think you're right. Kali has things well in hand," Daniel agreed. "Let's go find the girls."

He'd barely gotten the words out of his mouth when there was a loud scream from the other end of the hallway.

"Shit," Daniel said, and the two men took off at a run.

At first he let Jarvis lead the way, but when they got to the front door—and he saw the splintered wood—Daniel pushed past the lankier man and sprinted down the front steps.

But he needn't have run. He found the girls had things well in hand. Even Jennice had snapped out of her fugue and gotten into the act, both arms raised in the air as if she were casting a spell—and who's to say she wasn't. If the three Vargr skipping in a circle in front of her were any indication, then she was a very powerful lady, indeed.

A few feet away from Jennice, Clio and Noh were taking turns beating a large Vargr over the head with a rake and a shovel, respectively.

"She just made them start dancing," Clio called over to Jarvis and Daniel, as she took her turn with the rake. "It was amazing."

Kali appeared in the doorway behind Jarvis, and when she saw the Vargr at play, she began to laugh.

"Oh my God, those Vargr look like trained seals! What will white girl's friends think of next?"

She was out of the doorway in three steps and, in two more, was happily ripping the spinal columns out of each of the dancing Vargr. As Kali felled the third Vargr, Jennice's body began to twitch and then she collapsed onto the stairway, her face covered in sweat.

Jarvis knelt down beside her, taking her hand and holding it in between his own.

"Are you all right?" Jarvis asked.

"Just . . . exhausted."

She closed her eyes, letting herself lean against Jarvis for support. Whatever she'd been doing to keep the Vargr incapacitated had expended a lot of her energy.

Clio and Noh moved out of the way so Kali could have a go at their Vargr, but the Goddess ignored the rake and shovel, taking pity on the mongrel by smashing its head in with her foot, blood and brains spilling into the grass.

"Don't play with your food," she admonished Clio and Noh as she plucked another eyeball from the mess of brain and skull in the grass and ate it.

"That's pretty disgusting," Noh said, but there was no judgment in her voice.

"Eyeballs are a delicacy, ghost watcher," Kali said with disdain. "I can't help it if you white girls are squeamish."

Daniel had never heard the term "ghost watcher" before and that was probably because he knew Kali had made it up. But the sentiment was correct. Callie had told him stories about her time at the New Newbridge Academy, and all the odd things she and Noh had experienced together there. He knew Noh could see ghosts, or *detached souls*, as she liked to call them, and he knew this was why she'd been able to tell Jarvis was in the wrong body.

"Can you see the Vargr's souls when they die?" he asked her.

Noh shook her head.

"Over the years I've learned to tune my radar way down around Death," she said. "I feel them leaving their bodies, but unless I want to make a connection with them, I don't see them."

"I bet that took you a long time," Daniel said, and Noh nodded.

"You have no idea."

Over Noh's shoulder, Daniel could see Freezay—aided by a strange woman—dragging an unconscious Starr toward them.

"Caoimhe!" Jarvis shouted, getting up from his perch on the stairs.

There was no point in running to help them. They seemed to have Starr incapacitated. As they got closer, Daniel could see Caoimhe was not happy, her lips set in a firm line, dark eyes livid. From the flare of her nostrils, he intuited she'd rather be slamming Starr's face into the ground than gently carrying her back to Sea Verge for questioning.

"Would you care for any assistance?" Jarvis asked, trotting over to Freezay, but the taller man waved him away.

"I see you've been busy," Caoimhe said, surveying the multitude of mutilated Vargr corpses.

She dropped Starr's arm and Freezay did the same, letting the Siren's unconscious body flop onto the grass at their feet.

"Thank you for letting me know what's been happening, Daniel," Caoimhe added, looking pointedly at Jarvis.

"I—" Jarvis said, but she shook her head.

"It doesn't matter. I'm sure you were only doing what Callie asked of you."

Worried Callie had kept her birth mother in the dark about her situation, Daniel had decided to call Caoimhe from the road to let her know what was happening. He wasn't surprised to learn she hadn't heard a peep from her daughter. She'd listened silently as Daniel had spoken, then, when he was done, she'd told him thank you for the information and hung up on him. He knew Callie was just trying to protect them all with her information blackout, but, well-intentioned as it was, he did not appreciate being left out of the loop—and he'd gotten the impression Caoimhe would feel the same way.

And he was right. She'd shown up at Sea Verge like a momma bear protecting her cub, ready to fight, maim, or kill anyone who tried to hurt her daughter.

"Let's kill it," Kali said, stepping away from the headless corpse at her feet and crouching down beside Starr.

"No!" Clio said, physically putting herself between the Hindu Goddess and the unconscious Siren. "We need to find out what she knows first."

Kali wasn't impressed by Clio's argument.

"What can she know, baby Death?" Kali said as she stood up, the front of her sari a blood-stained mess. "Very little about the fate of your sister. I can promise you this."

"I don't care," Clio said—and she looked ready to throw down with Kali in order to get her way. "I want to hear what she has to say, then you can do whatever you want with her."

Kali mulled over Clio's offer, head cocked as she weighed the myriad of possibilities this presented.

"Deal."

She offered her hand to Clio and they shook on it.

"I think we'd better get moving," Jarvis said, looking nervously around the yard. "By wormholing here with an uninvited guest, Freezay destroyed the spell protecting the house. It's how the Vargr were able to gain entrance to Sea Verge and I assume they won't hesitate to press their advantage again—and soon."

"Speak of the Devil," Daniel said, as the plaintive baying of a male Vargr raised the hair on the back of his neck.

He turned to the others, his face grim.

"Let's get the hell out of here."

* * *

there was a welcome committee waiting for Bernadette at the end of the tram's loop. The twins had called in reinforcements, though none of the four Victorian-garbed young men they'd brought with them seemed very happy about having to chase a dead woman around an amusement park parking lot.

Bernadette didn't blame them. If she could go back in time and change the outcome of the afternoon's roller-coaster ride, by God she would. She didn't want these crazy monsters chasing her any more than the monsters wanted to be chasing her. She used the word "monster" because in her mind, only monsters would steal another person's soul—and she was pretty sure that's what these odd people were trying to do.

"Before I even think about letting you take me, I want to know why," Bernadette said, climbing out of the now-stationary tramcar.

She wished the tram driver would notice her, but like all the other living people she'd encountered since she'd died he seemed oblivious to the confrontation happening three cars behind him.

As if he'd heard her thoughts, the driver hopped out of his seat and jumped onto the asphalt, walking back toward her car as he untucked the tail of his white shirt from the waist of his pants. He stepped onto the running board of Bernadette's tramcar and began to futz with one of the burned-out light bulbs hanging from the ceiling. Though he was inches from her, he might as well have been a million miles away, and Bernadette wondered how often, as a living person, she'd been surrounded by ghostly figures without knowing it?

She'd never spent much time thinking about the mechanics of what happened to a soul after it died, other than the going to Heaven or Hell part. She'd just assumed you closed your eyes and died then when you opened your eyes again you were standing in front of St. Peter—or, if you weren't so lucky, you opened your eyes to find yourself being prodded in the rear by the business end of a pitchfork.

These were her preconceived ideas on the subject, but they did nothing to prepare her for what she'd encountered during the course of her death. All the hours spent in church, listening to the minister preach about charity, turning the other cheek, and believing in Jesus Christ above all else, had absolutely no bearing on the reality of what happened to your soul when you died.

The tram operator finished playing with the light bulb and returned to his seat. He started the engine with the twist of a shiny silver key and the tram gave a sharp jerk, shooting forward. Bernadette watched it zoom back toward the theme park entrance, leaving her in the lonely darkness of an empty parking lot.

While the driver had futzed with the light bulb, the twins had been conferring, their heads bent so close together their cheeks touched. Now that the tram driver was gone, they were taking their sweet time in responding to Bernadette and this made her edgy. When she finally got sick of waiting for an answer, she said:

"What if I won't go with you? What if I fight you or go on the run?"

This got their attention.

"For our needs, you must come willingly," the twins said in unison, their voices melding into one, only upping the creepiness factor and making Bernadette even more wary of their intentions.

"Well, how about I just keep running until you get tired of chasing," Bernadette said.

The twins laughed, their voices a cohesive cackle. That's when it dawned on Bernadette they had no intention of letting her go. They were just going to play with her until she gave in to them.

"We won't stop with you. If you give us trouble, we will take your daughter, your grandson . . . We will steal the souls of all the people you love," the twins said in their eerie, singular voice.

She knew they were using her grandson to manipulate her, but she couldn't take the chance that what they were saying was true. There was no way she would do anything to jeopardize Bart's life. Not now, not ever.

"If I go with you, you'll leave Bart alone?" she said, her voice tremulous.

The twins nodded.

"You have our word."

Resigned to her fate, she dropped her head and sighed.

"I'll come with you."

The twins shared a knowing smile. It was always easier when they crushed their prey's spirit.

there were too many of them to take one car, so they'd had to split up. Jennice and Noh had climbed into the backseat of Clio's Honda, while Jarvis took the front passenger spot and Clio manned the steering wheel.

As Clio watched Freezay and Caoimhe loading the Siren into the back of Daniel's car, she had the instinctive urge to change the lineup. It wasn't that she didn't trust Daniel and Freezay—actually, she didn't know who to trust anymore, but this wasn't why she had the desire to switch passengers. It was all very simple: She wanted to be the one to deal with the Siren when it regained consciousness.

"We should go now," Noh said, turning in her seat so she could stare out the back window at the pack of Vargr loping across the grass toward them.

Clio threw the gearshift into drive, slamming the accelerator pedal to the floor with her foot, and forcing the car forward. In the rearview mirror, she could see the Vargr racing to reach the cars before they made it onto the main road. By wormholing them into the backyard, their master had put them at a clear disadvantage and now they were trying to make up the difference. Luckily, this gave Clio and the others just enough of a head start to get away—and little did the hapless Vargr know that Kali, the bloodthirsty Goddess of Death and Destruction, was lying in wait for them just past the front entrance to Sea Verge.

Clio wasn't surprised when Kali volunteered to stay behind and take care of the newly arrived Vargr. Anyone could see she took great pleasure in killing the beasts, ripping off their heads, and feeding on their entrails.

It was decided that once she'd taken care of the remaining Vargr she'd wormhole out of Sea Verge and hopefully draw whoever was monitoring the wormhole network, letting the bad guys chase her until the rest of them could get to a safe place.

The new Vargr had descended upon them so quickly they really hadn't been able to strategize. Their cobbled-together plan consisted of going to a pre-arranged meeting point so they could regroup and question Starr.

It wasn't an amazing plan, but it would do in a pinch.

The meeting point was a long drive ahead of them, at a place Jarvis thought would be safe, but even this wasn't a guarantee. If Sea Verge could be breached, then nowhere was truly safe.

Clio hit the main road going seventy, the wheels screeching as she made a hard right turn onto the asphalt. In the rearview mirror, she saw Daniel's car easily keeping pace with her own and she was happy to notice he had a lead foot, too.

"I think we got away," Noh said, catching Clio's eye in the mirror.

Noh was right. Except for Daniel's car, the road was empty. No sign of pursuing Vargr, irate Hindu Goddesses, or missing-in-action sisters. Clio hoped this meant the enemy had encountered "the force of nature" known as Kali and were already being turned into lifeless meat puppets.

In death, a Vargr returned to its human body—unless its head was removed from its body and then it stayed in animal form. Kali had wanted to make a point to the Vargr's master, which was why she'd been ripping Vargr heads off left and right. She wanted Uriah Drood to know she meant business—and if the human police discovered these aberrations, these supernatural monsters that had no place in the human world, well, she didn't really care.

Still, the thought of the human police finding, and then freaking out over, all the half-human, half-Vargr bodies strewn across Sea Verge's front lawn worried Clio. The need for secrecy had been ingrained in her since she was a small child. Letting the human world know what you were, and the powers you possessed, was the ultimate of sins.

"How far away is it?" Clio asked Jarvis.

She only had a quarter of a tank of gas, which meant she was going to have to stop to fill up again soon.

"It's not terribly far—" Jarvis started to say, but the words were ripped from his mouth as the car suddenly shot forward, rocked by a massive explosion that came from behind them.

The velocity of the shockwave made the car start to fishtail as dirt and debris from the explosion filled the air. Clio spun the steering wheel hard, using all her upper body strength to keep the car on the road. She slammed her foot on the brakes, the car coming to a jerky stop, but still facing the right direction.

"What the hell just happened?!" Clio yelled, her whole body shaking with adrenaline as she turned around in her seat.

"Guys?"

Noh and Jennice were both staring out the back window. Clio followed their gazes and her mouth fell open . . . where Daniel's car should've been was only a fiery, smoking crater. The shock was so great for a moment no one said a word, and then out of the silence, she heard Noh say:

"I think Daniel's car just exploded."

fourteen

CALLIOPE

.

I used Jarvis's computer to send Daniel a song. I knew it was cheesy, but I wanted him to know I was thinking about him. Even if everything worked out badly and I ceased to exist, I wanted him to know his face would be the last thing I remembered as I disappeared.

It's funny what imminent destruction will do to a person. It clears out all the cobwebs in your mind, lets you see things the way they *really* are for once in your life. No more bullshit. No more false perceptions colored by our own egos: just the truth in high definition.

I didn't just love Daniel. I was *in* love with him—which was a very different thing. I'd been fighting off this need to love another person my whole life, something I think stemmed from my not-so-healthy fear of loss. I'd lost my best friends in a car crash when I was a teenager, and now I'd lost my dad, my mom, my crazy-ass homicidal sister . . . Jarvis and Runt had been in harm's way more times than I cared to think about—and the list just went on and on.

I'd met Daniel in the middle of all the insanity and I'd fought my feelings for him with all my energy, pushing him away and emotionally beating him up every chance I got. I guess unconsciously I was just trying to prove he would go away, too, if given half the chance.

I'd made our relationship about sex because sex, to me, was safe. It was just a physical battle of the bodies. Two people intermeshed for a few minutes and then a release . . . and then disconnect.

No feelings, just fucking.

I was a big, fat coward. I was scared of love. I was scared of Daniel . . . and I was scared of taking responsibility for my actions.

To that effect, I'd hidden behind my own immortality, so I didn't have to deal with what frightened me. You can only be laissez-faire about something that's "a given" in your life. I could rail against living forever because it was a luxury I didn't have to think about. I'd wanted to be a normal girl because I knew I was never going to be one.

I'd been living in Oblivious Land for a long time, in denial about so many important things in my life. All I wanted now was a one-way ticket out of there—and it seemed like dying might just be that ticket.

So I sent Daniel a silly little Dolly Parton song to tell him all of this. I wasn't sure if he would understand, or if that even mattered. It was enough to know how I felt and to own those feelings for the first time ever in my life.

"Time to go," Marcel said. He was crouched down beside me in the bushes, his face inches from mine.

The situation was not funny. Not even slightly funny, but I felt a hysterical laugh burbling up from my belly. I was able to contain it, so long as I didn't look at the object of my inappropriate hilarity, which was the black shoe polish Marcel had spread across his cheekbones and nose. He'd tried to get me to do the same, saying something about how we were on a Black Ops mission and camouflage was essential, but I politely declined the proffered face blacking.

Though she was as much a part of this "mission" as I was, Marcel hadn't offered Runt any of his shoe polish camouflage. I guess he thought her fur was dark enough already.

Runt had spent the past hour nestled against me, her head hidden inside the crook of my arm. I wasn't surprised to discover that her physical wounds were almost healed, but there was still no sign of her voice . . . and from what Jarvis had said, there probably never would be. I wanted to cry when I thought about her beautiful voice, lost forever, but I held my emotions in check. If I lost it, I would only be making it harder for her. So, I needed to stay strong for both of us.

"You think he's asleep already?" I asked as I sat up on my knees, trying to get a good look inside.

Marcel nodded.

"I do."

We'd been camped out in Purgatory for the past three hours, watching and waiting. I'd never been on a full-fledged stakeout before, but freezing your butt off while nestled inside a prickly bush wasn't my idea of a "good time." Of the three aspects of the Afterlife—Heaven, Hell, and Purgatory—I liked Purgatory second least, or second best, depending on how positive I was feeling at the time.

Except for the gargantuan brimstone skyscraper housing Death, Inc., Purgatory was a wasteland, devoid of indigenous life, and windy and miserable as all get-out. True, here and there you could find nomadic camps of escaped denizens from Hell who thought braving the Purgatorial badlands was better than being brutalized down in Hell, but other than those brave few, it was an empty landscape, drab and inhospitable.

No one in their right mind would choose such a desolate existence, one so far removed from all the modern conveniences—malls, 7-Elevens, fast-food joints, movie houses, yoga studios—so I had to assume the head of the Harvesters and Transporters Union was a total nut job. Because here, in this wasteland, was exactly where Uriah Drood had decided to build his compound.

If his "home"—and I use the term lightly here—was any indication of the wealth the union possessed, then I was definitely in the wrong business. The place made Sea Verge look like a McDonald's Playland. It was sprawling, with one main house and five gigantic outbuildings, a tennis court (because who doesn't like to play tennis in a wasteland?), and a stable someone had retrofitted into a massive garage.

The main house was crafted entirely out of glass, the large plate glass walls letting you see the lavish furnishings you would never be invited inside to inspect all up close and personal-like. The outbuildings were vertiginous rectangles constructed from high-gloss aluminum, but the pale blue light that infused all of Purgatory did nothing to illuminate their beauty, making them seem flat and drab instead of shiny and new.

I was very curious to find out what Uriah Drood was housing in those towering outbuildings, but we didn't have time to sneak a peek at them. Our goal was to get inside the main house and squeeze Drood until we got every last drop of information out of his protuberant gut.

"I'm sick of waiting," I said, standing up and shaking out my left leg, which had fallen asleep. "Let's do this thing."

Before we'd left Sea Verge, Jarvis, Marcel, and I had conferred on the best way to infiltrate Uriah Drood's compound. Since Jarvis had been inside the place—when the Harvesters and Transporters Union had originally threatened to go on strike, he and my dad had spent a tedious afternoon trapped inside Drood's conference room before the first round of negotiations began—he was the only one who knew all the glass walls were spelled so anyone could enter the house, but only those with a special counter-spell could leave it.

I thought this was an illogical way to protect your home, but Jarvis explained that Uriah Drood was like a spider and his home was just a giant web in which to entangle his prey.

This made me feel better.

Not.

Marcel had taken Jarvis at his word. If he was going to be dealing with a spider, he was going to go in prepared. He'd suggested we hit a hardware store before leaving for Purgatory—and the first thing he'd put in our shiny metal shopping cart, after he'd loaded up on shoe polish, of course, was a can of bug spray. I'd gone for the more "subtle" approach: a length of rope, a palette knife, a ball peen hammer, and a pair of supersharp wire cutters. I had a good idea of what I was going to be doing with my newly purchased tools and it was not pretty.

I'd also purchased a dark brown leather tool belt, one that snapped into place around my hips and made me feel like a DIY version of Lara Croft from *Tomb Raider*. I'd coiled the rope and clipped it into place on the left side of the belt, then

I'd slid the remaining tools into various other loops and pockets, so I jangled when I walked. I think Marcel was amused by my purchases, as was the gawky dude with the bright orange smock who rang us up at the checkout counter. He'd eyed my palette knife with what I thought was suspicion, but then he'd surprised me by asking if I wanted a "real" knife instead of the blunt one I'd chosen.

I might've taken him up on the offer, but I thought there was something rather ironic about using a painting knife to inflict pain—and I especially liked the idea I was turning torture into an art form. It appealed to my baser senses.

"Yes, now is the time," Marcel said as he stood up, leaving the cover of the bushes.

Silent as a cat, he began to steal toward one of the large plate glass walls, crossing the ten-foot gap separating the bushes from the house without incident.

"Here we go," I whispered to Runt as, tools jangling at my hip, we left the safety of the bushes to follow Marcel's path to the house.

When we caught up to him, he placed a finger to his lips, the universal symbol for silence, then, fascinated, I watched as he focused his energy on the window, lifting his left fist into the air and plunging it into the glass. Logic predicted his hand would shatter the pane, but logic wasn't working. As his flesh hit the pane, the glass transformed from a solid state into something resembling a clear gelatin mold. Marcel looked over at me and grinned, arm half deep in the gelatinous substance.

"Shall I?" he asked.

I watched as he pressed the rest of himself through the gelatin, disappearing into the interior of the house. Once inside, he turned and waved at me to follow him.

I looked down at Runt.

"You ready for this?" I asked.

She wagged her tail and I took that to mean, "yes."

With Runt at my heels, I closed my eyes and walked quickly toward the plate glass wall. I tensed, expecting the gelatinous substance to envelop my body—but this didn't happen. Instead, my nose and forehead smashed into an unyielding wall of glass.

"Ow!" I yelped, as a caromed off the glass and fell backward onto the ground.

Barred from entering the house, I'd been left out in the cold emptiness of the Purgatorial wasteland. Immediately, my fingers went up to my nose, the hot wetness they found there making me woozy.

"Runt?" I called, the hand covering my lower face muffling her name so it came out as "Rub."

I was worried she'd been hurt, too, but then I looked over and saw her face pressed up against the other side of the glass. She'd made it inside with Marcel, but she didn't look very happy about it. When she caught my gaze, she began to paw at the glass, fighting to get back outside to me.

That's when I remembered what Jarvis had said about Drood's compound being like a spider web—you could get in, but you couldn't get out.

I felt discombobulated as I climbed to my feet, and I had to fight the urge to give up and sit back down again. Instead, I took a tentative step toward the glass, my legs like shaky noodles not wanting to hold me up.

"I'm all right," I called to Runt, giving her a reassuring smile—though my nose hurt like a sonofabitch and I had the beginnings of a massive headache.

With a frantic energy I could feel even from outside, she continued to paw at the glass, her tail slapping against Marcel's leg in her panic.

"It's okay," I said, as I knelt down across from her and pressed my palm against the solid pane of glass. "I'll find a way in."

Runt snuffled, trying to get closer to my hand, but the glass made it impossible.

I felt awful. I was supposed to protect her, but here I was, on the other side of the glass, totally unable to help her if something bad happened.

Marcel said something to me, but I couldn't make out the words. I tried to read his lips, but discovered I sucked at lipreading. Finally, he pantomimed I should go around to the front door and meet them there.

I very much doubted I'd be able to get in that way, but I figured anything was worth a shot.

Following Marcel and Runt's lead, I walked around to the other side of the house, happy the building was made of glass, so I could keep an eye on Runt.

I'd expected Drood to have guards, razor wire, spotlights . . . anything a normal person would have to secure their home. But there was none of this, just a dark and empty house waiting for us to enter it.

Spider web.

The words echoed in my head.

Short and rotund with a baldpate and pale, bluish-tinged alabaster skin, Uriah Drood liked to wear expensively tailored suits that made him seem sleeker than he actually was, their dark silhouettes giving him a rather spider-like appearance, though I'd never noticed the resemblance before.

Marcel and Runt had stumbled into his web because he didn't think they were a threat. They were more like flies, or roly-poly bugs he could dispose of easily and without thought. I, on the other hand, frightened him.

That I frightened *anyone* was kind of amusing—that I frightened someone like Uriah Drood was amazing.

He may have blocked me from entering his house for now, I thought. *But between the three of us—me, Marcel, and Runt—I'm sure we can find a loophole to get me inside.*

I caught sight of the thin man with the weasely face and red hair just as we were nearing the front entrance. He was standing just beyond Marcel and Runt's field of vision, his body tucked into a shadowy doorway leading off into another wing of the house. I could see him clear as day—and I could also see the curved knife he was jauntily tossing back and forth between his hands. I raced to the glass and started to pound on its transparent surface, screaming at Marcel to look behind him.

The glass stood between us, making my words unintelligible. Marcel stared at me, trying to understand what I was saying. I stabbed the air with my finger, trying to get him to turn around, but it was too late, the man had already launched his attack.

I was trapped on the wrong side of the glass, unable to do anything but watch as Weasely Face raised his knife into the air and slashed down, shearing off Marcel's arm just below the elbow.

Blood streaked across the glass, blurring my view as Weasely Face drew back his knife to attack again. But Marcel was ready this time, twisting out of the way, so Weasely Face's blade sliced through empty air. Marcel dodged another thrust of the knife, jumping out of the way as Weasely Face pressed forward, attacking with unheralded violence.

With his uninjured hand, Marcel reached into his pocket and pulled out the bug repellent he'd picked up at the hardware store. Still sidestepping Weasely Face's frontal attack, he used his teeth to pop off the bug spray's lid, depressing the button with his thumb and shooting a stream of clear liquid directly into Weasely Face's eyes.

Weasely Face dropped the knife, his fingers tearing at his eyes as he tried to wipe the bug spray away. Runt used Marcel's distraction to sink her teeth into Weasely Face's ankle and, with a silent scream (at least on my end), the man went down like a sack of flour, clutching at his ankle with one hand and his eyes with the other.

Marcel turned to the glass and gave me a "thumbs up" sign. Then he went back to Weasely Face and began to kick him in the gut. Weasely Face writhed on the floor, each kick connecting with his soft belly until he got wise and twisted himself into a protective fetal position. Marcel shrugged and changed his tactic, slamming his huarache into the back of Weasely Face's head over and over again.

I felt a surge of joy as Marcel and Runt turned the tables on their attacker. I sighed, the tension going out of me as I rested my forehead against the glass, once more wishing I was inside the house with them, or they were outside the house with me.

When I looked up again, I was just in time to observe a tall, menacing figure emerge from the shadows and make a beeline for Marcel. I tried to catch Runt's attention, to let her know they weren't safe, but she was crouched in front of Weasely Face, guarding him for Marcel, and didn't see me. I began to beat on the window, screaming for them to watch out for this new assailant, but Marcel was too intent on beating the shit out of Weasely Face to notice my frantic pantomimes.

I screamed until my throat was raw, but it was futile. I was impotent. I had to watch, again, as Marcel was attacked from behind, the shadowy man grasping him around the back of the neck with pale white hands. The man lifted Marcel off his feet, twisting him in the air like a rag doll until he got a good grip on Marcel's throat. The Ender of Death began to flail, eyes going wide as a tourniquet of long white fingers cut off his air.

He's immortal, I thought. *They can make him pass out, but he won't die.*

Still it was a horrible scene to have to be a party to.

Marcel's eyes began to bug out of his head, his face turning puce as the man increased the pressure on his trachea. Runt made a dive for the man's leg, but he'd seen her go for Weasely Face and was prepared, kicking out with his foot to catch her in the belly. The movement propelled her backward and she slid across the concrete floor, crashing into a side table, where she lay, unmoving.

I beat my fists against the glass until they ached, but it was no good. My mind raced, trying to come up with a way to break the glass, so I could climb inside.

That's when I remembered my tool belt.

I reached down and ripped the ball peen hammer from its loop, hefting it in the air. Using all my strength, I slammed the head of the hammer into the windowpane, the force of the action jarring the bones in my hands and wrists and arms—but the glass held firm. I repeated the action two more times and found myself rewarded as a small crack appeared in the surface of the glass. I raised the hammer and pounded the butt end of the wooden handle against the crack, hitting it again and again with all my energy until the crack grew in size.

Still, it wouldn't break.

For the first time, the shadowy man's gaze strayed in my direction. My heart stopped as we locked eyes, and I felt the gorge rise in my throat, anger and impotence duking it out in my stomach for prominence.

This is impossible, I thought—but part of me knew it wasn't.

The shadowy man was my arch-nemesis, Frank.

I watched as the man who'd tried to kill me *and* ruin my relationship, dug his disgusting fingers into Marcel's throat.

You're supposed to be in prison, I thought, my mind spinning. *How can you be here?*

But then I understood.

The two worlds were merging, faster even than Jarvis or I

had believed possible . . . and Frank, or at least his alternate-universe version, was here in my world, moving with an ease I found very, very disturbing.

Oh, shit, I thought, fear clutching at my heart as I realized something even more distressing: If the alternate-universe version of Frank was Death in his own world, then he probably came to my world endowed with all the same powers I possessed.

Which meant he wasn't just choking Marcel, he was *killing* the Ender of Death.

fifteen

At first, Jarvis couldn't fathom what was happening, but then understanding blossomed in his chest as he sat back in the passenger seat and closed his eyes.

From the backseat, he heard Noh say: "I think Daniel's car just exploded."

He shook his head, trying to clear his thoughts.

Explosion, Daniel, car . . . *gone*.

The words repeated in his head like a mantra as Clio slammed her foot down on the brake, sending Jarvis flying into the dashboard.

"No!" he yelled, grabbing her arm. "Keep going!"

She glared at him, but stamped her foot back on the gas and the car screeched forward, catching air as it hit a speed bump, then landing again with a sickening *crunch*.

Jarvis didn't know why he'd grabbed Clio like that, but some instinct had warned him stopping to investigate would mean the end for everyone in the car—and his job, the only job he now possessed, was to keep the next two "possible" Deaths safe. He could do nothing for Daniel or the others right now and he was heartsick about it, but he had to put the safety of the women in his car first.

As he tried to reconcile these disparate feelings inside of

himself, Noh reached out and squeezed his shoulder. He swiveled in his seat to look at her and she smiled at him.

"Are you okay?"

He nodded, still shaken up.

"What happened to that car?" Jennice said, the tone of her voice skirting the edge of hysteria. "What the hell happened to that car!?"

Noh removed her hand from Jarvis's shoulder, placing it on Jennice's arm in a bid to calm her down.

"It's all right," Noh said. "There's no need to get upset."

Jarvis turned his head to look over at Clio, but she was staring blankly ahead, eyes locked onto the road. Her body language screamed "leave me alone!" so he did. There would be plenty of time to discuss what happened—and to figure out the how of it—when she wasn't so angry with him.

He reassured himself the others would be okay: Daniel was immortal. Freezay wasn't, but he had special abilities through his paternal line and he was a master detective. Starr, he had no idea. Caoimhe . . . ? Once again, he didn't know for sure, but he assumed she was immortal through her daughter. Even though Calliope hadn't known her birth mother until very recently, it didn't preclude Caoimhe from her rights as Calliope's mother; rights that included immortality.

"I think we should go back," Clio said, her cadence clipped.

She was looking at him in the rearview mirror, her eyes dark with emotion. It was obvious she was angry and he was the object of that anger.

"It would do no good," he said.

She shook her head.

"You don't know that."

Yes, he did know it, although he had no idea how to impart this to her without sounding ridiculous. She was right to want to help the others, but he knew in his gut if they went back, there'd be nothing but a wrecked car and a pack of Vargr eager to kill Jennice and Noh, and take Clio and Jarvis hostage, or worse.

"You must trust me. If we were to go back, Daniel and Freezay and the others wouldn't be there."

"They would've stopped for us," she yelled. "And we just left them there!"

Clio had her father's temper. She was perfectly fine until you told her "no" and then she came unglued. Jarvis didn't mind Clio yelling at him, but he was worried her anger was filtering back to Jennice, who was already skating on thin ice, emotionally.

"I don't want to go back!" Jennice screamed, pushing against Jarvis's seat with both feet like an irate child. "They're going to eat us!"

So much for worrying about Jennice—Jarvis could see she'd already moved into irrationality and there was nothing he could do about it except use Jennice's words to his advantage.

"Of course she's right, Clio," Jarvis said. "The girls are mortal. The Vargr will rip them limb from limb if they find us."

Clio saw what Jarvis was doing and fumed.

"That's underhanded, playing on their fear, Jarvis," she said, shaking her head. "Unconscionable."

He didn't know if "unconscionable" was the right word, and, frankly, he didn't care, so long as it brought him the outcome he wanted.

Clio returned her gaze to the road, ignoring him.

"We were never going back, Ms. McMartin," Jarvis said, using his calmest voice to placate her. "And I promise you are safe in this car."

She took his words at face value and it seemed to calm her down.

"Okay."

She settled back into her seat, arms crossed over her chest, breathing hard. Noh reached over and patted Jennice's arm with an almost maternal affection.

"It's okeydokey, I promise," he heard Noh saying before her voice dropped to a murmur.

He returned his attention to the road, making a mental note of their surroundings. He saw Clio was taking the Newport Bridge out of Rhode Island, heading toward Connecticut. They'd have to backtrack a bit to get where Jarvis intended them to go, but that was all right. As long as they were on the road, the car taking them far away from Sea Verge, then they would be all right.

In this situation, one of the oddities of wormholing would work to their benefit. Though it wasn't too hard to wormhole *out* of a moving vehicle, it was exponentially more difficult to wormhole *into* one. It could be done, but it required a terrible amount of energy and expertise. So long as they were in transit, Jarvis felt like he could relax a little, knowing it would be very tough for someone to get a bead on them.

"When we arrive in Warwick, wake me up, please," Jarvis said, closing his eyes.

He heard Clio give an angry snort, but otherwise there was only the hum of the car speeding down the road.

Sleep had been in short supply since Calliope had taken off for parts unknown with a wounded hellhound and Marcel, the Ender of Death. If Jarvis was going to keep his wits about him, then he was going to need a little shut-eye.

As selfish as that felt.

clio wanted to punch Jarvis in his smarmy, hipster face.

First, he'd ignored the suffering of their friends and made them drive on instead of helping. Then he'd almost incited Jennice into a full-on meltdown in order to get his way, and, finally, he'd gone to sleep while they were in the middle of a crisis. If he hadn't been wearing his seat belt now, Clio might've been tempted to slam on the brakes and let him know exactly how she felt about his selfish attitude.

Namely it sucked.

Part of her wished she'd stayed at home that evening, entertaining Indra's Bollywood cronies and drinking too much wine—and then when she woke up the next morning, she'd be sibling-less and totally oblivious to the fact.

I'm an evil human being, she thought. *I can't believe I even thought that.*

She was just being spiteful because she was angry. In her heart, she was terrified to live in a world her sister wasn't in. She and Callie had always been close, as much friends as sisters. They could laugh together, make fun of each other, and if either of them was ever in a pinch, they knew the other would be there to help, no questions asked.

Clio had never felt this way about their older sister, Thalia. One of her very first memories was of throwing her teddy bear out of her crib so Thalia would fetch it for her. But instead of playing by the rules, Thalia had ignored Clio, choosing to read a book rather than engage with her baby sister. It was Callie, not too far out of diapers herself, who went and got Teddy and brought him back to Clio—and as Callie had threaded Teddy through the crib's bars, Clio had felt an overwhelming love for her second-oldest sister. They'd played "throw Teddy" all afternoon, or at least until Clio had gotten tired and curled up in a ball for her nap.

No, she wasn't interested in living in a world where Callie didn't exist—it wasn't even a question. She just wished she didn't feel so completely powerless. It was the inability to help that was making her so angry she could hardly bear it.

She felt bad about being nasty to Jarvis. It wasn't his fault everything was going to shit, that they were trapped in a car heading to some "safe" spot where they would be forced to sit out the whole affair while Callie battled for her life. All she'd be able to do was send "happy thoughts" in Cal's direction—and this wasn't nearly enough for Clio. She was fixing for a fight because, more than anything else in the world, she hated being left out of the loop. And this was exactly what was happening: She was being forcibly removed from the equation.

There was little she could do to change her situation, especially since she was chained to Noh and Jennice.

Jarvis was right. If a Vargr got ahold of one of the girls, they'd turn them into mush in less than two seconds flat. She couldn't put either of the mortals in jeopardy; she had to find a way to separate herself from them, so she could do what she did best: help Callie fight bad guys.

She knew she had to think outside the box and she had to do it quickly.

That was when the gas gauge caught her eye.

Why hadn't she thought of this before? She began to formulate a plan, one leaving Jennice, Noh, and Jarvis safe and sound, but allowing her the freedom to find Callie and help her sister stop Uriah Drood from trying to destroy their universe.

They were less than fifteen miles to Warwick with more than enough gas to get there. But she didn't want to wait until then—she wanted out now.

"I need to get gas," she said to no one in particular as she flipped her turn indicator on and began the process of getting over, so she could turn off at the next exit.

There were two gas stations and a couple of fast-food joints coming up, any of which would be a good place to call up a wormhole, but she'd specified a gas station as her destination, so she turned into the one with the heaviest traffic: four cars and a motorcycle.

She pulled into the island farthest away from the convenience store part of the station and turned off the car. Jarvis stirred, and Clio was worried he was going to wake up and mess up her plan, but sleep caught him again and he began to snore.

"I'll pump," she said, though she was careful not to catch anyone's eye as she opened the driver's door and climbed out.

She pulled a credit card from her back pocket and slid it into the pump, choosing the premium grade of gasoline. Once she'd entered her zip code, she pushed the nozzle into the gas tank and let it go, watching as the pump began to rack up the dollars.

It was time to set her plan in motion.

She knocked on Noh's window and mouthed: "bathroom." Through the smoky glass, she could see Noh giving her the thumbs-up. Clio offered a short wave in reply and, without looking back, headed for the convenience store.

Once inside, she asked for the bathroom key, waiting as the clerk behind the counter looked up from his motorcycle magazine just long enough to gesture to a slimy-looking blue key ring that had the word "Woman's" stenciled on it in white paint. With a smile, she deftly palmed the key ring and continued on her way to the bathroom.

There was no line for the two-stalled bathroom—and she doubted she'd have been able to wait if there *had* been a line because the stench in the tiny space was so disgusting. As it stood, she had to hold her breath in order just to keep herself from gagging.

Not wanting to touch anything she didn't have to, she avoided the walls and the stall doors, setting the key ring down on the one rusted-out sink because, though it was covered in hard water stains, it looked as though it hadn't been touched in decades. What was supposed to pass as a soap dispenser hung from a rickety screw above the sink, though she doubted it saw much action—because soap diluted with tap water (like this was) did not really constitute soap. There were no paper towels in the aluminum dispenser, but this didn't surprise her, either. If no one washed their hands, then why would they need paper towels?

Gross.

She set aside her disgust and focused on what she'd come in here to do. Namely, leave the mortals behind so she could go find Callie and help her kick some Afterlife ass. The one thing she didn't know was where Callie and Marcel had gone. Jarvis hadn't been forthcoming on that front and she didn't dare go back out there to try to pick his brain. He'd figure out her motivations in two seconds flat and any plan she'd made would be null and void.

Where to try first?

She decided Purgatory would be her first destination: the Hall of Death, to be more precise. That way she could sneak a peek at the Death Records and see if they offered up any clues. She'd interned there one summer and knew her way around the records room, so it would be easy to find what she was looking for without getting caught.

She'd learned to call up wormholes when she was a kid—not that she'd shared this secret with anyone else. Even Callie didn't know the extent of her magical ability, or how early it'd manifested in her. She'd been nine years old when she'd discovered her powers, and this was well before she'd hit puberty, which was when most people came into their own magically. She'd been smart enough to know getting her powers at such a young age was *not* normal, that if she told her parents, or even Cal, what was going on, they'd have called in all kinds of specialists to poke and prod her—then they'd have barred her from attending public school with all of her Newport friends, forcing her, instead, to go to some magic handling school where she'd never learn anything about human math and science.

This was not the future she saw for herself, so she kept her mouth shut and was very, *very* careful about hiding her magical abilities from the prying eyes of others. Even when she'd hit puberty, she'd still been protective of her magical prowess, not wanting anyone to see just how powerful she was. Only once, when she was ten, had she almost been caught—and it was by her older sister Thalia.

Clio was at Sea Verge, playing in the back garden by the creepy bench overlooking the cliffs and the sea. She knew Callie didn't like the place, that someone had died there and the bench was a memorial to this person, but none of that bothered her. Then she'd noticed how freaked-out Callie got every time they played there, and so she'd fibbed and told her older sister the bench scared her, too, (though it really didn't) and this had seemed to make Callie feel better.

When Callie was at school during the fall and winter, Clio would go talk to the bench. She would apologize for not visiting during the summer and she'd explain why (that Callie was scared of it), and this seemed to make things okay between them (her and the bench) until the next summer when she'd ignore it all over again. The bench always listened, but never commented, so Clio felt it was safe to share her secrets with the cold, marble creature.

She told the bench about accidentally changing her toothbrush into a mouse, and how then, not knowing how to turn it back, she'd caught it and put it outside to live its new life without fear of being killed by any mousetraps.

The bench never judged, but sometimes when the wind was up and the water was crashing down below, Clio thought she heard the bench sighing. She could never say if what she heard was real or not, but, either way, it was a very sad sort of sound.

The morning Thalia had almost caught her, she'd been telling the bench about Callie's best friend, Noh, who'd come to visit the week before school started. Clio had found Noh fascinating. She was certain the older girl could see ghosts, but she hadn't been able to get a full confirmation, which was annoying.

After a while, her butt cold and wet from sitting in the dewy grass at the base of the bench, she'd had an epiphany. She would do a spell to make herself see ghosts just like Noh did. Then the next time Noh came to stay, Clio could impress her with her own abilities.

She'd decided to make up a spell right then and there.

Because she was a magician in hiding, she could only practice with spell books she'd snuck out of her dad's study. She was what one would call a self-taught magic practitioner. She had no idea she was following in the footsteps of many of history's most famous magic handlers, who eschewed books in favor of making up their own spells, which they then sold to spell-book writers, this trade ballooning the magic handlers' fortunes.

She'd learned all this later when she was old enough to study magical history, but at that point in time, she was just a ten-year-old girl who happened to be unwittingly following a long and powerful tradition she knew nothing about.

To make her spell, she'd call three magical symbols into her mind: the unicorn, the Christian cross, and an image of her father, who was Death, personified. She'd woven these three things together, tying them into a neat little bow she kept in her mind's eye. Next, she whispered a line she'd read in a book by Ray Bradbury—"*. . . by the pricking of my thumbs, something wicked this way comes . . .*"—then she'd closed her eyes and untied her mind bow, clapping her hands together once to give the spell power.

When she looked up again there was a shadow sitting on the bench in front of her. He looked at her with sad eyes, but didn't speak.

"Are you a ghost?" she'd asked, but he hadn't replied, just turned his gaze back to the sea, ignoring her.

That's when Thalia had spoken.

"What're you doing?"

Because she'd had her eyes closed, Clio didn't know how long her sister had been standing there watching her. Maybe ten seconds, maybe longer—but Thalia had a funny look in her eye.

"Nothing," Clio had said.

She could tell Thalia didn't believe her.

"It'd better be nothing."

And then her much older sister had turned and walked away. The spell had seemed to dissipate under Thalia's watchful gaze, and when Clio looked back at the bench, the ghost man was gone.

As Clio stood in the stinky gas station bathroom, her laser-like mind in the process of calling up a wormhole, she realized she hadn't thought about that day in a very long time. For a moment, she wondered why this was—but then the lights began to dim and a swirling hole of darkness opened up in the fabric of time and space.

It beckoned Clio to climb inside of it.

And she did.

the sky above the gas station changed from blue to gray so quickly, Noh thought it was a hallucination. She climbed out of the car with a speed she didn't know she possessed and ran toward the convenience store. Something terrible was about to happen and she needed to get to Clio before it was too late.

She didn't know time was not on her side.

As she yanked the glass convenience store door open, she caught sight of the blood and screamed. Her mind yelled at her to ignore what she was seeing and get out—and she'd been in enough bad situations to know when it was best to listen to your gut—so she backed onto the asphalt, pulling the door shut in front of her. She didn't need to be told twice to get out of there. She whirled on her heel, running as fast as she could toward the car.

She yanked the driver's-side door open and gave silent thanks Clio had at least left the keys in the ignition.

"What in the—" Jarvis said, as she turned the key and the car roared to life under them.

She didn't answer him, just put the car in gear and floored it, the Honda taking off like a shot and tearing the flexible hose arm right off the gas pump.

The cloud over the gas station was larger and fiercer looking than it'd been before she'd gone into the store. She knew this did not bode well for them. She wasn't immortal like Callie and Clio—and probably Jarvis, too—and if the forces that be were able to catch them, then she and Jennice would be killed.

No, not killed . . . *murdered.*

Never in a million years did she think her friendship with Callie would put her in this kind of mortal danger. Sure, she might've been arrested by the fashion police—Cal was a fashion-obsessed clothes whore—but attacked by scary werewolves who ate convenience store clerk's brains out of their skulls?

No how, no way.

"Where is Clio?!" Jarvis was shrieking in her ear, his eyes searching the skyline for a break in the gray cloud cover.

"She did that wormhole thing!" Noh shouted back at him. "The dead clerk, his ghost kept pointing at the bathroom and yelling the word *worms* over and over again."

It was the ghost she'd seen first, even before the blood. He was wild-eyed and terrified, fear making his form fade in and out of invisibility. When he'd heard the door chime at her entrance, he'd flared to life again, and started screaming at her, all the while pointing at the women's restroom, whose door was hanging off its hinges. That's when she'd noticed the six giant werewolf creatures eating the dead clerk's brains.

"Worms! Worms!!!" the ghost was screaming at her, gesticulating madly toward the exposed women's restroom.

This was when her survival instinct had kicked in and she'd gotten the hell out of there, leaving the poor convenience store clerk alone to observe his own, messy end—but thank God he'd been there. Because without him, she would've stumbled right into a werewolf ambush and that would've been the end of her.

"What are you saying? She called a wormhole?!"

There was real anguish in Jarvis's voice. Noh could see he was blaming himself for Clio's foolishness.

"She should never have . . . she let them pinpoint our location . . . my God, did she make it out?" Jarvis's words came in a jumble, his long face ashen.

"I think she made it out," Noh said, her eyes on the road while her foot kept the gas pedal pressed down to the floor. "I didn't see anything bad where she was concerned. Only the dead clerk."

"She as good as killed him," Jarvis whispered, his jaw taut as a piano wire. "She almost killed you, too."

Noh shook her head.

"It was an accident. She couldn't have known."

Jarvis wasn't listening. He was staring out the windshield, up at the pitch-black sky enveloping them.

"They have us in their sights," he said, more to himself than to Noh or Jennice. "We have to get away or they'll wash us off the road."

Jennice had been quiet until now, but at this, she leaned forward, resting both elbows on the passenger seat.

"What does that mean: 'wash us off the road'?"

Noh had an inkling about what Jarvis was going to say, but she let him explain.

"The weather. They're going to create a flash flood, or send a tornado, or who knows what else they're scheming . . . the fact is, they're going to kill us."

"Fuck that!" Noh said, slamming her foot on the gas and sending the car speeding ahead.

Jennice pitched forward and Jarvis threw out his arms to block her from coming into the front seat.

"What're you doing?" Jarvis cried, shooting Noh a scathing look as she pushed the accelerator even harder.

"I'm saving our skin, that's what," she said—and, boy, did she hope she was right. "Call up a stupid wormhole right now."

"And go where?!" Jarvis snarled at her.

She took a deep breath, let it out, and then smiled up at him.

"To where we're headed, anyway: the New Newbridge Academy."

sixteen

Freezay opened his lips to scream and seawater filled his mouth. It sluiced down his throat and into his lungs, where it burned like fire. He began to choke, seawater pressing down on him from all sides, wrapping him in its briny embrace. He opened his eyes—and got more burning for his trouble—but managed to keep them open through sheer force of will.

There was just enough light for Freezay to be able to make out where he was, even though this information would prove to be extremely unhelpful. It was as his lungs had suspected: He was underwater and—if the coral reef in front of him was any indication—in the ocean.

He began to flounder from lack of oxygen, pushing with his arms and legs to escape the hostile and airless environment he was trapped in. He was using up a lot of energy, yet he was getting nowhere. No matter how much he paddled, he just kept getting yanked back into place. Frustrated, he looked down at his feet and saw the reason for his lack of upward momentum.

A thin cord of filament had been tied around his ankle and then knotted to an arm of the coral reef. The filament had a little bit of give, but that was it.

He was stuck.

He felt something cold and gelatinous brush against the

back of his neck and he whirled around to see who was touching him, but there was no one there. His lungs were bursting from lack of air, and this was making his head hurt. Or maybe it was the pressure from being so far underwater that was making his head hurt . . . he just didn't know. Everything was so fuzzy it was hard to . . . stay . . . functioning . . . stay . . . *awake*.

Someone, or something, stabbed him before he could fully pass out. He screeched in pain, eyes opening, eyes burning again. He was still underwater, but the panic at being unable to breathe was abating. He realized this was because his lungs weren't screaming for air anymore. He opened his mouth, but instead of choking on the salt water, he let it fill his lungs—and it didn't hurt.

Whatever concoction he'd been stabbed with, it was allowing him to get oxygen directly from the seawater. He reached back with his hand, his fingers plumbing his skin for the injection/stab site, but all he found was a round lump, about the size of a hazelnut, protruding from his lower back. He pressed the bump, but nothing happened. No pain, no itching, no burning; he felt like a child who'd been inoculated from smallpox.

He felt better, being able to breathe, but there was still the small matter of being tied to an outcropping of coral. He bent in half, reaching down with both hands to get a grip on his ankle, but being weightless made this harder than it should've been. He kept reaching out, missing, reaching out again, still missing . . . finally, after four tries, he was able to grasp his knees in a bear hug and then grab his pant leg with his right hand. He felt around for the filament, found it nestled against his skin and his waterlogged sock then followed the curve of his ankle until he came to the knot that stood between him and his freedom.

His fingers were stiff. They wouldn't bend the way he wanted them to, so there was no point in trying to coax the knot out. Instead, he decided to slide three fingers between the filament and his skin, give it a good, hard yank, and snap it.

Things did not go as planned.

The filament was thinner and sharper than he'd anticipated—and it had no intention of snapping. It wanted to stick around for the long haul, so it showed him who was boss by cutting into the softness of his ankle like a razor blade. He stared at the thin trickle of blood as it left the wound and floated toward the surface like an elongated, red tapeworm.

He dragged his hand away from the filament then swore when he realized he hadn't just cut his leg, but had sliced the pads of his fingers, too. Only unlike his ankle, they didn't start hurting until he'd noticed them. He stuck the offending fingers in his mouth and sucked on them, trying to stanch the flow of blood.

Another brush from the cold, gelatinous thing made him gasp and the blood from his fingers shot out of his mouth in a plume of red. He spun around, and this time he got a good look at the creature harassing him: a yellowfin tuna the size and shape of a small torpedo.

As he watched, it circled back around and returned to him, nuzzling against his chin like a warm-blooded puppy dog instead of a cold-blooded fish.

We're not cold-blooded.

Freezay shook his head. He'd heard something, a voice.

I said that we're not cold-blooded.

The tuna was still up against his neck, pressing itself into his flesh.

Yes, I'm the one talking . . . telepathically . . . to you.

The tuna backed away so that they were no longer touching, and its voice faded.

Freezay stared at the fish.

The fish stared at Freezay.

Freezay raised his hand and beckoned the tuna to come close again. The tuna swam forward, pressing its side into Freezay's cheek.

There. Now we can talk again.

Freezay didn't know what to say to the tuna.

There's no need to be nervous.

The tuna's telepathic voice was very warm and feminine.

Oh, that's very sweet of you to say.

He decided he was being rude not to ask the tuna's name—

It's Skye. Like the Isle of.

The tuna's ability to predict his thoughts—

Just call me Skye. Calling me "the tuna" is so impersonal.

Freezay knew there was only one thing he needed to do. He needed—

To ask for my help? Yes, that's why I'm here.

He needed the tuna to untie him.

Your wish is my command.

The tuna swam away from his cheek then dove downward, toward the coral. Fascinated by the tuna's—Skye's—dexterity, Freezay stared as she bit into the filament until, suddenly, he was free, and his body began to ascend slowly up to the surface.

Skye swam after him, catching up to his floating form with zero exertion of effort. She slid her body against him so he could grab ahold of her long flank with both hands, reconnecting them.

There you go.

Freezay wanted Skye to know he would be eternally—

No need to be grateful. It was my pleasure.

With a smile and nod to the bizarreness of his situation, Freezay gave up on communication altogether and decided just to enjoy the ride—

Splendid idea, Skye, the tuna, replied telepathically.

it felt very strange to have one's whole body compressed into something the size and shape of a walnut. Thank God, it hadn't hurt—and boy had Bernadette expected it to hurt—so, at least there was that. She did have to admit not having a body made life a lot easier. For one thing, you didn't get cold. You didn't get hungry and tired either, which was nice. Your joints didn't ache like they normally did—she'd only recently been diagnosed with arthritis and hadn't been looking forward to taking all the toxic medicines she'd been prescribed, and that still didn't completely stop your immune system from destroying your joints from the inside out.

Of course, there were downsides to not having a body, too. Like being dead. This was a downside Bernadette could not get behind. Still, she would never have been able to squeeze her old body into a container as small as the one she was in right now. Heck, who was she kidding? She hadn't been able to get her bottom into a size-sixteen pant in years, and now, here she was, all nested up in a tiny green-glass perfume bottle.

After she'd agreed to do what they asked, the twins had been as sweet as pie—and they weren't half as scary once their friends were gone. They'd described what they wanted her to do (fold herself up into a tiny ball) and then they'd explained how she could then will her new, smaller self into the green-glass bottle they were holding between them.

She'd cottoned on pretty quickly, easily manipulating her essence into whatever shape she wanted. Getting into the bottle had been harder. Her soul hadn't wanted to go, had fought her efforts to force it inside. Finally, the gentle twin had removed an oval-shaped silver bell from her hair, ringing it three times in quick succession. The trilling sound had an immediate effect on Bernadette. She was at once totally free and, at the same time, totally enmeshed in the sound. It filled every ounce of her spirit and made her want to laugh and cry at the same time. It was orgasmic, as powerful as a religious epiphany, and she was afraid it might make her lose her mind if it'd gone on too long.

Not that she had a physical mind to lose. It was whatever made her *her*—her soul, maybe?—she was terrified of misplacing.

After what seemed like an eternity, the ringing stopped. Though the bell had only rung three times, it had felt like hours to Bernadette. That was when she'd had to remind herself she was on Afterlife time. Things worked differently in death than they did in life. Bells rang for hours instead of seconds, Victorian zombie twins came to collect you for nefarious purposes . . . and God was missing in action.

Bernadette decided she no longer felt like praying. It hadn't done much for her in life, and it had been less than helpful in death. The only thing she felt compelled to ask for—and it wasn't praying, it was just asking the universe for help—was the safety of her grandson, Bart. It was all she cared about in the entirety of the world, all she needed or wanted. If these Victorian zombies left Bart alone for eighty or ninety years, then all of her suffering, all of the terribleness of death, would be fine. Well, maybe not fine, but at least bearable.

She'd been in her green-glass prison for a long time when she suddenly realized someone had removed the top, and she was free to come out. She focused on her soul, pushing it from the confines of the perfume bottle, and then, suddenly, her soul was expanding, stretching back into its original, human form.

She felt so much better now that she wasn't in the bottle. She hadn't realized how constraining it'd been in there. She also hadn't realized her senses had shut down until her sight and hearing began to return in fits and starts. It reminded her of Bart's computer when he had to reboot it, all black screen and then a whirling ball of color.

When her eyes had finally adjusted and she was able to see again, she found herself goggling at her surroundings. She kept wanting to pinch herself, to make sure she was experiencing what she thought she was experiencing: a biblical frieze right out of the Old Testament come to life before her awestruck gaze.

As a child, she'd imagined the Red Sea as a bloody, foaming beast bowing before Moses's raised staff, parting so he could bring his people forth to a new life. Who cared if this new life entailed wandering in the desert for forty years? At least the Jews were free of Pharaoh's rule, right?

Reality dovetailed nicely with Bernadette's imagination. The sea before her was red and frothy, bubbling up with eddying pools of foam that reminded her of watery tentacles—yet, the man who stood at the edge of the cauldron-like sea, a thin metal staff in his raised hand, was not like any kind of Moses she'd ever dreamed of. He was tall and statuesque like a racehorse. He even had a horse's forelock of black hair draping his brow. His skin was the color of a ripe peach, firm and tan, and his pitch-black hair descended in luxuriant waves to his shoulder blades.

He was wearing a long, pale blue caftan that split at the neck—revealing a tuft of thick black chest hair—but covered the rest of him completely except where its sleeves fell back from the wrists of his upraised arms. He was doing something to the water, controlling it with his mind so it leapt and foamed, parting briefly every now and then to reveal a sandy, rock-strewn bottom. Then the water would fall against itself, covering the sea floor again.

The man half turned in Bernadette's direction and she saw dark eyes, thick eyebrows, and an equine shape to his face. He smiled at her, beckoning her forward with his free hand, and the warmth of his expression made Bernadette's heart flip-flop.

"Come!" he called, the smile never leaving his face.

She looked around, making sure he was really calling to her—there was no one else there, just an empty expanse of desert—then she took a tentative step toward him.

"Don't be afraid, Bernadette."

His voice was loud, but got softer as she crossed the divide between them. Like a promise, he held his hand out for her to take, his pianist's fingers trembling slightly. His features became doughier as she got closer to him, her relative closeness and the harshness of the desert sun finally revealing all of his flaws.

He wasn't nearly as handsome as she'd first thought. His eyes were too close, his chin too long, and his thick hair had chunky white dandruff peppered through it.

The only thing that held true was his smile. It never once lost its hold on her.

"Are you Moses?" Bernadette asked as soon as she'd reached him and his hand was grasping hers.

The man laughed, showing pristine white teeth.

"I'm just the Gatekeeper to the East . . . I have stood here for centuries, tasked with guiding souls to their proper destination."

"Oh," Bernadette said as the man's hand began to get sweaty, making it hard to hold.

She tore her eyes away from his puffy face, choosing to stare out at the roiling sea, instead. She didn't think it was a very heavenly sea, all red and swollen and seething—and it made her wonder where, exactly, she was . . . because she was starting to feel pretty certain this *wasn't* Heaven.

"Are you ready to walk the sea?" the man asked, continuing to smile down at her.

His smile hadn't seemed at all sinister at first, but now Bernadette couldn't look at it without getting creeped out. She hated to admit it, but the man was starting to make her feel very uncomfortable.

"I don't think I want to," she said. "No, I'm sure I don't."

She tried to remove her hand from the man's, but he held on tightly, not letting her go.

"Take me back home," she said.

The man gave her a sad smile, one more real than the one he'd first worn.

"There is no going back, Bernadette," he said, a mournful undertone to his words. "One can only go forward when one is on the path leading into the heart of Hell."

"**you can't go** back," Morrigan said, her red eyebrow arched in a look of pure disdain.

She was sitting on the edge of the bed beside Caoimhe, her long white fingers gently pulling at the tangled strands of her lover's hair.

"I have to, love," Caoimhe said.

She knew what Morrigan had done—because Morrigan had told her in detail—and she was very sorry her partner had wasted her energy. She wasn't going to stay in their lovely, sun-drenched Balmoral flat doing nothing as her daughter was erased from the world.

Of course she'd expected such resistance from her jealous wife, which was exactly why she'd told her nothing of Daniel's call. She'd just gotten her things in order, putting together her few meager possessions (most of what they owned jointly *really* belonged to Morrigan), so she would be ready to go to Sea Verge. She knew she'd arrived in time to stop that horrible Siren, Starr, from absconding into the sea, but then something had happened in the car and she'd blacked out, waking up here, in her bed with Morrigan at her side.

"I forbid it," Morrigan said, standing up and walking to the mantelpiece.

Stress had made the blue veins underneath her pale skin stand out and her prized red hair seemed limp. She was still a beautiful woman, but she looked wrecked.

"You can't forbid me to do anything, love," Caoimhe said, sitting up in bed, her head swimming. She remembered an explosion, a bright flare of orange, and knew this must be what was responsible for the vertigo she was experiencing. "I'm my own person."

She'd always been her own person. It was something she prided herself on. No one could ever say she was beholden to anyone or anything. Even when Morrigan had tried to force immortality upon her, Caoimhe had resisted—not because she didn't want to spend forever with her wife, but because she hadn't earned it, herself.

"I detest that about you, you bitch," Morrigan said, her back to Caoimhe. "So hatefully independent."

"Yes, it's the truth," Caoimhe said, slipping her feet into her slippers and standing up.

She felt woozy for a moment, but the feeling passed, and she was able to walk across the room without keeling over.

"It's also what you love about me," Caoimhe finished, wrapping her arms around Morrigan's slender waist.

She nuzzled against the soft fluff of hair at the nape of Morrigan's neck then pressed her lips to the warm flesh.

"You really are hateful," Morrigan said, trying to ignore Caoimhe's lips on her skin.

"I am?"

Morrigan nodded.

"Terribly hateful? Or just plain old hateful?" Caoimhe asked—and she thought she'd won Morrigan over.

"No," Morrigan said, pushing Caioimhe away. "You can't seduce me into doing what you like."

The jig was up. She wasn't going to get Morrigan's approval, no matter what she did. She'd hoped this wasn't going to be the case, but in her heart she'd suspected as much.

Her wife did not care for her daughter. Not because she disliked Calliope, personally, but because she hated anyone who took Caoimhe's attention away from her. It was a flaw in Morrigan's character, but through the years, Caoimhe had come to accept it was a part of who her lover was. She didn't try and change Morrigan—that would've been like squeezing blood from a rock—but she didn't reward the bad behavior, either.

"She's your boss and you're willing to just throw her under the bus," Caoimhe said, her tone harsh.

Selfishness was another of Morrigan's characteristics she didn't love.

"I'm just a lowly Vice-President," Morrigan whined.

"So?" Caoimhe said.

"So nothing," Morrigan replied. "If she can't take care of herself, then she doesn't deserve to be Death—"

Caoimhe rested her hands on her hips, the silky dressing gown she wore making her feel strangely vulnerable.

"That's enough! I don't want to hear another word against Callie."

Morrigan saw Caoimhe meant business and decided not to push the issue.

"Now, I'm going to meet Jarvis and the others at the agreed upon place and there's really nothing you can do to stop me," Caoimhe said, eyes narrowed.

"But isn't there?" Morrigan said, taking a step toward Caoimhe.

Caoimhe sensed Morrigan had something up her sleeve, and she knew it was not going to be pleasant. She tried to back away, to put as much distance between them as she could, but for every step back she took, Morrigan took one closer.

"What're you doing?" Caoimhe asked, her thighs pressed up against the top of the down-filled comforter.

"I'm saving your skin. That's what I'm doing."

Caoimhe sat down on the bed then yanked her legs up so she could roll across the bed.

"You can go wherever you like," Morrigan said, shrugging her bony shoulders. "But it's going to catch you."

Caoimhe felt funny. The vertigo had returned and now it was making her head spin. She was able to get to the other side of the bed, but her dismount left something to be desired. She landed on the floor, hitting her head against the nightstand.

"What did you do to me?" she slurred, glaring up at Morrigan, who'd circumvented the bed to be nearer to her.

"I only did what's best for you," Morrigan said, squatting down beside her, looking sad.

"The best . . . ?" Caoimhe moaned, understanding blossoming inside her skull—but it was too late to do anything about it.

The room dipped and swirled as she tried to hold on to consciousness . . . and then her vision blurred and everything faded to gray.

And then black.

seventeen

CALLIOPE

I felt like Alice, staring into the looking glass just before she stepped through it. I knew she was curious about what was waiting for her on the other side of the mirror, but the difference between us was that I knew the answer.

Death and the End of Death.

I pressed my hand against the wall, the cold glass pulling the heat from my flesh. I'd dropped the hammer on the ground in frustration after it'd cracked the glass, but refused to do anything more. Now I bent down and picked it up again, sliding it back into my leather tool belt.

The Alternate Frank, the one who came from a different universe, grinned at me as he stabbed his fingers into the smoothness of Marcel's throat, choking the life out of the Ender of Death. Marcel's eyes had begun to pop out of his head, the skin of his face and neck a fetid shade of purple. But the worst was his tongue. It was as if a giant pink slug had crawled out of his mouth and was flailing against his lips.

"Call a wormhole!" I screamed, my voice muted by the glass.

I knew Marcel couldn't hear or see me in the condition he was in, but I wasn't yelling at him. Instead, my eyes were trained on Runt, who was huddled in a ball, her front paw bent at a crooked angle. She was staring intently at my lips, her pink eyes flicking back and forth as she tried to decipher what I was saying.

"Wormhole!!" I cried, pounding on the glass with my hand. "Call a wormhole!!"

Understanding flared in her eyes, her tail thumping against the concrete floor.

Thank God, I thought. *She understood me.*

Jarvis had warned us no one could wormhole in or out of the inside of Uriah Drood's compound—so why had I asked Runt to do the impossible? Well, what very few people realized was hellhounds possessed their own special blend of magic. Which meant Runt wasn't being monitored by anyone.

The first time she'd dragged me into a wormhole of her calling, I was an emotional wreck afterward. Stepping into Runt's magic was like getting high on an eight-year-old girl's pretend tea party: Your soul felt all full of unicorns, kittens, cotton candy, and pretty pink and purple twinkle lights. You had so much happiness inside of you, you thought you were gonna burst. Then, when you finally stepped out of the wormhole, all of that happiness just . . . evaporated—and the loss of all those beautiful things hit you with a quiet intensity reminiscent of a sucker punch to the gut.

Coming down off a hellhound magic high was seriously depressing.

Anyway, the reason I'd asked Runt to call up a wormhole was twofold: I figured Uriah Drood probably hadn't calibrated his spell to affect hellhound magic and Runt was just close enough to Marcel she might possibly be able to save his life.

"Do it, Runt!" I screamed.

The Alternate Frank—as I now called him—seemed amused by my antics on the other side of the glass, but was much more interested in throttling Marcel, so he didn't really pay attention to *what* exactly I was saying. The one great thing about dealing with a narcissist is they're so caught up in the greatness of their own actions they discount what everyone else is doing.

Alternate Frank had no idea he was about to have his ass

handed to him on a plate. He was too busy luxuriating in the slow murder of the Ender of Death to be prepared for the on-slaught of goodness Runt unleashed on him.

I watched from the other side of the glass as Runt sat up, struggling a little to stand on her busted leg. She looked like she was all about the plan we'd come up with, and kept thwack-ing her tail excitedly against the leg of the side table she was standing next to. I closed my eyes and sent all the good vibes I had inside me toward the hellhound. If she could pull this off, the three of us might actually get out of Purgatory with our lives intact.

I opened my eyes, my confidence in Runt unimpeachable, and waited for her to get the ball rolling. She lowered her head in concentration and I felt the ground begin to tremble. The trembling grew in intensity until the sandy dirt was roiling underneath my feet. I had to lean against the glass wall in order to keep my balance, leaving my sweaty palm prints all over it.

Inside, Alternate Frank lost his balance, his grip on Mar-cel's throat slackening. He released Marcel, who fell forward, slamming his forehead into the wall. The taut skin opened in a spray of blood that arced across the glass, leaving a trail of bright red on the inside of the glass wall as he slid down its surface. He hit the floor, folding like a discarded marionette, his arms and legs akimbo.

Behind Marcel's body, Alternate Frank had planted his feet on the concrete floor, trying to keep his balance.

"Good job, girl!" I yelled at Runt, giving her the thumbs-up through the window.

She wagged her tail at me as she hobbled over to Marcel's limp body, her coat swathed in a dusky rose halo that shim-mered even in the blue Purgatorial light. When she got to Mar-cel, she looked up at me, uncertainly. I didn't need a diagram to know what she was thinking: She couldn't transport me away with her and Marcel because I was on the wrong side of the glass—and she didn't want to leave me here.

"Go!" I yelled, nodding my head. "Get Marcel away from here!"

Alternate Frank had pinpointed the source of the trouble and was now zeroing in on my puppy.

"Get out of here!" I screamed at Runt. "He's coming!!"

I pointed to Alternate Frank, who was attempting to walk across the floor as the ground rocked and rolled beneath his feet. Runt seemed to realize the time for indecision was over. Looking back at me with a baleful expression in her eyes, she gave a casual flick of her head and called up a wormhole—actually it was more like a golden, shimmering door—then used her teeth to drag Marcel's limp body through the doorway.

Alternate Frank leapt into the air, trying to follow Runt and Marcel on to their next destination, but he wasn't fast enough. The doorway disappeared with a *pop* and he belly flopped onto the floor, his chin slamming into the concrete.

I leaned against the glass, exhausted, my body shaking like I'd just run a marathon. I had to force myself to stop thinking about how close Alternate Frank had come to getting his hands on Runt. If she hadn't wormholed them out of there when she did—

No, I did not want to think about what would've happened.

The earthquake-like shaking had stopped immediately after Runt had disappeared inside the wormhole/doorway, so I could happily remove my hands from the glass wall I'd been using to steady myself.

Runt and Marcel were safe(ish) for now, and if I wanted to keep them that way, then I had to do something about Alternate Frank. This meant I had to either get past the stupid house spell or, if I was really smart, find a way to entice Alternate Frank outside.

I decided to try to entice him outside first and leave the spell breaking for another day.

"Hey, shithead!" I yelled, pounding on the glass wall with my fists.

Alternate Frank was still on the floor, not having moved from the spot where he'd landed after he'd missed the wormhole.

Obviously, he couldn't hear what I was saying, but my movement caught his eye. He turned his head to look at me, a ribbon of blood on his chin where he'd split his lower lip on the concrete.

The Frank from my universe wore blond muttonchops

which I would've called his "trademark" look, but Alternate Frank had no facial hair—and he was thinner than my Frank. Otherwise, they were exactly the same. Blond hair and eyebrows, light brown eyes, and a sexy sneer to their lips.

From the first moment I'd met my Frank on the porch of a magical house on stilts in the middle of the marshlands of Queens, New York, I'd been smitten. It was purely a visceral, sexual attraction, and like an idiot, I'd acted on it when I should've stayed far away. My indiscretion had almost ruined my relationship with Daniel—actually, who was I kidding, it *had* ruined my relationship with Daniel—but somehow we'd managed to work it out and get back together.

Which was an amazing feat in its own right.

"Come out here and try to kick my ass!" I yelled, banging my fists on the glass.

Alternate Frank set one hand on the floor, using it to lift his torso and head, then he rolled over on his side and pushed himself up into a sitting position, eyes latching onto mine. I could feel the hatred rolling off of him in waves—and I was happy I could incite so much emotion in an adversary.

Crawling over to the wall, he motioned for me to kneel down closer to him. When I didn't move, he gestured again, shaking his head. I knew there was glass between us, so he couldn't do anything too terrible to me, and this was what finally persuaded me to kneel down closer to him.

He leaned forward and spat at me, a ball of bloody mucus and saliva splatting on the surface of the glass. The action was so aggressive I sat back away from the glass wall.

"Schmuck head," I whispered, annoyed with myself for letting him get to me.

While I watched, he maneuvered around so his back was to the window. Using the glass to brace himself, he slid up the wall until he was back on his feet, but still leaning on the wall for support. He turned around so his face was pressed against the glass, his brown eyes leering in my direction.

My Frank may have been an asshole, but he wasn't a creepazoid. Not like Alternate Frank, who was just balls-to-the-wall *freaky.*

"Come out here and fight like a real man, you prick," I said, catching his eye and leering right back at him.

Alternate Frank intimidated me, but I sure as hell wasn't going to let him know that.

He stuck his tongue out at me and I noticed the tip was hanging from the rest of the muscle by a thread of flesh. I'd assumed the blood in his mouth had come from his split lip. I hadn't realized he'd bitten through his tongue when he'd belly flopped onto the concrete.

He seemed to enjoy my reaction to his mutilated tongue—so much so, he smushed the thing against the glass, licking upward and smearing his bloody saliva all over the glass. I knew he was hoping to get a rise out of me, so I yawned, letting him see how bored I was by his "tongue show."

"That's gross," I said. "Really disgusting. You're nasty, you know that?"

He grinned, showing me his bloodied teeth.

"Someone should punch you in the testicles," I added, giving him the finger. "We'll see how big your grin is then."

He laughed, more flecks of bloody saliva hitting the glass.

"I bet the girls stay far, far away from you back home."

I dropped the bird, but if I could've jammed that middle finger up his nose, I would have.

I guess I was feeling too pleased with myself and this caused me to let my guard down. Or maybe I just believed I was safe on my side of the glass. Either way, I was startled when Alternate Frank thrust his hand through the window and grabbed my throat with his bony fingers, making it impossible for me to draw a breath.

I reached down and pulled the ball peen hammer from my tool belt and started beating the shit out of Alternate Frank's wrist. The rest of him was still trapped behind the glass, so I couldn't hear him screaming. But I could see his face and how much pain my hammer was inflicting on him. Watching him writhe while I battered at him with my hammer made me so damn happy I started giggling.

I'd done a lot of damage in a relatively short amount of time, my hammer busting apart the flesh around his wrist, shattering bones so they poked through the skin. I was ready to get my carnage on and do even more damage with the wire cutters in my tool belt, but Alternate Frank got wise and yanked his hand back through the glass.

"Yeah, you wanna mess with me, you better go all the way," I hissed at him through the glass as he cradled his wounded arm to his chest.

He looked down at his arm then looked back up at me and smiled. I couldn't figure out why he was grinning at me like that—but then he held out his arm and showed me what was so amusing: He'd already begun to heal.

I watched, in awe, as the bone shards knitted themselves back together at a whirlwind pace, the massacred flesh beginning to reconstitute itself over them as soon as they were done reforming. When it was over, his skin was flawless, with zero trace of the abuse I'd just inflicted.

"Bastard," I murmured, wishing I boasted a healing time of 2.6 seconds.

Not knowing what else to do, I flipped Alternate Frank double birds and took off for the bushes, hoping he'd give chase—and I was not disappointed. Looking over my shoulder as I ran, I caught sight of my nemesis pushing through the spelled glass hands and face first. A second later, he was outside and in hot pursuit of yours truly.

I ran as fast as I could, jumping over the bushes where Marcel, Runt, and I had hidden earlier before heading out into the Purgatorial wasteland. The landscape was silent, no birds or insects chirping, nothing at all to mute the sound of my own heartbeat in my ears, or Alternate Frank's footfalls as he closed the distance between us.

As I ran, I stuck my hand into my tool belt, removing the palette knife from its loop and palming it in my right hand. I wasn't sure what exactly I was going to do with it, but I felt better having a weapon in my hand and I'd dropped my hammer back by Uriah Drood's house.

I felt a stitch forming in my side, the pain lancing up my torso, and my body immediately started to slow down. It wanted me to know it was not built for such hard-core physical exertion and was much happier at rest, at sleep, or at dinner—basically, any activity that didn't require too much physical activity. I was fast losing steam and I knew I needed to be proactive and come up with a plan, or Alternate Frank was going to catch me and then the ball was going to be in his court, not mine.

Stop, drop, and roll.

The words appeared in my mind like manna from Heaven and without any conscious thought, I did exactly as they demanded. I went down hard, using my velocity to roll to the left as dirt and sand flew into my face. I shut my eyes, but some of the debris made its way into my mouth and I found myself spitting out bits of sandy dirt.

I was still holding the palette knife in my hand as I crawled to my feet, so I brandished it in front of me, letting Alternate Frank see I had a weapon. He'd stopped a few feet away from me, and now stood watching, head cocked, as he tried to figure out what the hell I was doing. I guess it did look pretty odd, my whole stop, drop, and roll strategy, but I wasn't about to second-guess my intuition.

"Whatcha think you're gonna do with that stubby old thing?" he said.

I wasn't surprised to hear he and my Frank both shared a slow-as-molasses Southern drawl.

"I dunno," I said, shrugging as I looked down at the knife.

"It's not a real looker now, is it, sister?"

I had to agree. The palette knife was nothing to write home about, but I felt way more secure with it in my hand than I did without it. Still, I knew there was room to up my game. I reached down, extracting the wire cutters from my tool belt and holding them in my left hand.

Now I could defend myself with two weapons instead of one.

"I know I'm running the risk of sounding real corny here, but whatever," I said. "I don't think it's the size of your weapon, but how you stick it in that counts."

With that said, I didn't hesitate in my next action. I ran straight for Alternate Frank, my palette knife extended out in front of me like a sword aimed right for his chest. It was time to show Alternate Frank what I meant about "sticking it in." I jammed the knife's triangular head into his breast, the metal sliding through his shirt and flesh like they were made of butter.

He cried out, eyes wide with shock. He hadn't expected me to act so boldly, and now he was paying for having underestimated me. I pushed the palette knife in deeper, and I knew I'd hit my mark: The blade had pierced his heart. Even with my knife inside of it, it continued to beat, the knife's wooden handle reverberating with each contraction of the heart muscle.

I wasn't stupid enough to think I'd killed him. I knew better than that. I raised my wire cutters and punched them, pointed tip first, into the soft flesh of his temple. I yanked them out, releasing a flood of blood that poured down his face and onto his shirt, then I stabbed him again in the exact same place. The first hit dazed him, but it was the second one that dropped him to his knees. I kicked him in the gut and he flew backward, landing on his side, blood dripping into the sandy dirt. I squatted down beside him and quickly rolled him onto his back before pulling the rope off my tool belt so I could tie him up.

Halfway through binding him, he started to regain consciousness. I needed more time to secure him, so I slammed the wire cutters into his forehead and this seemed to knock him out again. I felt a little guilty about beating the shit out of him, but then I remembered how he'd kicked Runt and I didn't feel so bad anymore.

Tying his wrists as tightly as I could manage, I lassoed the other end of the rope around his ankles, pulling it taut and knotting it in place. It was a modified version of the hogtie, and I hoped it would keep Alternate Frank immobile and under my control.

"Take . . . it . . . out," Alternate Frank murmured.

"What?" I said, leaning close to his face.

"Take the little stubby thing out," he coughed.

I shook my head.

"Not gonna happen. You're just gonna have to suck it up for now."

Apparently, Alternate Frank didn't like being told *no*, and to show his displeasure, he coughed up a disgusting ball of saliva and snot and spat it at me. It hit me in the neck and I immediately stood up, wiping it away with the back of my hand.

"You're disgusting," I said.

He only laughed at me.

"And you're a pathetic attempt at Death, Calliope Reaper-Jones."

He could say whatever the hell he wanted because he was the one who was hog-tied in the dirt, not me.

"I think it's time to get out of here," I said, as I stepped over him and grabbed the taut part of the rope linking his ankles and wrists together, dragging him behind me as I walked.

I could hear him coughing, but I didn't give a shit if dirt and debris were flying in his face.

"Where the hell are you taking me, sis?" he yelped.

I didn't answer his question. I just kept walking.

"Where are we going?!" he yelled, trying to intimidate me with anger.

But I remained silent.

"Bitch," he grumbled.

I purposely veered toward a stretch of ground littered with small stones. It was fun to rake Alternate Frank over them, his yips of pain making me smile. I had no intention of telling my captive where I was taking him. He was the wily type, and I didn't want to give him any advantage over me.

The very idea of me being able to subdue Alternate Frank without any help was absolutely ludicrous—the man healed in seconds, for God's sake, and he was huge. Yet, here we were: me pulling him behind me like he was a little red human wagon.

It blew the mind.

I shook my head, happy to know I wasn't a total putz at being Death.

We hadn't gone very far when a cool wind kissed my face and I lifted my eyes from the ground, wondering where the hell the welcome breeze had come from in the emptiness of Purgatory. But my breath caught in my throat when I saw, like a much-wished-for mirage, a shimmering golden doorway standing open in the middle of the wasted Purgatorial landscape. I blinked just to make sure I wasn't imagining things. And then I saw who was waiting for me on the other side of the doorway: Runt and her father, Cerberus, the three-headed former Guardian of The North Gate of Hell.

With a squeal of joy, I began to run toward them, Alternate Frank bumping along behind me.

eighteen

Jennice had never heard of a "wormhole" before, but this didn't stop her from going through one.

After it was all over, and she'd made sure her limbs were still in the right places, she suddenly realized she hadn't eaten anything since breakfast. She was glad her stomach had been empty, or otherwise she might've thrown up all over the backseat of the car.

Even when she tried to think back to the moment when reality had done a flip-flop and everything she'd known about the world had changed, she still couldn't quite wrap her mind around it. It seemed like one minute Noh was speeding down the highway with Jarvis yelling at her, and then the next minute a huge swirling storm cloud was touching down on the road in front of them.

When Jennice saw the dark gray funnel ahead of them, she closed her eyes and began to pray—as if this would save her and everyone in the car from imminent death. She prayed Noh would turn the wheel, the car would miss the eye of the storm, and certain disaster would be averted. She knew this was just wishful thinking. They were going far too fast for the car to do anything but sail into the middle of the melee, but still she held out hope something or someone would save them.

Then everything went all wonky and her sense of reality shifted. Her body was tossed upside down and her stomach lurched, bile rising in her throat as she felt like a lone tennis shoe rotating around inside an industrial-sized dryer.

Ignoring the rising nausea, she opened her eyes and was shocked to find the car no longer speeding down a Rhode Island highway about to be sucked into a humongous storm cloud, but coasting, instead, down a tree-lined stretch of road toward a massive wrought iron gate towering above them.

The gate was closed, a thick chain and padlock wrapped around the latch in an attempt to keep out unwanted guests. Noh drove the car right up to the gates, easing down on the brake as she did. She threw the car in park and opened her door, climbing out and jogging over to the padlock. She grasped the lock, lifting it up in the air, then jiggled it a little bit before letting it go. She came back to the driver's seat and crawled inside, turning off the ignition.

"Well?" Jarvis asked.

He didn't sound too optimistic.

"It's spelled. But I know another way in."

"I hope so, or we'll be at their mercy again," Jarvis said, crossing his arms over his chest.

"It's pretty," Jennice said, studying the large, Gothic building standing just beyond the gate.

It was the first real, coherent thing she'd said in a while—and both Noh and Jarvis turned in their seats to look at her.

"I don't care where we are," she added, leaning into the seatback. "I'm just glad we got away from the werewolves."

It was true. She would've been happy in a maximum security prison, provided the guards could keep those hairy beasts away from her.

"They're not werewolves," Jarvis said.

"What are they, then?" Noh asked, as she got out of the car and slammed the door, leaving Jennice and Jarvis no choice but to climb out after her.

It took Jennice a moment to unbuckle her seat belt, so Jarvis and Noh were already ahead of her before she'd even managed to crawl out of the backseat. She had to scamper to catch up to them.

"They're called Vargr," Jarvis was saying as Jennice joined

them. "I can understand why you would call them 'were-wolves,' but I assure you, they're not."

"I think they wanted to eat us," Jennice said, shuddering at the thought.

While she'd tried to erase the last few hellish hours from her memory, flashes of Sea Verge and killing the Vargr, of the car blowing up and Clio disappearing . . . all the detritus of the terrifying day kept repeating on a loop inside her brain, the images making her stomach clench.

"Yes," Jarvis agreed, "they would've eaten you and Noh—and taken Clio and myself hostage."

Jennice hadn't really wanted her fears confirmed. She didn't like knowing there was something higher up the food chain than human beings.

"That would've sucked," Noh said, but Jennice could tell she wasn't really listening to their conversation, too busy tromping through the woods and looking for a way to bypass the all-encompassing wrought iron fence to really pay attention.

Every now and then Noh would stop and cock her head as though she were listening to someone—and then she'd continue on.

The fence stretched on ahead of them, the wrought iron supplemented now by the addition of large stretches of smooth stone walls, making the thing impossible to scale.

"What is this place?" Jennice asked, less curious and more worried it was getting dark and they were still outside, totally helpless if the Vargr decided to show up again.

"It's called the New Newbridge Academy. It's where Noh and Calliope attended boarding school. I chose it as our meeting place because it has magical wards protecting it—at least, if we can get inside the grounds."

Jennice was sufficiently impressed by the fact Noh and her friend Calliope had attended boarding school. Having gone to a traditional public school, she was in awe of a place like the New Newbridge Academy with its Gothic buildings, lush grounds, and all-over "spooky" vibe.

Suddenly Noh stopped beside the stone wall, gesturing for them to do the same.

"Yeah, that's the closest way in?" Noh asked—and, at first,

Jennice thought she was talking to Jarvis, but then realized this wasn't the case.

"Noh, who are you talking to?" Jennice asked, getting more spooked by the minute.

Noh held up a hand for Jennice to wait a moment, and then she said: "Thanks for that, Henry."

She blew a kiss into the air.

"That was Henry," she added, smiling. "He's one of my oldest friends. Callie knows him, too."

"Is he invisible?" Jennice asked, wondering if there were an army of invisible people surrounding them she couldn't see.

Noh shrugged.

"Kind of," she said, running her hands through her dark hair, then wrapping it in a knot at the nape of her neck. "He's a ghost."

"Oh," Jennice said—realizing she'd missed something important.

"You look so shocked," Noh laughed. "You just traveled through a wormhole without a whimper, but it's the dead people who freak you out?"

Jennice had to admit Noh was right. No point in getting worked up about someone seeing dead people when there were things like Vargr out there, trying to eat you.

"If her friend Henry has found a way into New Newbridge, then by all means we should follow," Jarvis said, holding out his arm for Jennice to take.

She accepted his assistance, glad for the arm to lean on. The floor of the woods was littered with stones and hidden tree roots—and it was getting darker, which made it hard to see where you were going or what you were stepping on.

Noh didn't wait for them to follow her, but took off, jogging ahead of them before disappearing behind a thicket of brambles growing against the stone wall.

"We're in!" Noh called, her disembodied voice echoing back to them.

Jarvis raised an eyebrow, but didn't hurry his pace.

"My life is full of impetuous women," he said, his tone wistful.

"I'm gonna try to keep it together from now on," Jennice

said, making up her mind to actually do what she was saying. "My mom calls me her rock, and usually I am. But then those Vargr . . ."

She didn't want to think about that stuff anymore. It was just too overwhelming. Thankfully, Jarvis sensed her hesitation and changed the subject.

"Looks as though we're here," he said, as they came to the spot where Noh had disappeared through the thicket of greenery.

Hidden behind the brambles was a small, arched doorway cut into the stone wall. The door was standing open and they could see Noh leaning against the doorframe, impatiently waiting for them.

"What took you guys so long?" she asked, grinning rakishly—and then she pulled them inside.

daniel felt bad about misleading everyone, but there was only one way to save Callie and it involved getting into bed with the enemy—at least a former enemy. But doing the right thing sometimes meant you had to make sacrifices.

He hadn't wanted to double-cross Freezay, but Watatsumi had insisted on it as part of the deal. He didn't know what beef the Water God had with the former detective from the Psychical Bureau of Investigations, but he'd wanted Freezay delivered to him posthaste.

Freezay was an adult who could take care of himself, and knowing this had assuaged Daniel's guilty conscience somewhat, but the Caoimhe deal was a bit harder to swallow.

Unbeknownst to Daniel, Watatsumi had made some kind of bargain with Caoimhe's girlfriend, Morrigan. Daniel didn't know the details, but whatever they'd decided between them, it meant that when Daniel delivered Freezay to Watatsumi, he'd also been forced to hand over Caoimhe, too. He hadn't liked the change in plans—hell, he'd been the one to bring Caoimhe into the loop, and now he felt like he was the one betraying her.

He assuaged his guilt by telling himself he was only doing what was necessary in order to get Callie out of this unharmed. He repeated the belief like a mantra, letting it ease his conscience whenever he found himself forced into an untenable situation (like with Caoimhe).

And even though he was aware Watatsumi did not have his, or anyone else's, best intentions at heart, Daniel felt like the end completely justified the means.

Now he just had to complete one more task and then he'd be able to use the wish-fulfillment jewel to take him to Callie—Watatsumi had promised him this.

There was only one problem with the task. It involved getting tangled up with someone he hated with every fiber of his immortal being: He was supposed to break Callie's ex-lover Frank out of Purgatorial prison.

Callie had assured him the thing with Frank was nothing, that they hadn't even had *real* sex, but he didn't believe her. He knew firsthand what a voracious sexual appetite she had, and he seriously doubted the fling was as benign has she'd let on. Even now, months later, just the thought of her being with Frank, of him touching any part of her, incensed Daniel.

In his past life, he'd had no problem using a little violence to get what he wanted, but that was something he thought he'd reconciled—then he'd met Callie and realized he'd found the one creature on Earth who could rekindle those urges.

He hated how out of control she made him feel, how everything she did affected him so intensely—even though this was probably the very reason he'd fallen in love with her. All he knew was she drove him to distraction and made him do things he never in a million years thought he'd do again.

Like breaking this guy, Frank, out of Purgatory.

Daniel had spent a lot of time at Death, Inc., when he'd worked for the Devil. He'd had to check Death Records on an almost daily basis, so he'd quickly learned the layout of the place and could move among its many floors, using secret passageways the original architects of the massive brimstone structure had included as a way for the Grim Reaper to move, unseen, through the building—while also keeping a watchful eye over his/her minions.

Daniel was using one of these passages now to circumvent the Hall of Death and go directly to the former prison wing.

In the years before Callie's dad had taken over Death, Purgatory had been more of a prison and less a way station between Heaven and Hell. Anyone who'd gone against the status quo had been remanded here, the chance for their souls to continue on to the recycling pool, forfeit. It'd been a Draconian system, one that'd taken someone idealistic and strong, like Callie's dad, to come in and restructure.

Everyone had expected the venture to fail, but to their surprise, the corporatization of Death into Death, Inc., had been a complete success. It was proof the Afterlife could be run with respect and dignity, not just an iron fist.

With the exception of one of the lower floors of prison cells, the Purgatorial prison wing had been torn down to make room for new support staff offices. This one remaining floor had been kept intact, and was only used for the most violent or treasonous of offenders. Frank was in the treasonous camp, having helped try to overthrow Callie's Reign of Death—and now, under direct orders from Callie, herself, his cell was the most heavily guarded one in the prison.

The passageway Daniel had chosen looked as though it hadn't been used in decades. There was a fine layer of dust on the ground, one soon covered in Daniel's advancing footprints. He'd brought a lighter with him, but he'd been able to see well enough so far he hadn't needed to use it, though he knew the next part of the journey would devolve into total darkness and then the lighter would become indispensable.

As if the building had read his mind, all the available light was extinguished and Daniel stopped in the middle of the path, digging into his pocket for the lighter. He knew the passageway was spelled to fall into darkness whenever an intruder tried to enter the prison wing, but he hadn't expected his presence to be noted so swiftly. He realized it was only a matter of time before the guards were sent in to find him. He needed to act quickly.

Fishing the lighter out of his pocket, he depressed the metal button so the flame flared to life, illuminating the space. Directly in front of him lay a large, arched black metal door marking the end of the passageway. Undaunted by the heavy padlock looped into its keyhole, he pulled a tiny book from his back pocket and held it out in front of him. With a silent *whoosh*, the door slid open and a ray of light from the other side of the doorway broke across his face. Finding the lighter no longer necessary, he extinguished the flame and put it back in his pocket.

He didn't feel bad about swiping the book from Jarvis. During the Vargr onslaught, he'd watched Callie's Executive Assistant rescue it from one of the bookcases and put it in his suit coat pocket. He'd already known he'd be braving Purgatory to rescue Frank, and he'd figured if the book just happened to be in his possession, it would make the whole endeavor much easier. Later, as they were leaving Sea Verge, he'd casually picked Jarvis's pocket, stealing the original copy of *How to Be Death* for himself.

It'd already proven to be a very wise impulse decision.

Daniel stepped through the arched doorway, leaving behind the dank, stone walls of the secret passage in favor of a well-lit hallway boasting the last fifteen prison cells in all of Purgatory. As he entered the hall, he pressed himself against the smooth concrete wall; while behind him, the arched doorway slammed shut and melted into the wall, leaving him unable to return the way he'd come. He looked in both directions, expecting one of the Bugbear guards to race into the hallway and call him out, but, to his surprise, this didn't happen. Instead, he was greeted by silence—and the eerie feeling he'd missed something important.

It was the smell that clued him in first.

It was the stench of purification and it led him to the prison cell across from the hall. The cell's door had been left wide open, boasting a ready escape for whatever prisoner had been locked inside. Daniel took a few tentative steps forward, eyes sweeping the interior of the cell—and this was how he found the corpse, its giant, curving body twisted at an unholy angle as it lay prone and bloodied on the cold, stone floor.

Hyacinth Stewart had been Callie's boss at House and Yard—back when Callie had still been in denial about her supernatural destiny and had insisted on forging a normal, human career path. Hyacinth had made Callie's "normal" life a living Hell and then when Cal had become Death, Hyacinth had shown her true supernatural colors.

And, needless to say, they had not been pleasant.

It turned out she was one of Watatsumi's henchmen, working with him to try to kill Callie, with the hopes of installing Frank in her place. When their nefarious plans had been foiled, Hyacinth had been arrested (along with Frank) and imprisoned here in Purgatory.

Now she was dead, her corpse slowly decomposing inside its air-conditioned prison cell.

Bile rose in his throat as the foul smell of rotting flesh filled his nostrils. He stumbled backward, his body pressing against the smooth concrete wall for support. He had the sinking feeling he'd arrived too late—but he had to be sure. He took off down the hall, eyes scanning the cells, searching for survivors and finding none, each cell occupant dead and accounted for.

This was when Daniel knew he'd failed in his task.

Watatsumi would not be pleased.

how was she supposed to know there were two Franks? She wasn't privy to all the supersecret stuff Watatsumi was up to. She didn't know there were two Franks running around—and that she could only trust one of them. Sure, she'd thought Frank was locked up in prison for being a bad boy, but people got out of jail all the time. She hadn't wanted to make him feel awkward—really she didn't care what he'd been up to or how he'd escaped from Purgatory—so she hadn't asked him any questions, they'd just spent a little time together then she'd agreed to do him a favor.

And now Watatsumi was all pissed off at her.

"But I got you that detective, so maybe you should just back off," she said, angrily.

She was lounging on a bed of floating kelp, her body pleased as punch to be back in the water after such a long time on dry land.

It's a real trial to stand on two legs when you're used to a fish tail, she thought as she dreamily admired her long green tail. It was a little scaly from being a pair of human legs for so long, but she knew once she'd exfoliated with a little sand, it would be fine.

She disliked using legs. It made her feel cheap. Pretending to be human was so beneath her it wasn't even funny. She didn't want to think about what it would've been like if Freezay had had his detective way with her. She'd probably be locked in some human jail cell—or, worse, stuck in an ocean-less Purgatory with Frank.

"You think acquiring the detective absolves you from any wrongdoing?" Watatsumi asked.

He was in his human form—which meant he was wearing his weird, old grass skirt and black kimono. The one that smelled funny even underwater. Starr didn't care much for Watatsumi's human form. She thought his face resembled a shriveled up prune, and shriveled up prunes were not very attractive, if you asked her.

She liked him so much more when he was in his sea serpent form. It kind of turned her on—something she wouldn't have believed possible when she was spending time with his human self. And though she'd never let him know this, she'd often wondered what it would be like to mate with him when he was all big and red and scaly.

Still, he'd never made a pass at her when he was a sea serpent. He'd only tried to get all up on her tail when he was in his wrinkled, human form—and that was the time when she had *zero* interest in him.

Gross.

"Well, I think it's worth something," she trilled.

She was in Watatsumi's jewel cave, or *lair*, as he liked her to call it. It was the place where he spent most of his time, making his nasty plans and fussing over his trove of hand-raised abalone. He was always tending to the mollusks, bringing in new species to take root on the walls of his cave. Starr thought it was strange how much time and energy he lavished on the underwater insects just so he could eat them.

Starr truly did enjoy spending time with Watatsumi, but the *real* reason she liked visiting his cave was because she was obsessed with all the shiny jewels lining its walls like glittering stars. And when Watatsumi was feeling especially generous, he'd even let her take her pick—though she was only allowed one jewel at a time. Starr was partial to the star sapphires (of course she was), but there were so many other beautiful jewels, ones in every size, shape, and color imaginable, she tried not to limit herself just to one type of gem.

When he was in his sea serpent form, she'd often accompanied Watatsumi out to some of his favorite haunts for a day of jewel collecting. He knew where all the rotting carcasses of long-forgotten shipwrecks lay strewn along the ocean floor, and he liked nothing more than sending his fleet of slave tuna down to pluck out the jewels from the bottom of the wreckage. The tuna would gobble up the jewels, stowing them in their mouths so they could bring them back to the lair where Watatsumi would then place them in different spots around the cave based on some weird catalog system of his own devising.

"Yes, you bringing me the detective might be worth something," Watatsumi said, thoughtfully, his eyes scanning the wall of jewels as if he'd been listening in on Starr's private thoughts. "But there is one thing . . ."

Starr waited for him to go on, but he remained silent.

"Go on," she said, finally. "Tell me what you're thinking . . ."

She hated his long silences. They drove her completely crazy, and, to her dismay, she always found herself filling them up with words.

"You're the only one to see this alternate version of Frank."

"That's true," she agreed—and she'd done more than just see him, but Watatsumi didn't need to know that.

Until that moment, Watatsumi had been sitting on his throne, one he'd had fashioned from the jaws of a great white shark he'd killed in hand-to-fin combat, but now he took to his feet, moving toward her, his wrinkled face unfathomable.

"Tell me all that happened between you."

Watatsumi was a space invader, always getting up in Starr's personal space in a way she didn't care for at all—and today was no exception. As he leaned in closer, eyes watching her intently, she could almost taste his breath: rank and fishy and totally unappealing.

"Leave nothing out," he said, black kimono lying open to the waist, revealing a healthy slice of well-toned torso.

With his salt-and-pepper hair and rheumy eyes, Watatsumi may have seemed like an old man, but Starr was always surprised when she caught a glimpse of his tight abs.

"We just . . . talked," Starr said. "You know, not about anything really important."

"And . . . ?" Watatsumi asked, encouraging her to continue.

He placed a long finger on her chest just in between her naked breasts, pushing in on the flesh with a marked show of aggression. She shrank back from him, floating backward in the water to get away from his touch.

"Are you scared of me?" Watatsumi asked, moving closer to her, and forcing her back up against the jeweled wall.

She didn't want to fuck Watatsumi. She didn't like how he looked or smelled, and his aggression was turning her off big-time.

"Did you screw him?" Watatsumi asked, closing the space between them and pressing his lips against her cheek, nuzzling her.

She could feel his cock poking into the soft flesh of her waist, long and hard. But the way he was brandishing it like a weapon felt cruel and she wanted absolutely nothing to do with it, or with him.

"Did I screw him?" she repeated huskily.

Watatsumi didn't say a word, just waited for her answer.

"No," she lied.

She heard Watatsumi's sharp intake of breath, felt him press himself along her body in a very demanding way—and she was disgusted.

"Get off me," she hissed, shoving him away from her—but he was stronger than she'd imagined, and he had no intention of letting her go.

"You little lying cunt," he said, grasping her arm.

His fingers dug into her skin and then she felt the water all around her get warm.

"What're you doing?" she cried, starting to panic because the Machiavellian look on Watatsumi's face was frightening her.

"Punishing a liar," he said as he grinned wickedly at her.

She tried to pull away from him, but before she could tear herself from his iron-like grip something sharp sliced into the taut flesh of her belly. She gasped, pain lancing up her middle then fanning out across her torso. She doubled over as a wave of nausea threatened to overwhelm her, but this passed quickly, and she was able to look down at her belly to find a piece of raw redwood protruding from her gut.

"What did you do?" she moaned, a trail of putrid-smelling bubbles rising from her lips and swirling around her head.

These were her last words.

Like a crab dumped into a pot of boiling water for someone's supper, Starr was engulfed in heat, her body seizing as her skin morphed from tan to pink to a nasty shade of scarlet. Her eyes became gelatinous blobs inside their orbital cavities, her cheeks and chin falling in on themselves. Flesh bloated and tore from the heat, blobs of fat pouring out of the ripped seams of skin and floating into the water, bobbing around the melting body.

"Stupid lying fish," Watatsumi said, as he released Starr's corpse, letting it rise like a dead goldfish to the top of the cave.

He looked down at his hands, at the redwood shard he'd pulled from the Siren's gut. He'd known he would have to dispatch Starr one day, and he was just glad her immortal weakness hadn't been as difficult to obtain as the promethium he'd used on Calliope Reaper-Jones.

Pleased with his handiwork, he watched as Starr's body floated aimlessly around the top of the cave, bumping into the ceiling and leaving bits of waterlogged flesh wherever it got lodged.

As much as he had once wanted to possess the Siren, he now felt nothing as he stared at her corpse. Finally, tired of having the thing making a mess of his lair, he snapped his fingers and the tuna came and took it away.

nineteen

The wormhole dropped Clio into one of the study rooms branching off from the main Hall of Death. Though there was no one in the room when she arrived, it looked as though someone had recently vacated the space. A thick book lay open on the rectangular wooden table, a brass reticle marking the reader's place in its pages. The acrid scent of a freshly extinguished candle tickled Clio's nose, enticing her to sneeze.

She looked around, making sure she was alone then she quickly walked to the doorway, popping her head out into the main hall. The Hall of Death was always busy, always swarming with strange people and creatures doing research, or looking at Death Records. During her internship, she'd gotten to know a lot of the regulars, helping them pull up hard-to-find rare documents from the library, or collect the other odds and ends they might need for their work. She'd been lucky to intern directly for Tanuki, who was in charge of the placing and fulfilling of all Death Record orders—and it was under his watchful eye that she'd spent her days.

She'd even been allowed into the Record Room where the actual Death Records were housed. It took over the whole top level of the Hall, and Clio likened its setup to a dry cleaner's clothing conveyor belt, where stacks of Death Records were grouped into specific categories, each one spinning like a giant Rolodex whenever an order was placed for retrieval. It was a highly complex, highly confusing system that ran on magic and was supposed to be tamper proof. So, unless you worked in the Hall of Death and had special dispensation to deal with the Death Records, you weren't allowed anywhere near the place. You could ask to see your own Death Record—and Tanuki would have it fetched for you—but that was it. Everyone else's Death Records were off-limits.

As Clio slipped into the stream of traffic heading down the main hallway, no one even glanced in her direction, and she was able to stay relatively obscured by the crowd as she followed the crush of bodies heading toward the front desk—but just before she arrived at the desk, she made a sharp right and slipped into a small depression in the wall.

She hadn't gone to the desk for help because she didn't know who was trustworthy anymore. She liked Tanuki, but he could have ulterior motives she knew nothing about. Besides, she was pretty sure there was a ladder leading to the Record Room hidden somewhere on either this wall or the one across the hall.

Once again, Clio found herself awed by the sheer beauty of the Hall of Death. It was part Gothic monastery, part Frank Gehry modern glass and metal monstrosity, but somehow these two disparate sensibilities worked well together. Clio had to admit she liked the modern part of the hall best, with its twisted metal framework and gaping transparent glass skylights that magically showed blue skies even though they didn't really exist. Everything above her head was stark and utilitarian—and utterly gorgeous—but she was a modernist, so she was slightly biased.

Clio began to explore the wall behind her, looking for the ladder. It only took her a few minutes, but she found the ladder concealed behind a thickly woven tapestry bearing a rendering of a golden cat and unicorn at play. Slipping behind the tapestry and reaching upward, her fingers brushed the limestone wall until she grasped the first metal rung of the ladder and pulled herself up. It was slow going from there, each subsequent rung embedded in the limestone just a tad farther away from the last, so you had to think about what you were doing, or risk going too fast and falling.

As she climbed, Clio noticed the rungs were engraved with etched pictographs. Some bore mythical beasts, while others were etched with strange shapes she'd never seen before. If she hadn't been gunning for the Record Room, she'd have stopped to study the strange images, but she was already feeling the press of time, so she kept pushing forward.

When she finally got to the top of the ladder, she hoisted herself up onto the landing and just lay there, trying to catch her breath. She was in pretty good shape, but that ladder was murder.

Climbing to her feet, she began her search, the overhead light following her as she strolled through the stacks, each section lighting up only after she'd moved past the warm glow of the previous one. She was on the lookout for the pink section of the Record Room—but since it was the smallest grouping of files, and the stacks were constantly on the move, it would prove hard to find.

She didn't sense the presence behind her, watching her as she walked through the stacks. She was too intent on finding the pink section to notice she was being followed—a faux pas that made her easy pickings.

"Here you are," she muttered as she finally found the stack she was looking for.

She reached out, her mind intent on finding Anjea's Death Record, but, suddenly, a hand emerged from the darkness, wrapping itself around her mouth. Without thinking, she slammed her elbow into her assailant's solar plexus—once, twice, three times—as hard as she could, but they wouldn't let go. If anything, they held on tighter, digging their fingers into her cheeks and lips.

"Settle down now."

The voice was a whisper in her ear, begging her to calm down.

"I'm not gonna hurt you."

She decided to hear the voice out. If it were lying, she'd go on the offensive and kick its ass six ways to Sunday.

"I'll let you go if you promise you won't scream."

Clio nodded.

"If you scream, they'll know where we are—and they're already hunting through this place looking for one or the other of us."

Her assailant released her and she spun around, trying to get a look at his/her face. Her assailant stood just outside of the light, but there was just enough overspill for her to make a positive identification.

"You're Frank. The real one," she said.

He nodded and stepped fully into the light, so she could see him.

Clio gasped.

The man was a pale, gaunt concentration camp victim in a short-sleeved orange jumpsuit.

"You know who I am? What I did?" he asked.

She nodded.

"You're so thin." The words just popped out of her mouth. She hadn't meant to be rude.

"He's taking over in this world and I'm wasting away because of it," Frank said. "At least your sister's just gonna disappear. That's lots better than this."

He gestured to his skinny arms, the flesh hanging from them like a skin-colored blanket draped over bone.

"What're you doing up here?" Clio asked, trying not to stare at Frank's skeletal frame.

"They came to kill me and everyone else on the prison floor," he replied. "I was the only one who got away—and up here seemed as safe a place to hide out as any."

Clio wanted to ask him more questions, but a *clanging* sound like the heel of a boot on a metal ladder rung, caused Frank to jump. He grabbed Clio's hand and pulled her behind him as he ran through the stacks, moving too fast for the lights to catch them and give away their location.

Behind her, Clio could hear chatter and then there was more clanking, the echo of more guards climbing up the ladder to find them.

"Wait," Clio hissed, trying to slam on the brakes.

Frank didn't want to stop, so she grabbed ahold of the conveyor part of one of the stacks, and the stack roared to life, spinning the folders like plastic-sheeted laundry.

"I know where to go," she whispered, as the stack whirled around them and the overhead light popped on, illuminating their hiding spot.

Frank's face was ashen, eyes fixed on the moving stack— and for the first time, Clio realized he wasn't being a jerk. He was just *terrified*.

"I promise it's a safe place," she added.

She let go of the stack and it stopped moving, but the light stayed on.

"All right," he said, and he let her drag him behind her as they ran, the lights bursting on above them in a riot of yellow and green.

She could hear their pursuers gaining on them, but she ignored her thudding heart and kept pressing on. She knew where they could hide and it wasn't very far.

"Here," she said, stopping abruptly and pointing at a ragged black hole cut into the wall in front of them.

"It was supposed to house a chute that would re-file the Death Records, but now it's just the entrance to a hidden passageway."

She didn't wait for Frank's reply, just squeezed his hand and urged him toward the gaping hole. They jumped together, neither of them making a sound as they disappeared into the darkness.

the first thing Freezay did when his head broke the surface of the water was to take a long, shuddering breath then dip his head back under the water, so he could thank his tuna savior.

But as he searched the cold, dark waters, eyes scanning for her silvery blue scales, he discovered she had gone. He spun around, searching the water for the tuna as he ignored the burning in his eyes, but there was no trace of her.

After a few minutes, he had to accept he was alone under the waves. He resurfaced again, his mind racing as he tried to imagine what it would be like to explain the odd experience to someone else—the idea that a telepathic tuna had saved his life sounded insane even to his own ears.

He started to laugh, the sound breaking from his lips uncontrollably: This was truly one of the most bizarre moments of his life.

He was still laughing when a beautiful blonde woman swam up to him and tapped him on the shoulder.

He did a double take. He'd thought he was alone out here on the water. Everywhere he looked there was nothing but ocean, no land as far as the eye could see, so where had the woman come from?

She gave him a weary smile, her cornflower blue eyes melancholy. She looked familiar, but he didn't think he'd ever met her before.

"We need to go now," she said, reaching down and grasping a piece of his shirt.

"Who are you?" Freezay asked, amazed by how beautiful she was even underneath all the sadness she radiated like perfume.

"It doesn't matter," she said, pulling him by the shirt and starting to swim. "Just know your plight . . . well, everyone underwater heard about your plight and I just couldn't, in good conscience, let you remain there."

"You sent Skye to rescue me."

She nodded.

"I didn't want anyone to know I was involved, so I sent Skye in my place."

"Well, please thank her for me," Freezay said. "She was amazing."

The woman smiled.

"Just so you know, you'll be able to breathe underwater for a few more hours. Any resistance your lungs give is purely psychological."

Then she dove underwater, taking Freezay with her. He didn't have time to take a breath or close his eyes, and his body started to panic, wanting to go back to the surface. He had to tell himself to relax and just go with the flow. He had no idea who this woman was, but she obviously wanted to help him—and whatever she had in store for him, it couldn't be any worse than drowning underwater tied to a piece of coral.

After he'd made the choice to go along with fate instead of fighting it, he felt a lot better and was able to enjoy being pulled through the water. Since he didn't have to do any work, he took the down time to study his new friend. From her lack of mermaid tail, he could see she wasn't a full-blooded Siren, but her legs and lower body were covered in scales and her feet were elongated like flippers, so there had to be some Siren blood there.

He appreciated the fact she was wearing a swimsuit, so he didn't have to stare at her nude body. He'd had a hard time with Starr's nudity—apparently he was a glutton for Siren punishment—and he didn't need another round of that. Things were just too crazy to throw sex and attraction into the mix.

He wanted to ask her where they were going, but he wasn't sure if talking worked underwater. He decided to give it a shot and see what happened.

"Where are we going?" he asked, expecting his words to get lost in the rush of water, but he was pleasantly surprised to hear his own voice echoing back very distinctly in his ears.

She turned her head, her mouth trained in his direction, but one eye still looking ahead.

"I'm taking you to land. I can't help you after that, but I can get you started on your journey."

She seemed to think this ended the discussion because she returned her attention back to swimming. Freezay didn't try to get more out of her, just chilled out and enjoyed the ride. It felt like eons since he'd been able to relax. If he thought back, really tried to place the last time he'd had this feeling, it would've been more than three weeks earlier.

He'd been between jobs—which was a rare thing for him. If he didn't keep his brain occupied, he got maudlin and did stupid things like drink two bottles of rum in an evening and get himself kicked out of his favorite bar. But for some reason fate had conspired to give him a night off, and this time he wasn't feeling all antsy on the inside like he usually did.

He'd taken up residence at the bar early, but he'd limited himself to one drink every two hours. Couple that with the greasy basket of fries and the cheeseburger he had taken his time over, and it had guaranteed him a stay at the bar until closing. He'd been a good boy that night, and the bartender, Jessica—a twenty-four-year-old, "Sister Golden Hair" song come to life—had taken pity on him and come back to his place after she'd tipped out, letting him make love to her until the sun had come up.

That was the last time he hadn't been totally stressed out—and it had been very, *very* nice.

"We're almost there," his guide said, turning back to give him a smile. "Another few minutes."

Freezay felt like they'd been traveling for hours, the blonde woman pulling him behind her like a swaddled child, but now as he looked around, expecting to see land, he found nothing but open sea. He had no idea where they were. They could've been in China for all he knew.

"Are we near the U.S.?" Freezay asked and the blonde laughed.

"Yes, you're in U.S. waters. In fact, we're just off the Massachusetts coastline."

"Well, that's a relief, I guess," he said.

He didn't know Massachusetts very well, so this was going to be interesting. A wet man with no money and no car was not what you wanted to be when you hit the streets of suburbia.

"Time to go up," she said, and began the ascent to the surface.

Twilight was fast approaching as they broke through the surface of the water. He squinted his eyes, but could barely make out the shape of the shoreline in the darkness.

"I'll tow you in closer," the blonde said, "but no land, all right?"

He nodded, just pleased to be sucking air again. The water breathing wasn't terrible, but it left a thick briny taste in his mouth.

It only took them a few minutes to reach a sandbar, and then Freezay could stand again.

"This is as far as I go," his guide said.

He stuck out his hand and she took it. They shook once and then he released her slender palm.

"Thank you, whoever you are," he said, giving her a wink. "My mystery woman."

She smiled, but her eyes were still sad. When she didn't take the bait, he shrugged—he wasn't going to get her name after all—then he stepped off the sandbar, dog-paddling toward the shore.

"Wait!" she called after him, and he stopped, turning back around and treading water.

He waited as she collected herself. It was hard to tell what she was thinking because twilight had finally overtaken the sky, hiding her face in shadow.

"Please tell Calliope and Clio I love them . . . and that I'm sorry."

She didn't wait for an acknowledgement, just dove into the waves and was gone.

there was a reason the Cult of Kali was so dark and violent: The woman had an almost insatiable thirst for blood. This she then passed down to her followers, and they obliged her accordingly with feasts of violence. She appreciated their devotion, but it wasn't enough. Every so often she liked to dip her hands into warm blood she'd drawn for herself.

The Vargr massacre had elicited enough blood to keep her happy for weeks. When she was done eviscerating and decapitating her enemies—and there were many of them—she found her body caked in their red, hot gore. It was quite an aphrodisiac. She was intoxicated by the taste and smell of herself and she swore she wouldn't bathe for at least twenty-four hours. She liked the feeling of viscera all over her skin.

And it wasn't a bad moisturizer, either.

As she surveyed the mess she'd made of white girl's pad, she remembered she'd left one of the Vargr alive and kicking. It was one of the smaller females, and she'd only broken its back, so it was incapacitated, but it wouldn't die, for now.

She marched back through the carnage, stepping on as many body parts as she could, enjoying the feel of crunching bones and matted fur under her feet. She'd decapitated most of her kills, but a few had escaped the treatment and those were the ones who hadn't changed back into human form. She felt sorry for the human ones. They looked weak and powerless next to their furry brothers and sisters.

That was one thing she did not want: to be powerless in

death. She didn't fear death, she relished it, and if she didn't die while in battle, then she would consider her demise a failure.

She couldn't remember exactly where she'd left the survivor, so she just started kicking the bodies as she walked until one of them groaned and she saw it still retained its head.

"Hey, fur ball," she said, giving the beast another kick in the flank. "I got something to tell you and you'd better listen well."

She squatted down next to the helpless creature, its blood-flecked tongue lolling in its mouth.

"Tell that master of yours that I got white girl's back," she said, whispering in the Vargr's ear. "So fuck the hell off."

She stood up and gave the beast a final kick.

"You gonna remember that, fur ball?"

The beast nodded weakly.

"Now I'm gonna send you back where you came from."

She slapped her hands together and a whirling vortex appeared in front of them. Slipping her hands under the wounded beast, she lifted it into the air and heaved it into the wormhole. Having received its due, the wormhole closed up like a lotus flower and disappeared.

Kali rubbed her hands together, pleased with her good work. She'd promised white girl she'd look after her, and Kali was not one to shirk her duties. Now she had another task to start on and she needed a little help for this one—namely, someone (Indra) whose golden tongue could persuade even a corpse to sit up and live again. She'd already let Indra know what was happening and that she was on her way to collect him. He had a vested interest in the outcome of this battle because he was in love with white girl's sister—and if he and Kali didn't help out, his lady was not gonna survive this hostile takeover. Immortal or not now, when white girl, aka Death, ceased to exist, then the bad boys would execute any of her remaining friends and family. Kali knew this for fact because if she were the one on the other side, she'd do the exact same thing.

Lucky for white girl, Kali had a soft spot for dipwads who threw girly magazines at her head (something Callie had done on their very first meeting). She would use everything in her power to keep white girl sitting pretty—and that meant getting her hands dirtier than they already were. Something she was very much looking forward to.

Surveying the damage, Kali saw her work at Sea Verge was done. She thought about taking a wormhole to Indra's house, but decided against it. As much as she liked killing Vargr, this was not the time for that—and hopping into a wormhole would only clue the bad boys in to where she was headed. True, she'd told Jarvis she would try to draw out their pursuers, but it had been a lie. She had other business to attend to, business that came directly from white girl's own mouth.

Instead, she made her way back to the garage, a separate building just down from the main house where she knew Jarvis kept the earthbound transportation. She was looking for something spiffy, preferably an automobile, but when she opened the garage door, her eye caught sight of something hot pink hiding in the corner underneath a white drop cloth.

"Now wait one minute," she whispered as she crossed the garage, making a beeline for the drop cloth–covered, hot pink thing.

Ripping away the covering, she gasped because what she saw underneath it made her heart do a little flip-flop.

"So. Damn. *Hot*," Kali breathed, as she stared, in utter fascination, at the hot pink Segway standing before her.

It looked as though the Goddess of Death and Destruction had found her mode of transportation.

twenty

CALLIOPE

Marcel was dead—at least this incarnation of him.

His body lay in the desert sand, the fierce light from the sun beating down on his twisted features: the purple tongue, the petechial hemorrhaging in his eyes, the splotchy fingerprints wrapping around his throat like a necklace. Rigor mortis hadn't set in yet, but it soon would. And I didn't want to think about what the desert heat would do to the body after a few hours on "broil."

I looked up at Cerberus, the giant, three-headed hellhound (I thought he resembled an overgrown black lab, but I would never tell him that), trying to ascertain his thoughts on what we should do next. I trusted him implicitly, not just because he was Daniel's friend and Runt's dad, but also because he was wise and didn't take shit from anyone.

I was beyond pleased that when Runt had made her wormhole jump she'd chosen to go to her dad—because anywhere Cerberus happened to be was what I would call "safe."

Cerberus's two dumb heads (they possessed the good-natured disposition of traditional dogs) were busy sniffing Marcel's corpse and enjoying the fine stench of death it was exuding, while the third head (I affectionately referred to him as "Snarly head") was busy watching me.

Snarly head was the thinking man's head and the only one you wanted to have a dialogue with. He differed physically, and in disposition, from his two brother heads because he was a Cyclops—his one giant yellow eyeball hardly ever blinked—and he was about as excitable as a rock. Let's just say whenever the two dumb heads were busy licking their shared balls, Snarly head was the only one who had the decency to look embarrassed by the spectacle.

I could tell Snarly head had lots to say on the subject of what we were gonna do with Marcel's body, but since I was Death, he wanted to be respectful and let me speak first, if I was so inclined. I had an idea of what I *thought* we should do, but was loath to say it out loud because it was so goddamned unorthodox it would probably get me yelled at.

I looked from Runt to Snarly head, then I took a breath and said, "I want to call him back from death."

No one yelled at me.

This was a good sign.

"Is it a terrible idea?" I asked, my energy flagging as the heat beat down on my head and I remembered where I was again.

As if I could ever really forget.

Hell was the place I hated most. The heat was infernal—it never let up even at night—and it was the scene of some of my most spectacular failures. And did I say I hated the place?

No, I despised it.

"I think you've had many ideas that were much worse," Snarly head said, his large yellow eye, unblinking.

"Really? You think this one might be okay?" I asked, surprised by his answer.

Snarly head nodded.

"What I think . . . is that your idea is worth a try."

I looked over at Runt, who was sitting in the sand beside her dad, black tail thumping. I took this as a sign she was telling me to go for it.

"What about this schmuck?" I said, pointing at Alternate Frank, who was still trussed up like a heifer. His pale skin wasn't used to Hell's furnace-like heat and he was only turning redder by the second.

Alternate Frank had been silent since we'd taken the wormhole into Hell, and as far as I was concerned, the longer he kept his mouth shut the better.

"You will need him," Snarly head said, turning so he could stare at my prisoner with his giant yellow eye. "Possibly as a bargaining piece—but you will also need to interrogate him, find out what he knows so you are then in synch with your enemy. So as much as I would like to tear him limb from limb and feed his carcass to the crows . . ."

I knew exactly how Snarly head felt. This was the man who was partially responsible for the attack on Runt, and who'd murdered Marcel, and God knew what else.

"Okay then, we hold on to him . . . for now," I said.

With the Alternate Frank situation settled, I returned to the next matter at hand: Marcel's reanimation.

I tried not to think about what this would mean for my future. If I brought Marcel back to life now, then I'd still be liable for my part of the agreement I'd made with him and Anjea in the Antarctic. The world would have its Golden Age of Death and then, when it was all over, I would be sacrificed to Marcel. It still might happen anyway—I didn't know if the bargain carried over to his next incarnation or not, but with my luck it probably did.

Still, if I took the gamble and let Marcel stay down for the count, then I *might* be able to marshal all my strength and wit together to beat Uriah Drood and his minions—but the likelihood of me being erased from the universe before that could happen was very high.

Logic won out over self-preservation.

"Let's do this thing," I said, kneeling down in the sand beside Marcel's inanimate corpse.

I placed my hands on his tortured face, the rigid, dead flesh making me queasy. I'd done this once before, unwittingly. It felt strange to be doing it now, on purpose.

"Live," I whispered.

There was a *crack* of rolling thunder above me and then the cloudless blue sky split in two, rain pouring down on us in warm, wet waves. I was soaked instantly and had to push my waterlogged hair out of my face so I could see.

I felt the muscles in Marcel's face shudder beneath my fingers and then his one good hand shot up and wrapped itself around my neck, pulling me down toward him. I was too surprised to pull away as his lips brushed mine. Heat and a powerful attraction exploded between us, and then, my body thrumming with power, he released me and tilted my head so he could whisper into my ear:

"You are brave."

I looked down into his eyes, the whites so bright they resembled bleached eggshells.

"You're welcome," I said.

I held out my hand and he took it, letting me help him to his feet as the water continued to beat down on us.

"We're in Hell?" he asked, looking around.

His experience in Hell had been about as wonderful as mine, so I doubted he was very happy to be here.

"Yup," I said, using my hands to slick my hair back off my face.

"Great," he said, arching an eyebrow before turning his attention to his murderer. "And what do we have here?"

He knelt down beside Alternate Frank, who was still lying trussed up in the (now) wet sand, looking as miserable as a drowned rat.

"We have to keep him alive," I said, shaking my head. "So, if you're thinking about doing something naughty—not gonna happen."

Marcel grabbed Alternate Frank by the chin and shoved his head back, then he leaned in close enough to whisper:

"One day I will cut your balls off and feed them to you."

"You can eat sh—" Alternate Frank started to say, but Marcel sucker punched him in the mouth and blood poured from the wound.

"You don't have the right to speak to me," Marcel hissed, the cords standing out on his neck.

He looked like he wanted to say more—a lot more—but I grabbed him by the shirt collar and pulled him to his feet.

"Do you know Cerberus?" I said, taking Marcel's good hand and leading him toward Snarly head. I didn't want him spilling any more of Alternate Frank's blood.

"We've . . . met," Marcel said as he and Snarly head eyed each other—but this was all either of them offered on the subject.

"All right, then," I said, changing the subject—my very obvious way of diffusing the situation. "Now what do we do?"

Marcel blinked at me, while Runt remained silent. Only Cerberus replied, but his words were not intended as an answer to my question.

"You're Death. It is your time to make the big decisions."

"Ha," I laughed, but Cerberus was right. It was time for me to get the show on the road.

I reached up and patted him on the chin, rubbing one of the spots I knew Runt liked. Cerberus closed his eye, leaning his head into my hand and enjoying the impromptu scratching session.

As we stood there, the rain stopped as suddenly as it'd begun. Nature's response to my powers was always an interesting thing to behold.

"Well, we don't have Drood," I said, shaking off some of the rainwater—I knew ten minutes under Hell's sun would have us all dry as a bone.

"We haven't even *seen* him," Marcel said. "But he seems to know what we're going to do before we do it."

That wasn't exactly true, but we had experienced a lot of bad luck since our arrival in Purgatory.

"I think shithead over there," I said, pointing to Alternate Frank, "was hiding out in Drood's compound. Someone brought him over to our world from his alternate universe and now he's just waiting until the two universes merge so he can take over."

Alternate Frank snorted.

"Have you got something to say?" I asked, glaring at him.

"Nope, got nothing to say to you, sis," he replied then spit out a tooth, his mouth still bloody where Marcel punched him.

"Can I kick him?" Marcel asked, glowering at Alternate Frank.

I shook my head.

"You can kick me, little priss," Alternate Frank said to Marcel. "But that don't mean I ain't gonna kick you back."

"Ignore him," I said, taking Marcel by the shoulders and forcibly turning him back around to look at me.

Marcel was like a small child with poor impulse control. I

was really gonna have to watch him, or else he was gonna beat Alternate Frank's face in when I wasn't looking.

"Drood knew you were coming," Marcel said, his nostrils flaring. "He'd spelled the house against you."

"It was a precaution," I disagreed. "The only person who knew where we were going was Jarvis—and I trust him as much as I trust myself."

Marcel raised an eyebrow.

"Oh, shut up," I said, punching him in his good arm. "I'm totally trustworthy."

Making fun of me seemed to have taken the edge off Marcel's bad mood. Not that I blamed him; he'd been clinically dead, for God's sake—and no one felt like doing the hokey pokey after something like that. I was just getting ready to say as much when I felt a concussive *boom* ratchet through my body, so loud I instinctively covered my ears to protect them.

"What the hell?" I said, as I removed my palms from the side of my head, only to discover that a cacophonous ringing in my eardrums was affecting my ability to hear properly.

Marcel, who was still facing me, pointed to something or someone just over my shoulder. I whirled around to discover Daniel walking toward me, the original copy of *How to Be Death*, the one written in Angelic tongue and impossible to read, held out in front of him like an offering.

He said something, but I could only make out a few of the words, the rest were gibberish.

I shook my head.

"I can't hear anything," I said. I knew I was speaking too loudly, but that's what happens when you can't hear anything. "How did you get the book and how did you get here?"

Once again, Daniel spoke, but all I managed to decipher was: Jarvis and massacre. Neither of those two words left me with a happy feeling in my stomach.

"Just . . . stop . . . for a minute," I said, shaking my head, as if this would somehow restore my hearing. "I can't hear anything."

Daniel nodded, letting me know he understood. I turned back to Marcel.

"Can *you* hear anything?"

He shrugged and I took that as a "yes." I switched my gaze from Marcel to Runt, who also nodded, and then, finally, to Cerberus, who was already talking to Daniel—so obviously his hearing hadn't been affected, either.

As I watched, Daniel grabbed Snarly head in a headlock and then the two of them, a grown man and a three-headed hellhound, were rolling around in the sand, tussling with each other. I'd seen them get all rowdy together before, and, I had to admit, it was pretty darn adorable.

But back to the problem at hand.

Why was I the only one who couldn't hear anything?

I leaned my head to the right and smacked the heel of my palm against my temple a couple of times then switched sides, repeating the process. This was something I'd done as a kid when I was trying to get the water out of my ear canal after I'd gone swimming. Needless to say, it didn't work in this water-less situation.

Daniel, clothes covered in dirt and sand, set his hand on my shoulder and I jumped. Not being able to hear made normal interaction nearly impossible.

Daniel held *How to Be Death* out for me to take, and I extended my palm, letting him slip the tiny tome into my hand. Instantly, my ability to hear returned in a rush and I was able to catch Cerberus saying:

". . . if Drood wants a battle, he's going to get one."

He was talking to Marcel, who was nodding.

"I can hear again," I said as I put the book into my back pocket and then grabbed Daniel, pulling him into me so I could squeeze him tight.

He seemed confused at first, but then he grinned and leaned down to kiss me.

"I missed you," I whispered in his ear, after we'd broken apart and I was carefully ensconced under his arm.

"I missed you, too," he said, pulling me even closer.

As for my temporary hearing loss, I was pretty sure it was the book's way of punishing me for not protecting it better. Here it was, down in Hell—which was probably the *worst* place for it—under the former Devil's protégé's control, so why wouldn't it be pissed off at me?

It was amazing how, as I'd learned to embrace my supernatural existence, I'd also had to accept that, sometimes, books and other curios behaved like human beings instead of inanimate objects.

"And then what happened?" Cereberus was asking Daniel, in what seemed to be a more thorough exploration of the subject they'd been talking about while I'd been partially deaf.

"Freezay and a Siren wormholed directly into Sea Verge, breaking a protection spell Jarvis had placed on the house and giving entrée to a pack of gnarly Vargr."

"Are they all right?" I asked, terror making me lightheaded. If anything had happened to Clio . . .

"Everyone got away. Kali showed up and took things in hand, giving the rest of us a chance to escape."

"Where are they now?" Marcel asked—and I could feel Daniel tense.

My boyfriend did *not* enjoy being interrogated. It did nothing but put him on the defensive and make him seem guilty, even when he wasn't.

"There was . . . Something happened," Daniel began, "and the car I was driving exploded—"

"Oh my God," I said, beginning to freak out again.

"I was able to wormhole everyone away, but then things went funny and we were separated. I called Morrigan to come get your mom—"

I took a step away from him, my thoughts spinning. What was Caoimhe doing at Sea Verge? I'd specifically told Jarvis not to let her know what was going on because I knew she'd be safer this way. And if, God forbid, there were any problems, or if I ceased to exist, I knew Morrigan would protect her. I may not have "loved" my birth mother's choice of partner, but I knew Morrigan was a gifted warrior, one who'd guard Caoimhe with her life.

"When I found out what was happening, I thought she needed to know," Daniel said, looking sheepish.

I took another step away from him and Runt padded over, leaning her head against my leg in a show of support.

"I was just doing what I thought was right," he added. "She's your mother. She deserves to know when her child is in danger."

I knew I shouldn't be angry with Daniel for doing what he

thought was best, but I was annoyed. Still, what was done was done and there was nothing I could do to change it—and knowing Caoimhe had actually come to Sea Verge to protect me did make me feel all warm and mushy on the inside.

It was amazing to realize Caoimhe had done more for me in the last twenty-four hours than my adopted mother had *ever* done. Caoimhe was willing to step up to the plate when the going got rough, while the woman who had raised me had run off to the sea, leaving Clio and me to fend for ourselves after our dad's death.

As much as I hated to compare the two women, Caoimhe was clearly the winner in my book.

"It's okay," I said, giving Runt a pat on the head before walking back over to Daniel. "I know you were just doing what you thought was best."

He grinned at me.

"Thank you for saying that, Cal. It's appreciated. I really was trying to help."

I let him take my hand again and I leaned against him, glad to have the comfort of his nice, warm body.

"So how did you find me?" I asked.

"The book brought me to you," he said, kissing the top of my head. "I asked it to find you and then I was here—though it wasn't like any wormhole I've ever been through. More like a doorway."

It sounded like the book had the same magical properties as the hellhound populace—which meant no one could track you when you were traveling by the *How to Be Death* book.

I was really starting to wish Jarvis were here with us. My Executive Assistant had an almost encyclopedic knowledge of magic and the Afterlife. If anyone knew what kind of magic the book and my hellhound friends were using, it would be Jarvis.

"I'm just glad you're here," I said, intertwining my fingers in his. "I'm sorry I didn't come find you. It was all just so crazy. Plus . . . I wanted to protect you guys, if, you know, I ceased to exist."

I felt stupid for not just going to him earlier, confiding in him about what was happening to me.

"It doesn't matter, Cal," he said, ruffling my hair. "We're together now."

I looked up at my big, strong boyfriend, happy to have him here with us on our journey. Cerberus and Runt seemed happy he was here, too—only Marcel was skeptical, continuing to give Daniel strange looks and asking inappropriate questions whenever I let him get a word in edgewise.

Which wasn't very often.

"So this is the guy who's going to take over Death, Inc., after Drood erases you from the history books?" Daniel asked, looking over at Alternate Frank.

"Yup," I said.

"You think you have the right to be here?" Daniel growled at Alternate Frank before giving Runt a quick pat on the head and then leaving me to walk over to the prisoner. "You think what you're doing is right? Ruining the Golden Age of Death just because you can, you selfish prick."

Like Marcel before him, I was afraid Daniel was gonna go to town on Alternate Frank, but he restrained himself.

"Calliope won't let me torture him," Marcel said to Daniel, in a matter-of-fact tone.

Daniel looked over at me.

"I think it's worth a try, Cal," he said.

I shook my head just as Alternate Frank began to laugh, his face so sunburnt I thought the skin was going to split over the sharpness of his cheekbones.

"Torture me all you want, sis," he said. "I'll die before I talk to the likes of you."

I raised an eyebrow in Daniel and Marcel's direction, as if to say: "See?"

Snarly head seconded my thought.

"Alive for now, boys," he said. "You'll be able to have your way with him soon enough."

Even though he was basically espousing what I was thinking, I was still disturbed by the lack of emotion in Snarly head's voice. I didn't like the vibe the men around me were putting out; it stunk of testosterone and anger.

"We'll just see what happens," I said, trying to diffuse the tension in the air. "Maybe Alternate Frank will be smart and decide to spill his guts of his own volition."

There was another cackle from Alternate Frank—but it was drowned out by the sound of a terrified, feminine scream.

One that was coming from not very far away.

I looked at the others.

"Cerberus, can you manage numb nuts over there?" I said, pointing at Alternate Frank.

Snarly head nodded, and one of the dumb heads used its teeth to grab ahold of the taut rope binding Alternate Frank's wrists and ankles together, then the dumb head hoisted the annoying little shit up into the air, ready to be transported. Alternate Frank did not take well to being manhandled and started screeching about wanting to be put down. The other dumb head decided what Alternate Frank was *really* saying was that he wanted to be licked, and it used its giant tongue to do as requested, licking Alternate Frank into a strained silence.

Then, together, the six of us took off in search of the owner of the scream.

twenty-one

Bernadette screamed again as the East Gatekeeper tried to shove her forward onto the path leading through the foaming red sea.

The Blood Sea.

"No! I won't go!" she cried, shoving him back.

She was bigger than him and had the terror of a pinioned heifer on the way to the slaughterhouse behind the shove. It sent the man in the caftan flying, his butt hitting the ground with a satisfying *thud*.

"If you think I enjoy forcing you souls down the path to attrition, then you are wrong," he said, glaring at her as he picked himself back up and dusted off his caftan. "I am just as much of a sinner as you."

They squared off against each other, neither one willing to give an inch.

Bernadette would never have gone with those horrible twins if she'd known they were taking her to Hell. No one had breathed a word about going to *Hell*. That was never part of the deal.

Even though he was bearing the brunt of her anger, she didn't blame the East Gatekeeper for her troubles. He had a job to do, and Bernadette understood this. She'd been the office manager at a dental practice for over twenty-two years, so she was no stranger to spotting a good work ethic when she saw one, and the East Gatekeeper was nothing, if not diligent. She wasn't trying to step on his toes or get him in trouble—she just didn't want to go to Hell.

"They never said anything about Hell," Bernadette breathed, her large bosom shifting up and down as she tried to catch her breath. "I'm not perfect, but I've done nothing in my life that would send me here."

The East Gatekeeper sighed. She was well aware he'd heard this excuse before.

"Sometimes we don't want to accept certain . . . things . . . about ourselves," he offered. "That doesn't mean we aren't at the place we're supposed to be."

Bernadette didn't like where he was going with this and was determined to nip it in the bud before he got any further. In life, she'd been extremely good at getting things done and she would just apply the same principle here: She would "common sense" the East Gatekeeper to death.

"There must be someone you can call? Someone who knows who is supposed to go to Hell and who is supposed to go to Heaven? A list perhaps?" Bernadette asked, setting her fists on her hips and cocking her head. "Someone upstairs, maybe?"

The East Gatekeeper knew a troublemaker when he saw one. They came through every now and then, caused a scene, and then ended up going to Hell anyway. He'd found it was easier to just prove to them they were in the wrong, and if they got violent, he'd call in the Bugbears. He hated to do it—with their prehensile tails and strange teddy bear–like features, the creatures that policed Hell gave him the willies—but sometimes it was necessary.

"Fine. I will consult the list. If I prove to you that you are on it," the East Gatekeeper said, "then you'll go without a fight."

Bernadette had righteousness on her side—and complete confidence in the life she'd lived on Earth.

"Go ahead. Make my day."

She'd always wanted to say that. She was a big Clint Eastwood fan, and had even gone with a few girlfriends to visit Carmel when he was the mayor of the tiny town, just to see if they could catch a glimpse of Dirty Harry. Of course, they hadn't sighted their idol, but they'd stayed in a lovely bed and breakfast overlooking the water and had eaten their way through a number of exquisite meals in the three days they were there.

"Give me one moment," the East Gatekeeper said.

He snapped his fingers twice, the sound echoing in the vastness of the desert, and a large scroll appeared before him on what amounted to a freestanding, wooden toilet paper holder. He took a pair of reading glasses from his caftan pocket and slid them onto his nose.

"This may take a few minutes . . . a lot of names here," he said, yanking on the end of the roll and starting to read.

"Take your time," Bernadette said, relaxing for the first time since she'd gotten there.

She'd been wrong to let those horrible Victorian twins browbeat her into submission. She'd let fear get in the way of common sense. It wasn't a bad response—she was a fierce grandmother and Bart's safety really was the most important thing—but if she went to Hell now, then she might never see her grandson again. She knew, in her grandmother's heart, Bart was going to go to Heaven, and if she were stuck here, in this overheated desert, there would be no reunion with him.

And this was not something she wanted to risk happening.

While she watched, the East Gatekeeper ran through the whole of the scroll with absolutely no luck and Bernadette could see his confusion. He cleared his throat, holding out his finger to let her know he'd need another minute, then he started back at the beginning. On this pass, he took his time with each name, the worried creases on his forehead elongating the closer he got to the end of the scroll.

"Not finding it?"

He looked up at her, brow furrowed.

"But I know your name," he said. "How can I know your name if you're not on the list?"

Bernadette shrugged.

"I have no idea, but does this mean I'm free to go?"

The East Gatekeeper shook his head.

"I need to get confirmation from the higher-ups."

He began to rub his chin in an obsessive manner, his eyes unfocused.

"Something is very, very wrong here . . ." he mumbled under his breath, returning to the scroll.

"Can I help you?" Bernadette asked. "I used to be an office manager. I'm very good with paperwork."

The East Gatekeeper, looking more befuddled than ever, shook his head.

"No, the offer is appreciated, but I don't think it would be wise."

"Why not?" Bernadette asked, crossing the space between them in one long stride—she knew a man who was ripe for being bossed when she saw one.

"Well, it's just not done . . ." he began, but trailed off.

"I won't tell anyone if you don't," she said, holding out her hand for him to shake.

He stared at her fingers, uncertainly. Finally, he sighed and took them in his own hand, pumping her arm up and down.

"Thank you," he said, and she could see he was grateful for any and all help she might offer . . . and she also sensed he was lonely.

Very lonely.

"I think if we're going to work together," Bernadette said, "we should be on a first name basis."

"Oh, yes, of course," he said, releasing her hand and giving her a shy smile.

"I'm Judas. Judas Iscariot, the Guardian of The East Gate of Hell."

Bernadette had not expected him to say that, but she supposed she wasn't totally surprised. Where else would Judas Iscariot, the betrayer of Jesus Christ, be, but in Hell?

Well, she'd never been one to judge. Sometimes bad things happened to good people—and Bernadette had always believed in the old adage: There but for the grace of God, go I.

"It's nice to meet you, Judas," she said, returning his smile. "Let's see if we can figure this thing out."

the screams had come from somewhere ahead of them, Cerberus had told Daniel. So this was the direction they took: Cerberus in the lead (with Alternate Frank dangling from the mouth of one of his dumb heads), he and Marcel behind the hellhound, and Callie and Runt bringing up the rear. The girls were slower than the boys and they had to be mindful of their speed, so they wouldn't lose the stragglers.

Daniel knew for a fact Runt was almost as fast as her father, Cerberus, but was going slow on purpose in order to stay close to Callie. His girlfriend had never been much of an athlete, but she looked exhausted now. He wondered when she'd last slept, and figured from the dark circles under her eyes it'd probably been days.

She caught him checking on her and winked at him.

He wanted to pick her up and throw her over his shoulder, and then get them both the heck out of Hell. He knew it wasn't her favorite place—she'd avoided it whenever possible, not even coming down to visit him when he'd taken over as Steward of Hell—and he understood her rationale, but it still kind of hurt his feelings. He'd long ago learned not to take Callie's slights personally because she had no idea some of the things she said and did were hurtful to him. He knew eventually they'd have to talk about it, but for now, he just took what she did with a grain of salt, knowing her intentions were good—and her heart was in the right place.

"The East Gate!" Cerberus called from the next dune.

Daniel picked up his pace, Marcel sticking close to him, and then they were cresting the dune and heading down the long stretch of sand toward the East Gate of Hell.

The East Gate was where the monotheists entered Hell—and this didn't just include the Judeo-Christian-Islamic religions, but also Hinduism and any other religion that worshipped a single God (who might or might not wear many masks). It was delineated from the outer deserts of Hell by the Scarlet Sea, through which all souls entering via this gate had to pass on their way to the interior of Hell. Judas Iscariot was the Gatekeeper and had been for centuries. He'd never given the Devil—or Daniel—any trouble and did his job well and without question.

Still, the stink of failure and loss enveloped the man, and anyone who spent time with him could see he was lonely and terribly guilt ridden. He did his penance in silence, never complaining, and seemed almost happy about being punished for his sins.

"It's just another soul," Daniel said, as he and Marcel caught up to Cerberus, who'd been waiting for them at the bottom of the dune.

Wiping the sweat from his brow—the heat and physical exertion had soaked him—Daniel turned around to make sure Callie and Runt were still behind them. The girls, at their slower pace, had just crested the dune and were making their way down.

Daniel saw Judas Iscariot had caught sight of them and was waving them forward.

"He may need help," Cerberus said, inclining his head. "He's called for the scroll."

Cerberus had been the Guardian of the North Gate of Hell for many years and knew the drill. If Judas Iscariot had called for the Scroll of Names, then there was some contention between the soul and their proposed destination. Usually this was just a dodge, some soul trying to get out of its punishment. But, occasionally, some paper pusher at Death, Inc., made a mistake and a soul was sent to the wrong place.

The most infamous case concerned Heinrich Himmler and Heaven. Needless to say, there'd been a lot of irate people in Heaven who'd immediately notified the powers that be, letting them know a terrible mistake had been made. They'd found Himmler hiding in a cupcake shop in the Elysian Heights section of Heaven, pretending he was a German dog trainer named Heinrich Hitzinger, who had no idea who "this Heinrich Himmler person" they were searching for was.

"What's going on?" Callie asked, as she caught up with Daniel—and a moment later, Runt padded up behind her.

"He's got the Scroll of Names out," Daniel said. "It means he and the soul are in disagreement about where the soul should be going."

Callie nodded, shading her eyes with her hand.

"I think he's trying to get your attention," she said, pointing to Judas Iscariot, who was waving for them to join him, his reading glasses held aloft from his face so he could see them better.

"We should go," Cerberus said.

No one disagreed.

They moved toward the Scarlet Sea as a group, but this time Callie held Daniel's hand as they walked.

Judas Iscariot didn't wait for them to reach him. He took off, holding his caftan up to his knees so he wouldn't trip over it as he ran. The soul in contention, an older woman with a massive bosom housed inside a flowery top, came with him, too. She had thick gray hair and a doughy, grandmotherly face, but like an old battleship, she was more than formidable.

"How did you know?" Judas Iscariot said, his eyes full of awe.

"The Scroll of Names," Cerberus said, as if this explained everything.

Judas Iscariot was floored. He looked at Cerberus reverently.

"Of course, the Scroll of Names."

It was the grandmotherly soul who stepped in and cleared things up. Otherwise the inscrutable Judas Iscariot/Cerberus back-and-forth might have gone on forever.

"I got railroaded into coming to Hell by a pair of twins dressed up as Victorian dollies. They strong-armed me here against my will, but they never said a word about 'here' being Hell."

She gave one big definitive nod, letting them know she was done, then she turned to look at Judas Iscariot for confirmation.

"It's true," he said, smiling shyly at the older woman. "Bernadette isn't on the Scroll of Names. Someone brought her here by mistake. And there are other names missing."

He pointed back to the Scarlet Sea, where the scroll waited.

"So many in the past weeks. I knew their names, so I never once thought to double-check any of them against the scroll."

"I hardly ever checked the scroll when I was at the North Gate," Cerberus said. "It wasn't necessary."

Judas Iscariot looked uneasy now, his eyes flicking back to the grandmother.

"Go on, Judas," she said. "Tell them what you told me."

He swallowed, wrapping his arms around himself, protectively.

"Sometimes, I get lonely—" He stopped, his cheeks turning bright red, as he realized how what he'd said could be misconstrued. "Oh, no, no, no . . . nothing like *that*! Not sexual, but just . . . friendly. I get lonely for someone to talk to."

Callie released Daniel's fingers and walked over to Judas Iscariot. She placed her hand on his shoulder and smiled warmly up at him.

"And then, one day, someone to talk to just magically showed up at the Gate," she said, her voice soft and gentle.

Judas Iscariot nodded.

"He said he was working on something secret, something for God."

Callie nodded.

"And he asked for your help?"

Judas Iscariot shook his head violently.

"No, nothing like that. He only said he was lonely, too, working on this secret project for God, and that he'd seen me here and thought we might talk."

He looked over at the grandmother, who gave him a thumbs-up.

"So we would talk every now and then when his work brought him near the East Gate," Judas finished.

Callie patted his arm, her dark eyes catching his own, letting him know he was doing well.

"I think the man, your friend, put a spell on you," she said. "He implanted names into your head so he could run souls into Hell, souls that didn't belong there, for his own not-so-nice purposes."

With those words, Judas Iscariot broke down, his entire body wracked with sobs. The grandmother was instantly at his side, holding him. Callie continued to pat his shoulder.

"I . . . I am . . . I wanted to be . . . *forgiven* . . . and now . . . I've ruined myself . . . again."

He fell to his knees, hands clasped together reverently, eyes heavenward.

"Please God . . . smite me . . . here," he sobbed. "Take away . . . this . . . terrible suffering."

But there was no answer from above.

Callie knelt down in front of him, took his hands in hers and said:

"It's not your fault. I promise you when this is all over we will find a way to end your suffering, but right now, I need you to tell me about the man who tricked you. Because he's trying to destroy our world and you are the only one who can help us stop him."

from his perch on a faraway dune, the Man in Gray watched the drama unfold. He saw the tortured Judas Iscariot fall to his knees, begging for mercy. Saw the little Death go to him, take his hands in hers, ask him for his help . . . he watched it all.

And he felt nothing.

Not that this surprised him. He'd long ago ceased experiencing emotions like regret, guilt, and sorrow. He knew little of those—but hate and anger and bitterness . . . he was cut from their cloth. They swelled in his chest, filling the place where a human heart should be. He fed on their whispers, lived for how they vilified humanity and all the creatures that existed alongside of the humans. No one had ever had sympathy for him, and so he had sympathy for no one.

He knew Judas Iscariot would spill his guts. It was a given. That was why the Man in Gray had chosen his words carefully, made sure the traitor of Jesus only knew a few limited things about him and his work. He could've shared more, would've shared more, had he been able to permanently secure the other man's silence.

But this wasn't available to him.

He'd very much wanted to share his thoughts with someone—and maybe he *had* shared more than he should've with Judas Iscariot. Just because of that need, of that wanting to be heard and understood. If anyone could understand his feelings, it was Judas. They were both sinful criminals, both forced to do God's bidding. It was God who'd created them to be what they were; God who'd instilled in them the needs and wants of a human being—and the brains to think all these dark and terrible thoughts with. The Man in Gray didn't believe in free will. He knew humans were programmed to do as they were told, even though sometimes the things asked of them got them eternal punishment at God's own hand.

The Man in Gray hated God for this, and what better way to punish the Creator than to destroy his master creation: humanity.

He would erase the human race and no one, not even little Death, was going to get in his way. It did worry him slightly he was relying on Drood's minions to stop Death and her friends— she should never have been allowed to meet Judas Iscariot, or get this far into Hell in the first place. He realized, once again, he may have misjudged things. It looked as though he was going to have to look after this loose end himself.

And then he had an epiphany.

A grand idea filled his body and made him shudder with excitement. It was so simple and amazing he didn't know why he hadn't thought of it before. He would let Death and her friends plunder Judas Iscariot's mind and find whatever information the Man in Gray had left in there. If Death was as formidable as she should be, she would figure out the Man in Gray's little ruse and come to *The Pit* to try and stop him.

And that was where he would be waiting.

The thought of Death inside *The Pit* made him gleeful. If he could harness the power of Death's soul, then there was nothing he might not accomplish. He imagined Death's face as the power from *The Pit* spun out of control and the two universes did more than just collide . . . they cancelled each other out.

Boom!

The end of Earth, and its Afterlife, forever!

It didn't bother him one iota he would be incinerated along with the rest of Earth. He was looking forward to oblivion, something that'd been denied him for what felt like an eternity. He just wished he could be there to see God's face when it happened. This would be the ultimate fuck you: God, turning to see who had done this horrible deed, and finding it was none other than he, the Man in Gray, who'd destroyed the world.

And then the Man in Gray—who was once Enoch, writer of the Angelic book that bespoke the End of Days—would see everything he had wrought, and behold, it would be *very* good.

twenty-two

Jarvis had never been to the New Newbridge Academy. He knew of it, of course, because Calliope had been invited to attend when she was a child—the only one of Death's children to be offered a place at the school, but anything he had heard about the school came from Calliope's own mouth or from the school's reputation, which had preceded it.

As he'd walked across the lawn toward the burnt-out building on the far side of the property, he'd had to admit the place was beautiful. The Gothic architecture, the brick facades, the greenery as far as one's eye could see—he understood now why Noh and Calliope felt so connected to the school. It was magical.

Night had finally descended on them like a heavy blanket as they'd trooped, single file, across the lawn. Jennice had quickened her pace in time with the dissipating twilight until she was almost on top of Jarvis. He'd sensed her fear and offered her his hand, which she'd greedily accepted. Thankfully, her fingers were warm, and not at all clammy.

"Henry wants us to go this way," Noh was saying, as she led them through the darkness toward the side entrance of the burnt-out building.

"This place is creepy," Jennice whispered in Jarvis's ear as they came to the undamaged side door and watched as Noh eased it open, eliciting a loud *creeeak* from the rusty hinges.

"It's not really scary," Noh promised, patting the doorframe like an old friend. "This is just where all the ghosts live, so they want us where they can keep an eye on us, in case any bad guys do the old 'showing up unannounced' trick."

She stepped through the doorway and disappeared inside. Jennice looked at Jarvis, who shrugged.

"It can't hurt to go in," he said, uncertainly.

"But it's haunted."

That was an understatement. If what Noh said was true, then the place was crawling with ghosts.

Noh had tried to explain this to them earlier, as they'd entered the school grounds and begun the walk toward the main buildings.

"The New Newbridge Academy is special. The ghosts of kids who've died while attending the school . . . well, they tend to stick around—and there are a lot of them because the school has been around for a long time."

She'd said all of this without interruption, though every now and then she'd paused, head cocked as though she were listening to someone. The someone in question was her ghostly friend, Henry, who was the one guiding them through the main buildings toward the burnt-out one in the back.

"The building we're going to may look like it should be condemned, but I promise you, it's safe," Noh had said, trudging ahead like a schoolmarm, leading a bunch of errant children.

"Where is everyone?" Jennice asked quietly, her eyes scanning the buildings for "living" occupants.

"The school closed down last year, so right now there's no one here," Jarvis replied.

Calliope had been most upset when she'd gotten the news, but her hands had been so full between her day job—she'd been the Assistant to the Vice-President of Sales at a company called House and Yard—and learning to take over the family business, that there was nothing she could do to stop it.

"My aunt taught at New Newbridge for years," Noh said, "but things change, ya know. Nothing you can do about that. Still, it's a good old place. Lots of magic here."

This was the very reason he'd suggested they come to the New Newbridge Academy. It was magically secure and there were no living creatures to get caught in the middle of all the craziness. As they crossed the threshold of the decrepit building, Jarvis could only hope whatever magic still remained at New Newbridge would keep them safe.

"Follow me," Jarvis said, taking Jennice's hand and guiding her through the doorway.

Noh was waiting for them, a small brass candleholder with a lit candle resting in her hand.

"Come this way," she said in a low, spooky voice then she giggled. "Seriously, stop looking like you ate a bug, Jennice. It's a-okay here. I swear. I spent half my childhood running around this place. It's the place I love the most in all the world."

The side door they'd entered the building through had brought them into a large, and long disused, laundry room. Cobwebs hung from the ceiling, and dirt and debris littered the floor; the industrial washers and dryers were caked with crud. The only living creatures that had spent any time here in recent years were of the rodent persuasion. Jarvis could see rat droppings mixed in with the dirt.

Very unsanitary.

"Henry says no one's seen anything," Noh told them. "So I think we're okay for now."

Jarvis tended to agree with her. The New Newbridge Academy had a long tradition of protecting the supernatural children of the East Coast of the United States. It was why Calliope and Clio's dad had finally relented and let Calliope attend the school. He'd wanted to keep his middle child under his thumb in Newport; hire tutors and personally make sure she was protected at all times—but it'd been Calliope's (adopted) mother who'd encouraged him to send her to the boarding school.

He knew Calliope believed she'd been sent away because she was unwanted, but this was hardly the case. The decision to send her to the New Newbridge Academy had been a very difficult one—and probably the smartest, too, because even back then there were people who wanted to do away with the special little girl.

In fact, as if to prove Calliope's (adopted) mother right in insisting they send the girl to New Newbridge, the only major attempt on her life had come when she was home from boarding school. She'd been involved in a terrible car accident. The perpetrators had been under the (misguided) impression her immortal weakness was steel and they had engineered a car crash in order to get rid of her—instead that'd taken the lives of Calliope's two best friends from Newport. The choice had been made *not* to tell her she was the cause of her friends' deaths; her parents thought the guilt would be too much for Calliope to bear.

Jarvis had believed they were making a huge mistake and had fought to tell the girl the truth. He'd seen her change dramatically after the accident—and not for the better. She'd turned inward, an angry, sullen teenager replacing the gregarious, giggling girl who'd skipped around Sea Verge, bringing light and happiness wherever she went.

The powers that be had been wrong to keep her in the dark. This only allowed her pain and anger to fester. The girl's fate was going to include guilt no matter how they tried to protect her. Better to help her embrace what she was instead of letting her grow up to loathe all the things that made her unique. Jarvis had watched as Calliope had turned away from her immortality and her family, trying to mold herself into a "normal" girl. It was a horrible transformation to behold—and it had torn Calliope's father apart to watch it.

Neither Death nor his middle daughter had ever been the same after that.

"Let's go to the back stairs and then up to Henry's room," Noh said, urging them forward with the candle. "It's lovely there."

How anything could be lovely in the upstairs of a burned-out building, Jarvis didn't know, but he followed Noh out of the laundry room and into a smaller, dustier hallway. Here there was a dilapidated stairwell leading to the upper levels of the building, and as Jarvis and Jennice watched, Noh traversed it like a mountain goat, nimbly maneuvering her way around the broken steps.

"You think it'll hold us?" Jennice asked.

"We shall know soon enough," Jarvis said, putting his foot on the first step, then letting his weight settle.

Luckily, the step appeared to hold him.

"It's all right," Jarvis continued. "Just step where I step and you should be fine."

"She went up these things pretty fast," Jennice said. "You sure she's not a ghost, too?"

This made Jarvis laugh.

"If she's a ghost, then I want to be exactly like her when I die."

The funny thing was he wasn't joking. Noh was growing on him. Ghostly or not, she, like Calliope, was definitely a force to be reckoned with—and Jarvis had a soft spot for strong-willed women. In fact, the woman Jarvis was currently smitten with put Calliope and Noh *both* to shame. His special lady friend, Minnie, was like Mother Nature to their gale force winds.

He wondered how Minnie was doing and if she knew what was happening down here on Earth. He doubted she, or God, her boss, missed anything—they always seemed to have a finger on the pulse of humanity.

To his surprise, thinking about Minnie made him feel better. He found he didn't really mind being in a dirty building with cobwebs and mouse droppings, chaperoning two will-o'-the-wisp girls. Just knowing Minnie was out there, waiting for him made him feel as though everything would be all right in the end.

These thoughts were interrupted when Jarvis's sensitive nose decided it'd had enough of dusty, dirty environs and let out a massive sneeze that rattled his body. This was followed by a second, and even more explosive sneeze, which forced Jarvis to reach into his suit coat pocket for his handkerchief.

His hand found the handkerchief easily enough, but as he reached around inside the pocket, it was with dawning horror Jarvis discovered something else was not where it was supposed to be: The original, Angelic copy of *How to Be Death* was gone.

they'd been able to dodge their pursuers by following the secret passageway. Until it dead-ended at a blank brick wall. The lighting inside the passage was so low Clio had to use her hands to search the walls, hoping to find a secret button or latch that would allow them to continue onward, but she came back empty-handed.

"Now whadda we do?" Frank asked, but it was less a question and more a whine of defeat.

Clio was never one to give up easily.

"We turn around and go back the way we came. They have to be gone by now, I would think. It's been hours."

Clio hoped she was right. It did feel like they'd been walking for hours—but with the ever-present gray limestone floor and walls, it was hard to get a bearing on how long they'd actually been inside the passage.

"You think that's such a good idea?" Frank asked.

He looked even worse than when she'd first discovered him. His cheeks were razor blades protruding from the sides of his face, his eyes all bruised and sunken in. Whatever process was causing this marked change in Frank, it was progressing at an alarming rate. She just hoped she could get him out of Purgatory before he totally wasted away.

"I don't have another plan up my sleeve, so . . ." She trailed off, happily daring him to come up with something better— anything to keep them out of the bad guys' clutches.

Frank shook his head, and they were both horrified when a handful of his hair fell out, floating to the floor.

"Jesus," Clio breathed, as Frank's face tightened and he reached up, gently patting his scalp.

Even more hair came out in his hand and he lurched forward, his gait unsteady. Clio grabbed him around the waist, so he wouldn't fall over then helped him to sit down on the cold, stone floor. Once he was on his butt, he promptly rolled into the fetal position and began to rock back and forth against the wall.

Because he was doing it so silently, it took Clio a moment to realize Frank was crying—the tip-off was his skinny rib cage moving up and down in an exaggerated manner as the sobs wracked his body. It was pathetic to watch Frank cry, his whole body overtaken by emotion. Clio wanted to avert her eyes, walk away, and give him some privacy, but compassion filled her veins and she knelt down beside him, her hand reaching out to touch his wasted cheek.

"Does it hurt?" she asked, and he nodded.

"I feel all achy and feverish, like I got the flu," he whispered, the tears still coursing down his face. He reached up and wiped them away, but it was a futile gesture because there were already more coming.

"Okay, we have to get you out of here. Damn the assholes, we're taking a wormhole. I don't care if they follow us," she said, putting her hand on Frank's shoulder.

"You know, you remind me of a friend I once had," Frank said suddenly. "He was brave like you, willing to fight the good fight."

It felt strange having Frank describe her as "brave" because all she felt right then was weak and scared. The polar opposite of brave.

"He died when we were real young—"

Frank was still talking and Clio realized he was delirious.

"I let him down, though. Shoulda been there when he needed me, but I was sick . . . and I let him down. Then the animals got him."

"I can't imagine that's true—" she began to say, but Frank only shook his head, the violence of the action bouncing his skull off the limestone. Clio knew it must've hurt him, but Frank seemed to have embraced the pain as his punishment.

"You don't know . . . you don't know," he moaned.

"Okay, we're gonna get you out of here now."

But Frank wasn't listening. His eyes were rolled up in his head, fluttering back and forth like moth wings.

"Frank?" Clio said, shaking him. He didn't respond, his rigid body starting to thrash. She watched in dismay as his head slammed into the limestone wall over and over again.

Clio didn't know what to do. She'd never seen anyone have a seizure before, didn't know how to help him. She just had to sit there and wait until it was over.

"Frank?" she kept asking, trying to break through to him, but he was gone, trapped inside his flailing body.

When it was finally finished, Frank slumped against the wall, his limp body unable to move. His eyes were unfocused, but Clio could see he was still conscious and alive inside.

She didn't waste another second, just used her powers to call up a wormhole right there in Death, Inc., under everyone's nose.

It appeared with a low rumbling that came to a crescendo as a flash of light rent the air in front of them.

"Let's scram," she said, dragging Frank toward the shimmering tear in the fabric of space/time.

He opened his mouth, trying to speak, but Clio shushed him.

"Not the time," she said—and then she pulled him through the wormhole behind her.

The magic hit her hard enough to take her breath away. And if *she* was feeling it, then she knew it was even worse for Frank. She'd always made fun of Callie for her hatred of traveling by wormhole, but if this was Cal's experience every time she took one, then Clio finally understood her dislike.

She felt as though she and Frank were socks in a washer, getting all tumbled around on the heavy cycle. It wasn't the end of the world, but it wasn't fun, either; especially for Frank, who was already hurting so much.

This thought made her wonder if the reason for someone having a terrible wormhole experience might lie in the psyche of the person doing the traveling. Callie was predisposed to hate the experience, so her brain created what she was expecting—and she had a feeling Frank, sick as he was, might be of the same mind as her sister.

Like two rag dolls, the wormhole spit Clio and Frank out in the middle of a gravel driveway, a few feet away from Clio's Honda Element. She had no idea where they'd ended up, just that she'd asked the wormhole to bring them to her car, wherever it might be. She *had* expected to find Jarvis and Noh with the Element, so it was kind of a disappointment to pick herself up and discover the car was abandoned.

"Damn," she muttered under her breath as she scooted over to Frank, who was lying on his side in the gravel, his skin pale blue in the moonlight.

"Callie, I'm sorry I almost killed ya," Frank said, reaching up with a shaking hand and trying to touch Clio's cheek. "It wasn't my idea. I always had a little soft spot for ya."

Shit, he thinks I'm Callie, Clio thought. *This is awkward.*

"I, uh, forgive you."

He patted her cheek.

"Thank you. Thank you for that."

He closed his eyes—and Clio had never before been so happy to have someone fall into unconsciousness. As much as she loved Callie, she just didn't have the wherewithal to deal with her sister's fucked-up love life right then.

With Frank down for the count, Clio took a moment to investigate her surroundings.

The car seemed to have been abandoned in favor of going on foot. Clio assumed the reason for this choice had been the giant wrought iron gate and heavy spelled padlock blocking the entrance—and she figured (rightly) no one was getting past the gate without a key or a counter spell.

She didn't know what to do. She'd really been hoping to find Jarvis and the others, but now she was at a loss.

Without thinking, she yelled Jarvis's name into the night sky.

That was silly, she thought, her only response coming from the crickets humming in the grass.

She sat back down in the gravel beside Frank.

She wasn't sure what to do next. She could try and drag Frank with her while she explored the grounds, looking for a way inside, or she could just leave him "resting" in the gravel— but neither option seemed very appealing.

"Shit," she said under her breath, pulling her knees up to her chest and resting her chin between her kneecaps. She knew she needed to make a plan, but she was just so frickin' tired all she wanted to do was curl up in a ball and go to sleep.

And then she remembered something important; something she should've thought of immediately.

Clio had a cell phone.

It was just too bad she didn't get a chance to use it.

caoimhe woke up in the muted silence that comes just before first light. Her head ached something fierce and her eyelids didn't want to cooperate, unwilling to open no matter how fervently she begged. So she just lay there, trying to remember what she'd done to give herself such a massive hangover. Had she been at the pub all night? She didn't think so, but no matter how hard she fought to recall the previous evening, nothing came back to her.

She focused, instead, on asking her head to stop aching— and what a joke this was. She felt like her brain had zero control over her body these days, and even less so when she was hungover. Finally, after an age, she was able to crack on eye open and get a glimpse of her surroundings. She was happy to discover she was in her own bed, in her own bedroom, in her own flat. It'd been a long time since she'd woken up in a strange place with this kind of hangover, but there'd been a time in her life—not long after she'd given Calliope up to the girl's father—that she'd tried to blot out her pain in alcohol and a string of very unfulfilling sexual dalliances with random strangers.

Her memory failed her for a moment, or maybe she'd just zoned out. But now something, some idea she was missing, started to eat at her. She ran back through her thoughts, trying to discover what the missing link was . . . alcohol, hangover, random hookups, and one's own bed . . . *Calliope*.

That was it. That was the disconnect: her daughter Calliope.

Her energy returned like a shot of adrenaline and she sat up, her body filled with purpose. She slid her legs over the side of the bed so the soles of her feet touched the floor—and the room shifted to the right, her head pounding with blood as she fought to remain upright in the wake of the vertigo.

"Don't make a sound."

She raised her head, fighting the woozy feeling trying to overtake her, and saw a tiny owlet perched on the bottom of the window frame just across from where she was sitting. It was too chilly to have the window open, but for some unknown reason, either she or Morrigan had left it open a crack, and now a little creature had taken this as an open invitation to enter the flat.

"What—" Caoimhe started to say, but the owlet shushed her with a *squawk* from its miniature beak, its downy brown feathers ruffling in annoyance.

"Quiet."

The owlet was looking at something over Caoimhe's shoulder. Caoimhe turned to find Morrigan asleep in the bed beside her, her partner's red hair splayed across the white pillow like blood splatter.

"Morrigan shouldn't know you're here?" Caoimhe asked, whispering her question.

The tiny owlet bobbed up and down, letting Caoimhe know this was the correct answer.

"She won't help you," the owlet said. *"She wants to keep you for herself."*

Caoimhe's brain was assailed by a flash of memory, something she didn't want to remember, but was important to hold on to.

Morrigan at the fireplace. Morrigan turning as Caoimhe scuttled across the bed, trying to escape.

Caoimhe closed her eyes, trying to catch more of the memory, but this was all her brain seemed to have cataloged. Of course, just this little bit was enough to make her understand the owlet's need for secrecy.

"I may not look like myself, but my owlet has kindly allowed me to share this body with it," the creature was saying, and Caoimhe had to rip herself out of her own head to make sure she was following the owlet's words.

"I came to you once, long ago when you were with child—"

Caoimhe's breath caught in her throat. This wasn't just an owlet—this was Anjea, the Vice-President in Charge of Australia for Death, Inc. The seer who'd come to her when she was pregnant with Calliope and told her her child was special and must be protected at all costs. It was because of this woman she'd given Callie up and been excommunicated from her daughter's life.

"What happened to you?" Caoimhe whispered, her body trembling with fear.

The owlet sighed, ruffling its feathers as it prepared to give her a thorough explanation.

"I knew they would come for me, so I took the precaution of splitting my soul between my body and my owlet. They came as I had predicted they would and I left my body before they could destroy it," the owlet that was Anjea said. *"It was the only way to make sure I would survive to help your daughter."*

Calliope was in danger. Caoimhe could taste it. She wondered if this was why Morrigan had been after her in the memory. If Morrigan knew something was terribly wrong and was trying to stop her from helping Callie . . . ? She shuddered, the thought too hideous to follow any further.

The owlet seemed to be reading her mind.

"Morrigan has made a deal with the God Watatsumi to support his Death, Frank, in favor of your daughter. She will stop you from going to Calliope if you wake her."

Caoimhe nodded she understood, though, if what the owlet said was true, she knew she would never return to Morrigan's bed again.

"Calliope needs our help now," the owlet continued. *"I've come to fetch you. Will you go with me?"*

"If it's to help Calliope, then I'd follow you anywhere."

Silent as a mouse, Caoimhe stood up and, ignoring her dizziness, crossed the room to her dresser. Easing the dresser drawer open as quietly as possible, she pulled out a soft white T-shirt and began the ritual of dressing.

twenty-three

CALLIOPE

Judas Iscariot had been letting way too many souls into the interior of Hell. He'd had no idea he was doing it because someone had put a spell on him, making him an unwitting poppet in a nasty game of "steal the souls." But now Judas knew what had been done to him, he was beside himself with guilt. The trick would be to calm him down enough to glean what we could about his mystery friend. I was convinced the friend would turn out to be Enoch, the guy Jarvis had mentioned in conjunction with the human translation of my *How to Be Death* book, but we would just have to wait and see what information we could cadge out of Judas.

Of course, all of this was way easier said than done.

"No more crying," I said, patting Judas's arm. "We need you to tell us everything about this mystery guy."

Judas nodded then bit his lip.

"He called himself 'the Man in Gray.'"

I wanted to say: Well, that's a stupid name.

But instead, I said:

"That's great. A great descriptor."

I looked over at Daniel and Marcel, who were standing by the bloodred sea marking the entrance to the East Gate of Hell.

They were whispering together, heads lowered so I couldn't make out what they were saying.

I decided to ignore their conspiring and concentrate on Judas. He seemed comfortable with me, Runt, Cerberus, and Bernadette (the soul who'd clued us into the discrepancies between who was *actually* on the scroll and who was a plant from the Man in Gray), but every so often he would look sideways at the boys as if he were afraid they were going to come over and attack him.

"Look right here," I said, drawing Judas's focus away from Daniel and Marcel and back to me. "Where were the souls you let in supposed to go? Did he ever say anything about that?"

Judas looked nonplussed. There were tears in the corners of his eyes, and I saw before me a beaten man, one who cowed before everyone and everything because of the centuries spent existing under the weight of such immense guilt.

"No, he didn't say a thing about anything like that. We never talked about souls."

"It's okay," Bernadette said, coming over and wrapping an arm around Judas's shoulder. "No one's trying to make you feel bad. This is all very important. Just think hard and we'll see what's hidden in that noggin of yours."

Turning the "grandmotherly setting" to high, she squeezed him to her and he finally started to calm down.

"He did sometimes refer to something he called *The Pit*," Judas whispered. "It was where he was doing his top-secret project."

Cerberus gave a start and my gaze slid to him. Something Judas said had registered with Snarly head. I could see it in his large, unblinking eye.

"What?" I asked.

Snarly head frowned, shook his head.

"It could be nothing—"

"If you're thinking it, then it's not nothing," I said.

I could tell Snarly head was pleased with my compliment.

"She'ol," he continued, more brusquely. "It has been called *The Pit* by many. It's where Enoch has spent these many centuries in imprisonment."

"Doesn't sound like he's imprisoned there anymore," Daniel offered.

I had to agree with Daniel. It looked like someone had sprung him from jail in order to further their own ends.

"Do we know where *The Pit* is?" I asked.

Daniel and Cerberus exchanged a look. Ugh, more male conspiring—it drove me nuts. If we were going to play girls against boys, then I was taking Judas for the girl's team. The boys could just hang out in the desert all by themselves and we ladies (and Judas Iscariot) would go fix the problem without them.

"Obviously you guys know something you're not telling me," I said, letting them see my annoyance.

"We've been having problems with that part of Hell for a while now," Daniel said, rubbing the weariness from his eyes. "It's always been kind of a no-man's-land, but since the Devil was deposed, it's gotten even worse. Besides, She'ol has always been the purveyance of the Angels—until recently. Since they've opted to stay mostly out of the human world these days, places like She'ol have been up in the air, as far as who has control over them."

"So someone like Enoch could be AWOL and no one would have any idea he was even gone."

At least Snarly head had the courtesy to look sheepish about not divulging this pertinent piece of information until now. Did they not think I'd want to know something like this? I mean, c'mon menfolk.

"Boys, I think it's high time you led us into the interior of Hell and showed us *The Pit*. This way we can actually try to stop the whole universe-collision-extravaganza before it's too late."

I let my gaze linger on Alternate Frank, who was hanging upside down from the dumb head's mouth, drool covering his torso. He did not look happy about it.

"Because if you want Alternate Frank here in charge, then just keep doing what you're doing," I added. "You might as well be working for the other team, the way you're withholding info."

I wanted the boys to understand who they were going to be dealing with in the future if they didn't get their butts in gear and start sharing all their information with me. Because Alternate Frank wouldn't be half as cool as I was—especially when he remembered how "nicely" they'd treated him.

"I know the way, too, and I'd like to go with you. To make up for my mistake," Judas said, a hangdog expression on his gaunt face.

It was the meekest call to arms I'd ever heard, but since he was the only one offering, I happily took him up on his services.

"Thank you, Judas. You can definitely go with us."

Judas looked surprised to be taken so seriously—especially by someone like me (Death)—and he stood a little taller after that.

"Are you guys coming?" I asked, as Runt, Bernadette, and I followed Judas toward the red sea.

"Hold on," Daniel said.

Me and my mostly female crew stopped near the water's edge, waiting.

"Someone has to stay behind and man the East Gate," he finished lamely.

"Not Cerberus," I said, raising one eyebrow to show I meant business. I wasn't going to this "*Pit*" place without Cerberus. He was one scary-ass mofo and I wanted him there with me if I ran into any trouble.

Daniel was at a loss. Obviously *he* was going to come with us—and there was no way Marcel was going to stay behind since he considered himself to be my "champion" and was all about dogging my every step, ostensibly for "protection."

"I could do it," Bernadette said quietly, all eyes turning in her direction.

"I don't think—" Daniel began, but I interrupted him.

"Great idea. Daniel, swear her in."

My boyfriend was incredulous—I don't think he'd ever been bossed so thoroughly before. He gave me a sidelong glance then shook his head, letting me know I was going to get an earful later. I hated to be a bitch, but I was more than willing to take one for the team if it meant we got the show on the road.

"Bernadette," Daniel said, purposely not looking in my direction. "With this dispensation, you are now the Guardian of the East Gate of Hell. May this confer all powers of the office to you forever and always, or until I, or my successors, should choose to revoke them. Good luck to you."

The words were no sooner out of his mouth than she began

to transform. Gone was the elderly woman we'd first met, replaced now by a ravishing young woman with dark brown hair
and raffish eyes. She held up her hands, eyes goggling at how
smooth and unlined they were. Then she touched her face, her
fingers trembling as she felt the tender, young flesh.

"I'm . . . *young* again," she breathed, tears trickling down
her cheeks. "Thank you. Thank you so much."

"My pleasure," Daniel said, and he genuinely seemed
pleased to have brought her so much joy.

As we left the newly improved Bernadette standing by the
edge of the bloodred sea, one hand on the scroll, the other waving us good-bye, I wondered how she would take to her new
job. She had a no-nonsense quality about her I really responded
to. Maybe if I got out of this thing with my life still intact, I'd
lure her away from Hell with a cushy job at Death, Inc.

I was tired of all the underhanded subterfuge, the diehard
political affiliations . . . the narcissism and bad behavior at
Death, Inc. I could really stand to have a few more people
working for me who I could trust to be on my side when the
going got tough.

I found myself at the back of the group with Daniel and
Runt as we hit the path leading into the thick of the bloodred
sea. As we walked, the water boiled and oozed around us, giving our group a bit of shade from the oppressive heat—and
giving me a little relief from the intense sweating my body had
been doing since I'd arrived in Hell.

"I'm sorry," I whispered as I reached out and took Daniel's
hand. He seemed surprised, but didn't pull away. "I shouldn't
have snapped at you. It was shitty."

He shrugged—which meant he agreed with my estimation
I'd been shitty to him.

"Mad at me?" I asked, pushing him a little.

He shook his head.

"I'm never mad at you. I just wish . . ."

He didn't finish the thought.

"Wish what?" I asked, starting to feel a little defensive.

"I just wish sometimes you would think before you speak."

"Woah," I said, his words yanking me out of my repentant
mood.

Was I just supposed to censor everything I said and did so I wouldn't offend my boyfriend? That sounded about as exciting as having my teeth pulled without Novocain.

"I don't want to talk about it right now, okay, Cal?" he said. "Can we deal with this stuff later when you're not acting all annoyed?"

Let's just say the word "annoyed" didn't even begin to cover how I was feeling.

"Sure, whatever," I said, dropping his hand and picking up my pace. "C'mon, Runt."

Runt and I took off, leaving Daniel to bring up the rear all by himself.

to get to *The Pit*, or She'ol—or whatever you chose to call it—you had to trek through some really rank parts of Hell. Not that I'd spent much time in the interior of Hell (zero time actually), so it wasn't like I had anything to compare it to. Still, I knew the nasty parts of town when I saw them . . . and our journey took us right through them.

It'd taken us a while to get beyond the bloodred sea—the path, which was sandy and irregularly planed, like the bottom of any good body of water should be, kept the going slow. We had to pick our way around sinkholes whose terminuses lay miles below us, and avoid spots where flash floods washed across the path, dragging away any stragglers who didn't start running as soon as they felt the ground rumbling beneath them.

By the time we'd reached the end of the path and stepped back onto dry land, I was really stewing over what Daniel had said to me. I didn't want to be angry with him, but I couldn't stop myself from growling on the inside.

Stupid, stupid liking of boys, I thought, anger burbling up every time I replayed our conversation in my head.

I decided the best thing I could do was to just stay away from him until I'd calmed down—and he seemed to be in agreement. A few minutes after the fight, he'd passed me by on his way to catch up with Marcel and Cerberus.

Thankfully, Runt had chosen to stay by my side, sticking as close to my heels as possible as we walked—and I found myself talking to her as we trudged along the path, even though I knew she couldn't answer me.

"Am I an evil bitch?" I asked as we'd skirted the edge of one of the larger potholes.

"I mean. If I am, just smack me with your tail."

She looked up at me with sad eyes then gave me a half-hearted swipe with her tail.

"So I'm half a bitch?"

Tongue lolling from the heat, she smacked me harder on the leg.

I guess that's a yes, I thought.

We'd gone on like this for a while—me asking Runt if I was an ass, her half smacking me with her tail—and then Runt had encouraged me to pick up my pace, so we could catch up with the boys.

I was sure she and I could take care of ourselves if we'd gotten separated, but she was being really pushy about us staying close to the rest of our party. I chose to stick by Marcel and Cerberus, basically ignoring Daniel. He did the same by walking with Judas—though he looked rather bored by the East Gatekeeper's nonstop chatter.

I'd known what kind of stuff happened in Hell, the debasement and humiliation, but the stories didn't prepare me for the reality of what I saw.

Each "neighborhood" of Hell (I use the term very loosely) was set up so you would eke out your punishment time alongside the other true believers from your religion or philosophical way of thinking. Since we'd entered the interior of Hell via the East Gate, we got to walk through a number of the monotheist neighborhoods. For me, it was like stepping into another world: Tenement-like wattle-and-daub buildings crowded on top of each other, people herded together like cattle as they stared blankly out at us through holes in the crumbling walls. Even the roads and alleyways were dilapidated, a sheen of human excrement and dirt covering everything we saw.

There were demons everywhere—you knew who and what they were by the studded leather bodysuits they wore—and they did the enforcing, making sure the souls carried out the duties assigned to them in Hell. Some of the demons were humanoid, others more oddly shaped, their skins the texture and color of rotting fruit. But every single one of them wore the same miserable expression on their face.

I thought the demons looked about as happy to be trapped in Hell as the souls being punished.

Just to give you a sampling of what I saw down there:

We passed a demon standing on top of a naked woman. The woman was lying at the base of a giant pile of horseshit, her mouth wide open, guzzling down the excrement as the demon prodded her with a stick.

Every other prod, she crawled forward an inch, her body tunneling further into the pile.

It was so disgusting I had to turn my head away.

Another demon—this one was bright blue, but otherwise humanoid—stood over a semi-circle of naked human men sitting on the ground. At first, they appeared to be doing intricate beadwork, but upon closer inspection, I realized they were actually sewing thousands of sequins onto brassieres.

I pointed to the men, asking Snarly head who the sequined bras were for. His answer was sad, though rather apropos:

"The demons put on a drag show every Friday night in the Fallen Angel Quarter. The men you see before you are here because they bullied a homosexual to death on Earth. This is their punishment: sewing sequins on brassieres for drag queens."

It was a trip to hear Snarly head use the word "brassieres" in a sentence, but the mood of the place kept my laughter in check.

"I heard the drag shows are supposed to be amazing down here," I said.

Snarly head nodded then suddenly flicked his gaze behind him to make sure the dumb head carrying Alternate Frank still had a good hold on the prisoner, before returning his gaze back to me.

"If we were here for different reasons, we would go see a show. It's well worth the price of admission," he added.

"And what's the price of admission?" I asked curiously.

"A kiss."

"That doesn't sound too bad," I said.

Snarly head looked down at Runt, who was trotting between us. Whatever he was going to say was naughty enough he didn't want his daughter to hear.

"Go walk over by Daniel," he said to her.

Runt shook her head defiantly, but I reached down and patted her on the head.

"Your dad can tell me later," I said to her—and Runt thumped my leg with her tail, telling me if I ever got the four-one-one, she wanted all the details.

Though we got some funny stares, we were mostly left alone as we journeyed through the different "neighborhoods" occupying the East Gate of Hell. The demons seemed to know who we were, and every now and then one of them would bow to Daniel, but that was it. The poor souls there for punishment hardly even looked at us.

Our path led us through a number of different Christian sects, wove us in and out of the Jewish quarter, and then finally dumped us out of the monotheist section via one of the Hindu neighborhoods. Judas had taken a very direct route to guide us through the eastern part of Hell, so we only saw a fraction of the different neighborhoods—and even this was almost more than I could handle.

At the end of the Hindu area, we'd watched three human men being force-fed raw hamburger by a bored-looking demon with pale green skin, four arms, and a quintet of triple-D breasts. She was daintily picking up large chunks of meat from a fly-ridden wheelbarrow then ramming the raw flesh down the men's throats. If they threw it back up, she would get a trowel, shovel up the regurgitated meat, and force it back into their mouths.

I watched, disgusted, as the men cried while they chewed.

"Don't look at that," Marcel said, holding up his hand to block my view.

"Stop it," I said, pushing his hand away. "What kind of a Death am I if I'm too much of a pussy to look at what really happens here in Hell?"

Marcel thought about what I'd said, rolling it around in his mind before finally agreeing.

"You're right, Death. It would make you a pussy."

Well, I didn't want anyone to think I was a pussy, so after that exchange, I kept my eyes glued to every indignity and atrocity we passed. Needless to say, I was very happy when we left the misery behind us so we could venture farther into the interior of Hell, where this She'ol was supposedly located.

"This is creepy," I said to Marcel, as the last of the tenements dropped away behind us, and we crossed into what appeared to be an expansive junkyard.

As far as the eye could see, the horizon was littered with junk. Empty rusted-out cars, metal pieces of God knew what, trash, broken toys, torn sheaves of paper—I didn't know where all the trash came from or what it was supposed to represent, but it smelled awful. Like piss and vomit and rotting garbage, all mixed together in a sickly sweet bouquet.

"It smells like death," I said to Marcel, who was standing beside me.

He grinned back at me—and out of the corner of my eye I caught Daniel staring at us.

"Excuse me," I said to Marcel then I headed over to where Daniel stood talking with Cerberus and Judas.

They were trying to decide which way we were going to go through the junkyard. There seemed to be some disagreement as to which path was safest, with Judas and Cerberus of one mind and Daniel of another.

"Can I talk to you for a minute?" I asked Daniel.

He glanced at the others then nodded.

"Okay, sure."

Daniel followed me back toward the Hindu tenements until we were far enough away from the others they couldn't accidentally eavesdrop on us. I had no interest in having a personal conversation with Daniel while everyone listened in and judged us.

"Look," I said, turning on my heel, and spinning around to face him. "I love you and I'm sorry. I'm down to talk about all the other stuff later, but I just wanted you to know that."

He ran his hands through his hair, messing it up in the front, and I had to stop myself from reaching out to smooth it down.

"Me, too," he said. "That I'm sorry and that I love you."

"Good," I said, holding out my hand for him to shake. "Friends again?"

He took my hand then used it to pull me in closer.

"More than friends."

He kissed me hard on the lips, his tongue slipping inside my mouth, tasting me. I melted into him, enjoying the intensity of the embrace as his body pushed against mine hungrily. But instead of continuing the kiss as I'd expected him to, he suddenly pushed me away. I stared back at his handsome face, shocked by his raw, sexual aggression.

"Don't forget. There's more where that came from if you're a good girl," he said, enjoying my dazed expression—he'd never been so dominant before and I had to admit it kind of turned me on.

I nodded, my body wanting more right then and there, but he just grinned down at me and took my hand, leading me back to where the others were still waiting.

Daniel was in a much better mood after that. Even letting Cerberus and Judas have their way, so we ended up taking the safer but longer path through the hellish junkyard. As we climbed through the trash, I stayed close to Daniel and Runt—and Marcel stayed close to me. Normally this would have gotten on my nerves, but for some reason I didn't mind having a makeshift honor guard.

"What's with the junkyard?" I asked Daniel as we picked our way through a mangled VW minibus, three decapitated dolls sitting in the driver's seat.

"It's not junk, Cal," he said, offering me his hand as we climbed up onto the roof then clambered down the front bumper. "It's all the sorrow of human existence concretized into stuff"—he indicated the junk—"and it can be toxic."

"How so?"

Runt had circumvented the VW instead of climbing through it, and this had somehow gotten her ahead of us. We found her waiting by the engine of an old lawn mower, tail thwacking against a rusted-out metal filing cabinet.

"Find yourself in the wrong part of the junkyard," Daniel said. "Touch the wrong thing, and you'll end up as part of the scenery."

I'd been about to touch a piece of metal signage wrought in the shape of a snail, but I thought better of it and yanked my hand away.

"What?" I said, upset, as Daniel laughed at me.

"We're in a safe part. Nothing around here will get you. It's why Cerberus and Judas wanted to come this way."

Suddenly I heard a high-pitched whine coming from just ahead of us. This was followed by a sharp, angry bark.

"Runt!" I screamed and started blindly running in the direction of the barking, almost tripping on an exposed piece of metal sticking out of the ground.

"Hold up, Cal!" I heard Daniel yell behind me, but I kept running.

I found the hellhound pup standing on the bottom of an upside-down rowboat and I fell to my knees beside her, wrapping my arms around her neck.

"Runt!" I cried, hugging her tightly.

"It's all right, Cal," she said, licking my face. "No one's hurt. It's just, well, Dad . . ."

She looked over at Cerberus, who was standing a few feet away from us amidst a sea of junked cars. He wore a stunned expression on the faces of all three of his heads.

"What's happened?" Daniel said, racing to my side and kneeling down beside me to make sure Runt and I were okay.

Marcel and Judas joined the party a moment later, having had to backtrack to find us.

Only then did Snarly head finally speak:

"I don't know how he did it, but your Alternate Frank has escaped."

twenty-four

Freezay's shoes made funny *splotching* noises as he jogged along the sidewalk. He felt awkward, all cold and wet and alone, as he made his way down the well-kept suburban street, but he tried not to think about where he was—just focused his mind, instead, on where he wanted to be going.

He'd swum until he'd hit the beach and then he'd started running, his feet sinking into the sand as the tiny grains did everything in their power to slow him down. He'd ignored the pain in his calves, pushing himself to pick up the pace as he hit the stairwell leading up to the road, and then taking the stairs two at a time.

He didn't know why he felt compelled to run, but the sensation of his body being in forward locomotion was ecstatic. Even the ache in his calves was tolerable, making him feel alive for the first time in days. He was happy to be moving, to be stretching his muscles and using the pent-up energy he always carried around inside of him.

This was the energy that got him into trouble. Energy he had to slake with activity, or else it would make him cross lines he shouldn't be crossing. It was what had gotten him kicked out of the Psychical Bureau of Investigations—

No, he didn't want to think about that right now. He'd made

a mistake, asked the wrong questions, and turned himself into the enemy. It was dead and done now. Nothing left to say or do, but move forward with his life and not dwell in the past.

As he jogged down the street, a quiet stretch of sidewalk and asphalt lined with clapboard houses and small dune-like yards full of beach grass, he began to assemble the puzzle in his mind's eye. There was enough light from the moon and the streetlights above him to get the gist of where he was headed, and he found he quite enjoyed running in the semi-darkness. It was cold out, the wind causing the skin underneath his wet clothes to pimple with gooseflesh. He ignored the chill, pushing himself harder as he let his mind wander where it wanted, picking up the pieces of the plot and fitting them together where he could.

He had a cell phone, but it was for sure waterlogged, and he didn't know who he would've called anyway. He was on his own for now and he'd best use his time wisely, best put his thinking cap on and figure out what kind of mess Calliope had gotten herself into before it was too late.

He didn't know what'd happened to Caoimhe and Daniel and Starr, but he suspected—no, he *knew* there was something fishy about the car explosion. It had Starr's fingerprints all over it, but he couldn't be 100 percent certain she was responsible. Sure, she was a little bitch and she'd made a number of sly moves, had manipulated him, and dragged him around by the penis, but it didn't mean she was responsible for the car getting blown up.

The more he thought about it, the less it jibed with the Siren's modus operandi. She was a narcissist, one who favored easy manipulations to turn a situation in her favor—so, why go to all the trouble of blowing up a car and tying him to a coral reef? How did she benefit?

As an investigator, he'd learned early on that a rush to judgment usually meant you were missing some of the more pertinent pieces of information. He knew Starr had an angle—because everyone had one—he just didn't know what it was.

So, who had wanted him dead and why? Who had a vested interest in seeing him wiped off the face of the Earth for good?

He wracked his brains, thinking of old cases, people who held grudges, angry men and women he'd brought to justice.

His gut told him it would be someone connected to the ocean, someone who felt safest working in water, as water had been their weapon of choice.

And then it hit him—he knew who Starr was working for.

Years ago, Freezay had had a run-in with one of the Japanese Sea Gods. Watatsumi was the schmuck's name and he'd lived in a squirrelly underwater grotto deep in the waters off the Eastern Seaboard. A real piece of work, he'd been using wish-fulfillment jewels to seduce wealthy, seagoing human beings. Once he'd suckered them in with the jewel's magic, he'd turn his victims into tuna, treating the poor human-fish hybrid creatures as though they were his own personal slaves.

Freezay's department had put a stop to Watatsumi's little sideline business, but he remembered the Japanese Sea God's name had come up more recently in connection with Callie and one of the other "possible" Deaths. The guy called Frank, who was now doing time in a Purgatorial prison for trying to murder Callie with . . . *a wish-fulfillment jewel.*

Now all the pieces of the puzzle were fitting together.

"So, you still run when you're thinking."

The voice came out of the darkness. It was so unexpected Freezay lost his rhythm and tripped, landing hard on the road, hands and knees slamming into uneven asphalt. He could feel the skin on his palms tearing and the small lacerations filling up with blood.

"Shit, I'm sorry I scared you like that," Caoimhe said, stepping into the light and kneeling down beside him.

He noticed the tiny owlet on her shoulder and wondered why she had Anjea's bird with her. The last time he'd seen the creature, it'd helped him catch a killer at the Haunted Hearts Castle.

"What're you doing with Anjea's little guy?" he said gruffly as he begrudgingly let her help him back onto his feet.

He immediately saw she was wearing a white shirt with no bra—and he found it really hard not to look at the way her breasts strained against the cottony material. Damn, he just seemed to have no control over his libido these days.

To his embarrassment, she caught him just as he was dragging his eyes away from her breasts.

"You're so predictable."

He shrugged, glad it was too dark for her to see how red his cheeks were.

"That's what makes me, me."

At least he knew better than to outright lie when he was caught being naughty.

"The owlet is how we're getting out of here, so be nice to her," Caoimhe said, abruptly changing the subject.

They were standing in a pool of light beneath one of the overhead streetlights and it was hard not to stare at Caoimhe. She was that beautiful.

"So I ended up underwater. Some Japanese Water God jonesing for my death," he said, wiping his bloody palms on his ocean-damp pants. "But Calliope's mother, the half Siren who raised her, came and saved my ass. She's playing hooky in the ocean and she looks like shit warmed over."

Caoimhe snorted.

"You've always had a way with words, haven't you, Free."

It was a cheeseball nickname, one she'd given him years before—but it made him feel all mushy she was using it. It'd been so long since she'd called him *anything*.

"I like when you call me that," he said, taking a step closer to her. Her body was so ridiculously warm and he was so god-damned cold.

She put a hand up between them, blocking him from getting too close.

"I know you too well to trust you."

But she wasn't angry—and she was right. He *was* getting fresh with her at a very inopportune moment.

"So now you know where I ended up," he said, stepping back and giving her room to breathe again. "What happened to you?"

She rocked back and forth on her heels, choosing her words carefully.

"Morrigan . . . I think she bargained with someone—maybe your Japanese Water God—for my safe return."

This was an odd twist to the story.

"Go on," he said.

She clasped her hands, rubbing them together nervously.

"I don't know details. I woke up and, I think, she'd drugged me, to keep me from helping Callie."

Caoimhe looked down at her hands, and Freezay could see she was trying not to cry.

"Stop looking so pretty when it's fucking freezing out," he said, trying to make her laugh.

She knew what he was doing, and smiled up at him, gratefully.

"After that, Anjea—who's in the, uhm, *owlet* right now—came to my window. She can help us find Callie."

Freezay stared at the tiny brown creature on Caoimhe's shoulder.

"Anjea's in there?" he asked, uncertainly.

Caoimhe nodded.

"Uh-huh, she's in there all right. But she hasn't, uh, talked since we left my flat in Dublin."

"She always was an obstinate old thing," Freezay said.

Then he turned and addressed the bird.

"You got someplace you want us to go? Let's go."

the ghosts were quick to let Noh know someone had arrived. She'd immediately asked them if this someone was good or bad. The ghosts had answered with a resounding: "Both."

This answer had not inspired much confidence in Jennice. Plus, she'd just gotten used to being in Henry's attic room, the only place in the whole building that was clean and warm, and now Noh and Jarvis wanted to follow the ghosts out to the front grounds again, to see this Mr. or Ms. Bad *and* Good. She wanted to tell them she was just gonna stay up here in the nice, warm attic room all by herself, but the thought that she wasn't alone, that there were little kid ghosts all over the place she couldn't see, gave her the willies. So, she'd decided she'd rather go outside with the living people she knew than stay inside with the dead people she didn't.

Saying good-bye to safety, she followed Jarvis and Noh as they made their way back to the rickety stairwell. She'd felt bad about gripping Jarvis's hand when they'd climbed the stairs the first time—especially when she'd realized her thumbnail had actually poked bloody, crescent-shaped holes in his palm.

She'd felt awful and had wanted to heal the wounds for him,

but Jarvis had demurred. He said pain was good; it reminded him he was still alive.

When he'd discovered his book was missing, she'd thought he really *was* going to die. All the color had drained from his face and he'd made these strange mewling noises, almost like he'd turned into a panicky baby kitten. She'd patted him on the back, thinking maybe he'd swallowed funny when he was sneezing, but he'd waved her away. Though not before she'd noticed his whole body was trembling.

Jennice was an observant woman. She'd seen the trembling and had immediately known something terrible had happened. Noh, on the other hand, was too busy talking to her dead school friends to notice Jarvis's distress, and by the time she'd turned around to see what was keeping them on the stairwell, he'd already collected himself.

But Jennice had seen the whole thing—and though he acted like everything was fine, she noticed his hands still shook slightly whenever he used them to gesticulate while he was talking.

Something he did a lot.

"Do you want to hold on to me?" Jarvis asked, offering her his arm.

She shook her head; she was a big girl and she was going to get down those stairs under her own steam even if it killed her.

"I think I got it," she said, hoping she sounded confident.

Jarvis didn't seem at all put off by her refusal, just gestured for her to go ahead of him.

Noh was already halfway down the stairs, chattering to herself. At least that's what it looked like to Jennice. It was really weird to think Noh was *actually* talking to a ghost.

Very weird.

The stairs were less rickety than they looked, and she was able to make it down without incident by taking her time and holding on to the thick wooden banister. Jarvis was nothing but kindness, not once hurrying her or making her feel bad for going so slowly. She thought he was a real peach and hoped she hadn't made a total fool out of herself in front of him. In the space of a few hours, he'd seen all of her insecurities, all of her powers, had been a party to the murder of a bunch of bad were-wolf people—and he still seemed to like her.

If something like that doesn't bond you with someone, Jennice thought, *then I don't know what does.*

"Henry says more people are here now," Noh called back to Jennice and Jarvis, waiting for them before she left the stairwell and headed for the laundry room. "He says we need to hurry."

Jennice walked faster, Jarvis at her heel as they passed the broken-down washing machines and dryers, then headed out the side door. Once they were outside, Jarvis took the lead, calling back to Jennice over his shoulder:

"Stay behind me and let me do what needs doing. Do you understand?"

He didn't wait for her answer, just took off after Noh, who was already running across the grass like a two-legged pony. Jennice didn't want either of them to get too far ahead of her, so she fast-walked, making sure to keep Jarvis's retreating back within her line of sight.

She was too far away to see what was going on when she heard Noh scream:

"Get off of her!"

Jennice didn't think this sounded too good, so she slowed her pace, wanting to do as Jarvis asked and stay out of the way.

Then she heard Noh yell:

"Kick him in the gnards, Clio!"

She hadn't heard someone say the word "gnards" in forever. Now she kind of wanted to see what was happening up ahead. She started fast-walking again, finally catching up with Noh, who was standing at the gate, waving her fists in the air like a boxer.

On the other side, Jennice could see Clio and a man she didn't know wrestling on the ground. The man was trying to push Clio's face into the gravel, but Clio was stronger than she looked, elbowing him in the gut then rolling out of his grip as he grabbed his stomach and doubled over in pain.

"Kick his ass, Clio!" Noh yelled, jumping up and down, arms swinging wildly. "Beat the shit outta him!"

Jennice looked around for Jarvis, but he was nowhere to be seen. When she turned back to the action, the man was on his feet again and gunning for Clio. He was quite a bit taller than her, and not a physically bad-looking guy, but the nasty expression he wore on his face made him seem mean and unattractive to Jennice.

"So, it was all some kind of sick game, huh?" Clio said, her words coming out in an angry burst. "One minute you're all sick and dying, and the next you're attacking me?"

The man was only half listening to Clio, too busy plotting his next attack strategy to really take in what she was saying—and then suddenly Jarvis was there, coming out of the darkness at a run, heading straight for Clio's attacker. The guy didn't see Jarvis coming, and when her friend slammed into him with the power and speed of a small locomotive, the bad guy went down—and *stayed* down.

"Go, Jarvis!" Noh screamed, still jumping up and down like a cheerleader. "You nailed him."

Jarvis had managed to climb back onto his feet, but now he was bent over at the waist, trying to catch his breath. He waved Noh's odd compliment away with a trembling hand.

"No, I did not *nail* him, but thank you for the support."

Jennice giggled. She knew it wasn't really funny, but, actually, it kinda was. Her giggles started Noh giggling and then the two of them fell into each other's arms as hysterical laughter poured out of them. Even Jarvis, who'd often been accused of being humorless, cracked a smile.

"Yes, that's what she said," he added. "The nailing bit. That's a 'that's what she said' joke I just made, you know."

Clio snorted then ran over and grabbed Jarvis in a bear hug.

"That's not really how you do that—" she started to say, but then stopped herself, not wanting to rain on his parade. "Thank you for saving my ass."

"That's what she said . . . ?" Jarvis inquired—his grasp of the "that's what she said" joke less than tenuous.

Jennice and Noh had finally started to calm down, but this put them over the edge again. Now Jennice was laughing so hard, she was crying.

"We need to get the two of you back over the gate," she heard Jarvis telling Clio as she and Noh finally stopped laughing.

"Let us come help," Jennice said, feeling better now she'd almost laughed herself silly.

There was just something about laughter that sent all of

your worries packing. At least that was what Jennice's mom had always said—and Jennice had to agree.

"Come around then—" Jarvis started to say, but his words were lost as one of those crazy wormhole things appeared in front of him, the energy it released so powerful, it knocked both Jennice and Noh off their feet.

"Look out!" Noh screamed, using the gate to claw herself back to her feet.

Jarvis and Clio turned around just as a thin guy with ginger hair and a weasel-like face emerged from the wormhole, followed by two much larger companions, both of whom came to stand menacingly behind him.

"Get 'em!" Weasely Face cried—and then the two larger men took off, running straight toward Jarvis.

"No!" Jennice screamed, raising her hands into the air in her panic.

But there was nothing she could do.

She was on the wrong side of the gate.

noh watched, horrified, as the two giant men went in for the kill. They were going to turn Jarvis into a pile of pulp if someone didn't do something and fast—but she was trapped on the other side of the gate, and short of magically pulling a tommy gun out of her pocket, she was screwed.

"No!" Jennice screamed, raising her arms in the air in front of her.

Noh watched, fascinated, as the two large men, both the size of small mountains, suddenly stopped in their tracks, as though someone had yanked them back by unseen strings.

"Is she doing that?" Noh asked Henry, who was floating beside her. "I can't see anything."

The ghostly boy nodded. He was about thirteen, with short brown hair and a pair of dark brown eyes trained right on Jennice.

"Yes, I believe she is. I can see this funny green light coming out of her hands and going into those men."

A girl in a riding habit and boots, her long hair plaited in two braids hanging down her back, nodded her head in agreement.

"Yes, definitely," the girl said. "I can see it and Henry can see it. How about you, Nelly?"

Nelly had short, dark hair that made her look more like a boy than a girl. She had floated away from Trina—the girl with the braids—and toward the gate, and now she was running her ghostly hands through the green light, trying to figure out what it was made of.

"Remember the kid who came to Newbridge right before Noh? The one who went around healing all the sick birds that one winter?"

The other two nodded.

"You never told me about this," Noh said, feeling left out.

"It wasn't a big deal," Henry sighed. "It was just something silly the kid did."

It always made Noh sad she wasn't a ghost like her friends. It felt like they had "in jokes" she wasn't privy to because she was alive. If she were dead, then she'd know all the ghost stories instead of having to have them explained to her, which would be nice for a change.

"Well, that kid had the same kinda light. Only his was blue," Nelly said as he followed the green light back to Jennice's hands, still examining it.

"It's probably whatever color your aura is," Trina said with authority. She was a terrible know-it-all sometimes, which drove the others crazy.

As the ghosts continued to debate the possibility of magical powers being colored by one's aura, Noh tiptoed over to Jennice and rested a hand on her upper arm, whispering in her ear:

"Shut their brains off. Don't kill them, just put them into a deep, deep sleep."

Like a sleepwalker, Jennice nodded.

"Okay."

Like a shot, the men fell to their knees, dropping face-first onto the gravel. Jarvis grinned back at Jennice and Noh, his face filled with relief.

"What did you do to my guys!?" Weasely Face screamed at Jarvis.

Even from her vantage point, Noh could see the man was terrified of Jennice's strange power.

"I did nothing to your men," Jarvis said, pointing to Jennice.

"She did—and you'd best get out of here if you don't want to be next."

Weasely Face looked from Jarvis to Jennice then back again.

"I'm out of here," he shrieked and tore off down the gravel driveway like a dog with its tail between its legs.

They all watched him go, then Jarvis turned back to Jennice and Noh.

"As I was saying before we were so rudely interrupted. Help me get this unconscious person"—he pointed to the first man, the one Clio had been brawling with—"inside these gates, please."

"On it," Clio said, reaching down and grabbing the guy's feet.

Jarvis took the man's arms and they hoisted him into the air. As they waddled slowly down the driveway toward the secret entrance Henry had shown them earlier, Noh heard Jarvis saying:

"You led those men right here. You know that, don't you? Just like you almost got us all killed at that gas station by wormholing off to God knows where. You are a selfish, selfish individual . . ."

Noh couldn't hear Clio's answer, but she was extremely happy she wasn't the one who'd stirred Jarvis's ire. He may have been a bit light in the heels, but he was a force to be reckoned with when you got him all hot and bothered.

"You did good, kiddo," Noh said, as Jennice dropped her hands.

"Did I kill them?" she asked, her body swaying unsteadily.

Noh patted her on the arm.

"No, you did not. You made them go to sleep, just like I told you to."

Relieved, Jennice walked over to the gate and leaned against it, exhausted.

"Thank God," she said, sweat beading on her upper lip. She wiped it away with the back of her hand. "Thank God for you, Noh."

"I like her. She's magical," Trina said, floating over to Jennice and giving the unsuspecting "realie" a ghostly hug. "Realie" was what the ghosts called the living.

"She's pretty great," Nelly said matter-of-factly—and Henry nodded his head in agreement.

Though she wished Jennice could hear the compliments being bestowed upon her, Noh was kind of glad her new friend couldn't see the three chatty ghost kids as they floated in the air around them.

It would've given Jennice a heart attack.

twenty-five

Daniel watched Callie being torn between two disparate emotions: dread about what'd happened to Alternate Frank and joy that Runt could talk again. He was curious as to which emotion was going to win out. If he were a betting man—which he wasn't, anymore—he'd have gone with joy . . . and would've been amply rewarded for his choice.

"Your voice," Callie cried, throwing her arms around the hellhound puppy. "You can talk again!"

She was laughing and crying at the same time, arms looped around Runt's neck, as she rocked back and forth, giddy with happiness.

"It's a miracle," she added, kissing Runt's cheek.

"It was Jarvis," Runt corrected, but sweetly.

"Yes, it was totally Jarvis," Callie agreed, as she wiped away tears of joy, unable to contain her excitement.

Finally, after too much hugging and kissing and crying for Daniel's taste, she let Runt go, and finally began to address the other issue at hand.

"So what happened?" Callie asked Cerberus.

There was no blame in her tone, but everyone could see the three-headed hellhound, who should've been overjoyed at his daughter's miraculous recovery, was inconsolable. Daniel guessed Cerberus felt as though he'd let everyone down by allowing Alternate Frank to slip through his teeth.

"I don't know," Cerberus said, his usually gruff voice a tremolo of emotion. "He was there and then he wasn't."

Runt padded over to her dad, leaning her body against one of his massive legs.

"He vanished," she said. "I was on the rowboat and I could see him. He lifted his head as if he was listening to something, a piece of music or someone singing a song, and then he smiled. But it wasn't a nice smile."

Daniel watched Callie watching Runt and Cerberus. He knew from experience hellhounds were biologically unable to tell a lie—and he hoped Callie was aware of this fact, too.

"And then he vanished," Runt finished sitting down on her haunches and looking over at Callie for approval.

Callie's pale face was flushed from the hellish heat, her dark hair lying limply around the base of her neck. She looked even more like an innocent little girl than she usually did.

"Do you think this means the two universes are almost done merging?" she asked, directing her question to Daniel and Marcel.

Daniel had always thought she was beautiful—and her inability to see her own beauty was one of the most charming things about her—but now, when she gave him such a serious look with those dark eyes and soft lips, he found her utterly ravishing. He couldn't help but look over at Marcel, wanting to know if the Ender of Death was as attracted to Callie as he was.

He'd never been a jealous guy. He hadn't really needed to be before he'd met Callie. He'd found other women were entranced by his power and did whatever he asked of them because of it. They would never have thought once, let alone twice, about cheating on him.

Callie, on the other hand, was stubbornly independent and did whatever she wanted—but because of these facets of her personality, and her sexual dalliance with Frank, he'd become hyper aware of other men's gazes . . . other men's attraction to his woman.

He felt like an asshole, hating this self-fulfilling prophecy he was creating in his own head. The more he worried about her leaving him, the more he created situations in which she would be well within her rights to go.

Like the argument back at the Scarlet Sea—he'd told himself to keep his mouth shut, but what had he done instead? He'd snapped back at her, gotten defensive, and pushed her away. He'd always saddled Callie with the "pushing away the ones you loved" issue, but, whether he wanted to admit it to himself or not, he was just as guilty of doing it as she was.

Daniel knew he was being ridiculous. There was no lust, no love, no sexual interest of any kind in Marcel's eyes when he looked at Callie. Marcel was the Ender of Death, for Christ's sake. All he wanted was to get rid of Callie so he could destroy the next Death after her and the next one after that and the next one after that . . . on and on into perpetuity.

Damn, I am losing my shit, Daniel thought, massaging his temples with the heels of his palms. He needed some serious couch time with a shrink. Any shrink.

He heard his name being called and looked up, all thoughts of future psychoanalysis sessions put on the back burner.

"Daniel?" Callie said, her eyes telegraphing this was not the first time she'd called his name.

"Uhm, yes," he said, for the life of him unable to remember the question she'd just asked him.

His affirmation wasn't the greatest, most informed answer he could've given, but it seemed to satisfy her.

He could feel his heart beating sluggishly in his chest and he realized all he wanted was for everyone to take their eyes off of him—he was getting panicky and he just wanted to be left alone.

Instead, his mind kept flashing to the Edgar Allan Poe story "The Tell-Tale Heart." He had a guilty little secret, too—only his wasn't hiding beneath the floorboards. His was old and scary and smelled like rotten fish . . . and had a name: Watatsumi.

Using the wish-fulfillment jewel, Daniel had done as Watatsumi had asked, blowing up his car in front of Clio and Jarvis, so they'd think he and the others were either dead or missing in action—obviously he'd only created *the illusion* of an explosion, or one of them would really be dead and the others would be singed pieces of humanoid shish kebab. Next, he'd used the jewel to wipe his passengers' memories. Then he'd used the jewel again to transport the car and its occupants to a predetermined location where Watatsumi had been waiting to meet them.

When they'd arrived at the strip of lonely beachfront on the outskirts of Queens, New York—really it was more of a floating island made of reeds and mud than a beach—he'd climbed out of the driver's seat, stretched his legs, and looked around.

He couldn't help but think of Callie as he stared out at the Manhattan skyline. She loved New York like a love-struck teenager; blatantly ignoring its flaws, while blindly extolling its virtues. It was kind of cute how passionate she was about the city, even though it boasted one of her most egregious temptations.

Shopping.

And New York City had the best of it: Barneys, Saks Fifth Avenue, Bloomingdale's—plus all those cute little boutique clothing stores Manhattan was famous for.

God, he'd been spending way too much time with Callie. He *actually* knew the name of her favorites stores, places of such conspicuous consumption—places he'd eschewed before he'd met her—he was ashamed of himself for having ever set foot in them.

Annoyed with himself, he turned away from the Manhattan skyline. It seemed like any spare moment he had was taken up with thoughts of her. He'd always been obsessive, constantly lost in details, to the detriment of everything and everyone else around him. It was one of the things that'd made him so good at being the Devil's protégé, though this thought had him cringing.

"You're right on time."

The wrinkled, old Japanese Water God had snuck up behind him without even a rustle of warning from the ratty grass skirt he wore.

"I try to be punctual," Daniel said, taking the wish-fulfillment jewel from his pocket, so the small piece of orange beryl warmed his hand.

"Everything went well?" Watatsumi asked, staring across the water, eyes focused on something Daniel couldn't see.

"I did what you asked of me," Daniel said.

Watatsumi didn't look at him, just kept staring out at the sea.

"Now I take the fish and the detective and send the mother home to her lady friend."

"You sent the Siren to get Freezay, didn't you?" Daniel asked.

Watatsumi nodded, grinning at Daniel like a small child with a secret.

"She thought it was Frank, but no, it was Sumi. Sumi pretending to be someone else and getting a good fuck for his pleasure."

The wizened old man cackled, his shoulders shaking.

"You're . . . an interesting fellow," Daniel said, uncertainly.

"Don't judge me," Watatsumi said harshly. "You're here right now, aren't you?"

The old God was right. Daniel was here, listening to this crap, but at least he had his reasons—and the main one was the wish-fulfillment jewel he was already holding in his hand.

"Okay, so you send Caoimhe home," Daniel said, ignoring the old man's nasty grin. "You take the other two and then I'm outta here."

Watatsumi slapped Daniel on the back. It was supposed to be fraternal, but it hurt.

"When the time comes, and it will be soon, the jewel will bring us together," Watatsumi said. "I will have the prison. You will bring Death."

When he said he would bring the prison, what Watatsumi meant was he would bring Pandora's Box. Well, it was more of a jar, really, but it was the only magical artifact Daniel knew that could contain someone like the Man in Gray, as apparently Enoch was calling himself these days.

Pandora's Box and the wish-fulfillment jewel were the enticements Watatsumi had used to get Daniel on his side, and Daniel had accepted because he could think of nothing else that would put a stop to the two universes merging.

Of course, he knew Watatsumi was one of the worst double-crossers in the history of the business. The minute he thought he could get rid of Callie and install his protégé, Frank, in her place, he would try and do it.

But Daniel was prepared for this eventuality.

He hadn't been the Devil's own protégé for nothing.

Lost in thought, he realized someone was saying his name again and Daniel looked up to find Callie standing beside him, her face flushed with worry.

"Daniel, we're pushing on," she said, touching his cheek.

The press of her hand against his skin yanked him out of his head and he blinked, trying to collect his thoughts.

"Okay," he said, forcing a smile.

She gave him a funny look, opened her mouth to say something to him, but thought better of it.

"Let's go," he said, taking her hand—and then careful not to say or do anything suspicious, Daniel guided the others through the rest of the junkyard without further incident.

It was one of the most stressful things he'd ever done.

clio had taken the tongue-lashing as her due. She'd clearly deserved it, running off like she had at the gas station and then allowing those three jerks to follow her to the New Newbridge Academy. No, Jarvis wasn't wrong, per se, but he *was* missing the point. She'd done these things with a purpose. She wasn't just going to sit around while her sister was erased from their world; she was going to do everything in her power to stop it from happening.

Noh had tried to speak up for her, but Jarvis had waved the other girl away. He wasn't interested in excuses. He just wanted to yell at someone. Clio understood this, having felt that way, herself, all day long—but she'd done something proactive with the feeling, and now they had their hands on Frank, one of the vehicles by which the bad guys had sought to destroy her sister.

"I get that you're pissed, Jarvis," she said as they carried Frank's limp body across the lawn, on their way to the burnt-out building where, according to Noh, all the ghosts lived.

Clio had never been to the New Newbridge Academy before—she was a little kid when Callie had started school here, so no one had ever thought to bring her along for a visit. If they had, she knew she would've fought to stay because the place was amazing: dark, creepy, and eerie.

Three of her favorite adjectives.

"It was thoughtless, thoughtless, *thoughtless—*"

Jarvis was still muttering about her selfishness, her narcissism, her *whatever*, but he was losing steam. The invective was more benign, his energy spent. Now he just looked worn-out instead of apoplectic.

"I know it seems that way, and I'm sorry to have put you in any danger," Clio said, interrupting him. "But you're a big boy who can take care of things. I knew you didn't need me. And I was right. Because here you are."

He rolled his eyes, breathing hard as they lugged Frank's deadweight around the side of the building and then through a door leading into a ramshackle laundry room.

"Why don't you put him here?" Noh said, her voice carrying through the doorway as she and Jennice followed them inside.

Pushing her way past them, Noh gestured for them to follow her into what had once been a sitting room, but was now just a cobweb-covered space with a fireplace, an overstuffed couch, and two dirty but comfortable-looking tweed armchairs. They waited as Noh cleared the dust from the couch, then she and Jarvis hoisted Frank onto it, sending a cloud of dust into the air that made Jarvis sneeze.

"Damnable dust," he wheezed, yanking his handkerchief from his pocket and blowing his nose.

When he was done, he re-pocketed the handkerchief and gazed at the women in his care. Clio could see his mind turning, and she assumed he was wondering what horrible thing he'd done in a previous life to get saddled with these three crazy ladies.

"You can't keep me here!"

Frank was up off the couch and on his feet before any of them realized he was conscious. He went for Clio first because she was closest. She had no time to duck as his fist sailed through the air, slamming into her jaw with enough force to snap her head back.

She'd taken a punch to the face before, but this one was worse. Pain flooded through her jaw like wildfire, its path indiscriminate and devastating. Black spots blossomed in her vision, obscuring her sight. Instinctively, her hands went to her face, her fingers probing for broken bones and for blood. She found the broken bones in short supply, but the blood was free flowing from a gash inside her mouth where her teeth had cut into the soft, pink flesh of her cheek. The blood was salty and metallic tasting as it filled her mouth, making her gag. She found herself spitting up saliva and blood in such quantity it ran down her chin and onto her shirt.

She was helpless to do anything to stop Frank as he went for Jarvis next, head butting him in the gut while the lanky hipster tried to pummel him with balled fists. The force of the impact sent the two men tumbling over the couch. Frank got up first and drew back his fist, letting it fly. The punch caught Jarvis in the nose—and Clio gasped as blood arced through the air, splattering on the wall.

Weaving on his feet, his eyes rolling back into his head, Jarvis mumbled something unintelligible, then pitched forward onto his face.

Knockout.

Frank had already moved on to Jennice. She was trying to subdue him the way she'd done with the two large men outside, but she was having trouble.

"I saw what you did, girl," Frank said. "That sure was something. I could use a lady with your talents."

Jennice's brow furrowed as she channeled all the power she possessed directly at Frank. But he only laughed, crossing the space between them in two steps and gripping her by the throat with one hand, easily lifting her into the air.

"Leave her alone!" Noh screamed from across the room.

She ran forward, gunning for Frank, but he held out his free hand, and without even swiveling his head to look at her, said:

"I wish you dead."

As her thick dark hair swished across her face, Noh froze midstride, her long legs folding underneath her as if all the bones had suddenly been yanked from her body. As she crumpled to the ground, her chin slammed into the wooden floor with a heavy *thwack* that made Clio's blood run cold. Clio stared as Noh just lay there on the floor, unmoving, her long limbs splayed out at awkward angles.

Clio held her breath as she waited for Noh to pop back up and laughingly say: "C'mon, guys, can't you take a joke?"

But no matter how much she wanted it, Clio knew Noh wasn't going to get back up again.

"Oh my God!" Jennice screamed. "What have you done!?"

She pounded on Frank's chest, screaming and crying, as she completely lost her shit. Clio dropped to her knees at Noh's side, lifting the girl's wrist—it was *so* cold—and feeling for a pulse, but there was nothing. Not even a flutter.

"I'm so sorry," she whispered to her sister's best friend, patting Noh's long hair, amazed to discover how soft it was.

"Sonofabitch!" she heard Jennice shriek—and that's when something snapped inside of Clio.

She climbed to her feet, her body thrumming with rage. It boiled in her veins, driving her to snuff out Frank like a cockroach under her heel. She screamed, the sound primitive and guttural as it tore out of her throat, causing the wound inside her cheek to start bleeding again. But she was incensed and felt not pain, but adrenaline pumping through her body. She grabbed one of the heavy, tweed armchairs and lifted it high over her head, growling as she slammed it into Frank's back.

The force of the blow caused him to drop Jennice—who fell against the wall, weeping—but it didn't knock him off his feet as she'd expected. Instead, he whirled around, eyes full of hate as they latched onto Clio. He looked ready to wish them all dead, but she didn't give him a chance to get the words out. Jumping on top of him, she rammed her fist into his mouth and they fell to the ground, Clio instantly winning the upper hand and clambering on top of Frank to straddle his torso with both legs.

"Fuck you, you bastard," she breathed, overcome by the need to stop him, no matter what the cost.

With one graceful move, she removed her fist from his mouth and bent down over him, planting her lips over his and sealing his mouth shut with her own.

But this wasn't a kiss given out of love or passion. It was not something to be savored and cherished. No, this kiss was bestowed with burning hatred.

Frank shrieked, thrashing under Clio's weight as she sought out his floundering tongue with her teeth and bit the thing clean off at the root. She sat up, her face a bloody mess, and spit the offensive piece of muscle onto the dirty floor. Jennice had the presence of mind to reach out with her foot and kick it away, the tongue skittering across the floor before disappearing underneath the skirt of the couch.

"We need to tie him up," Jarvis said.

He was standing above her now, lower face covered in blood, nose bent too far to the left.

With their matching beards of blood, she was sure they made quite a disgusting pair.

Clio felt hysteria burbling up inside her, looking for a release. She wanted to laugh, to get all the bad stuff out of her, but she couldn't do it. She was afraid if she started laughing now . . . she might never stop.

noh looked down at her body, sad to see it lying on the floor, devoid of life. Her hair was spread across her face so she couldn't see her eyes or mouth, but she thought this was probably for the best. She felt bad her passing had made everyone cry—especially Jennice. She'd really grown to like the funny little healer.

As she floated beside them, she so badly wanted to let them know it was okay, that she wasn't unhappy about her death, and they shouldn't feel bad about it, either—but she had no way of sharing this important information with them.

While Jarvis and Clio looked for rope to tie up Frank, Noh floated over to Jennice, who sat on the floor by the body, holding Noh's lifeless hand. She reached out with ghostly fingers and tried to touch Jennice's hair, but Noh's arm sailed right through her friend's head.

"Are you all right?"

It was Trina, floating beside her, except now her body was more solid and full of color than Noh had ever seen it before.

"You look alive," Noh said.

Nelly popped up beside Trina and giggled.

"You look dead."

Noh supposed she did. She stared down at her ghostly body and that's when she realized something amazing: She wasn't an adult anymore. She was a kid again, practically the same age she'd been when she'd first started at The New Newbridge Academy. She lifted her hands to her hair and found the ponytail she used to wear when she was younger. She even had on her mother's silver hair clip, a fact that thrilled her.

"I wish I could tell them it's all right, that I might even be happier now," Noh said, brow furrowing. "They're so sad and it's not a sad day, at all. It's actually a happy one."

The others had no answer for Noh. The realies were her domain, not theirs.

"Where's Henry?" she asked suddenly.

Trina rolled her eyes.

"He's upstairs being all moody."

Noh grinned as the need to find Henry and tell him what had happened to her filled her with unbridled excitement.

"Well, I'd better go up there and show him my new ghost body," she said—and then she was gone. The empty body on the floor, the one that'd housed her soul for so many "living" years, well, she'd already forgotten about it.

twenty-six

CALLIOPE

There was something "off" about Daniel.

He was skittish, his gaze sliding away without ever quite looking me in the eye. His thoughts seemed to wander even in the middle of a conversation, so when someone asked him a question, he stared blankly back at them—something I'd never seen him do before. This was the antithesis of the Daniel I knew. My experience was with Mr. Present, Mr. Right There In The Moment, Mr. Sensitive and Thoughtful. This other Daniel was a stranger to me, one I didn't enjoy—and I worried it was my fault.

I'd been a jerk and hurt his feelings, not just on this one occasion, but here and there for the entirety of our relationship. I'd thought this was how relationships worked, a constant battle for balance, and the understanding that sometimes you hurt the other person's feelings. I mean, God, Daniel had hurt my feelings so many times I'd stopped counting. But it didn't mean I loved him any less.

Part of me wondered if the distracted behavior was the product of all the stored-up hurt and anger Daniel had been carrying around because of me and, soon, he'd decide to shut me out entirely and that would be the end of our relationship.

I could take the fighting, the screaming, the anger, but what really ripped me apart was the distance. For the first time in our relationship, I was beginning to feel as though Daniel had put a wall between us, one I could never hope to surmount.

It was an extremely depressing thought.

I did my best to act natural, but inside I was gutted. I wished Jarvis or Clio was there to talk to. They were both so pragmatic. They'd tell me I was being silly, that there was absolutely nothing to be paranoid about—and I'd believe them.

Kind of.

I stuck close to Daniel as we left the junkyard behind us and traversed even more desert, cooing at him like a lovesick dove while he smiled back at me, his eyes empty. I found I couldn't stop myself from fawning all over him; the colder he behaved toward me, the more I fought for his attention. Runt had chosen to stay by my side, and I realized she knew something was wrong because she wouldn't stop whining. She just kept looking back and forth between us, and emitting this weird, incessant doggie whine that drove me bat-shit crazy.

Still, I was ecstatic she'd gotten her voice back, and if it meant I had to endure the doggie whining to have her whole again, then so be it—but it was pretty damn distracting.

"I think we're almost to the edge," Judas said, running ahead of the rest of us and pointing to the "edge" of the desert.

I followed his gaze until I saw what he was talking about.

Way ahead of us, just beneath the horizon, the rolling dunes of sand were gradually giving way to flat orange rock.

"That's the She'ol?" Marcel asked, slowing down so he could walk abreast of Daniel and me.

"No, those are just the Cliffs of Tranquility," Daniel said, using the tail of his shirt to wipe the sweat from his face. "The She'ol is at the very bottom."

"And you knew there was something fishy going on here," Marcel said, rather pointedly, "but decided not to tell anyone about it."

"What are you trying to say?" Daniel snarled, stopping in the middle of the sand and staring at the Ender of Death.

Marcel held his ground, not the least bit intimidated by Daniel's gruff tone. The two of them stood there, facing each other, toe-to-toe, both red-faced and sweaty, but so different looking it was almost comical. Where Marcel was blond and cherubic, with pre-Raphaelite features, Daniel was all Black Irish and exquisite, ice blue eyes.

"No fighting," I said, deciding to intervene before someone lost their cool and things got out of control. "Marcel didn't mean anything. He was just making conversation."

Marcel raised a pale eyebrow.

"I very much meant something by that, Death. I wanted to know why they've left this place to its own devices for so long."

Runt had taken off to get Cerberus and Judas, and they'd arrived just in time to hear the tail end of the conversation.

"Daniel has not been in charge very long," Snarly head said, his terse tone a warning to Marcel to tread carefully. "We've been cleaning up the Devil's mess as best we can, but there is much to do and not enough help to do it. Besides, it belongs to the Angels—it's not officially in Hell's jurisdiction."

Marcel considered this for a moment, then nodded for Snarly head to continue.

"The She'ol *is* on our list and it will be dealt with eventually. The general populace of Hell needed our attention first."

While Snarly head was working hard to defend him, Daniel was busy getting the funny, faraway look in his eyes again. I doubted he'd even heard a word Snarly head had just said. I wanted to punch him in the arm and drag him back to reality, but I didn't want to give Marcel any ammunition.

"Happy?" I said to Marcel, thinking if I put him on the defensive, then he'd back off.

"For now, Death. For now."

I tried to catch Snarly head's eye, but he was staring at Daniel with a worried expression on his face.

Even Judas looked worn-out. The bottom of his blue caftan was filthy and he'd twisted his long hair into a loose topknot to keep himself cool, revealing a swath of patchy red psoriasis scales on his neck and the base of his scalp.

Not that I was judging anyone. I was sure I didn't look much better myself.

After the "almost" confrontation, we walked the rest of the way in silence, each of us keeping to ourselves. Which turned out to be a good thing because we heard the inhuman wailing long before we reached the edge of the rock cliffs.

Daniel had drifted away as we walked, until he was closer

to Cerberus and Judas than to me. Marcel took up Daniel's slack, staying back with Runt and me.

"Do you hear that?" Marcel asked, cocking his head to the side.

The wailing was low and indistinct, but I'd heard it, too.

"The She'ol," I said.

The Ender of Death covered his mouth with his hand, still listening.

"They're singing."

I had a hard time believing whoever was down there was singing. It sounded more like moaning to me.

"Are you sure?"

He shrugged and kept walking.

"I think so."

I didn't believe it was possible to get any hotter than I already was, but the closer we got to the She'ol, the more I sweated. Every other step, I had to stop and wipe my face with the inside of my shirt.

"It's hotter, isn't it?" I asked Marcel. "I'm not making it up, right?"

Earlier, his pale skin had turned light pink then a deeper shade of rose and now his cheeks were fire-engine red.

"You're not crazy," he said. "It's hotter."

"Like an oven," I added. "And we're the rump roast."

He grinned at me.

"I think you're the silliest Death of all."

The Ender of Death had existed from the very beginning of time. He lived from incarnation to incarnation, always in mortal flesh; unlike Death, who was immortal and ruled as long as he or she wanted, or was able, to stay in power. The Ender of Death was the equal and opposite of Death—and, sadly, it seemed they would forever remain in constant battle.

The Ender of Death had murdered my father, and if things worked out, when the Golden Age of Death had passed, he would murder me, too. This was his job, just like it was mine to keep Death running smoothly.

"How many Deaths have there been?" I asked.

I'd never been curious about this stuff before, but for some reason I was enjoying my chat with Marcel and wanted to hear him tell me stories. Besides, he knew more than anyone about where I'd come from because he'd personally known each and every one of my Death forefathers and mothers.

"Countless," he replied, but I could tell he was counting them in his head.

I never got to find out the answer to my question because it was at that very moment we reached the edge of the cliff.

Cerberus, Judas, and Daniel were already there, the three of them standing together by the lip of the drop-off, gazing down at what was happening below. Runt raced past me, going to sit by her dad as Marcel and I joined the others.

The noise was louder now, rising up toward the sky. Marcel and I had both been wrong. It wasn't wailing, exactly, but it wasn't singing, either.

"What the hell are they doing?" I asked, because I couldn't believe what I was seeing.

My Harvesters and Transporters were down by the She'ol, herding souls into a bright orange metal octagon shaped like a starship. No, *not* a starship: *a Gravitron*. Like the carnival kind I'd ridden on a hundred times, or more, as a kid. It even had a flashing neon sign on top of it that read:

The Pit

"*The Pit*? You gotta be kidding me," I said, darkly.

"I think the Man in Gray has a sense of humor," Marcel said, sagely.

"Or else he's just a big fan of the literal," I shot back.

That's when I realized the whining/singing noise we'd heard was actually coming from *The Pit* itself. After a certain number of souls were pushed through its entrance, the mechanized metal door would ease shut and then the thing would slowly burrow down into the ground and spin. It went faster and faster, picking up speed—this was what created the whining/singing noise—until electricity began to crackle around it. As soon as this happened, a neon orange lightning bolt of pure energy would shoot out of the top of the machine and disappear into the sky—and then it would get just a little bit hotter.

I could tell the machine had been going for a while, because it'd already turned much of the sky above it into an angry shade of burnt orange. I wondered if the machine was seeding the atmosphere of Hell with pure soul energy, something that was, from the looks of things, very unstable.

"Who knew a Gravitron in Hell would signal the end of the universe as we know it," I said.

"Don't you mean the collision of two universes into one?" Judas asked. "That's what you said before."

I shook my head.

"I don't think so."

I tried to catch Daniel's eye, but he was too entranced by *The Pit* to notice, so I gave up, addressing myself to the others.

"This isn't about getting rid of me in favor of Alternate Frank," I continued. "This is about destroying life as we know it, period. You don't build something like that machine down there, with that kind of energy production, unless you want to cross the streams."

Snarly head and Judas looked at me, uncomprehending.

"It's a *Ghostbusters* reference," Marcel said.

I'd expected Daniel to be the one to get it—we'd watched *Ghostbusters* like a zillion times on my computer while lying on the bed in my old Battery Park City apartment in Manhattan—but he was all checked out.

"So, do we just go down there?" Runt asked.

Whenever Runt spoke, I was reminded of how much television she'd watched with Clio before she'd learned to talk because of how much she sounded like Cate Blanchett in the movie, *Elizabeth*.

"You're not going down there," Snarly head said, the tone of his voice brooking no argument.

"Yes, I am," she said. "You're not the boss of me."

I'd never heard Runt talk back to her dad before. Heck, I'd never heard *anyone* talk back to Cerberus before, but it worked. He bowed all three of his heads (Snarly *and* the two dumb ones), letting Runt know he was acquiescing to her demand.

"If that is your wish, Daughter, then I cannot stand in the way of your destiny."

"Pop, I just want to help Callie," she said. "She needs me."

I'd learned early on that trying to talk Runt out of doing something was pointless. The little hellhound was going to do what she wanted whether you liked it or not—just like someone else I knew.

Me.

"That's all well and good," Marcel said, "but what's your plan? You can't just go down there without an idea of how to disarm the machine."

Luckily, Daniel chose that moment to finally return to reality.

"I think I should go down there on my own," he said, eyes feverish. "I'm the Steward of Hell and it's my job to find out what they're doing."

"Those stupid idiots are building their own funeral pyre," I said. "They don't know it, but that's what they're doing."

"Yes, Daniel should go down there with Judas," Marcel said, nodding in agreement. "He should act as though he's just realized there's a problem. Tell them he's interrogated Judas, who's told him about the extra souls coming in through the East Gate."

I didn't like this plan because it put Daniel in unnecessary danger. What was the point of him going down there when they'd immediately sniff him out as an enemy?

"It's just a distraction," Daniel added as if he'd read my mind. "It'll give the rest of you time to get down there and stop the machine."

This part of the plan seemed amenable to the others, but Snarly head asked the one question we were all thinking.

"How?" he wanted to know. "How do we stop the machine?"

I had the answer to this one in my back pocket, and Daniel had been the one to unwittingly give it to me.

"The book," I said, pulling the original copy of *How to Be Death* from my pocket. "This is the key to everything."

"But you can't even read it," Daniel said.

He was missing the point.

"I don't have to read it," I said. "I just have to throw it in there with all those human souls. It'll blow *The Pit* sky-high."

Cerberus got it first.

"The book can't be touched by human hands, or the human self combusts," he said, nodding his head. "You believe that goes for human *souls*, too?"

"Yes," I said. "Yes, I do. I think it's the magic inside of us that protects us from this book. Not just immortals, but anyone with supernatural powers. And those are all human souls down there, without any magic. So no protection."

"I think Cal's right," Daniel said—and I wanted to cry, I was so pleased he had my back. "It's the only chance we have."

His gaze was on me as he spoke and I felt all the love we'd had and would always have for each other flowing between us—and I knew every fight, every cold shoulder, every stupid misunderstanding was forgiven in that moment.

Thank you, Daniel, I mouthed.

He smiled at me—and had I known it would be for the last time, I might've stopped him, made him kiss me, or stroke my hair, or I don't know what . . . but I didn't know. How could I know?

I couldn't.

So I let him go.

He gave me a final wave—and then he and Judas took off down the steep mountain path that would lead them from the top of the cliff down to *The Pit* of Hell.

twenty-seven

Anjea, in her owlet form, brought them to the edge of the Cliffs of Tranquility. Caoimhe thought she'd never been in a place so hot before in her life. Even breathing the air scorched her lungs. The heat was making her woozy, so she grasped Freezay's arm. She didn't know if it was a smart move. She wasn't trying to encourage him, but maybe—just maybe—she wasn't trying *not* to encourage him, either.

She was done with Morrigan. She knew this at least.

She'd put up with her partner's petty jealousies for far too long, and now that they'd extended to her daughter, Calliope, well, Morrigan could just go fuck herself.

It was like a weight being lifted off Caoimhe to finally be done with the relationship—though it was strange to think that until she'd made the decision in her head, she hadn't known what a relief it would be.

I should've been footloose and fancy free years ago, she thought to herself.

Then she looked over at Freezay, the big lug, and found she was glad to have him there with her.

She'd fancied herself in love with him once. She'd been a kid back then, wet behind the ears with no male or female experience to speak of, working at the PBI as Manfredo Orwell's Second Assistant. This entailed picking up his dry cleaning, fetching his coffee . . . doing whatever Second Assistants did.

He'd taken her with him on a routine recruiting trip to California to see a young man about a position in the company. She'd been tasked with fetching this young man, a Mr. Edgar Freezay, and bringing him back to Manfredo.

From her boss's description, she'd expected Freezay to be a smarmy, narcissistic boy, but she wasn't any of those things. He was blond and handsome, but too awkward and tall to be completely comfortable in his own body . . . and he was earnest.

When she'd introduced herself to him, he'd looked at her with those bedroom eyes, long lashed and seductive, as though he knew her, knew her deep down to the core, and, in that instant, she was hooked. But then he hadn't asked for her number, or how he might contact her—and that was that.

So time passed, the summer ended, and she'd found she'd almost forgotten him. And then suddenly he was thrust back into her life again.

It was two weeks before the annual Death Dinner and Masquerade Ball and she was sitting at her desk, secretly reading *The Stranger* instead of doing her work, when he'd stumbled into her office. As soon as he saw her, he'd stopped, a deer frozen in the headlights.

"How may I help you?" she'd asked, quietly setting her book down on her lap so she wouldn't get in trouble.

"I was, uh, wrong office."

He was gone as quick as a jackrabbit.

She stared after him for a few moments, confused by his odd behavior, then she went back to her book.

"Excuse me?"

She looked up again and he was standing in the doorway, holding a bedraggled-looking daisy in his hand.

"Did you steal that from the receptionist's desk?" she asked, knowing full well he had.

He looked sheepish, but nodded.

"I wanted to ask you to dinner and I didn't want to do it empty-handed."

He offered her the daisy. She thought about refusing it, but decided to take it, instead.

"I'll pick you up after work," he said, grinning stupidly down at her. "That okay with you, Caoimhe?"

He'd remembered her name.

"Works for me, Mr. Freezay."

Now his stupid grin grew even wider: She'd remembered *his* name.

They'd spent the next two weeks together and it was like a dream . . . then they'd gone to the Death Dinner and Masquerade Ball.

And that one night had torn them apart forever.

She hadn't thought about those days in a long time, so she was surprised by how fresh the memories seemed, like they'd happened only yesterday.

"Look down there," Freezay said, pulling her from her thoughts in order to point to the crazy assemblage of bodies below them.

There were Harvesters and Transporters scurrying around like worker ants outside of a giant orange octagonal building with a sign on it, reading:

The Pit

"What the hell is that?" Caoimhe asked, fascinated by the carnival vibe of the building and its surroundings.

"Don't know," Freezay replied, uncertainly. "But it's not good, whatever it is."

Caoimhe felt the owlet on her shoulder give a strand of her hair a gentle tug, telling her it was time to go.

"Shall we go down there?" she said.

Freezay nodded,

"Looks like down's the only way *to* go."

She let him take her hand.

"Follow me," he said, leading her toward the path that would take them from the top of the cliff to its bottom.

It was slow going. The path was slippery, with chunks of orange rock breaking off underneath their feet as they walked. Caoimhe was glad to have Freezay to lean on, to keep her upright whenever her ankle would twist, or she'd start to lose her footing. She found herself clinging to him as though he were a solid, immovable mountain.

When they finally reached the bottom of the cliff, Caoimhe had to rest her head against Freezay's arm. She thought she was going to pass out because the heat was even worse down here than it'd been on the cliff.

"You okay?" he asked, and she nodded.

"Fine, just . . . it's very hot down here."

"Ain't that the truth," he replied.

She closed her eyes for a second, savoring the nearness of this big, strong man, then her mind flashed to Calliope and she knew they had to hurry.

"She needs us," Caoimhe said, her eyes fluttering open.

She started to run, fear for her daughter making her fly. And Freezay stayed right beside her, keeping up with her panicked pace.

They hit the crowd of Harvesters and Transporters first. She and Freezay had both expected interference, but, instead, they received no resistance from the strange, Victorian-garbed creatures. The Harvesters and Transporters were too busy running around the orange rock floor, holding their eyes and screaming.

"What happened to them?" Caoimhe asked, as Freezay grabbed her hand again and began to maneuver them through the hysterical crowd.

"Don't know," Freezay said, shoving a tall man in a stove-pipe hat out of his way.

He didn't like the Harvesters and Transporters, never had and never would. They'd elected Uriah Drood as their union president, which to Freezay said more than anything about their motives. Any union that had someone like the sniveling pig Drood as their representative deserved what they got.

"Help me!" screamed a tiny woman in a beetle black dress, gray gauzy bits of fabric floating at her throat and wrists. She was thrashing around, holding her arms out in front of her as though she was blind.

"What happened to you?" Caoimhe said, grabbing the woman by the arm.

The woman began to shake, her small body trembling.

"He opened the jar—"

"What jar?" Caoimhe asked.

The woman shook her head, trying to erase the memory from her brain.

"Pandora's Box. He opened it and it burned out the fake eyes Mr. Drood had given us, so now we can't see at all."

The woman gave up these lasts words with a sob, and Caoimhe let her go.

"I guess that's how he bribed them," Freezay said. "None of them have real eyes, just empty black holes where eyes should be, and they're horribly self-conscious about it."

The crowd was getting rowdier now, more hysterical.

"It'll be easier to get through here if I carry you," Freezay said. "Is that all right?"

Embarrassed for God knew what reason, she nodded and let him pick her up. It felt nice to have him carry her through the crowd, protecting her with his own body. Still, even with her in his arms, it took them more than a few minutes to weave through the crowd of bleating Victorians. Finally, they made it to the edge only to discover there was a low fence made of giant concrete blocks surrounding the octagonal orange building. This was what was keeping the crowd away from *The Pit*. Inside the fence Caoimhe saw two bodies huddled together by the entrance to the octagon. One of them resembled her daughter. Her heart skipped a beat as she tried to see if it was Callie or not.

"We need to go in," she heard the owlet whisper in her ear.

"Take us inside," she said to Freezay.

"Your wish is my command," he replied, as he set her down carefully on top of the fence then climbed up after her.

howard had not liked being in that jar. Had not liked being carried around like a genie in a bottle. Had not liked being kicked out of the jar and forced to go through Hell. Had not liked anything that'd happened to him since he'd died.

He wanted to see his wife. He wanted to rest. He wanted to just be left the goddamned hell alone.

Instead, he was in this animal-like pen with a bunch of other angry dead people. Every so often a few of those Victorian bastards would come in and drag a bunch of souls out, but none of them ever returned, so no one knew where they were being taken.

He was about ready to start yelling—*Attica! Attica! Attica!*—when another host of Victorians came in, corralling him and a bunch of others and herding them out of the pen. He didn't know if he should be irate or overjoyed at this turn of events—but he knew if he'd had his druthers, he'd still be sitting in that rest home playing cards and eating glorified baby food.

The Victorians didn't speak to them, not anymore—*but they'd sure done a lot of talking to get me into that jar, by God,* he thought. Well, if they didn't want to talk to him, then he didn't want to talk to them, either.

After they were a few feet away from the pen, the souls were forced to line up, in single file, one dead person in front of another. Howard slid in between a little girl with short red hair and a young African American woman in surgical scrubs. He wondered what had happened to the doc so that she'd died with her scrubs on. He figured it wouldn't hurt to ask, so he tapped her on the shoulder. She turned around, a serious expression on her face.

"How'd you die?" Howard asked.

She shook her head and indicated she didn't speak English.

He made the universal signal for slitting your throat and she laughed, said something in her native tongue. She could see it wasn't translating, so she began to shake and jump up and down.

It took a few seconds, but he got it: earthquake.

"Earthquake," he said, offering her his hand. She took it and they shook.

The Victorians came around again and the long line of souls began to walk across the plane of orange rock. Howard was just happy to be moving, even if he didn't know where he was going. He figured it couldn't get any worse than it already was—but he'd figured wrong.

When he saw the old Gravitron buried in the dirt, he got a funny feeling in his gut. You could call it intuition, or just a funny feeling in your gut, but Howard always trusted it—and it was telling him to turn around and run far, far away as fast as his legs could carry him.

* * *

gerald was the last one in the big orange machine. He hadn't wanted to go inside, but they'd made him. He didn't like carnivals or roller-coaster rides and this smacked of both.

The inside of the machine was filled with soft black velvet seats, one for each customer, Gerald realized. *Maybe this isn't going to be so awful, after all,* he thought. Maybe when this was done, they'd let him be alive again and he could find Molly and go home—because he missed his Vespa something fierce and hoped whoever found her took good care of her and only gave her Supreme gasoline.

Since Gerald was the last person inside the ride, he was the last person to sit down. But as soon as he'd found his seat, the music began to play. It was funny music, like what they played at a carnival, and it made the room start to spin. Gerald didn't like it. It was going too fast and the music was going too fast, too.

"Stop it!" Gerald screamed—and he wasn't the only one. Other people were screaming, too. Some of them were even crying.

No one outside was listening, or if they were, they didn't care. The room just spun faster and faster and *faster* until Gerald couldn't think anymore.

And then there was no need for Gerald to think.

Because Gerald didn't exist.

harold was in the group that didn't make it into the Gravitron for the first ride. He was annoyed about this. Frustrated he had to stand around and watch as someone else got to do something, *anything*, before he did.

While the Victorians herded the luckier souls into the ride, Howard occupied himself by trying to communicate with the doctor. She seemed very nice, even if he had no idea what she was saying. He wanted to impart his name to her, but this simple thing was proving very confusing.

He would say: "Me, Howard." She would say: "Meoward."

It went on like this until they'd closed the door of the Gravitron and started the machine up. That's when everyone around him stopped doing whatever they were doing and started watching the big orange thing as it began to whirl. Like him, they wanted to know what the ride was going to do to them.

They didn't have to wait long for their answer.

Howard thought the Gravitron spun around so fast it looked like a whirling dervish, but as it burrowed in the ground and shot out its load of bright orange energy, Howard changed his mind.

There was nothing magical about the Gravitron, if that's even what it was, and Howard was pretty damn sure it wasn't.

What he did know, though, was the machine was the scariest thing he'd ever seen.

twenty-eight

All he had to do was get down there, take out the wish-fulfillment jewel, and then Watatsumi would show up with Pandora's Box—and the box would solve all of Daniel's problems.

"Are you okay?" Judas Iscariot asked as they neared the end of the path.

"Fine," Daniel said, but he was sweating profusely, his body aching from heat and stress. "Just want to get down there and stop this madness."

He didn't want to talk to Judas Iscariot anymore, so he picked up his pace, keeping his thoughts to himself as he left the other man behind him. He just needed to get down there and everything would be all right. He'd explain everything to Callie, tell her why he'd done what he'd done, and she'd forgive him because it'd all been for her.

He tried to imagine her reaction in his mind, but couldn't. Maybe he was drawing a blank because he was afraid of what his mind might conjure. That it might not be the reaction he wanted.

"Nearly there," Judas Iscariot called, from behind him.

Yes, I'm not blind, Daniel thought. *I can see we're almost there.*

But where was "there" really? He saw the odd Harvester and Transporter scurrying around, but they hardly seemed to notice Daniel and Judas Iscariot. Beyond them stood a silent herd of souls, their eyes dripping with fear after watching their compatriots go into *The Pit* and get annihilated.

He didn't blame them for being scared.

The Pit was scary.

He searched the area, looking for Uriah Drood, or this elusive Man in Gray, but he saw no one who fit either description. He stopped by a low concrete block fence and waited for Judas Iscariot to catch up. It took the slight man a few seconds, but he finally saw Daniel and jogged over to him.

"Thought I'd lost you," Judas Iscariot said, looking sheepish.

Daniel didn't feel like making small talk, but he supposed he had to.

"So, you see your friend in gray anywhere?" Daniel asked, but Judas Iscariot shook his head.

"He's not really my friend."

Daniel didn't give two shits if he was Judas Iscariot's friend or not.

"I don't see Drood here, either," Daniel said, changing the subject.

"You think they're in it together?" Judas Iscariot asked.

"Yes," Daniel said.

"Me, too," Judas Iscariot agreed.

Daniel was getting impatient. He wanted Watatsumi to come now. He pulled the orange wish-fulfillment jewel from his pocket, letting it sit in his palm.

"What's that?" Judas Iscariot asked.

"Nothing."

But Daniel sounded like a liar, and he knew it.

"It's a wish-fulfillment jewel," he added, finally, feeling bad about being such a jerk to the other man.

Judas Iscariot stared at it, then he held out his hand, palm up.

"Can I touch it?"

Daniel raised an eyebrow.

"No, I don't think that's a good idea."

They were pressed up against the fence now, another crush of dead souls having been brought in just as the last group was forced inside *The Pit*.

"Please," Judas Iscariot asked.

"I don't know—"

"I promise I won't bother you again."

The man looked so pathetic Daniel felt sorry for him. Against his better judgment, he lifted his arm and let the jewel drop into Judas Iscariot's upturned palm. They just stood like that, both of them staring at the jewel in Judas Iscariot's hand almost as if it held the answers to the universe inside of it—and maybe it did.

"So, this jewel will give me whatever I wish for?" Judas Iscariot asked.

Daniel nodded.

"Within reason."

Judas Iscariot looked up, eyes begging Daniel to understand.

"I'm sorry," he whispered then he gazed down at the jewel: "I wish to not exist anymore."

What happened next was over so quickly Daniel didn't have time to process it.

First, the jewel in Judas Iscariot's hand began to glow like a hot coal, cooking the soft flesh of his palm. Instinctively, he yanked his hand back, trying to dislodge the jewel from his skin, but no matter how hard he shook his hand, the jewel wouldn't budge, preferring to stay affixed to Judas Iscariot's palm.

He whimpered as the overheated jewel bit into his skin, melting the top layer of dermis so it could burrow deeper inside his flesh. He screamed, terrified as the jewel disappeared inside his hand, the tissue around the wound turning red and inflamed looking—but it didn't stop there. The redness began to take over his hand, streaks of orange shooting up his forearm. He grabbed his wrist, trying to stop the orange from spreading.

It was a moot point. Daniel could already see the orange traveling up the man's neck, sending tendrils of color up into his cheeks. It was like watching a time-lapse video of someone's entire body being overtaken by blood poisoning.

"Help me," Judas Iscariot cried, eyes beseeching Daniel to do something—but there was nothing to be done, the jewel was almost finished.

Judas Iscariot lifted his hands, the sleeves of his pale blue caftan falling back so he could stare in horror at the reddish-orange flesh of his arms. When he looked up at Daniel again, even the whites of his eyes were orange.

He began to cry, tears the color of tangerine Kool-Aid sliding down his cheeks. He opened his mouth to speak, but no words came out, just a slow and steady hiss, like the sound of someone letting the air out of a balloon. Daniel watched in dismay as Judas Iscariot began to deflate. His skin lost its elasticity, shrinking down and flattening out, until, finally, there was nothing left of him, but a paper doll made of skin. Even his head had collapsed in on itself.

The Judas Iscariot paper doll bowed, so light now, it just floated to the ground. It lay against the orange rock, which it was almost the same color as, and then it began to melt away until there was only a puddle of orange water on the ground at Daniel's feet.

Daniel stared in disbelief at the spot where Judas Iscariot had been standing only seconds before. Suddenly the puddle changed from orange to indigo and began to expand, taking over a larger and larger space until Daniel had to climb on top of the concrete block fence to escape it. The growing puddle caught the attention of the Harvesters and Transporters, and they began to descend on it in droves. Even the souls were curious, crowding around the other side of the fence to see what was happening.

A form began to take shape in the water. At first it was just a dark and wavering presence, but then it coalesced into something more solid as it ascended from the depths of the water and broke through the surface. It rose above the indigo water like an avenging angel, a dark cloak hiding its identity from the spectators—and then it dropped the cloak and Daniel gasped.

Watatsumi hung in the air, glowering down at everyone. He'd replaced his uniform of black kimono and grass skirt with an eggshell-colored caftan that fell to his ankles. He held out his arms, waggling his fingers, and the surface of the puddle began to bubble. As he raised his arms, a barnacle-encrusted clay jar rose from the depths of the water, dripping seaweed as it floated in the air in front of him.

Watatsumi turned to Daniel and grinned like a crocodile,

his teeth long and razor-sharp. Daniel understood, then, what his fate would've been had he tried to use the wish-fulfillment jewel for anything other than what Watatsumi had intended: *He* would've been the puddle on the ground, not poor, tortured Judas Iscariot—a man whose guilt had been his final undoing, though in a way he got what he'd asked for.

"You should know better than to double-cross a double-crosser," Watatsumi said, losing the grin as he snapped his fingers and the water in the still-growing puddle began to boil, steam pouring from its surface.

Another figure emerged from the depths, but this one was not shrouded like Watatsumi had been. He was tall and lanky with light blond hair and a bedraggled orange jumpsuit. He lifted his head, eyes wild as two spitting cats, and Daniel saw the dried blood caking the lower half of his face . . . and the way his hands were bound together by lengths of sheer white fabric.

"Oh, Jesus," Daniel murmured under his breath.

It was Alternate Frank.

jarvis watched as Clio yanked a set of sheers from one of the windows and tore them lengthwise, using the fabric to make jerry-rigged coils of rope. She bound Frank's wrists and feet with the fabric, then turned him on his stomach so she and Jennice wouldn't have to look at his face. Jarvis was still in shock, so he didn't care which way they placed Frank on the ground.

That Noh was dead seemed impossible—it all had to be some terrible mistake. Jarvis's eyes kept sliding back to the spot where her body lay, Jennice beside her, holding on to one of Noh's lifeless hands. He'd tried to get Jennice to move away from the corpse, but she'd yelled at him, telling him to mind his own business—then gone back to stroking Noh's hair with her free hand.

From the way she was concentrating, Jarvis thought she might be trying to heal Noh. He didn't have the heart to tell her it was useless. When Death decreed you dead, well, you were dead—at least to that body. He'd gone through the experience not very long ago, which was why he was in an ill-fitting body instead of the one he'd been born into. He'd loved his faun's body, the beautiful cloven hooves and thick Tom Selleck mustache he'd worked for years to cultivate.

All of it was gone now because of a bizarre twist of fate.

"He really had me going," Clio said.

She was perched on the couch, staring into the empty fire grate. She was covered in blood, but she wouldn't let Jarvis go find anything to wash her with. She seemed to think the blood was a badge of courage.

Jarvis thought it was unhygienic.

"Whom?" Jarvis asked.

"Frank," she said, still staring at the grate.

"How so?" he asked.

He'd taken up residence in the remaining armchair and was holding a handkerchief to his own bloody nose.

"When he found me at Death, Inc., I thought he was dying. His body was so gaunt, even his face. It was awful."

Jarvis looked over at Frank, who hadn't moved since they'd bound him.

"He doesn't look too bad," Jarvis said. "Except for his face."

"I know," Clio agreed. "It's so weird. He looks fine now, but before . . . he was different. Sickly, delirious. He had a seizure right in front of me. Then we got here. He was still all messed up and then *bam* he was suddenly okay again. I don't know how he did it."

Jarvis didn't like what Clio was saying. Not at all.

"He didn't seem angry before?" Jarvis asked.

Clio shook her head then looked up, making eye contact with Jarvis for the first time since she'd ripped a man's tongue out of his mouth with her bare teeth.

"No, the opposite. He was sad, kept apologizing to me, confusing me with Callie."

Jarvis pocketed his bloody handkerchief and stood up. He circumvented the broken armchair resting in the middle of the floor and walked over to where Frank was lying. He knelt down beside him, gazing at Frank's face intently.

"I wish he could speak," Jarvis said, sighing. "Then maybe we would have an idea what's been happening."

He'd decided to keep the three of them (four, if you included Frank) here at the New Newbridge Academy until he had some idea of the lay of the land. Clio had argued against this, but Noh's death had taken the fire out of her, and she'd given in. Jarvis didn't like being cooped up here any more than she did, but they had Jennice to think of. She wasn't immortal and it would be hard to defend her if there were any more attacks.

"You don't think . . ." Clio said, but she didn't finish her thought.

"I don't think what?" Jarvis asked, standing back up.

Clio was looking at him, her expression uncertain.

"That this isn't Frank."

Jarvis didn't know what she was talking about. She could see his confusion, so she explained:

"It's not the Frank from our universe."

Jarvis instantly understood.

"This is the Alternate Frank."

Clio nodded.

"Yes. It appears the two universes are almost one now. Meaning the Alternate Frank and the Frank from our universe have merged."

Below him, Frank snickered. The man may have been outwardly ignoring them, but he was obviously paying close attention to their every word.

"You think this is funny," Clio snarled, jumping up off the couch and crossing the room in two long strides, squatting down beside him and grabbing a handful of hair so she could yank his head off the ground.

He gave an involuntary groan, but didn't cry out.

"It's not funny, you sonofabitch," she said, almost spitting as she leaned down to stick her face in his. "So don't you dare laugh."

Suddenly, she sat back, unclenching her fingers from his hair like she'd been burned.

"What the—" she said, but the words ceased in her throat as Frank's body flickered once, twice, and then disappeared, leaving nothing behind but the empty floor.

the man in Gray knew the time to show himself had arrived. He was tired of waiting, and, besides, he'd let the others play without him long enough.

He'd been watching the drama unfold from the lip of his secret cave, a place he'd discovered by accident while building *The Pit*. He had no idea what purpose the cave had been created for, but long ago someone had seen fit to cut it into the side of the cliff face—and for that, he was grateful.

Drood had tried to make him stay in Purgatory at his compound, but the Man in Gray had hated it there. Eventually he'd won out and been allowed to stay where he'd wanted, but not before poor Uriah Drood had realized he'd gotten way more than he'd bargained for when he'd released the Man in Gray from his prison.

Drood hadn't wanted him to build the new Pit on top of the old She'ol, but the Man in Gray had liked the irony. His idea of crafting a machine of destruction on top of a hole that'd been his home for so many centuries, and then christening it *The Pit* in honor of this former prison, had been a stroke of sheer genius.

He still couldn't believe how smoothly it'd all gone after that. He'd bent Drood to his will and then bribed the Harvesters and Transporters with shiny new eyeballs in order to entice them to work around the clock, getting the machine built in almost no time at all. Of course, he'd actually had to produce the shiny new eyeballs to secure their cooperation, but all the magical effort he'd spent had been more than worth it.

Funny how vain the creatures were, with their boring Victoriana obsession and compulsion to buy sunglasses to hide empty eye sockets. He'd never have guessed something as simple as an eyeball would buy him such goodwill—but once he and Drood had crafted the spell, they'd been willing to do whatever he asked of them.

Watching from his cave, he found himself bored by the little Japanese God's grandstanding. It was annoying to think someone could actually come along, believing they were in charge of the show, when he, the Man in Gray, was so obviously the ringmaster.

Hopping off the lip of his cave, he dropped five feet down to another outcropping of orange rock, then followed the cliff face down, jumping from outcropping to outcropping, until he'd reached the bottom.

He was curious to finally see the little Death up close and

personal. She, the Ender of Death, and their hellhounds had taken the long way down the cliffs. They thought they were being sly, that they could surprise him, but he'd been watching them all day. No one could hide from the Man in Gray. Not when they were on his turf.

Because he was coming from the opposite cliff face, his path was shielded from view by *The Pit* itself. So he took his time, strolling leisurely across the orange rock floor, passing the fenced-off area where the Harvesters and Transporters kept the souls—or the "fuel," as he'd coined them. He ignored their anguished cries for help as he walked by them, his eyes on the prize just on the far side of *The Pit*.

He came to the low, concrete block fence and leapt on top of it, walking its length like a tightrope. He waved to the "fuel" then followed the curve of the fence around to the other side. Spread out before him stood all the Harvesters and Transporters, their new eyes fixed on the floating Japanese man and the creature he'd just called forth from the depths of his magical, indigo puddle.

The Man in Gray wanted to laugh. That anyone would choose to show up for their big coup via puddle was just ludicrous.

"And whatever do you think you're doing?" the Man in Gray called out in a loud voice, skipping along the curve of the low, concrete fence.

His entrance scored a loud cheer from the assemblage and he raised his hands above his head, fingers spread in double victory.

"What are *you* doing here?" growled the Japanese God as he turned to see what all the fuss behind him was about.

The Man in Gray could tell the God was not pleased to see him there, that he resented anyone trying to steal his little Water God thunder.

Now you know how it feels, the Man in Gray mused.

"I'm the Man in Gray and this is my party. So, the real question is, what are *you* doing here?"

The Japanese God stared at him. He seemed confused by the turn of events.

"*You* are the Man in Gray?" he asked.

The Man in Gray nodded.

"That's me. The Man in Gray, at your service."

The Japanese God snickered, something about the situation having amused him. Now if there was one thing the Man in Gray hated, it was someone laughing *at* him. It made him very mad, indeed.

The Japanese God pointed his finger at the blond man in the orange jumpsuit.

"Get rid of him, Frank."

The man called Frank held up his wrists.

"But I'm all tied up."

This seemed to annoy the Japanese God, but he lifted a hand, waving it around, and instantly Frank was free of his bindings.

"Thank you," Frank said, giving his liberator a small bow—but if the Japanese God thought this Frank—this *Alternate Frank*—was going to do his bidding, well, he was sadly mistaken.

This Alternate Frank came from another universe and he belonged to the Man in Gray.

It was funny how mistaken Uriah Drood had been about his own plan. He'd wanted the Man in Gray to use his Angelic knowledge of the book *How to Be Death* to create *The Pit* and generate enough energy to merge their universe and another—where an alternate Death was in charge—so he could get rid of the little Death, Calliope Reaper-Jones. The Man in Gray had known Drood's plan was only the beginning of what *The Pit* could do. The original Angelic copy of *How to Be Death*, the book he'd been banished to She'ol for memorizing, had instructions on how to jump-start the Apocalypse. *The Pit* would and could do that, and the merging of these two universes would be the first act.

This was where the subterfuge began.

To further his own agenda, he'd had to play along with Drood, never letting the other man suspect that he meant to use *The Pit* to destroy humanity—and the easiest way to do this was to distract him, to give him access to the Alternate Frank, the one who was already Death in his own universe. The Man in Gray had used a wormhole—one calibrated to travel through-out space/time—in order to invite this Alternate Frank to return with him to their universe and, as his bribe, he offered this Alternate Frank the ability to rule as Death in *two* universes instead of just one.

This had all been easy to set in motion.

And as *The Pit* had sucked up more and more souls, the two universes had begun to merge. Because she had no counterpart in the other universe, Calliope Reaper-Jones couldn't be completely eradicated until the two universes were one—unlike the two Franks, who would slowly become *one* Frank over the course of the entire merger. The Man in Gray had explained this to Drood, and Drood had decided to give his weasel-faced enforcer and goons the job of chasing down Calliope's friends and family and destroying them in front of her.

Drood wanted the little Death to suffer—and suffer she would if the Man in Gray had anything to say about it.

Amazingly, Drood had never suspected the Man in Gray's ruse. He'd been pleased as punch, hiding the Alternate Frank in his compound until *The Pit* could complete the "merger" of the two universes. The cherry on top of all this madness was Drood had even allowed the Man in Gray to "share" his body with him. Little did he know the Man in Gray was terrible at sharing.

As was evidenced now by the Man in Gray's inability to share the spotlight with Watatsumi.

"Go get rid of *him*, Frank," the Man in Gray said, pointing a finger at the Japanese God.

Upon hearing the Man in Gray's command, Frank leapt at Watatsumi, wrapping his long fingers around the old man's throat.

The two men fell into the puddle of water and began to writhe around in it, each one trying to get the upper hand.

"Drood!?" a man's voice yelled from the crowd, and the Man in Gray turned around to see who wanted him.

He was glad of the reminder, actually. He'd almost forgotten he was still in Drood's body, he'd gotten so used to wearing it. Of course, it was far too big for him—Drood had been a gluttonous piggy—but it had suited his purposes . . . until now.

Now he had his eyes set on the body of the man yelling at him. It belonged to the little Death's boyfriend, the Steward of Hell. It was an attractive enough skin suit, one he could climb into easily enough, and then when the little Death showed up, she would have no idea her boyfriend was no longer inside of it.

Pleased with his plan, he stepped out of Drood's body, letting it fall off of him like a cloak, the skin suit turning to dust as soon as it was free of his shade.

Good riddance, he thought as he floated away from the fence and toward his new body.

When he arrived at his destination, he was surprised by how little resistance the Steward of Hell put up. With barely a fuss at all, the Man in Gray slipped inside of his new body and took over.

twenty-nine

CALLIOPE

I had just landed on the last outcropping of rock on the far side of the cliff face when there was a tremendous *boom* and the ground shook so hard I was thrown to my knees. The *boom* was followed by a series of screams that grew in intensity before finally subsiding into silence. It reminded me of the summer I'd spent in Rome with Noh and her aunt when we were both juniors in high school. Every time there'd been a soccer game, the entire city would be deathly quiet and then suddenly erupt in cheers or screams whenever a goal was scored or lost.

"What was that?" Runt said, jumping onto the outcropping beside me.

She was followed by Cerberus and then Marcel, bringing up the rear.

"Don't know," I said. "But I can't imagine it's good."

I gestured for the others to follow me as I climbed back onto my feet then leapt off the outcropping, landing on the bottom of the valley floor. I hadn't liked Marcel and Daniel's plan to begin with, and now I couldn't help but worry something had gone terribly wrong.

It was much easier going over the smooth orange rock now that we were on a level plane. We were coming from a less direct route, one I'd hoped would keep us out of sight, and we'd encountered no one on our climb down. Now we came to a corral full of human souls trapped inside a makeshift paddock. They yelled at us to stop and help them, and it broke my heart not to be able to take care of them right then and there, but we needed to get to *The Pit* and help Judas and Daniel.

We came to the edge of the first set of cliffs and then had to go around them to finally get our first view of *The Pit*.

"Oh, shit," I said, as we rounded the corner and came face-to-face with a riot of Harvesters and Transporters. They were crying and screaming as they held their hands over their faces.

"What's happened?" I whispered to Marcel, as we stood by the sheer cliff wall, staring at the madness that'd been set loose around us.

He shook his head, as confused by what he was seeing as I was.

"They're holding their eyes," Snarly head said, craning his neck in the direction of two men in rust red suits, their hands pressed into the flesh of their orbital bones.

"But they don't have eyes," I said, surprised because I thought it was a given everyone knew that Harvesters and Transporters only had black holes for eye sockets. That they "saw" via their hearing.

"My eyes!" sobbed one of the two men as he ran past us, completely unaware we were even there.

"I'm sure we'll find out more the closer we get," Snarly head said.

We walked through the throng of hysterical Harvesters and Transporters, doing the best we could to avoid accidentally running into them or knocking them over.

"This is nuts," I said to Runt, who'd stuck to my side like glue ever since we'd left the—relative—safety of the rock out-croppings.

"They've gone mad," she agreed, the two of us dodging unwieldy Victorians at every step.

"Oh, my God," I hissed, stopping in my tracks as I saw the bodies of Alternate Frank and Watatsumi—what the hell was *Watatsumi* even doing here?—lying on their sides in the middle of a shallow puddle, their fingers wrapped around each other's throats.

I could tell they were both dead by the glassy blue of their skin and the way their eyes were glazed and unblinking. Beside them lay a clay jug, its body broken into a dozen jagged pieces.

I had no idea what the jar was for, or what had killed Frank and Watatsumi, or why the Harvesters and Transporters were going crazy all around us . . . but I was about to find out.

"Callie?"

Daniel was standing at the entrance to *The Pit*. He looked a little worse for wear, but he was alive and smiling at me—and that's all I cared about.

"Daniel!" I cried and ran to him, letting him pick me up and swing me around.

"What happened to you?" I said, as he squeezed me tight and then let me go, setting me down on my own feet, but still holding me around the waist.

"It was crazy," he said. "I had to break open Pandora's Box, but it didn't do what I thought it would do."

"What did you think it would do?" I asked, uncertainly—I knew nothing about Pandora, or her box.

"It didn't stop the Man in Gray from taking over my body."

Daniel's arms tightened around my waist.

"I don't understand?" I said, his words not computing.

"You don't need to," he said then he yanked me off my feet and began to drag me toward the inside of *The Pit*.

As soon as Marcel and Cerberus realized what was happening, they took off after us, but it was too late. Daniel had pressed a button on the inside wall and the mechanized door was already shutting tight behind us.

Outside, I could hear Runt barking, her yips frantic, and then there was a loud *clang* as Cerberus rammed his body into the door, trying to force it open.

Daniel held on to my arm, leading me past the front entrance and into the black velvet interior of *The Pit*. The first thing I noticed as my eyes adjusted to the darkness was *The Pit* was jam-packed with souls, all bunched inside, waiting for us. None of them spoke, just stared at us, the stench of their terror, palpable.

I tried to give them a reassuring smile, but it did nothing to allay their fears.

"Well . . . ?"

"It's very, uhm, spacious," I said, trying to be agreeable. "Just like I remember from going to the carnival when I was a kid."

"Go on," he said, pleased I was complimenting his creation.

If I hadn't realized it before, I was well aware of it now. I wasn't talking to Daniel anymore. This was the Man in Gray.

"I love the black wall-to-wall carpeting," I said. "And those seating/standing cubicles are just like what you'd find in a real Gravitron. You did a great job."

"I did, didn't I?" he purred.

"You sure did," I agreed.

He walked me over to one of the only vacant black velvet cubicles, and settled me inside it.

"Why don't you have a seat," he said. "Maybe we can chat a little before I blow us sky-high."

A least now I knew what his intentions were—and I also knew he had no idea I was carrying the original, Angelic copy of *How to Be Death* in my back pocket.

"Sure," I said, making myself sound game. "And I had a question for you, actually, too."

He sat down on the floor in front of me, just far enough away I couldn't reach him with a kick.

"You want to know why I'm doing all this, don't you?"

I shook my head.

"In time," I replied, "but tell me something else first—"

"Anything!"

I leaned back in my cubicle, my head sinking into the black velvet headrest.

"Is Daniel still in there with you?"

The Man in Gray licked his lips and acted as if he were thinking over the question.

"Mmmh, no," he said finally. "No, I'm afraid not. That big boom you heard was him going bye-bye."

"How?" I found myself saying, but another part of me was disappearing, flying far away from *The Pit* and from the Man in Gray and even from Hell.

"He thought he could trick me, get me in his body then push over that stupid jar. But he miscalculated. That wasn't Pandora's Box."

"What is Pandora's Box?" I repeated, confused.

The Man in Gray shook his head as though I'd just said something stupid.

"Your boyfriend had some deal going with that Japanese God. I believe he'd been told if he helped him, then they could use Pandora's Box to stop me, save you, save the world . . . How should I know the details?"

I didn't believe him.

"Daniel would never have anything to do with Watat-sumi—"

"I watched the whole thing go down," the Man in Gray said. "I didn't get the details, but your boyfriend definitely thought that clay jar was Pandora's Box."

Oh, Daniel, I thought. *What did you get yourself mixed up in?*

"So what was it, then?"

The Man in Gray shrugged.

"Whatever it was, it destroyed the spell Uriah Drood and I had crafted to give the Harvesters and Transporters new eyes, and it also killed Frank and his Japanese 'friend.' Luckily I'd pushed your boyfriend out of his body just in the nick of time and was able to run in here and save myself."

The Man in Gray was an asshole. He'd been buried in the She'ol for far too long and it'd warped him beyond all hope of repair.

"His shade could still be here," I said, wanting to hold on to anything that might mean Daniel was out there somewhere, waiting for me to find him.

"No," the Man in Gray said. "Whatever was in that jar, it got him. He's not on this plane anymore. The body would know it."

Damn, Daniel, I thought. *Damn you and your stupid hero-ics and your need to fix everything.*

"Don't be sad he's gone," the Man in Gray continued. "We're all going to be annihilated shortly anyway."

"How's that?" I said.

He got up and walked back over to the entrance of *The Pit,* pulling a piece of velvet fabric away from the wall and reveal-ing a tiny keyboard. All around me the souls began to tremble in their seats, dead human beings who just wanted to get through the Afterlife and return to the recycling pool, all so they could take another shot at an Earthly existence.

"How's that?" I repeated.

He pressed a few more keys and then the room began to spin.

"I've already annihilated enough human souls that one more round in *The Pit*, especially with you in it, should be enough to get the Apocalypse started."

Oh, shit. I'd seen the seething orange sky, and now I knew what it meant. This wasn't just about merging universes; it was about utter annihilation.

"You'd sacrifice yourself?" I asked, incredulous.

He nodded, happy to finally be able to tell someone the intricacies of his plan.

"Yes, of course I would. Because the end is nigh, and there is nothing God can do to stop it once the Apocalypse has been set into motion."

"You hate God that much?" I asked, surprised by the vehemence of his words.

"Even more than you can imagine."

As we'd been talking, *The Pit* had picked up speed, spinning faster and faster and making me dizzy enough I found it hard to breathe.

"What if I told you I had *How to Be Death* in here with me right now?" I asked, ready to play my one and only trump card.

This gave the Man in Gray pause.

"But you don't."

I reached into my back pocket and pulled the book out for him to see.

"But I do—and there are enough human souls in here that if you annihilate them, the book is gonna mix with their energy and blow your little machine to smithereens all before you can get your little Apocalypse jump-started. Or finish merging these universes."

The Man in Gray reached for the keyboard, but the room was spinning too fast and I could see his fingers jerking over the keyboard. *The Pit* was coming to the climax of its final ride. Soon it would be over—one way or another.

Without thinking, I leapt out of my seat and ran across the

room, my eyes focused on the keyboard. I could feel *The Pit* shuddering as it started to rip everyone inside apart, atom by atom.

"No!" I screamed, my fingers finally finding purchase on the keyboard, hitting all the buttons until I felt the machine begin to decelerate and then come to a complete stop. The dead souls on board, shocked at not being obliterated, started to clap, their relief eliciting thunderous applause.

I looked over at the Man in Gray, but all I could see was Daniel—even though I knew he wasn't there anymore.

"Why?" the Man in Gray asked, looking up at me with wet, puppy-dog eyes.

I shook my head. A million answers floated through my mind, but I settled on one:

"Because you don't get to be the one to end our world."

He thought about it for a moment then nodded.

"Yes, I suppose that was asking for too much."

I walked up to Daniel and kissed him softly on the lips. Then I stepped back and to the Man in Gray, who wasn't immortal, just tired and sad, whispered:

"I wish you dead."

caoimhe and freezay found me cradling Daniel's body by the entrance to *The Pit*. I knew he wasn't inside it anymore, but I just couldn't let go—because letting go meant I had to let *him* go.

And I wasn't ready to do that.

"Baby, you have to stop," Caoimhe said, wrapping her arms around my shoulders and rocking me.

I shook my head.

"Please? For me?"

Her words penetrated, but I found I just didn't care.

Runt had crawled up beside me, nuzzling her pink nose into my waist. She didn't try to talk to me, just pushed herself against my shoulder, letting me know she was there.

"Baby, please," Caoimhe whispered—and then Clio was there holding me, too.

All the women in my life, all the ones I loved more than

anything else in the world were trying their damnedest to keep me anchored here, to stop me from floating away.

But I was too far gone to care.

I don't know how they pried my fingers off him, how they pulled me away from the man I loved, and took me back to Sea Verge, but they did.

They did.

epilogue

Kali and Indra had done as Calliope had asked, and now the young man was holding on to Kali's waist as she drove the hot pink Segway down the long drive leading to Sea Verge. Indra would never have deigned to travel by Segway, so he'd followed behind her in his red mini-convertible with the white racing stripes down its side.

In retrospect, Kali decided her friend was a genius and this was why she'd created this contingency plan. She'd put Kali in charge of overseeing it, and had hinted it might be nice to include Indra in its execution, too, because he could sweet-talk a lady out of her undergarments—never mind make a kid understand he was one of the three "possible" Deaths-in-Waiting.

Well, execute it, they had.

"This place is huge," the kid said, the wind whipping his long dark hair into his face.

"You ain't seen nothing yet, Nature Boy," Kali said, using her new nickname for the kid.

They followed the driveway down to the house, sunlight bombarding their eyes and making it hard to see, but once they'd crossed into the shade, Kali saw Clio and Jarvis outside, waiting for them.

Jennice had come out, too, but she was sitting on the front

steps, a little removed from the others. Apparently, Noh's death had been very hard on her—and then she'd come home to find her beloved mother had passed away, too. Kali thought it was almost too much to bear for someone so young, but Jennice was trying to put a good face on it—though anyone with eyes could see how much she was suffering.

And Kali hated suffering—unless she was the one causing it.

"Get off me, Nature Boy," Kali said as she brought the Segway to a stop and she and the kid hopped off.

His name was Geir. He was nineteen and from Iceland, but going to school in Boston. He was skinny, wore a kilt, and kept his hair in long waves down his back, but Kali had caught him staring at her chest. So she figured it meant he liked women despite appearances to the contrary.

"Hi, Geir. I'm Clio."

He dropped his backpack and took Clio's hand, grinning at her. They both had sharp, chiseled features, dark hair and eyes, and very long, feminine lashes—which made Kali decide they looked more like siblings than complete strangers to one another.

One did have to take into account the supernatural world was very incestuous, so the two of them may have had common ancestors somewhere in their lineage.

"It's lovely to meet you, Geir," Jarvis said, also extending his hand for the boy to take.

It was an awkward handshake, but since they were both awkward men—neither of whom seemed at home in his own skin—it was fine.

Jennice was the last one to meet the Icelander, and while they were being introduced, Clio ran to Indra, letting him enfold her in his strong arms.

Kali had known Indra for a long time, and she'd never seen him act so silly headed around a woman before. He got this goofy look on his face whenever Clio's name came up in conversation, and the way he was cuddling her, well, Kali saw babies in the future.

Cute, little, annoying Eurasian babies. Yuck, it disgusted her just thinking about all that cuteness.

"Shall we go in, then?" Jarvis said, interrupting Indra and

Clio's public display of affection—something Kali would have to thank him for later.

"Yes, let's go see dipwad," Kali agreed.

Then the six of them went inside.

callie was in her dad's study, going through his books, deciding which ones she would keep and which ones she would donate to the Hall of Death's reading room. The place had been a mess when she'd gotten back. Two Vargr attacks had not been good for the old house, but it'd forced Callie to start to think about redecorating. If she was going to live here, she might as well make it look the way she wanted, instead of the way her parents had kept it.

"They're here," Runt said, trotting into the room, a pretty pink bow tied around her neck.

"What's with the bow?" Callie asked, admiring the hell-hound's new accoutrement. "Did Caoimhe give it to you before she left?"

Caoimhe and Freezay had left for California that morning. They were going to close up Freezay's bungalow and pack up the odds and ends he wanted to bring back with him to New-port. For now, he and Caoimhe were going to stay with Callie at Sea Verge. That way Freezay could work for Death, Inc., as Callie's new Head of Death Security—and Caoimhe, well, she could work on being a mom.

"Jennice," Runt said, flopping on the floor at Callie's feet. "She thinks it makes me look more like a girl."

Callie snorted.

"I think you're pretty darn girly as you are," Callie said, kneeling down to pat the pup's head.

There was a flutter of wings at the window and Callie stood up.

"I'd better let Anjea in."

"She eats mice," Runt said, matter-of-factly.

"Yes, she does," Callie said, opening the window so the owlet could come inside.

She flew around the room once, as if she were checking the lay of the land, then she landed on Callie's shoulder. The owlet didn't talk very much, and when she did, it was usually only to Callie. Today was no exception.

"Come to check out the new recruit, have you?" Callie asked the owlet, who merely began to groom her wings, ignoring the question.

"I think he's cute for a human kind of a person," Runt said, padding over to the window so she could try and catch another glimpse of Geir.

"No way, no how," Callie said, picking up another book while Anjea continued to groom herself. "You are not old enough to like boys."

"That's what you think," Runt said, hightailing it out of the room just as Jarvis led the crowd in from the outside.

"This is Geir, Calliope," Jarvis said, pushing the young man toward Callie.

He blushed as he held out his hand, and Callie bypassed it in favor of a hug.

"I'm so glad you're here, Geir," she said, pulling him to her.

"It is my pleasure," he replied, blushing even more as she released him from the embrace.

"Why doesn't everyone sit down," Kali said, winking at Callie. "Dipwad wants to talk now."

Callie and Jarvis had brought in some folding chairs, arranging them so there were seats for everyone.

"Yep, you guys have a seat so old dipwad here," Callie said, "can talk."

The others did as she requested, and once they were settled in, she began.

"My name is Calliope Reaper-Jones, and I am the Grim Reaper. I run Death like my father before me did, as a corporate entity called Death, Inc. I am its President and CEO, and I make all the big decisions"—she winked at Jarvis here—"but not without the help of my friends."

She sat down on the edge of the desk, facing her audience, and ran her fingers along the old desk set that had once belonged to her dad.

"Clio, Geir, and Jennice, whether you know this, or have only guessed at it, you are the next three 'possible' Deaths."

Only Geir seemed a little bewildered by everything he was

hearing. Clio wore a serious expression and Jennice just looked sad.

"I want the three of you to work for me. To learn how Death, Inc., works so if something happens to me, whoever takes my place will be prepared."

Outside a seabird screeched and everyone looked to the window, expecting something supernatural to happen—but sometimes a seabird was just a seabird, and so they all settled back to let Callie finish her pitch.

"I wasn't prepared. I was thrust into something overwhelming and I caused more trouble than good," she said. "My dad was trying to protect me, but, instead, he just made my life harder. I don't want that for you. I want you to step into your destiny with your eyes wide open, to choose your fate so it doesn't choose you."

She clapped her hands together and stood up.

"That's it. That's the spiel. Do you want to come live with me at Sea Verge and learn to make the Afterlife a better place?"

No one clapped.

But no one said *no*, either.

kali found her friend sitting on an old bench out by the cliffs, looking out at the water and listening to the waves. She sat down beside her, but didn't speak. Finally, after a few minutes she grew impatient and punched Callie in the arm.

"Hey!" Callie said, rubbing the spot where Kali had hit her—she already knew from experience she was going to have a bruise there the next day.

"I need to tell you some stuff, white girl."

"Okay," Callie said, still rubbing her arm. "Tell me."

"It's about Daniel," Kali sighed.

Callie had been waiting for this, expecting it, so she just nodded.

"Once upon a time, when you weren't even embryonic, dip-wad, there was a guy."

"This sounds like one of those alternative fairytales," Callie said, but shut up when Kali threatened to punch her again.

"As I was saying," Kali continued. "He was a guy. Just a guy. No one famous or special, but he wanted to be, so he made a deal with the Devil and, for his immortality, he agreed to do terrible things."

Callie turned her gaze back to the sea now, letting Kali talk.

"We're talking bad shit, white girl, the worst stuff in the Devil's arsenal. He lived like this for a long time and then one day something happened and he changed. He didn't want to do the bad stuff anymore, but he was stuck. And then you"—here, she poked Callie in the ribs—"you set him free. And he fell in love with you. But he was still always fighting the bad stuff, and it was still always threatening to win."

Callie shook her head, her eyes filling with tears.

"He was so much better than me. He wanted only good things for everyone—"

Kali reached down and took Callie's hand.

"But he thought bad things first, just chose not to act on them. He wanted to do the opposite of what was inside of him."

Callie nodded.

"Okay, sure, whatever—"

"No," Kali said, squeezing her hand. "Not *whatever*. This is hard for you to understand because even though you make mistakes, you see the good things first. That's you're nature, dipwad. It's what makes you a dipwad, for God's sake."

"I do bad stuff," Callie said. "All the time."

Kali laughed at her.

"*I* do bad stuff, white girl. My nature is to rip heads off and drink blood. I see Daniel for what he was because we were the same."

Callie started crying then, rubbing at her eyes with the back of her hands.

"Oh, God . . ."

"Stop," Kali said, taking her hand. "Now listen to me. You made Daniel a better person. And you have to know that he was trying to protect you by accepting Watatsumi's help—but being back in a mindset where he had to lie to you messed him up. He thought the end justified the means, white girl. Only he couldn't handle it. He was like an addict getting back on the drugs—and that's what killed him, in the end."

Callie took a deep breath, letting it out slowly.

"I loved him. I don't care what he did. I just want him and Noh to be alive again."

"I can see that," Kali said.

"At least with Noh I can go to New Newbridge and visit her—and I actually think she's happier being a ghost than she ever was as a living person."

When Callie looked down at her hands again, they were shaking.

"But Daniel . . . he's not anywhere."

Kali put her arm around her friend's shoulder and drew her in, hugging her tightly.

"He's in your heart, dipwad."

Yes, he's in my heart, Callie thought, as she stared out at the mercurial sea.

He would always be in her heart.

She just wished it were enough.